Bello:
hidden talent rediscovered

Bello is a digital only imprint of Pan Macmillan,
established to breathe new life into previously published,
classic books.

At Bello we believe in the timeless power of the imagination,
of good story, narrative and entertainment and we want to use
digital technology to ensure that many more readers
can enjoy these books into the future.

We publish in ebook and Print on Demand formats
to bring these wonderful books to new audiences.

www.panmacmillan.co.uk/bello

T0353270

Frances Hodgson Burnett

Frances Hodgson Burnett (1849–1924) was born in Manchester and spent her early years there with her family. Her father died in 1852, and eventually, in 1865, Frances emigrated to the United States with her mother and siblings, settling with family in Knoxville, Tennessee. Frances began to be published at the age of 19, submitting short stories to magazines and using the proceeds to help support the family. In 1872, she married Swan Burnett, a doctor, with whom she had two sons while living in Paris. Her first novel, *That Lass o' Lowrie's*, was published in 1877, while the Burnetts were living in Washington D.C.

Following a separation from her husband, Burnett lived on both sides of the Atlantic, eventually marrying for a second time, however she never truly recovered from the death of her first son, Lionel. Best known during her lifetime for *Little Lord Fauntleroy* (1886), her books for children, including *The Secret Garden* and *The Little Princess*, have endured as classics, but Burnett also wrote many other novels for adults, which were hugely popular and favourably compared to authors such as George Eliot.

Frances Hodgson Burnett

ROBIN

First published in 1922 by Stokes

This edition published 2014 by Bello
an imprint of Pan Macmillan, a division of Macmillan Publishers Limited
Pan Macmillan, 20 New Wharf Road, London N1 9RR
Basingstoke and Oxford
Associated companies throughout the world

www.panmacmillan.co.uk/bello

ISBN 978-1-4472-6842-0 EPUB
ISBN 978-1-4472-7049-2 HB
ISBN 978-1-4472-6841-3 PB

Visit **www.panmacmillan.com** to read more about all our books
and to buy them. You will also find features, author interviews and
news of any author events, and you can sign up for e-newsletters
so that you're always first to hear about our new releases.

The Years Before

Outline arranged by Hamilton Williamoon

THE HEAD OF THE HOUSE OF COOMBE

In the years when Victorian standards and ideals began to dance an increasingly rapid jig before amazed lookers-on, who presently found themselves dancing as madly as the rest—in these years, there lived in Mayfair, in a slice of a house, Robert Gareth-Lawless and his lovely young wife. So light and airy was she to earthly vision and so diaphanous the texture of her mentality that she was known as "Feather."

The slice of a house between two comparatively stately mansions in the "right street" was a rash venture of the honeymoon.

Robert—well born, irresponsible, without resources—evolved a carefully detailed method of living upon nothing whatever, of keeping out of the way of duns, and telling lies with aptness and outward gaiety. But a year of giving smart little dinners and going to smart big dinners ended in a condition somewhat akin to the feat of balancing oneself on the edge of a sword.

Then Robin was born. She was an intruder and a calamity, of course. That a Feather should become a parent gave rise to much wit of light weight when Robin was exhibited in the form of a bundle of lace.

It was the Head of the House of Coombe who asked:

"What will you do with her?"

"Do?" Feather repeated. "What is it people 'do' with babies? I don't know. I wouldn't touch her for the world. She frightens me."

Coombe said:

"She is staring at me. There is antipathy in her gaze." He stared back unwaveringly also, but with a sort of cold interest.

"The Head of the House of Coombe" was not a title to be found in Burke or Debrett. It was a fine irony of the Head's own. The peerage recorded him as a marquis and added several lesser attendant titles.

To be born the Head of the House is a weighty and awe-inspiring thing—one is called upon to be an example.

"I am not sure what I am an example of—or to," he said, on one occasion, in his light, rather cold and detached way, "which is why I at times regard myself in that capacity with a slightly ribald lightness."

A reckless young woman once asked him:

"Are you as wicked as people say you are?"

"I really don't know. It is so difficult to decide," he answered. "Perhaps I am as wicked as I know how to be. And I may have painful limitations or I may not."

He had reached the age when it was safe to apply to him that vague term "elderly," and marriage might have been regarded as imperative. But he had remained unmarried and seemed to consider his abstinence entirely his own affair.

Courts and capitals knew him, and his opportunities were such as gave him all ease as an onlooker. He saw closely those who sat with knit brows and cautiously hovering hand at the great chess-board which is formed by the map of Europe.

As a statesman or a diplomat he would have gone far, but he had been too much occupied with Life as an entertainment, too self-indulgent for work of any order. Having, however, been born with a certain type of brain, it observed and recorded in spite of him, thereby adding flavour and interest to existence. But that was all.

Texture and colour gave him almost abnormal pleasure. For this reason, perhaps, he was the most perfectly dressed man in London.

It was at a garden-party that he first saw Feather. When his eyes fell upon her, he was talking to a group of people and he stopped speaking. Some one standing quite near him said afterwards that he had, for a second or so, became pale—almost as if he saw something which frightened him. He was still rather pale when Feather lifted her eyes to him. But he had not talked to her for fifteen minutes before he knew that there was no real reason why he should ever again lose his colour at the sight of her. He had thought, at first, there was.

This was the beginning of an acquaintance which gave rise to much argument over tea-cups regarding the degree of Coombe's interest in her. Remained, however, the fact that he managed to see a great deal of her. Feather was guilelessly doubtless concerning him. She was quite sure that he was in love with her, and very practically aware that the more men of the class of the Head of the House of Coombe who came in and out of the slice of a house, the more likely the dwellers in it were to get good invitations and continued credit.

The realisation of these benefits was cut short. Robert, amazingly and unnaturally, failed her by dying. He was sent away in a hearse and the tiny house ceased to represent hilarious little parties.

Bills were piled high everywhere. The rent was long overdue and must be paid. She had no money to pay it, none to pay the servants' wages.

"It's awful—it's awful—it's awful!" broke out between her sobs.

From her bedroom window—at evening—she watched "Cook," the smart footman, the nurse, the maids, climb into four-wheelers and be driven away.

"They're gone—all of them!" she gasped. "There's no one left in the house. It's empty!"

Then was Feather seized with a panic. She had something like hysterics, falling face downward upon the carpet and clutching her hair until it fell down. She was not a person to be judged—she was one of the unexplained incidents of existence.

The night drew in more closely. A prolonged wailing shriek tore through the utter soundlessness of the house. It came from the night-nursery. It was Robin who had wakened and was screaming.

"I—I *won't*!" Feather protested, with chattering teeth. "I won't! I *won't*!"

She had never done anything for the child since its birth. To reach her now, she would be obliged to go out into the dark—past Robert's bedroom—*the* room.

"I—I couldn't—even if I wanted to!" she quaked. "I daren't! I daren't! I wouldn't do it—for a *million pounds*!"

The screams took on a more determined note. She flung herself on her bed, burrowing her head under the coverings and pillows she dragged over her ears to shut out the sounds.

Feather herself had not known, nor in fact had any other human being known why Lord Coombe drifted into seeming rather to follow her about. But there existed a reason, and this it was, and this alone, which caused him to appear—the apotheosis of exquisite fitness in form—at her door.

He listened while she poured it all forth, sobbing. Her pretty hair loosened itself and fell about her in wild but enchanting disorder.

"I would do anything—*any one* asked me, if they would take care of me."

A shuddering knowledge that it was quite true that she would do anything for any man who would take care of her produced an effect on him nothing else would have produced.

"Do I understand," he said, "that you are willing that *I* should arrange this for you?"

"Do you mean—really?" she faltered. "Will you—will you—?"

Her uplifted eyes were like a young angel's brimming with crystal drops which slipped—as a child's tears slip—down her cheeks.

The florist came and refilled the window-boxes of the slice of a house with an admirable arrangement of fresh flowers. It became an established fact that the household had not fallen to pieces, and its frequenters gradually returned to it, wearing, indeed, the air of people who had never really remained away from it.

As a bird in captivity lives in its cage and, perhaps, believes it to be the world, Robin lived in her nursery. She was put to bed and taken up, she was fed and dressed in it, and once a day she was taken out of it downstairs and into the street. That was all.

It is a somewhat portentous thing to realise that a newborn human creature can only know what it is taught. To Robin the Lady Downstairs was merely a radiant and beautiful being of whom one might catch a glimpse through a door, or if one pressed one's face against the window pane at the right moment. On the very rare occasions when the Lady appeared on the threshold of the day-nursery, Robin stood and stared with immense startled eyes and answered in a whisper the banal little questions put to her.

So she remained unaware of mothers and unaware of affection. She never played with other children. Andrews, her nurse—as behooved one employed in a house about which there "was talk" bore herself with a lofty and exclusive air.

"My rule is to keep myself to myself," she said in the kitchen, "and to look as if I was the one that would turn up noses, if noses was to be turned up. There's those that would snatch away their children if I let Robin begin to make up to them."

But one morning, when Robin was watching some quarrelsome sparrows, an old acquaintance surprised Andrews by appearing in the Gardens and engaged her in a conversation so delightful that Robin was forgotten to the extent of being allowed to follow her sparrows round a clump of shrubbery out of sight.

It was while she watched them that she heard footsteps that stopped near her. She looked up. A big boy in Highland kilts and bonnet and sporran was standing by her. He spread and curved his red mouth, then began to run and prance round in a circle, capering like a Shetland pony to exhibit at once his friendliness and his prowess. After a minute or two he stopped, breathing fast and glowing.

"My pony in Scotland does that. His name is Chieftain. I'm called Donal. What are you called?"

"Robin," she answered, her lips and voice trembling with joy. He was so beautiful.

They began to play together while Andrews' friend recounted intimate details of a country house scandal.

Donal picked leaves from a lilac bush. Robin learned that if you laid a leaf flat on the seat of a bench you could prick beautiful patterns on the leaf's greenness. Donal had—in his rolled down stocking—a little dirk. He did the decoration with the point of this while Robin looked on, enthralled.

Through what means children so quickly convey to each other the entire history of their lives is a sort of occult secret. Before Donal was taken home, Robin knew that he lived in Scotland and had been brought to London on a visit, that his other name was Muir, that the person he called "mother" was a woman who took care of him. He spoke of her quite often.

"I will bring one of my picture-books to-morrow," he said grandly. "Can you read at all?"

"No," answered Robin, adoring him. "What are picture books?"

"Haven't you any?" he blurted out.

She lifted her eyes to the glowing blueness of his and said quite simply, "I haven't anything."

His old nurse's voice came from the corner where she sat.

"I must go back to Nanny," he said, feeling, somehow, as if he had been running fast. "I'll come to-morrow and bring *two* picture books."

He put his strong little eight-year-old arms round her and kissed her full on the mouth. It was the first time, for Robin. Andrews did not kiss. There was no one else.

"Don't you like to be kissed?" said Donal, uncertain because she looked so startled and had not kissed him back.

"Kissed," she repeated, with a small caught breath. "Ye—es." She knew now what it was. It was being kissed. She drew nearer at once and lifted up her face as sweetly and gladly as a flower lifts itself to the sun. "Kiss me again," she said, quite eagerly. And this time, she kissed too. When he ran quickly away, she stood looking after him with smiling, trembling lips, uplifted, joyful—wondering and amazed.

The next morning Andrews had a cold and her younger sister Anne was called in to perform her duties. The doctor pronounced the cold serious, and Andrews was confined to her bed. Hours spent under the trees reading were entirely satisfactory to Anne. And so, for two weeks, the soot-sprinkled London square was as the Garden of Eden to Donal and Robin.

In her fine, aloof way, Helen Muir had learned much in her stays in London and during her married life—in the exploring of foreign cities with her husband. She was not proud of the fact that in the event of the death of Lord Coombe's shattered and dissipated nephew her son would become heir presumptive to Coombe Court. She had not asked questions about Coombe. It had not been necessary. Once or twice she had seen Feather by chance. She was to see her again—by Feather's intention.

With Donal prancing at her side, Mrs. Muir went to the Gardens to meet the child Nanny had described as "a bit of witch fire dancing—with her colour and her big silk curls in a heap, and Donal staring at her like a young man at a beauty."

Robin was waiting behind the lilac bushes and her nurse was already deep in the mystery of "Lady Audley."

"There she is!" cried Donal, as he ran to her. "My mother has come with me. This is Robin, mother! This is Robin."

Her exquisiteness and physical brilliancy gave Mrs. Muir something not unlike a slight shock. Oh! No wonder, since she was like that. She stooped and kissed the round cheek delicately. She took the little hand and they walked round the garden, then sat on a bench and watched the children "make up" things to play.

A victoria was driving past. Suddenly a sweetly hued figure spoke to the coachman. "Stop here," she said. "I want to get out."

Robin's eyes grew very round and large and filled with a worshipping light.

"It is," she gasped, "the Lady Downstairs!"

Feather floated near to the seat and paused, smiling. "Where is your nurse, Robin?" she asked.

"She is only a few yards away," said Mrs. Muir.

"So kind of you to let Robin play with your boy. Don't let her bore you. I am Mrs. Gareth-Lawless."

There was a little silence, a delicate little silence.

"I recognized you as Mrs. Muir at once," added Feather, unperturbed and smiling brilliantly. "I saw your portrait at the Grovenor."

"Yes," said Mrs. Muir, gently.

"I wanted very much to see your son; that was why I came."

"Yes," still gently from Mrs. Muir.

"Because of Coombe, you know. We are such old friends. How queer that the two little things have made friends too. I didn't know."

She bade them good-bye and strayed airily away.

And that night Donal was awakened, was told that "something" had happened, that they were to go back to Scotland. He was accustomed to do as he was told. He got out of bed and began to dress, but he swallowed very hard.

"I shall not see Robin," he said in a queer voice. "She won't find me when she goes behind the lilac bushes. She won't know why I don't come." Then, in a way that was strangely grown up: "She has no one but me to remember."

The next morning a small, rose-coloured figure stood still for so long in the gardens that it began to look rigid and some one said, "I wonder what that little girl is waiting for."

A child has no words out of which to build hopes and fears. Robin could only wait in the midst of a slow dark rising tide of something she had no name for. Suddenly she knew. He was *gone*! She crept under the shrubbery. She cried, she sobbed. If Andrews had seen her she would have said she was "in a tantrum." But she was not. Her world had been torn away.

Five weeks later Feather was giving a very little dinner in the slice of a house. There was Harrowby, a good looking young man with dark eyes, and the Starling who was "emancipated" and whose real name was Miss March. The third diner was a young actor with a low, veiled voice—Gerald Vesey—who adored and understood Feather's clothes.

Over coffee in the drawing-room Coombe joined them just at the moment that Feather was "going to tell them something to make them laugh."

"Robin is in love!" she cried. "She is five years old and she has been deserted and Andrews came to tell me she can neither eat nor sleep. The doctor says she has had a shock."

Coombe did not join in the ripple of laughter, but he looked interested.

"Robin is a stimulating name," said Harrowby. "*Is* it too late to let us see her?"

"They usually go to sleep at seven, I believe," remarked Coombe, "but of course I am not an authority."

Robin was not asleep, though she had long been in bed with her eyes closed. She had heard Andrews say to her sister Anne:

"Lord Coombe's the reason. She does not want her boy to see or speak to him, so she whisked him back to Scotland."

"Is Lord Coombe as bad as they say?" put in Anne, with bated breath.

"As to his badness," Robin heard Andrews answer, "there's some that can't say enough against him. It's what he is in this house that does it. She won't have her boy playing with a child like Robin."

Then—even as there flashed upon Robin the revelation of her own unfitness—came a knock at the door.

She was taken up, dressed in her prettiest frock and led down the narrow stairway. She heard the Lady say:

"Shake hands with Lord Coombe."

Robin put her hand behind her back—she who had never disobeyed since she was born!

"Be pretty mannered, Miss Robin my dear," Andrews instructed, "and shake hands with his Lordship."

Each person in the little drawing-room saw the queer flame in the child-face. She shrilled out her words:

"Andrews will pinch me—Andrews will pinch me! But—No—No!"

She kept her hands behind her back and hatred surged up in her soul.

In spite of her tender years, the doctor held to the theory that Robin had suffered a shock; she must be taken away to be helped by the bracing air of the Norfolk coast. Before she went, workmen were to be seen coming in and out of the house. When she returned to London, she was led into rooms she had never been in before—light and airy rooms with pretty walls and furniture.

It was "a whim of Coombe's," as Feather put it, that she should no longer occupy the little dog-kennels of nurseries, so these new apartments had been added in the rear. A whim of his also that Andrews, whose disciplinary methods included pinching, should be dismissed and replaced by Dowson, a motherly creature with a great deal of common sense. Robin's lonely little heart opened to her new nurse, who became in time her "Dowie."

It was Dowson who made it clear to Lord Coombe, at length, that Robin had reached the age when she needed a governess, and it was he who said to Feather a few days later:

"A governess will come here to-morrow at eleven o'clock. She is a Mademoiselle Vallé. She is accustomed to the education of young children. She will present herself for your approval."

"What on earth can it matter?" Feather cried.

"It does not matter to you," he answered. "It chances for the time being to matter to *me*."

Mademoiselle Vallé was an intelligent, mature French woman, with a peculiar power to grasp an intricate situation. She learned to love the child she taught—a child so strangely alone. As time went on she came to know that Robin was to receive every educational advantage, every instruction. In his impersonal, aloof way Coombe was fixed in his intention to provide her with life's defences. As she grew, graceful as a willow wand, into a girlhood startlingly lovely, she learned modern languages, learned to dance divinely.

And all the while he was deeply conscious that her infant hatred had not lessened—that he could show her no reason why it should.

There were black hours when she was in deadly peril from a human beast, mad with her beauty. Coombe had almost miraculously saved her, but her detestation of him still held.

Her one thought—her one hope—was to learn—learn, so that she might make her own living. Mademoiselle Vallé supported her in this, and Coombe understood.

In one of the older London squares there was a house upon the broad doorsteps of which Lord Coombe stood oftener than upon any other. The old Dowager Duchess of Darte, having surrounded herself with almost royal dignity, occupied that house in an enforced seclusion. She was a confirmed rheumatic invalid, but her soul was as strong as it was many years before, when she had given its support to Coombe in his unbearable hours. She had poured out her strength in silence, and in silence he had received it. She saved him from slipping over the verge of madness.

But there came a day when he spoke to her of this—of the one woman he had loved, Princess Alixe of X—:

"There was never a human thing so transparently pure, and she was the possession of a brute incarnate. She shook with terror before him. He killed her."

"I believe he did," she said, unsteadily. "He was not received here at Court afterward."

"He killed her. But she would have died of horror if he had not struck her a blow. I saw that. I was in attendance on him at Windsor."

"When I first knew you," the Duchess said gravely.

"There was a night—I was young—young—when I found myself face to face with her in the stillness of the wood. I went quite mad for a time. I threw myself face downward on the earth and sobbed. She knelt and prayed for her own soul as well as mine. I kissed the hem of her dress and left her standing—alone."

After a silence he added:

"It was the next night that I heard her shrieks. Then she died."

The Duchess knew what else had died: the high adventure of youth and joy of life in him.

On a table beside her winged chair were photographs of two women, who, while obviously belonging to periods of some twenty years apart, were in face and form so singularly alike that they might have been the same person. One was the Princess Alixe of X— and the other—Feather.

"The devil of chance," Coombe said, "sometimes chooses to play tricks. Such a trick was played on me."

It was the photograph of Feather he took up and set a strange questioning gaze upon.

"When I saw this," he said, "this—exquisitely smiling at me in a sunny garden—the tomb opened under my feet and I stood on the brink of it—twenty-five again."

He made clear to her certain facts which most persons would have ironically disbelieved. He ended with the story of Robin.

"I am determined," he explained, "to stand between the child and what would be inevitable. Her frenzy of desire to support herself arises from her loathing of the position of accepting support from me. I sympathise with her entirely."

"Mademoiselle Vallé is an intelligent woman," the Duchess said. "Send her to me; I shall talk to her. Then she can bring the child."

And so it was arranged that Robin should be taken into the house in the old fashioned square to do for the Duchess what a young relative might have done. And, a competent person being needed to take charge of the linen, "Dowie" would go to live under the same roof.

Feather's final thrust in parting with her daughter was:

"Donal Muir is a young man by this time. I wonder what his mother would do now if he turned up at your mistress' house and began to make love to you." She laughed outright. "You'll get into all sorts of messes but that would be the nicest one!"

The Duchess came to understand that Robin held it deep in her mind that she was a sort of young outcast.

"If she consorted," she thought, "with other young things and shared their pleasures she would forget it."

She talked the matter over with her daughter, Lady Lothwell.

"I am not launching a girl in society," she said, "I only want to help her to know a few nice young people. I shall begin with your children. They are mine if I am only a grandmother. A small dinner and a small dance—and George and Kathryn may be the beginning of an interesting experiment."

The Duchess was rarely mistaken. The experiment was interesting. For George—Lord Halwyn—it held a certain element of disaster. It was he who danced with Robin first. He had heard of the girl who was a sort of sublimated companion to his grandmother. He had encountered companions before. This one, as she flew like a blown leaf across the floor and laughed up into his face with wide eyes produced a new effect and was a new kind.

He led her to the conservatory. He was extremely young and his fleeting emotions had never known a tight rein. An intoxicating hot-house perfume filled his nostrils. Suddenly he let himself go and was kissing the warm velvet of her slim little neck.

"You—you—you've spoiled everything in the world!" she cried. "Now"—with a desolate, horrible little sob—"now I can only go back—*back*." She spoke as if she were Cinderella and he had made the clock strike twelve. Her voice had absolute grief in it.

"I say,"—he was contrite—"don't speak like that. I beg pardon. I'll grovel. Don't— Oh, Kathryn! Come here!"

This last because his sister had suddenly appeared.

Kathryn bore Robin away. Boys like George didn't really matter, she pointed out, though of course it was bad manners. She had been kissed herself, it seemed. As they walked between banked flowers she added:

"By the way, somebody important has been assassinated in one of the Balkan countries. Lord Coombe has just come in and is talking it over with grandmamma."

As they neared the entrance to the ballroom she paused with a new kind of impish smile.

"The very best looking boy in all England," she said, "is dancing with Sara Studleigh. He dropped in by chance to call and grandmamma made him stay. His name is Donal Muir. He is Lord Coombe's heir. Here he comes. Look!"

He was now scarcely two yards away. Almost as if he had been called he turned his eyes toward Robin and straight into hers they laughed—straight into hers.

The incident of their meeting was faultlessly correct; also, when Lady Lothwell appeared, she presented him to Robin as if the brief ceremony were one of the most ordinary in existence.

They danced for a time without a word. She wondered if he could not feel the beating of her heart.

"That—is a beautiful waltz," he said at last, as if it were a sort of emotional confidence.

"Yes," she answered. Only, "Yes."

Once round the great ballroom, twice, and he gave a little laugh and spoke again.

"I am going to ask you a question. May I?"

"Yes."

"Is your name Robin?"

"Yes." She could scarcely breathe it.

"I thought it was. I hoped it was—after I first began to suspect. I *hoped* it was."

"It is—it is."

"Did we once play together in a garden?"

"Yes—yes."

Back swept the years, and the wonderful happiness began again.

In the shining ballroom the music rose and fell and swelled again into ecstasy as he held her white young lightness in his arm and they swayed and darted and swooped like things of the air—while the old Duchess and Lord Coombe looked on almost unseeing and talked in murmurs of Sarajevo.

Chapter 1

It was a soft starlit night mystically changing into dawn when Donal Muir left the tall, grave house on Eaton Square after the strangely enchanted dance given by the old Dowager Duchess of Darte. A certain impellingness of mood suggested that exercise would be a good thing and he decided to walk home. It was an impellingness of body as well as mind. He had remained later than the relative who had by chance been responsible for his being brought, an uninvited guest, to the party. The Duchess had not known that he was in London. It may also be accepted as a fact that to this festivity given for the pleasure of Mrs. Gareth-Lawless' daughter, she might not have chosen to assume the responsibility of extending him an invitation. She knew something of his mother and had sometimes discussed her with her old friend, Lord Coombe. She admired Helen Muir greatly and was also much touched by certain aspects of her maternity. What Lord Coombe had told her of the meeting of the two children in the Gardens, of their innocent child passion of attraction for each other, and of the unchildlike tragedy their enforced parting had obviously been to both had at once deeply interested and moved her. Coombe had only been able to relate certain surface incidents connected with the matter, but they had been incidents not easy to forget and from which unusual things might be deduced. No! She would not have felt prepared to be the first to deliberately throw these two young people across each other's paths at this glowing moment of their early blooming—knowing as she did Helen Muir's strongly anxious desire to keep them apart.

She had seen Donal Muir several times as the years had passed and had not been blind to the physical beauty and allure of charm the rest of the world saw and proclaimed with suitable adjectives. When the intimate friend who was his relative appeared with him in her drawing-room and she found standing before her, respectfully appealing for welcome with a delightful smile, this quite incomparably good-looking young man, she was conscious of a secret momentary disturbance and a recognition of the fact that something a shade startling had happened.

"When a thing of the sort occurs entirely without one's aid and rather against one's will—one may as well submit," she said later to Lord Coombe. "Endeavouring to readjust matters is merely meddling with Fate and always ends in disaster. As an incident, I felt there was a hint in it that it would be the part of wisdom to leave things alone."

She had watched the two dancing with a kind of absorption in her gaze. She had seen them go out of the room into the conservatory. She had known exactly when they had returned and, seeing the look on their young faces, had understood why the eyes of the beholders followed them.

When Lord Coombe came in with the ominous story of the assassination at Sarajevo, all else had been swept from her mind. There had been place in her being for nothing but the shock of a monstrous recognition. She had been a gravely conscious looker-on at the slow but never ceasing growth of a world peril for too many years not to be widely awake to each sign of its development.

"Servia, Russia, Austria, Germany. It will form a pretext and a clear road to France and England," Lord Coombe had said.

"A broad, clear road," the Duchess had agreed breathlessly—and, while she gazed before her, ceased to see the whirl of floating and fluttering butterfly-wings of gauze or to hear the music to whose measure they fluttered and floated.

But no sense of any connection with Sarajevo disturbed the swing of the fox trot or the measure of the tango, and when Donal Muir walked out into the summer air of the starlit street and lifted his face, because already a faint touch of primrose dawn was showing itself on the eastern sky, in his young world there was only recognition of a vague tumult of heart and brain and blood.

"What's the matter?" he was thinking. "What have I been

doing—What have I been saying? I've been like a chap in a dream. I'm not awake yet."

All that he had said to the girl was a simple fact. He had exaggerated nothing. If, in what now seemed that long-ago past, he had not been a sturdy, normal little lad surrounded by love and friendliness, with his days full of healthy play and pleasure, the child tragedy of their being torn apart might have left ugly marks upon his mind, and lurked there, a morbid memory. And though, in time, rebellion and suffering had died away, he had never really forgotten. Even to the cricket-playing, larking boy at Eton there had now and then returned, with queer suddenness, recollections which gave him odd moments of resurrected misery. They passed away, but at long intervals they came back and always with absolute reality. At Oxford the intervals had been longer but a certain picture was one whose haunting never lost its clearness. It was a vision of a colour-warm child kneeling on the grass, her eyes uplifted, expressing only a lonely patience, and he could actually hear her humble little voice as she said:

"I—I haven't anything." And it always roused him to rage.

Then there was the piteous break in her voice when she hid her eyes with her arm and said of her beast of a mother:

"She—doesn't *like* me!"

"Damn! Damn!" he used to say every time the thing came back. "Oh! damn!—damn!" And the expletive never varied in its spontaneity.

As he walked under the primrose sky and breathed in the faint fragrant stir of the freshening morning air, he who had always felt joyously the sense of life knew more than ever before the keen rapture of living. The springing lightness of his own step as it rang on the pavement was part of it. It was as though he were still dancing and he almost felt something warm and light in his arm and saw a little head of dark silk near his breast.

Throughout his life he had taken all his joys to his closest companion and nearest intimate—his mother. Theirs had not been a common life together. He had not even tried to explain to himself the harmony and gaiety of their nearness in which there seemed no separation of years. She had drawn and held him to the wonder of her charm and had been the fine flavour of his existence. It was actually true that he had so far had no boyish love affairs because he had all unconsciously been in love with the beautiful completeness of her.

Always when he returned home after festivities, he paused for a moment outside her bedroom door because he so often found her awake and waiting to talk to him if he were inclined to talk—to listen—to laugh softly—or perhaps only to say good-night in her marvel of a voice—a marvel because its mellow note held such love.

This time when, after entering the house and mounting the stairs he reached her door, he found it partly open.

"Come in," he heard her say. "I went to sleep very early and awakened half an hour ago. It is really morning."

She was sitting up in a deep chair by the window.

"Let me look at you," she said with a little laugh. "And then kiss me and go to bed."

But even the lovely, faint early light revealed something to her.

"You walk like a young stag on the hillside," she said. "You don't want to go to sleep at all. What is it?"

He sat on a low ottoman near her and laughed a little also.

"I don't know," he answered, "but I'm wide awake."

The English summer dawn is of a magical clear light and she could see him well. She had a thrilled feeling that she had never quite known before what a beautiful thing he was—how perfect and shining fair in his boy manhood.

"Mother," he said, "you won't remember perhaps—it's a queer thing that I should myself—but I have never really forgotten. There was a child I played with in some garden when I was a little chap. She was a beautiful little thing who seemed to belong to nobody—"

"She belonged to a Mrs. Gareth-Lawless," Helen interpolated.

"Then you do remember?"

"Yes, dear. You asked me to go to the Gardens with you to see her. And Mrs. Gareth-Lawless came in by chance and spoke to me."

"And then we had suddenly to go back to Scotland. I remember you wakened me quite early in the morning—I thought it was the middle of the night." He began to speak rather slowly as if he were thinking it over. "You didn't know that, when you took me away, it was a tragedy. I had promised to play with her again and I felt as if I had deserted her hideously. It was not the kind of a thing a little chap usually feels—it was something different—something more. And to-night it actually all came back. I saw her again, mother."

He was so absorbed that he did not take in her involuntary movement.

"You saw her again! Where?"

"The old Duchess of Darte was giving a small dance for her. Hallowe took me—"

"Does the Duchess know Mrs. Gareth-Lawless?" Helen had a sense of breathlessness.

"I don't quite understand the situation. It seems the little thing insists on earning her own living and she is a sort of companion and secretary to the Duchess. Mother, she is just the same!"

The last words were a sort of exclamation. As he uttered them, there came back to her the day when—a little boy—he had seemed as though he were speaking as a young man might have spoken. Now he was a young man, speaking almost as if he were a little boy—involuntarily revealing his exaltation.

As she had felt half frightened years before, so she felt wholly frightened now. He was not a little boy any longer. She could not sweep him away in her arms to save him from danger. Also she knew more of the easy, fashionably accepted views of the morals of pretty Mrs. Gareth-Lawless, still lightly known with some cynicism as "Feather." She knew what Donal did not. His relationship to the Head of the House of Coombe made it unlikely that gossip should choose him as the exact young man to whom could be related stories of his distinguished relative, Mrs. Gareth-Lawless and her girl. But through the years Helen Muir had unavoidably heard things she thought particularly hideous. And here the child was again "just the same."

"She has only grown up." His laugh was like a lightly indrawn breath. "Her cheek is just as much like a rose petal. And that wonderful little look! And her eyelashes. Just the same! Do girls usually grow up like that? It was the look most. It's a sort of asking and giving—both at once."

There it was! And she had nothing to say. She could only sit and look at him—at his beautiful youth all alight with the sudden flame of that which can set a young world on fire and sweep on its way either carrying devastation or clearing a path to Paradise.

His own natural light unconsciousness was amazing. He only knew that he was in delightful high spirits. The dancing, the music, the early morning, were, he thought, accountable for it.

She bent forward to kiss his cheek and she patted his hand.

"My dear! My dear!" she said. "How you have enjoyed your evening!"

"There never was anything more perfect," with the light laugh again. "Everything was delightful—the rooms, the music, the girls in their pretty frocks like a lot of flowers tossed about. She danced like a bit of thistledown. I didn't know a girl could be so light. The back of her slim little neck looks as fine and white and soft as a baby's. I am so glad you were awake. Are you sure you don't want to go to sleep again?" suddenly.

"Not in the least. Look at the sun beginning to touch the tips of the little white clouds with rose. That stir among the leaves of the plane trees is the first delicious breath of the morning. Go on and tell me all about the party."

"It's a perfect time to talk," he laughed.

And there he sat and made gay pictures for her of what he had seen and done. He thought he was giving her mere detail of the old Duchess' dance. He did not know that when he spoke of new tangos, of flowers, of music and young nymphs like tossed blossoms, he never allowed her for a moment to lose sight of Mrs. Gareth-Lawless' girl. She was the light floating over his vision of the happy youth of the assembly—she was the centre—the beginning and the ending of it all.

Chapter 2

If some uncomplex minded and even moderately articulate man or woman, living in some small, ordinary respectable London house and going about his or her work in the customary way, had been prompted by chance upon June 29th, 1914, to begin to keep on that date a day-by-day diary of his or her ordinary life, the effects of huge historic events, as revealed by the every-day incidents to be noted in the streets, to be heard in his neighbours' houses as well as among his fellow workers, to be read in the penny or half-penny newspapers, would have resulted—if the record had been kept faithfully and without any self-conscious sense of audience—between 1914 and 1918 in the gradual compiling of a human document of immense historical value. Compared with it, the diaries of Defoe and Pepys would pale and be flavourless. But it must have been begun in June, 1914, and have been written with the casualness of that commonplace realism which is the most convincing realism of all. It is true that the expression of the uncomplex mind is infrequently articulate, but the record which would bring home the clearest truth would be the one unpremeditatedly depicting the effect produced upon the wholly unprepared and undramatic personality by the monstrous drama, as the Second Deluge rose for its apparent overwhelming, carrying upon its flood old civilisations broken from anchor and half submerged as they tossed on the rising and raging waves. Such a priceless treasure as this might have been the quite unliterary and unromantic diary of any—say, Mr. James Simpson of any house number in any respectable side street in Regents Park, or St. Johns Wood or Hampstead. One can easily imagine him, sitting in his small, comfortable parlour and bending over his blotting-pad in unilluminated cheerful absorption after his day's work.

It can also without any special intellectual effort be imagined that the record might have begun with some such seemingly unprophetic entry as follows:—

"June 29th, 1914. I made up my mind when I was at the office to-day that I would begin to keep a diary. I have thought several times that I would, and Harriet thinks it would be a good thing because we should have it to refer to when there was any little dispute about dates and things that have happened. To-night seemed a good time because there is something to begin the first entry with. Harriet and I spent part of the evening in reading the newspaper accounts of the assassination of the Austrian Archduke and his wife. There seems to be a good deal of excitement about it because he was the next heir to the Austrian throne. The assassination occurred in Bosnia at a place called Sarajevo. Crawshaw, whose desk is next to mine in the office, believes it will make a nice mess for the Bosnians and Servians because they have been rather troublesome about wanting to be united into one country instead of two, and called Greater Serbia. That seems a silly sort of reason for throwing bombs and killing people. But foreigners have a way of thinking bombs settle everything. Harriet brought out her old school geography and we looked up Sarajevo on the map of Austria-Hungary. It was hard to find because the print was small and it was spelt Saraievo—without any j in it. It was just on the line between Bosnia and Servia and the geography said it was the chief city in Bosnia. Harriet said it was a queer thing how these places on maps never seemed like real places when you looked them up and just read their names and yet probably the people in them were as real to themselves as we were, and there were streets in them as real as Lupton Street where we were sitting, finding them on the map on the sitting-room table. I said that bombs were pretty real things and the sound of this one when it exploded seemed to have reached a long way to judge from the newspapers and the talk in London. Harriet said my putting it like that gave her a queer feeling—almost as if she had heard it and it had made her jump. Somehow it seemed something like it to me. At any rate we sat still a minute or two, thinking it over. Then Harriet got up and went into the kitchen and made some nice toasted cheese for our supper before we went to bed."

Men of the James Simpson type were among the many who daily passed Coombe House on their way to and from their office work. Some of them no doubt caught sight of Lord Coombe himself as he walked or drove through the entrance gates. Their knowledge of him was founded upon rumoured stories, repeated rather privately among themselves. He was a great swell and there weren't many shady things he hadn't done and didn't know the ins and outs of, but his remoteness from their own lives rendered these accepted legends scarcely prejudicial. The perfection of his clothes, and his unusual preservation of physical condition and good looks, also his habit of the so-called "week-end" continental journeys, were the points chiefly recalled by the incidental mention of his name.

If James Simpson, on his way home to Lupton Street with his friend Crawshaw, chanced to see his lordship's car standing before his door a few days after the bomb throwing in Sarajevo, he might incidentally have referred to him somewhat in this wise:—

"As we passed by Coombe House the Marquis of Coombe came out and got into his car. There were smart leather valises and travelling things in it and a rug or so, as if he was going on some journey. He is a fine looking man for one that's lived the life he has and reached his age. I don't see how he's done it, myself. When I said to Crawshaw that it looked as if he was going away for the week end, Crawshaw said that perhaps he was taking Saturday to Monday off to run over to talk to the Kaiser and old Franz Josef about the Sarajevo business, and he might telephone to the Czar about it because he's intimate with them all, and the whole lot seem to be getting mixed up in the thing and writing letters and sending secret telegrams. It seems to be turning out, as Crawshaw said it would, into a nice mess for Servia. Austria is making it out that the assassination really was committed to stir up trouble, and says it wasn't done just by a crazy anarchist, but by a secret society working for its own ends. Crawshaw came in to supper and we talked it all over. Harriet gave us cold beef and pickled onions and beer, and we looked at the maps in the old geography again. We got quite interested in finding places. Bosnia and Servia (it's often spelled Serbia) are close up against Austria-Hungary, and Germany and Russia are close against the other side. They can get into each other's countries without much travelling. I heard to-day that Russia will have to help Servia if she has a row with Austria. Crawshaw says that will give Germany the chance she's been waiting for and that she will try to get through Belgium to England. He says she hates England. Harriet began to look pale as she studied the map and saw how little Belgium was and that the Channel was so narrow. She said she felt as if England had been silly to let herself get so slack and she almost wished she hadn't looked at the geography. She said she couldn't help thinking how awful it would be to see the German army marching up Regent Street and camping in Hyde Park, and who in goodness' name knew what they might do to people if they hated England so? She actually looked as if she would have cried if Crawshaw and I hadn't chaffed her and made her laugh by telling her we would join the army; and Crawshaw began to shoulder arms with the poker and I got my new umbrella."

In this domesticated and almost comfortable fashion did the greatest tragedy the human race has known since the beginning of the world gradually prepare its first scenes and reveal glimpses of itself, as the curtain of Time was, during that June, slowly raised by the hand of Fate.

This is not what is known as a "war story." It is not even a story of the War, but a relation of incidents occurring amidst and resulting from the strenuousness of a period to which "the War" was a background so colossal that it dwarfed all events, except in the minds of those for whom such events personally shook and darkened or brightened the world. Nothing can dwarf personal anguish at its moment of highest power; to the last agony and despairing terror of the heart-wrung the cataclysm of earthquake, tornado, shipwreck is but the awesome back drop of the scene.

Also—incidentally—the story is one of the transitions in, and convulsive changes of, points of view produced by the convulsion itself which flung into new perspective the whole surface of the earth and the races existing upon it.

The Head of the House of Coombe had, as he said, been born at once too early and too late to admit of any fixed establishment of tastes and ideals. His existence had been passed in the transition from one era to another—the Early Victorian, under whose disappearing influences he had spent his youth; the Late Victorian and Edwardian, in whose more rapidly changing atmosphere he had ripened to maturity. He had, during this transition, seen from afar the slow rising of the tidal wave of the Second Deluge; and in the summer days of 1914 he heard the first low roaring of its torrential swell, and visualised all that the overwhelming power of its bursting flood might sweep before it and bury forever beneath its weight.

He made seemingly casual crossings of the Channel and journeys which were made up of the surmounting of obstacles, and when he returned, brought with him a knowledge of things which it would have been unwise to reveal carelessly to the general public. The mind of the general public had its parallel, at the moment, in the temperature of a patient in the early stages of, as yet, undiagnosed typhoid or any other fever. Restless excitement and spasmodic heats and discomforts prompted and ruled it. Its tendency was to nervous discontent and suspicious fearfulness of approaching, vaguely formulated, evils. These risings of temperature were to be seen in the very streets and shops. People were talking—talking—talking. Ordinary people, common people, all kinds of classes. The majority of them did not know what they were talking about; most of them talked either uneducated, frightened or blustering nonsense, but everybody talked more or less. Enormous numbers of newspapers were bought and flourished about, or pored over anxiously. Numbers of young Germans were silently disappearing from their places in shops, factories and warehouses. That was how Germany showed her readiness for any military happening. Her army was already trained and could be called from any country and walk in life. A mysterious unheard command called it and it was obliged to obey. The entire male population of England had not been trained from birth to regard itself as an immense military machine, ready at any moment for action. The James Simpson type of Englishman indulged in much discussion of the pros and cons of enforced military training of youth. Germany's well known contempt of the size and power of the British Army took on an aspect which filled the James Simpsons with rage. They had not previously thought of themselves as martial, because middle-class England was satisfied with her belief in her strength and entire safety. Of course she was safe. She always had been. Britannia Rules the Waves and the James Simpsons were sure that incidentally she ruled everything else. But as there stole up behind the mature Simpsons the haunting realization that, if England was "drawn in" to a war, it would be the young Simpsons who must gird their loins and go forth to meet Goliath in his armour, with only the sling and stone of untrained youth and valour as their weapon, there were many who began to feel that even inconvenient drilling and discipline might have been good things.

"There is something quite thrilling in going about now," said Feather to Coombe, after coming in from a shopping round, made in her new electric brougham. "One doesn't know what it is, but it's in the air. You see it in people's faces. Actually shop girls give one the impression of just having stopped whispering together when you go into a place and ask for something. A girl who was trying on some gloves for me—she was a thin girl with prominent watery eyes—had such a frightened look, that I said to her, just to see what she would say—'I wonder what would happen to the shops if England got into war?' She turned quite white and answered, 'Oh, Madam, I can't bear to think of it. My favourite brother's a soldier. He's such a nice big fellow and we're so fond of him. And he's always talking about it. He says Germany's not going to let England keep out. We're so frightened—mother and me.' She almost dropped a big tear on my glove. It *would* be quite exciting if England did go in."

"It would," Coombe answered.

"London would be crowded with officers. All sorts of things would have to be given for them—balls and things."

"Cannon balls among other things," said Coombe.

"But we should have nothing to do with the cannon balls, thank goodness," exhilaration sweeping her past unpleasant aspects. "One would be sorry for the Tommies, of course, if the worst came to the worst. But I must say army and navy men are more interesting than most civilians. It's the constant change in their lives, and their having to meet so many kinds of people."

"In actual war, men who are not merely 'Tommies' actually take part," Coombe suggested. "I was looking at a ball-room full of them the night after the news came from Sarajevo. Fine, well-set-up youngsters dancing with pretty girls. I could not help asking myself what would have happened to them before the German army crossed the Channel—if they were not able to prevent the crossing. And what would happen to the girls after its crossing, when it poured over London and the rest of England in the unbridled rage of drunken victory."

He so spoke because beneath his outward coldness he himself felt a secret rage against this lightness which, as he saw things, had its parallel in another order of trivial unawareness in more important places and larger brains. Feather started and drew somewhat nearer to him.

"How hideous! What do you mean! Where was the party?" she asked.

"It was a small dance given by the Duchess, very kindly, for Robin," he answered.

"For Robin!" with open eyes whose incredulity held irritation. "The old Duchess giving parties to her 'useful companion' girl! What nonsense! Who was there?" sharply.

"The young fellows who would be first called on if there was war. And the girls who are their relatives. Halwyn was there—and young Dormer and Layton—they are all in the army. The cannon balls would be for them as well as for the Tommies of their regiments. They are spirited lads who wouldn't slink behind. They'd face things."

Feather had already forgotten her moment's shock in another thought.

"And they were invited to meet Robin! Did they dance with her? Did she dance much? Or did she sit and stare and say nothing? What did she wear?"

"She looked like a very young white rose. She danced continually. There was always a little mob about her when the music stopped. I do not think she sat at all, and it was the young men who stared. The only dance she missed—Kathryn told her grandmother—was the one she sat out in the conservatory with Donal Muir."

At this Feather's high, thin little laugh broke forth.

"He turned up there? Donal Muir!" She struck her hands lightly together. "It's too good to be true!"

"Why is it too good to be true?" he inquired without enthusiasm.

"Oh, don't you see? After all his mother's airs and graces and running away with him when they were a pair of babies—as if Robin had the plague. I was the plague—and so were you. And here the old Duchess throws them headlong at each other—in all their full bloom—into each other's arms. I did not do it. You didn't. It was the stuffiest old female grandee in London, who wouldn't let *me* sweep her front door-steps for her—because I'm an impropriety."

She asked a dozen questions, was quite humorous over the picture she drew of Mrs. Muir's consternation at the peril her one ewe lamb had been led into by her highly revered friend.

"A frightfully good-looking, spoiled boy like that always plunges headlong into any adventure that attracts him. Women have always made love to him and Robin will make great eyes, and blush and look at him from under her lashes as if she were going to cry with joy—like Alice in the Ben Bolt song. She'll 'weep with delight when he gives her a smile and tremble with fear at his frown.' His mother can't stop it, however furious she may be. Nothing can stop that sort of thing when it once begins."

"If England declares war Donal Muir will have more serious things to do than pursue adventures," was Coombe's comment. He looked serious himself as he said the words, because they brought before him the bodily strength and beauty of the lad. He seemed suddenly to see him again as he had looked when he was dancing. And almost at the same moment he saw other scenes than ball-rooms and heard sounds other than those drawn forth by musicians screened with palms. He liked the boy. He was not his son, but he liked him. If he had been his son, he thought—! He had been through the monster munition works at Essen several times and he had heard technical talks of inventions, the sole reason for whose presence in the world was that they had the power to blow human beings into unrecognisable, ensanguined shreds and to tear off limbs and catapult them into the air. He had heard these powers talked of with a sense of natural pride in achievement, in fact with honest and cheerful self gratulation.

He had known Count Zeppelin well and heard his interesting explanation of what would happen to a thickly populated city on to which bombs were dropped.

But Feather's view was lighter and included only such things as she found entertaining.

"If there's a war the heirs of great families won't be snatched at first," she quite rattled on. "There'll be a sort of economising in that sort of thing. Besides he's very young and he isn't in the Army. He'd have to go through some sort of training. Oh, he'll have time! And there'll be so much emotion and excitement and talk about parting forever and 'This may be the last time we ever meet' sort of thing that every boy will have adventure—and not only boys. When I warned Robin, the night before she went away, I did not count on war or I could have said more—"

"What did you warn her of?"

"Of making mistakes about the men who would make love to her. I warned her against imagining she was as safe as she would be if she were a daughter of the house she lived in. I knew what I was talking about."

"Did she?" was Coombe's concise question.

"Of course she did—though of course she pretended not to. Girls always pretend. But I did my duty as a parent. And I told her that if she got herself into any mess she mustn't come to me."

Lord Coombe regarded her in silence for a moment or so. It was one of the looks which always made her furious in her small way.

"Good morning," he said and turned his back and walked out of the room. Almost immediately after he had descended the stairs she heard the front door close after him.

It was the kind of thing which made her feel her utter helplessness against him and which enraged all the little cat in her being. She actually ground her small teeth.

"I was quite right," she said. "It's her affair to take care of herself. Would he want her to come to *him* in any silly fix? I should like to see her try it."

Chapter 3

Robin sat at the desk in her private room and looked at a key she held in her hand. She had just come upon it among some papers. She had put it into a narrow lacquered box when she arranged her belongings, after she left the house in which her mother continued to live. It was the key which gave entrance to the Gardens. Each householder possessed one. She alone knew why she rather timidly asked her mother's permission to keep this one.

"One of the first things I seem to remember is watching the gardeners planting flowers," Robin had said. "They had rows of tiny pots with geraniums and lobelia in them. I have been happy there. I should like to be able to go in sometimes and sit under the trees. If you do not mind—"

Feather did not mind. She herself was not in the least likely to be seized with a desire to sit under trees in an atmosphere heavy with nursemaids and children.

So Robin had been allowed to keep the key and until to-day she had not opened the lacquer box. Was it quite by accident that she had found it? She was not quite sure it was and she was asking herself questions, as she sat looking at it as it lay in her palm.

The face of the whole world had changed since the night when she had sat among banked flowers and palms and ferns, and heard the splashing of the fountain and the sound of the music and dancing, and Donal Muir's voice, all at the same time. That which had happened had made everybody and everything different; and, because she lived in this particular house and saw much of special people, she realised that the growing shudder in the life about her was only the first convulsive tremor of an earthquake. The Duchess began to have much more for her to do. She called on her to read special articles in the papers, and to make notes and find references. Many visitors came to the house to discuss, to plan, to prepare for work. A number of good-looking, dancing boys had begun to come in and out in uniform, and with eager faces and a businesslike military air which oddly transformed them. The recalcitrant George was more transformed than any of the rest. His eyes looked almost fierce in their anxious intensity, his voice had taken on a somewhat hard defiant ring. It could not be possible that he had ever done that silly thing by the fountain and that she had splashed him from head to foot. It was plain that there were young soldiers who were straining at leashes, who were restless at being held back by the bindings of red tape, and who every hour were hearing things—true or untrue—which filled them with blind fury. As days passed Robin heard some of these things—stories from Belgium—which caused her to stare straight before her, blanched with horror. It was not only the slaughter and helplessness which pictured itself before her—it was stories half hinted at about girls like herself—girls who were trapped and overpowered—carried into lonely or dark places where no one could hear them. Sometimes George and the Duchess forgot her because she was so quiet—people often forgot everything but their excitement and wrath—and every one who came in to talk, because the house had become a centre of activities, was full of new panics or defiances or rumours of happenings or possibilities.

The maelstrom had caught Robin herself in its whirling. She realised that she had changed with the rest. She was no longer only a girl who was looked at as she passed along the street and who was beginning to be happy because she could earn her living. What was every girl in these days? How did any girl know what lay before her and those who protected the land she lived in? What could a girl do but try in some way to help—in any way to help the fight and the fighters. She used to lie awake and think of the Duchess' plans and concentrate her thought on the mastering of details. There was no hour too early or too late to find her ready to spring to attention. The Duchess had set her preparations for future possibilities in train before other women had quite begun to believe in their existence.

Lady Lothwell had at first laughed quite gaily at certain long lists she found her mother occupied with—though this, it is true, was in early days.

But Robin, even while whirled by the maelstrom, could not cease thinking certain vague remote thoughts. The splashing of fountains among flowers, and the sound of music and dancing were far away—but there was an echo to which she listened unconsciously as Donal Muir did. Something she gave no name to. But as the, as yet unheard, guns sent forth vibrations which reached far, there rose before her pictures of columns of marching men—hundreds, thousands, young, erect, steady and with clear eyes—marching on and on—to what—to what? Would *every* man go? Would there not be some who, for reasons, might not be obliged—or able—or ready—until perhaps the, as yet hoped for, sudden end of the awful thing had come? Surely there would be many who would be too young—or whose youth could not be spared because it stood for some power the nation needed in its future.

She had taken out and opened the lacquered box while thinking these things. She was thinking them as she looked at the key in her hand.

"It is not quiet anywhere now," she said to herself. "But there will be some corner under a tree in the Gardens where it will *seem* quiet if one sits quite still there. I will go and try."

There were very few nursemaids with their charges in the place when she reached it about an hour later.

The military element filling the streets engendered a spirit of caution with regard to nursemaids in the minds of their employers. Even those who were not young and good-looking were somewhat shepherded. The two or three quite elderly ones in the Gardens cast serious glances at the girl who walked past them to a curve in the path where large lilac bushes and rhododendrons made a sort of nook for a seat under a tree.

They could not see her when she sat down and laid her book beside her on the bench. She did not even open it, but sat and looked at the greenery of the shrubs before her. She was very still, and she looked as if she saw more than mere leaves and branches.

After a few minutes she got up slowly and went to a tall bush of lilac. She plucked several leaves and carried them back to her bench, somewhat as if she were a girl moving in a dream. Then, with a tiny shadow of a smile, she took a long pin from under the lapel of her coat and, leaning forward, began to prick out a pattern on the leaf she had laid on the wooden seat. She was in the midst of doing it—had indeed decorated two or three—when she found herself turning her head to listen to something. It was a quick, buoyant marching step—not a nursemaid's, not a gardener's, and it was coming towards her corner as if with intention—and she suddenly knew that she was listening as if the intention concerned herself. This was only because there are psychological moments, moods, conditions at once physical and mental when every incident in life assumes the significance of intention—because unconsciously or consciously one is *waiting*.

Here was a crisp tread somehow conveying a suggestion of familiar happy eagerness. The tall young soldier who appeared from behind the clump of shrubs and stood before her with a laughing salute had evidently come hurriedly. And the hurry and laughter extraordinarily brought back the Donal who had sprung upon her years ago from dramatic ambush. It was Donal Muir who had come.

"I saw you from a friend's house across the street," he said. "I followed you."

He made no apology and it did not even cross her mind that apology was conventionally necessary. He sat down beside her and his effect—though it did not express itself physically—was that of one who was breathing quickly. The clear blueness of his gaze seemed to enfold and cover her. The wonderfulness of him was the surrounding atmosphere she had felt as a little child.

"The whole world is rocking to and fro," he said. "It has gone mad. We are all mad. There is no time to wait for anything."

"I know! I know!" she whispered, because her pretty breast was rising and falling, and she had scarcely breath left to speak with.

Even as he looked down at her, and she up at him, the colour and laughter died out of him. Some suddenly returning memory brought a black cloud into his eyes and made him pale. He caught hold of both her hands and pressed them quite hard against his bowed face. He did not kiss them but held them against his cheek.

"It is terrible," he said.

Without being told she knew what he meant.

"You have been hearing new horrible things?" she said. What she guessed was that they were the kind of things she had shuddered at, feeling her blood at once hot and cold. He lifted his face but did not release her hands.

"At my friend's house. A man had just come over from Holland," he shook himself as if to dismiss a nightmare. "I did not come here to say such things. The enormous luck of catching sight of you, by mere chance, through the window electrified me. I—I came because I was catapulted here." He tried to smile and managed it pretty well. "How could I stay when—there you were! Going into the same garden!" He looked round him at the greenness with memory awakening. "It's the same garden. The shrubs have grown much bigger and they have planted some new ones—but it is the same garden." His look came back to her. "You are the same Robin," he said softly.

"Yes," she answered, as she had always answered "yes" to him.

"You are the same little child," he added and he lifted her hands again, but this time he kissed them as gently as he had spoken. "God! I'm glad!" And that was said softly, too. He was not a man of thirty or forty—he was a boy of twenty and his whole being was vibrating with the earthquake of the world.

That he vaguely recognised this last truth revealed itself in his next words.

"It would have taken me six months to say this much to you—to get this far—before this thing began," he said. "I daren't have run after you in the street. I should have had to wait about and make calls and ask for invitations to places where I might see you. And when we met we should have been polite and have talked all round what we wanted to say. It would have been cheek to tell you—the second time we met—that your eyes looked at me just as they did when you were a little child. I should have had to be decently careful because you might have felt shy. You don't feel shy now, do you? No, you don't," in caressing conviction and appeal.

"No—no." There was the note of a little mating bird in the repeated word.

This time he spread one of her hands palm upward on his own larger one. He looked down at it tenderly and stroked it as he talked.

"It is because there is no time. Things pour in upon us. We don't know what is before us. We can only be sure of one thing—that it may be death or wounds. I don't know when they'll think me ready to be sent out—or when they'll be ready to send me and other fellows like me. But I shall be sent. I am sitting in a garden here with you. I'm a young chap and big and strong and I love life. It is my duty as a man to go and kill other young chaps who love it as much as I do. And they must do their best to kill me, 'Gott strafe England,' they're saying in Germany—I understand it. Many a time it's in me to say, 'Gott strafe Germany.'"

He drew in his breath sharply, as if to pull himself together, and was still a moment. The next he turned upon her his wonderful boy's smile. Suddenly there was trusting appeal in it.

"You don't mind my holding your hand and talking like this, do you? Your eyes are as soft as—I've seen fawns cropping among the primroses with eyes that looked like them. But yours *understand*. You don't mind my doing this?" he kissed her palm. "Because there is no time."

Her free hand caught at his sleeve.

"No," she said. "You're going—you're *going*!"

"Yes," he answered. "And you wouldn't hold me back."

"No! No! No! No!" she cried four times, "Belgium! Belgium! Oh! Belgium!" And she hid her eyes on his sleeve.

"That's it—Belgium! There has been war before, but this promises from the outset to be something else. And they're coming on in their millions. We have no millions—we have not even guns and uniforms enough, but we've got to stop them, if we do it with our bare hands and with walls of our dead bodies. That was how Belgium held them back. Can England wait?"

"You can't wait!" cried Robin. "No man can wait."

How he glowed as he looked at her!

"There. That shows how you understand. See! That's what draws me. That's why, when I saw you through the window, I had to follow you. It wasn't only your lovely eyes and your curtains of eyelashes and because you are a sort of rose. It is you—you! Whatsoever you said, I should know the meaning of, and what I say you will always understand. It's as if we answered each other. That's why I never forgot you. It's why I waked up so when I saw you at the Duchess'." He tried to laugh, but did not quite succeed. "Do you know I have never had a moment's real rest since that night—because I haven't seen you."

"I—" faltered Robin, "have wondered and wondered—where you were."

All the forces of nature drew him a little nearer to her—though the gardener who clumped past them dully at the moment only saw a particularly good-looking young soldier, apparently engaged in agreeable conversation with a pretty girl who was not a nursemaid.

"Did you come here because of that?" he asked with frank anxiety. "Do you come here often and was it just chance? Or did you come because you were wondering?"

"I didn't exactly know—at first. But I know now. I have not been here since I went to live in Eaton Square," she gave back to him. Oh! How good and beautiful his asking eyes were! It was as he drew even a little nearer that he saw for the first time the pricked lilac leaves lying on the bench beside her.

"Did you do those?" he said suddenly quite low. "Did you?"

"Yes," as low and quite sweetly unashamed. "You taught me—when we played together."

The quick emotion in his flushing face could scarcely be described.

"How lovely—how *lovely* you are!" he exclaimed, almost under his breath. "I—I don't know how to say what I feel—about your remembering. You little—little thing!" This last because he somehow strangely saw her five years old again.

It was a boy's unspoiled, first love making—the charming outburst of young passion untrained by familiar use to phrases. It was like the rising of a Spring freshet and had the same irresistible power.

"May I have them? Will you give them to me with your own little hand?"

The happy glow of her smiling, as she picked them up and laid them, one by one, on his open extended palm, was as the glow of the smiling of young Eve. The dimples playing round her mouth and the quiver of her lashes, as she lifted them to laugh into his eyes, were an actual peril.

"Must I give you the pin too?" she said.

"Yes—everything," he answered in a sort of helpless joy. "I would carry the wooden bench away with me if I could. But they would stop me at the gate." They were obliged to treat something a little lightly because everything seemed tensely tremulous.

"Here is the pin," she said, taking it from under the lapel of her coat. "It is quite a long one." She looked at it a moment and then ended in a whisper. "I must have known why I was coming here—because, you see, I brought the pin." And her eyelashes lifted themselves and made their circling shadows again.

"Then I must have the pin. And it will be a talisman. I shall have a little flat case made for the leaves and the sacred pin shall hold it together. When I go into battle it will keep me safe. Bullets and bayonets will glance aside." He said it, as he laid the treasure away in his purse, and he did not see her face as he spoke of bullets and bayonets.

"I am a Highlander," he said next and for the moment he looked as if he saw things far away. "In the Highlands we believe more than most people do. Perhaps that's why I feel as if we two are not quite like other people,—as if we had been something—I don't know what—to each other from the beginning of time—since the 'morning stars first sang together.' I don't know exactly what that means, or how stars sing—but I like the sound of it. It seems to mean something I mean though I don't know how to say it." He was not in the least portentous or solemn, but he was the most strongly feeling and *real* creature she had ever heard speaking to her and he swept her along with him, as if he had indeed been the Spring freshet and she a leaf. "I believe," here he began to speak slowly as if he were thinking it out, "that there was something—that meant something—in the way we two were happy together and could not bear to be parted—years ago when we were nothing but children. Do you know that, little chap as I was, I never stopped thinking of you day and night when we were not playing together. I *couldn't!*"

"Neither could I stop thinking," said Robin. "I had dreams about seeing your eyes looking at me. They were blue like clear water in summer. They were always laughing. I always *wanted* them to look at me! They—they are the same eyes now," in a little rush of words.

Their blueness was on hers—in the very deeps of their uplifted liquidity.

"God! I'm *glad!*" his voice was on a hushed note.

There has never been a limner through all the ages who has pictured—at such a moment—two pairs of eyes reaching, melting into, lost in each other in their human search for the longing soul drawing together human things. Hand and brush and colour cannot touch That which Is and Must Be—in its yearning search for the spirit which is its life on earth. Yet a boy and girl were yearning towards it as they sat in mere mortal form on a bench in a London square. And neither of them knew more than that they wondered at and adored the beauty in each other's eyes.

"I didn't know what a little chap I was," he said next. "I'd had a splendid life for a youngster and I was big for my age and ramping with health and strength and happiness. You seemed almost a baby to me, but—it was the way you looked at me, I think—I wanted to talk to you, and please you and make you laugh. You had a red little mouth with deep dimples that came and went near the corners. I liked to see them twinkle."

"You told me," she laughed, remembering. "You put the point of your finger in them. But you didn't hurt me," in quick lovely reassuring. "You were not a rough little boy."

"I wouldn't have hurt you for worlds. I didn't even know I was cheeky. The dimples were so deep that it seemed quite natural to poke at them—like a sort of game."

"We laughed and laughed. It *was* a sort of game. I sat quite still and let you make little darts at them," Robin assisted him. "We laughed like small crazy things. We almost had child hysterics."

The dimples showed themselves now and he held himself in leash.

"You did everything I wanted you to do," he said, "and I suppose that made me feel bigger and bigger."

"*I* thought you were big. And I had never seen anything so wonderful before. You knew everything in the world and I knew nothing. Don't you remember," with hesitation—as if she were almost reluctant to recall the memory of a shadow into the brightness of the moment—"I told you that I had nothing—and nobody?"

All rushed back to him in a warm flow.

"That was it," he said. "When you said that I felt as if some one had insulted and wronged something of my own. I remember I felt hot and furious. I wanted to give you things and fight for you. I—caught you in my arms and squeezed you."

"Yes," Robin answered.

"It was because of—that time when the morning stars first sang together," he answered smiling, but still as *real* as before. "It wasn't a stranger child I wanted to take care of. It was some one I had—belonged to—long—long and long. I'm a Highlander and I know it's true. And there's another thing I know," with a sudden change almost to boyish fierceness, "you are one of the things I'm going to face cannon and bayonets for. If there were nothing else and no one else in England, I should stand on the shore and fight until I dropped dead and the whole Hun mass surged over me before they should reach you."

"Yes," whispered Robin, "I know."

They both realised that the time had come when they must part, and when he lifted again the hand nearest to him, it was with the gesture of one who had reached the moment of farewell.

"It's our garden," he said. "It's the *same* garden. Just because there is no time—may I see you here again? I can't go away without knowing that."

"I will come," she answered, "whenever the Duchess does not need me. You see I belong to nobody but myself."

"I belong to people," he said, "but I belong to myself too." He paused a second or so and a strange half puzzled expression settled in his eyes. "It's only fair that a man who's looking the end of things straight in the face should have something for himself—to himself. If it's only a heavenly hour now and then. Before things stop. There's such a lot of life—and such a lot to live for—forever if one could. And a smash—or a crash—or a thrust—and it's over! Sometimes I can hardly get hold of it."

He shook his head as he rose and stood upright, drawing his splendid young body erect.

"It's only fair," he said. "A chap's so strong and—and ready for living. Everything's surging through one's mind and body. One can't go out without having *something*—of one's own. You'll come, won't you—just because there's no time? I—I want to keep looking into your eyes."

"I want you to look into them," said Robin. "I'll come."

He stood still a moment looking at her just as she wanted him to look. Then after a few more words he bent low and kissed her hands and then stood straight again and saluted and went away.

Chapter 4

There was one facet of the great stone of War upon which many strange things were written. They were not the things most discussed or considered. They were results—not causes. But for the stress of mental, spiritual and physical tempest-of-being the colossal background of storm created, many of them might never have happened; but the consequences of their occurrence were to touch close, search deep, and reach far into the unknown picture of the World the great War might leave in fragments which could only be readjusted by centuries of time.

The interested habit of observation of, and reflection on, her kind which knew no indifferences, in the mind of the Duchess of Darte, awakened by stages to the existence of this facet and to the moment of the writings thereupon.

"It would seem almost as if Nature—Fate—had meant to give a new impulse to the race—to rouse human creatures to new moods, to thrust them into places where they see new things. Men and women are being dragged out of their self-absorbed corners and stirred up and shaken. Emotions are being roused in people who haven't known what a real emotion was. Middle-aged husbands and wives who had sunk into comfortable acceptance of each other and their boys and girls are being dragged out of bed, as it were, and wakened up and made to stand on their feet and face unbelievable possibilities. If you have boys old enough to be soldiers and girls old enough to be victims—your life makes a sort of *volte face* and everyday, worldly comforts and successes or little failures drop out of your line of sight, and change their values. Mothers are beginning to clutch at their sons; and even self-centred fathers and selfish pretty sisters look at their male relatives with questioning, with a hint of respect or even awe in it. Perhaps the women feel it more than the men. Good-looking, light-minded, love-making George has assumed a new aspect to his mother and to Kathryn. They're secretly yearning over him. He has assumed a new aspect to me. I yearn over him myself. He has changed—he has suddenly grown up. Boys are doing it on every hand."

"The youngest youngster vibrates with the shock of cannon firing, even though the sound may not be near enough to be heard," answered Coombe. "We're all vibrating unconsciously. We are shuddering consciously at the things we hear and are mad to put a stop to, before they go further."

"Innocent little villages full of homes torn and trampled under foot and burned!" the Duchess almost cried out. "And worse things than that—worse things! And the whole monstrosity growing more huge and throwing out new and more awful tentacles every day."

"Every hour. No imagination has yet conceived what it may be."

"That is why the poor human things are clutching at each other, and finding values and attractions where they did not see them before. Colonel Marion and his wife were here yesterday. He is a stout man over fifty and has a red face and prominent eyes. His wife has been so occupied with herself and her children that she had almost forgotten he existed. She looked at and listened to him as if she were a bride."

"I have seen changes of that sort myself," said Coombe. "He is more alive himself. He has begun to be of importance. And men like him have been killed already—though the young ones go first."

"The young ones know that, and they clutch the most frantically. That is what I am seeing in young eyes everywhere. Mere instinct makes it so—mere uncontrollable instinct which takes the form of a sort of desperateness at facing the thousand chances of death before they have lived. They don't know it isn't actual fear of bullets and shrapnel. Sometimes they're afraid it's fear and it makes them sick at themselves and determined to grin and hide it. But it isn't fear—it's furious Nature protesting."

"There are hasty bridals and good-bye marriages being made in all ranks," Coombe put in. "They are inevitable."

"God help the young things—those of them who never meet

again—and perhaps, also, some of those who do. The nation ought to take care of the children. If there is a nation left, God knows they will be needed," the Duchess said. "One of my footmen who 'joined up' has revealed an unsuspected passion for a housemaid he used to quarrel with, and who seemed to detest him. I have three women in my household who have soldier lovers in haste to marry them. I shall give them my blessing and take care of the wives when they are left behind. One can be served by old men and married women—and one can turn cottages into small orphanages if the worst happens."

There was a new vigour in her splendid old face and body.

"There is a reason now why I am the Dowager Duchess of Darte," she went on, "and why I have money and houses and lands. There is a reason why I have lived when it sometimes seemed as if my usefulness was over. There are uses for my money—for my places—for myself. Lately I have found myself saying, as Mordecai said to Esther, 'Who knowest whether thou art not come to the kingdom for such a time as this.' A change is taking place in me too. I can do more because there is so much more to do. I can even use my hands better. Look at them."

She held them out that he might see them—her beautiful old-ivory fingers, so long stiffened by rheumatism. She slowly opened and shut them.

"I can move them more—I have been exercising them and having them rubbed. I want to be able to knit and sew and wait on myself and perhaps on other people. Because I have been a rich, luxurious old woman it has not occurred to me that there were rheumatic old women who were forced to do things because they were poor—the things I never tried to do. I have begun to try."

She let her hands fall on her lap and sat gazing up at him with a rather strange expression.

"Do you know what I have been doing?" she said. "I have been praying to God—for a sort of miracle. In their terror people are beginning to ask their Deity for things as they have never done it before. We are most of us like children waking in horror of the black night and shrieking for some one to come—some one—any one! Each creature cries out to his own Deity—the God his own need has made.

Most of us are doing it in secret—half ashamed to let it be known. We are abject things. Mothers and fathers are doing it—young lovers and husbands and wives."

"What miracle are you asking for?"

"For power to do things I have not done for years. I want to walk—to stand—to work. If under the stress of necessity I begin to do all three, my doctors will say that mental exaltation and will power have caused the change. It may be true, but mental exaltation and will power are things of the soul not of the body. Anguish is actually forcing me into a sort of practical belief. I am trying to 'have faith even as a grain of mustard seed' so that I may say unto my mountain, 'Remove hence to yonder place and it shall be removed.'"

"'The things which I do, ye shall do also and even greater things than these shall ye do.'" Coombe repeated the words deliberately. "I heard an earnest middle-aged dissenter preach a sermon on that text a few days ago."

"What?"—his old friend leaned forward. "Are *you* going to hear sermons?"

"I am one of the children, I suppose. Though I do not shriek aloud, probably something shrieks within me. I was passing a small chapel and heard a singular voice. I don't know exactly why I went into the place, but when I sat down inside I felt the tension of the atmosphere at once. Every one looked anxious or terrified. There were pale faces and stony or wild eyes. It did not seem to be an ordinary service and voices kept breaking out with spasmodic appeals, 'Almighty God, look down on us!' 'Oh, Christ, have mercy!' 'Oh, God, save us!' One woman in black was rocking backwards and forwards and sobbing over and over again, 'Oh, Jesus! Jesus! Oh, Lord Jesus!'"

"Part of her body and soul was lying done to death in some field—or by some roadside," said the Duchess. "She could not pray—she could only cry out. I can hear her, 'Oh, Lord Jesus!'"

Later came the morning when the changed George came to say good-bye. He was wonderfully good-looking in his khaki and seemed taller and more square of jaw. He made a few of the usual young jokes which were intended to make things cheerful and to treat affectionate fears lightly, but his good-natured blue eye held a certain deadly quiet in its depths.

His mother and Kathryn were with him, and it was while they were absorbed in anxious talk with the Duchess that he walked over to where Robin sat and stood before her.

"Will you come into the library and let me say something to you? I don't want to go away without saying it," he put it to her.

The library was the adjoining room and Robin rose and went with him without any comment or question. Already the time had come when formalities had dropped away and people did not ask for trivial explanations. The pace of events had become too rapid.

"There are a lot of chances when a man goes out—that he won't come back," he said, still standing after she had taken a place in the window-seat he guided her to. "There are not as many as one's friends can't help thinking—but there are enough to make him feel he'd like to leave things straight when he goes. What I want you to let me say is, that the minute I had made a fool of myself the night of the dance, I knew what an ass I had been and I was ready to grovel."

Robin's lifted face was quite gentle. Suddenly she was thinking self-reproachfully, "Oh, poor boy—poor boy!"

"I flew into a temper and would not let you," she answered him. "It *was* temper—but there were things you didn't know. It was not your fault that you didn't." The square, good-natured face flushed with relief, and George's voice became even slightly unsteady.

"That's kind of you," he said, "it's *kind* and I'm jolly grateful. Things mean a lot just now—with all one's people in such a state and trying so pluckily to hide it. I just wanted to make sure that you knew that *I* knew that the thing only happened because I was a silly idiot and for no other reason. You will believe me, won't you, and won't remember it if you ever remember me?"

"I shall remember you—and it is as if—that had never happened at all."

She put out, as she got up, such a kind hand that he grasped it almost joyously.

"You have made it awfully easy for me. Thank you, Miss Lawless." He hesitated a second and then dropped his voice. "I wonder if I dare—I wonder if it would be cheek—and impudence if I said something else?"

"Scarcely anything seems cheek or impudence now," Robin answered with simple sadness. "Nothing ordinary seems to matter because *everything* is of so much importance."

"I feel as if what I wanted to say was one of the things that *are* important. I don't know what—older people—or safe ones—would think about it, but—" He broke off and began again. "To *us* young ones who are facing—It's the only big thing that's left us—in our bit of the present. We can only be sure of to-day—"

"Yes—yes," Robin cried out low. "Only to-day—just to-day." She even panted a little and George, looking into her eyes, knew that he might say anything, because for a reason she was one of the girls who in this hour could understand.

"Perhaps you don't know where our house is," he said quite quickly. "It is one of those in the Square—facing the Gardens. I might have played with you there when I was a little chap—but I don't think I did."

"Nobody did but Donal," she said, quickly also. How did she know that he was going to say something to her about Donal?

"I gave him the key to the Gardens that day," he hurried on. "I was at the window with him when he saw you. I understood in a minute when I saw his face and he'd said half a dozen words to me. I gave him my key. He has got it now." He actually snatched at both her hands and gripped them. It was a *grip* and his eyes burned through a sort of sudden moisture. "We can't stay here and talk. But I couldn't *not* say it! Oh, I say, be *good* to him! You would, if he had only a day to live because some damned German bullet had struck him. You're life—you're youngness—you're *to-day*! Don't say 'No' to *anything* he asks of you—for God's sake, don't."

"I'd give him my heart in his two hands," gasped Robin. "I couldn't give him my soul because it was always his."

"God take care of the pair of you—and be good to the rest of us," whispered George, wringing her hands hard and dropping them.

That was how he went away.

A few weeks later he was lying, a mangled object, in a field in

46

Flanders. One of thousands—living, laughing, good as honest bread is good; the possible passer-on of life and force and new thinking for new generations—one of hundreds of thousands—one of millions before the end came—nice, healthy, normal-minded George, son and heir of a house of decent nobles.

Chapter 5

And still youth marched away, and England seemed to swarm with soldiers and, at times, to hear and see nothing but marching music and marching feet, though life went on in houses, shops, warehouses and offices, and new and immense activities evolved as events demanded them. Many of the new activities were preparations for the comfort and care of soldiers who were going away, and for those who would come back and would need more care than the others. Women were doing astonishing work and revealing astonishing power and determination. The sexes mingled with a businesslike informality unknown in times of peace. Lovely girls went in and out of their homes, and from one quarter of London to another without question. They walked with a brisk step and wore the steady expression of creatures with work in view. Slim young war-widows were to be seen in black dresses and veiled small hats with bits of white crape inside their brims. Sometimes their little faces were awful to behold, but sometimes they wore a strained look of exaltation.

The Dowager Duchess of Darte was often absent from Eaton Square. She was understood to be proving herself much stronger than her friends had supposed her to be. She proved it by doing an extraordinary amount of work. She did it in her house in Eaton Square—in other people's houses, in her various estates in the country, where she prepared her villagers and tenants for a future in which every farm house and cottage must be as ready for practical service as her own castle or manor house. Darte Norham was no longer a luxurious place of residence but a potential hospital for wounded soldiers; so was Barons Court and the beautiful old Dower House at Malworth.

Sometimes Robin was with her, but oftener she remained at Eaton

Square and wrote letters and saw busy people and carried out lists of orders.

It was not every day or evening that she could easily find time to go out alone and make her way to the Square Gardens and in fact it was not often to the Gardens she went. There were so many dear places where trees grew and made quiet retreats—all the parks and heaths and green suburbs—and everywhere pairs walked or sat and talked, and were frankly so wholly absorbed in the throb of their own existences that they had no interest in, or curiosity concerning, any other human beings.

"Ought I to ask you to come and meet me—as if you were a little housemaid meeting her life-guardsman?" Donal had said feverishly the second time they met.

A sweet flush ran up to the roots of her hair and even showed itself on the bit of round throat where her dress was open.

"Yes, you ought," she answered. "There are no little housemaids and life-guardsmen now. It seems as if there were only—people."

The very sound of her voice thrilled him—everything about her thrilled him—the very stuff her plain frock was made of, the small hat she wore, her way of moving or quiet sitting down near him, but most of all the lift of her eyes to his—because there was no change in it and the eyes expressed what they had expressed when they had first looked at him. It was a thing which moved him to-day exactly as it had moved him when he was too young to explain its meaning and appeal. It was the lovely faith and yearning acceptance of him as a being whose perfection could not be questioned. There was in it no conscious beguiling flattery or appraisement—it was pure acceptance and sweet waiting for what he had to give. He sometimes found himself trembling with his sense of its simple unearthliness.

Few indeed were the people who at this time were wholly normal. The whole world seemed a great musical instrument, overstrung and giving out previously unknown harmonies and inharmonies. Amid the thunders of great crashing discords the individual note was almost unheard—but the individual note continued its vibrations.

The tone which expressed Donal Muir—in common with many others of his age and sex—was a novel and abnormal one. His being no longer sang the healthy human song of mere joy in life and living. A knowledge of cruelty and brutal force, of helplessness and despair, grew in him day by day. Causes for gay good cheer and laughter were swept away, leaving in their places black facts and needs to gaze at with hard eyes.

"Do you see how everything has *stopped*—how nothing can go on?" he said to Robin on their second meeting in the Gardens. "The things we used to fill our time and amuse ourselves with—dancing and tennis and polo and theatres and parties—how jolly and all right they were in their day, but how futile they seem just now. How could one even stand talk of them! There is only one thing."

The blue of his eyes grew dark.

"It is as if a gigantic wall were piling itself up between us and Life," he went on. "That is how I see it—a wall piling itself higher every hour. It's built of dead things and maimed and tortured ones. It's building itself of things you can't speak of. It stands between all the world and living—mere living. We can't go on till we've stormed it and beaten it down—or added our bodies to it. If it isn't beaten down it will rise to heaven itself and shut it out—and that will be the end of the world." He shook his head in sudden defiant bitterness. "If it can't be beaten down, better the world *should* come to an end."

Robin put out her hand and caught his sleeve.

"It will be beaten down," she cried. "You—*you*—and others like you—"

"It will be," he said. "And it's because, when men read the day's news, almost every single one of them feels something leaping up in him that seems strong enough to batter it to earth single-handed."

But he gently put out his own hand and took in it the slim gloved one and looked down at it, as if it were something quite apart and wonderful—rather as if hands were rare and he had not often seen one before.

There was much sound of heavy traffic on the streets. The lumbering of army motor trucks and vans, the hurry of ever-passing feet and vehicles, changed the familiar old-time London roar, which had been as that of low and distant thunder, into the louder rumbling of a storm which had drawn nearer and was spending its fury within the city's streets themselves. Just at this moment there arose the sound of some gigantic loaded thing, passing with unearthly noises, and high above it pierced the shrilling of fifes.

Robin glanced about the empty garden.

"The noise seems to shut us in. How deserted the Gardens look. I feel as if we were in another world. We are shut in—and shut out," she whispered.

He whispered also. He still looked down at the slim gloved hand as if it had some important connection with the moment.

"We have so few minutes together," he said. "And I have thought of so many things I must say to you. I cannot stop thinking about you. I think of you even when I am obliged to think of something else at the same time. I am in a sort of tumult every moment I am away from you." He stopped suddenly and looked up. "I am speaking as if I had been with you a score of times. I haven't, you know. I have only seen you once since the dance. But it is as if we had met every day—and it's true—I am in a sort of tumult. I think thousands of new things and I feel as if I *must* tell you of them all."

"I—think too," said Robin. Oh! the dark dew of her imploring eyes! Oh! the beat of the little pulse he could actually see in her soft bare throat. He did not even ask himself what the eyes implored for. They had always looked like that—as if they were asking to be allowed to be happy and to love all kind things on earth.

"One of the new things I cannot help thinking about—it's a queer thing and I must tell you about it. It's not like me and yet it's the strongest feeling I ever had. Since the War has changed everything and everybody, all one's feelings have grown stronger. I never was furious before—and I've been furious. I've felt savage. I've raged. And the thing I'm thinking of is like a kind of obsession. It's this—" he caught her hands again and held her face to face with him. "I—I want to have you to myself," he exclaimed.

She did not try to move. She only gazed at him.

"Nobody else *has* me—at all," she answered. "No one wants me."

The colour ran up under his fine skin.

"What I mean is a little different. Perhaps you mayn't understand it. I want this—our being together in this way—our understanding and talking—to be something that belongs to *us* and to no one else. It's too sudden and wonderful for any one but ourselves to understand. Nobody else *could* understand it. Perhaps we don't ourselves—quite! But I know what it does to *me*. I can't bear the thought of other people spoiling the beauty of it by talking it over and looking on." He actually got up and began to walk about. "Oh, I *ought* to have something of my own—before it's all over—I ought! I want this miracle of a thing—for my own."

He stopped and stood before her.

"My mother is the most beloved creature in the world. I have always told her everything. She has always cared. I don't know why I have not told her about—this—but I haven't and I don't want to—now. That is part of the strange thing. I do not want to tell her—even the belovedest woman that ever lived. I want it for myself. Will you let me have it—will you help me to keep it?"

"Like a secret?" said Robin in her soft note.

"No, not a secret. A sort of sacred, heavenly unbelievable thing we own together."

"I understand," was Robin's answer. "It does not seem strange to me. I have thought something like that too—almost exactly like."

It did not once occur to them to express, even to themselves, in any common mental form the fact that they were "in love" with each other. The tide which swept them with it had risen ages before and bore them on its swelling waves as though they were leaves.

"No one but ourselves will know that we meet," she went on further. "I may come and go as I like in these hurried busy hours. Even Lady Kathryn is as free as if she were a shop girl. It is as you said before—there is no time to be curious and ask questions. And even Dowie has been obliged to go to her cousin's widow whose husband has just been killed."

Shaken, thrilled, exalted, Donal sat down again and talked to her. Together they made their plans for meeting, as they had done when Andrews had slackened her guard. There was no guard to keep watch on them now. And the tide rose hour by hour.

Chapter 6

Aunts and cousins and more or less able relatives were largely drawn on in these days of stress and need, and Dowie was an efficient person. The cousin whose husband had been killed in Belgium, leaving a young widow and two children scarcely younger and more helpless than herself, had no relation nearer than Dowie, and had sent forth to the good woman a frantic wail for help in her desolation. The two children were, of course, on the point of being added to by an almost immediately impending third, and the mother, being penniless and prostrated, had remembered the comfortable creature with her solid bank account of savings and her good sense and good manners and knowledge of a world larger than the one into which she had been born.

"You're settled here, my lamb," Dowie had said to Robin. "It's more like your own home than the other place was. You're well and safe and busy. I must go to poor Henrietta in Manchester. That's my bit of work, it seems, and thank God I'm able to do it. She was a fine girl in a fine shop, poor Henrietta, and she's not got any backbone and her children are delicate—and another coming. Well, well! I do thank God that you don't need your old Dowie as you did at first."

Thus she went away and in her own pleasant rooms in the big house, now so full of new activities, Robin was as unwatched as if she had been a young gull flying in and out of its nest in a tall cliff rising out of the beating sea.

Her early fever of anxiety never to lose sight of the fact that she was a paid servitor had been gradually assuaged by the delicate adroitness of the Duchess and by the aid of soothing time. While no duty or service was forgotten or neglected, she realised that life was passed in an agreeable freedom which was a happy thing. Certain hours and days were absolutely her own to do what she chose with. She had never asked for such privileges, but the Duchess with an almost imperceptible adjustment had arranged that they should be hers. Sometimes she had taken Dowie away on little holidays to the sea side, often she spent hours in picture galleries or great libraries or museums. In attendance on the Duchess she had learned to know all the wonders and picturesqueness of her London and its environments, and often with Dowie as her companion she wandered about curious and delightful places and, pleased as a child, looked in at her kind at work or play.

While nations shuddered and gasped, cannon belched forth, thunder and flaming, battleships crashed together and sudden death was almost as unintermitting as the ticking of the clock, among the thousands of pairing souls and bodies drawn together in a new world where for the time being all sound was stilled but the throb of pulsing hearts, there moved with the spellbound throng one boy and girl whose dream of being was a thing of entrancement.

Every few days they met in some wonderfully chosen and always quiet spot. Donal knew and loved the half unknown remote corners of the older London too. There were dim gardens behind old law courts, bits of mellow old enclosures and squares seemingly forgotten by the world, there were the immensities of the great parks where embowered paths and corners were at certain hours as unexplored as the wilderness. When the Duchess was away or a day of holiday came, there were, more than once, a few hours on the river where, with boat drawn up under enshrouding trees, green light and lapping water, sunshine and silence, rare swans sailing serenely near as if to guard them made the background to the thrill of heavenly young wonder and joy.

It was always the same. Each pair of eyes found in the beauty of the other the same wonder and, through that which the being of each expressed, each was shaken by the same inward thrill. Sometimes they simply sat and gazed at each other like happy amazed children scarcely able to translate their own delight. Their very aloofness from the world—its unawareness of their story's existence made for the perfection of all they felt.

"It could not be like this if any one but ourselves even *knew*," Donal said. "It is as if we had been changed into spirits and human beings could not see us."

There was seldom much leisure in their meetings. Sometimes they had only a few minutes in which to exchange a word or so, to cling to each other's hands. But even in these brief meetings the words that were said were food for new life and dreams when they were apart. And the tide rose.

But it did not overflow until one early morning when they met in a gorse-filled hollow at Hampstead, each looking at the other pale and stricken. In Robin's wide eyes was helpless horror and Donal knew too well what she was going to say.

"Lord Halwyn is killed!" she gasped out. "And four of his friends! We all danced the tango together—and that new kicking step!" She began to sob piteously. Somehow it was the sudden memory of the almost comic kicking step which overwhelmed her with the most gruesome sense of awfulness—as if the world had come to an end.

"It was new—and they laughed so! They are killed!" she cried beating her little hands. He had just heard the same news. Five of them! And he had heard details she had been spared.

He was as pale as she. He stood before her quivering, hot and cold. Until this hour they had been living only through the early growing wonder of their dream; they had only talked together and exquisitely yearned and thrilled at the marvel of every simple word or hand-touch or glance, and every meeting had been a new delight. But now suddenly the being of each shook and called to the other in wild need of the nearer nearness which is comfort and help. It was early—early morning—the heath spread about them wide and empty, and at that very instant a skylark sprang from its hidden nest in the earth and circled upward to heaven singing as to God.

"They will take *you*!" she wailed. "*You—you!*" And did not know that she held out her arms.

But he knew—with a great shock of incredible rapture and tempestuous answering. He caught her softness to his thudding young chest and kissed her sobbing mouth, her eyes, her hair, her little pulsing throat.

"Oh, little love," he himself almost sobbed the words. "Oh, little lovely love!"

She melted into his arms like a weeping child. It was as if she had always rested there and it was mere Nature that he should hold and comfort her. But he had never heard or dreamed of the possibility of such anguish as was in her sobbing.

"They will take you!" she said. "And—you danced too. And I must not hold you back! And I must stay here and wait and wait—and *wait*—until some day—! Donal! Donal!"

He sat down with her amongst the gorse and held her on his knee as if she had been six years old. She did not attempt to move but crouched there and clung to him with both hands. She remembered only one thing—that he must go! And there were cannons—and shells singing and screaming! And boys like George in awful heaps. No laughing face as it had once looked—all marred and strange and piteously lonely as they lay.

It took him a long time to calm her terror and woe. When at last he had so far quieted her that her sobs came only at intervals she seemed to awaken to sudden childish awkwardness. She sat up and shyly moved. "I didn't mean—I didn't know—!" she quavered. "I am—I am sitting on your knee like a baby!" But he could not let her go.

"It is because I love you so," he answered in his compelling boy voice, holding her gently. "Don't move—don't move! There is no time to think and wait—or care for anything—if we love each other. We *do* love each other, don't we?" He put his cheek against hers and pressed it there. "Oh, say we do," he begged. "There is no time. And listen to the skylark singing!"

The butterfly-wing flutter of her lashes against his cheek as she pressed the softness of her own closer, and the quick exquisite indrawing of her tender, half-sobbing childish breath were unspeakably lovely answering things—though he heard her whisper.

"Yes, Donal! Donal!" And again, "Donal! Donal!"

And he held her closer and kissed her very gently again. And they sat and whispered that they loved each other and had always loved each other and would love each other forever and forever and forever. Poor enrapt children! It has been said before, but they said it again and yet again. And the circling skylark seemed to sing at the very gates of God's heaven.

So the tide rose to its high flowing.

Chapter 7

The days of gold which linked themselves one to another with strange dawns of pearl and exquisite awakenings, each a miracle, the gemmed night whose blue darkness seemed studded with myriads of new stars, the noons whose heats or rains were all warm scents of flowers and fragrant mists, wrought themselves into a chain of earthly beauty. The hour in which the links must break and the chain end was always a faint spectre veiled by kindly mists which seemed to rise hour by hour to soften and hide it.

But often in those days did it occur that the hurrying and changing visitors to the house in Eaton Square, glancing at Robin as she sat writing letters, or as she passed them in some hall or room, found themselves momentarily arrested in an almost startled fashion by the mere radiance of her.

"She is lovelier every time one turns one's head towards her," the Starling said—the Starling having become a vigorous worker and the Duchess giving welcome to any man, woman or child who could be counted on for honest help. "It almost frightens me to see her eyes when she looks up suddenly. It is like finding one's self too close to a star. A star in the sky is all very well—but a star only three feet away from one is a kind of shock. What has happened to the child?"

She said it to Gerald Vesey who between hours of military training was helping Harrowby to arrange a matinee for the benefit of the Red Cross. Harrowby had been rejected by the military authorities on account of defective sight and weak chest but had with a promptness unexpected by his friends merged himself into unprominent, useful hard work which frequently consisted of doing disagreeable small jobs men of his type generally shied away from.

"Something has happened to her," answered Vesey. "She has the flight of a skylark let out of a cage. Her moving is flight—not ordinary walking. I hope her work has kept her away from—well, from young gods and things."

"The streets are full of them," said Harrowby, "marching to defy death and springing to meet glory—marching not walking. Young Mars and Ajax and young Paris with Helen in his eyes. She might be some youngster's Helen! Why do you hope her work has kept her away?"

Vesey shook his Greek head with a tragic bitterness.

"Oh! I don't know," he groaned. "There's too much disaster piled high and staring in every one of their flushing rash young faces. On they go with their heads in the air and their hearts thumping, and hoping and refusing to believe in the devil and hell let loose—and the whole thing stares and gibbers at them."

But each day her eyes looked larger and more rapturously full of heavenly glowing, and her light movements were more like bird flight, and her swiftness and sweet readiness to serve delighted and touched people more, and they spoke oftener to and of her, and felt actually a thought uplifted from the darkness because she was like pure light's self.

Lord Coombe met her in the street one evening at twilight and he stopped to speak to her.

"I have just come from Darte Norham," he said to her. "The Duchess asked me to see you personally and make sure that you do not miss Dowie too much—that you are not lonely."

"I am very busy and am very well taken care of," was her answer. "The servants are very attentive and kind. I am not lonely at all, thank you. The Duchess is very good to me."

Donal evidently knew nothing of her reasons for disliking Lord Coombe. She could not have told him of them. He did not dislike his relative himself and in fact rather liked him in spite of the frigidity he sometimes felt. He, at any rate, admired his cold brilliance of mind. Robin could not therefore let herself detest the man and regard him as an enemy. But she did not like the still searching of the grey eyes which rested on her so steadily.

"The Duchess wished me to make sure that you did not work too enthusiastically. She desires you to take plenty of exercise and if you are tired to go into the country for a day or two of fresh air and rest. She recommends old Mrs. Bennett's cottage at Mersham Wood. The place is quite rustic though it is near enough to London to be convenient. You might come and go."

"She is too kind—too kind," said Robin. "Oh! *how* kind to think of me like that. I will write and thank her."

The sweet gratitude in her eyes and voice were touching. She could not speak steadily.

"I may tell her then that you are well taken care of and that you are happy," the grey eyes were a shade less cold but still searching and steady. "You look—happy."

"I never was so happy before. Please—please tell her that when you thank her for me," was Robin's quite yearning little appeal. She held out her hand to him for the first time in her life. "Thank you, Lord Coombe, for so kindly delivering her beautiful message."

His perfect manner did not record any recognition on his part of the fact that she had done an unexpected thing. But as he went on his way he was thinking of it.

"She is very happy for some reason," he thought. "Perhaps the rush and excitement of her new work exalts her. She has the ecstasied air of a lovely child on her birthday—with all her world filled with petting and birthday gifts."

The Duchess evidently extended her care to the extent of sending special messages to Mrs. James, the housekeeper, who began to exercise a motherly surveillance over Robin's health and diet and warmly to advocate long walks and country visits to the cottage at Mersham Wood.

"Her grace will be really pleased if you take a day or two while she's away. She's always been just that interested in those about her, Miss," Mrs. James argued. "She wouldn't like to come back and find you looking tired or pale. Not that there's much danger of that," quite beamingly. "For all your hard work, I must say you look—well, you look as I've never seen you. And you always had a colour like a new-picked rose."

The colour like a new-picked rose ran up to the rings of hair on the girl's forehead as if she were made a little shy.

"It is because her grace has been so good—and because every one is so kind to me," she said. "Kindness makes me happy."

She was so happy that she was never tired and was regarded as a young wonder in the matter of work and readiness and exactitude. Her accounts, her correspondence, her information were always in order. When she took the prescribed walks and in some aloof path or corner met the strong, slim khaki-clad figure, they walked or stood or sat closely side by side and talked of many things—though most of all they dwelt on one. She could ask Donal questions and he could throw light on such things as young soldiers knew better than most people. She came into close touch—a shuddering touch sometimes it was—with needs and facts concerning marchings and trenches and attacks and was therefore able to visualise and to speak definitely of necessities not always understood.

"How did you find that out?" little black-clad Lady Kathryn asked her one day. "I wish I had known it before George went away."

"A soldier told me," was her answer. "Soldiers know things we don't."

"The world is made of soldiers now," said Kathryn. "And one is always talking to them. I shall begin to ask them questions about small things like that."

It was the same morning that as they stood alone together for a few minutes Kathryn suddenly put her hand upon Robin's shoulder.

"You never—*never* feel the least angry—when you remember about George—the night of the dance," she pleaded shakily. "Do you, Robin? You couldn't *now*! Could you?"

Tears rushed into Robin's eyes.

"Never—never!" she said. "I always remember him—oh, quite differently! He—" she hesitated a second and began again. "He did something—so wonderfully kind—before he went away—something for me. That is what I remember. And his nice voice—and his good eyes."

"Oh! he *was* good! He was!" exclaimed Kathryn in a sort of despairing impatience. "So many of them are! It's awful!" And she sat down in the nearest chair and cried hopelessly into her crushed handkerchief while Robin tried to soothe—not to comfort her. There was no comfort to offer. And behind the rose tinted mists her own spectre merely pretended to veil itself.

When she lay in bed at night in her quiet room she often lay awake long and long for pure bliss. The world in which people were near—*near*—to one another and loved each other, the world Donal had always belonged to even when he was a little boy, she now knew and lived in. There was no loneliness in it. If there was pain or trouble some one who loved you was part of it and you, and so you could bear it. All the radiant mornings and heavenly nights, all the summer scents of flowers or hay or hedges in bloom, or new rain on the earth, were things felt just as that other one felt them and drew in their delights—exactly in the same way. Once in the night stillness of a sweet dark country lane she had stood in the circle of Donal's arm, her joyous, warm young breast against his and they had heard together the singing of a nightingale in a thicket.

"Let us stand still," he had whispered close to her ear. "Let us not speak a word—not a word. Oh! little lovely love! Let us only *listen*—and be happy!"

Almost every day there were marvels like this. And when they were apart she could not forget them but walked like a spirit strayed on to earth and unknowing of its radiance. This was why people glanced at her curiously and were sometimes vaguely troubled.

Chapter 8

The other woman who loved and was loved by him moved about her world in these days with a face less radiant than the one people turned to look at in the street or in its passing through the house in Eaton Square. Helen Muir's eyes were grave and pondered. She had always known of the sometime coming of the hour in which would rise the shadow—to him a cloud of rapture—which must obscure the old clearness of vision which had existed between them. She had been too well balanced of brain to allow herself to make a tragedy of it or softly to sentimentalise of loss. It was mere living nature that it should be so. He would be as always, a beloved wonder of dearness and beauty when his hour came and she would look on and watch and be so cleverly silent and delicately detached from his shy, aloof young moods, his funny, dear involuntary secrets and reserves. But at any moment—day or night—at any elate emotional moment *ready*!

She had the rare accomplishment of a perfect knowledge of *how to wait*, and to wait—if necessary—long. When the first golden down had shown itself on his cheek and lip she had not noticed it too much and when his golden soprano voice began to change to a deeper note and annoyed him with its uncertainties she had spared him awkwardness by making him feel the transition a casual natural thing, instead of a personal and characteristic weakness. She had loved every stage of innocence and ignorance and adorable silliness he had passed through and he had grown closer to her through the medium of each, because nothing in life was so clear as her lovely wiseness and fine perceptive entirety of sympathy and poise.

"I never have to explain really," he said more than once. "You would understand even if I were an idiot or a criminal. And you'd understand if I were an archangel."

With a deep awareness she knew that, when she first realised that the shadow was rising, it would be different. She would have to watch it with an aloofness more delicate and yet more warmly sensitive than any other. In the days when she first thought of him as like one who is listening to a far-off sound, it seemed possible that in the clamour of louder echoes this one might lose itself and at last die away even from memory. It was youth's way to listen and youth's way to find it easy to forget. He heard many reverberations in these days and had much reason or thought and action. He thought a great deal, he worked energetically, he came and went, he read and studied, he obeyed orders and always stood ready for new ones. Her pride in his vigorous initiative and practical determination was a glowing flame in her heart. He meant to be no toy soldier.

As she became as practical a worker as he was, they did much together and made plans without ceasing. When he was away she was always doing things in which he was interested and when he returned he always brought to her suggestions for new service or the development of the old. But as the days passed and became weeks she knew that the far-off sound was still being listened to. She could not have told how—but she knew. And she saw the beloved dearness and beauty growing in him. He came into the house each day in his khaki as if khaki were a shining thing. When he laughed, or sat and smiled, or dreamed—forgetting she was there—her very heart quaked with delight in him. Another woman than Robin counted over his charms and made a tender list of them, wondering at each one. As a young male pheasant in mating time dons finer gloss and brilliancy of plumage, perhaps he too bloomed and all unconscious developed added colour and inches and gallant swing of tread. As people turned half astart to look at Robin bending over her desk or walking about among them in her modest dress, so also did they turn to look after him as he went in springing march along the streets.

"Some day he will begin to tell me," Helen used to say to herself at night. "He may only *begin*—but perhaps it will be to-morrow."

It was not, however, to-morrow—or to-morrow. And in the midst of his work he still listened. As he sat and dreamed he listened and sometimes he was very deep in thought—sitting with his arms folded and his eyes troubled and questioning of the space into which he looked. The time was really not very long, but it began to seem so to her.

"But some day—soon—he will tell me," she thought.

One afternoon Donal walked into a room where a number of well-dressed women were talking, drinking tea and knitting or crocheting. It had begun already to be the fashion for almost every woman to carry on her arm a work bag and produce from its depths at any moment without warning something she was making. In the early days the bag was usually highly decorated and the article being made was a luxury. Only a few serious and pessimistic workers had begun to produce plain usefulness and in this particular Mayfair drawing-room "the War" as yet seemed to present itself rather as a dramatic and picturesque social asset. A number of good-looking young officers moved about or sat in corners being petted and flirted with, while many of the women had the slightly elated excitement of air produced in certain of their sex by the marked preponderance of the presence of the masculine element. It was a thing which made for high spirits and laughs and amiable semi-caressing chaff. The women who in times of peace had been in the habit of referring to their "boys" were in these days in great form.

Donal had been taken to the place by an amusement-loving acquaintance who professed that a special invitation made it impossible to pass by without dropping in. The house was Mrs. Erwyn's and had already attracted attention through the recent *débuts* of Eileen and Winifred who had grown up very pretty and still retained their large, curious eyes and their tendency to giggle musically.

In very short and slimly alluring frocks they were assisting their mother in preparing young warriors for the seat of war by giving them chocolate in egg-shell cups and little cakes. Winifred carried a coral satin work-bag embroidered with carnations and was crocheting a silk necktie peculiarly suited to fierce onslaught on the enemy.

"Oh!" she gasped, clutching in secret at Eileen's sleeve when Donal entered the room. "There he is! Jack said he would make him come! Just *look* at him!"

"Gracious!" ejaculated Eileen. "I daren't look! It's not safe!"

They looked, however, to their irresistible utmost when he came to make his nice, well-behaved bow to his hostess.

"I love his bow," Eileen whispered. "It is such a beautiful *tall* bow. And he looks as good as he is beautiful."

"Oh! not *good* exactly!" protested Winifred. "Just *sweet*—as if he thinks you are quite as nice as himself."

He was taken from one group to another and made much of and flattered quite openly. He was given claret cup and feathery sandwiches and asked questions and given information. He was chattered to and whispered about and spent half an hour in a polite vortex of presentation. He was not as highly entertained as his companion was because he was thinking of something else—of a place which seemed incredibly far away from London drawing-rooms—even if he could have convinced himself that it existed on the same earth. The trouble was that he was always thinking of this place—and of others. He could not forget them even in the midst of any clamour of life. Sometimes he was afraid he forgot where he was and might look as if he were not listening to people. There were moments when he caught his breath because of a sudden high throb of his heart. How could he shut out of his mind that which seemed to *be* his mind—his body—the soul of him!

It was at a moment when he was thinking of this with a sudden sense of disturbance that a silver toned voice evidently speaking to him attracted his attention.

The voice was of silver and the light laugh was silvery.

"You look as if you were not thinking of any of us," the owner said.

He turned about to find himself looking at one of the prettiest of the filmily dressed creatures in the room. Her frock was one of the briefest and her tiny heels the highest and most slender. The incredible foot and ankle wore a flesh silk stocking so fine that it looked as though they were bare—which was the achievement most to be aspired to. Every atom of her was lovely and her small deep-curved mouth and pure large eyes were like an angel's.

"I believe you remember me!" she said after a second or so in which they held each other's gaze and Donal knew he began to flush slowly.

"Yes," he answered. "I do—now I have looked again. You were—The Lady Downstairs."

She flung out the silver laugh again.

"After all these years! After one has grown old and withered and wrinkled—and has a grown-up daughter."

He answered with a dazzling young-man-of-the-world bow and air. He had not been to Eton and Oxford and touched the outskirts of two or three London seasons, as a boy beauty and a modest Apollo Belvidere in his teens, without learning a number of pleasant little ways.

"You are exactly as you were the morning you came into the Gardens dressed in crocuses and daffodils. I thought they were daffodils and crocuses. I said so to my mother afterwards."

He did not like her but he knew how her world talked to her. And he wanted to hear her speak—The Lady Downstairs—who had not "liked" the soft-eyed, longing, warm little lonely thing.

"All people say of you is entirely true," she said. "I did not believe it at first but I do now." She patted the seat of the small sofa she had dropped on. "Come and sit here and talk to me a few minutes. Girls will come and snatch you away presently but you can spare about three minutes."

He did as he was told and wondered as he came nearer to the shell fineness of her cheek and her seraphic smile.

"I want you to tell me something about my only child," she said.

He hoped very much that he did not flush in his sometimes-troublesome blond fashion then. He hoped so.

"I shall be most happy to tell you anything I have the honour of knowing," he answered. "Only ask."

"You would be capable of putting on a touch of Lord Coombe's little stiff air—if you were not so young and polite," she said. "It was Lord Coombe who told me about the old Duchess' dance—and that you tangoed or swooped—or kicked with my Robin. He said both of you did it beautifully."

"Miss Gareth-Lawless did—at least."

He was looking down and so did not chance to see the look of a little cat which showed itself in her quick side glance.

"She is not my Robin now. She belongs to the Dowager Duchess of Darte—for a consideration. She is one of the new little females who are obstinately determined to earn an honest living. I haven't seen her for months—perhaps years. Is she pretty?" The last three words came out like the little cat's pounce on a mouse. Donal even felt momentarily startled.

But he remained capable of raising clear eyes to hers and saying, "She was prettier than any one else at the Duchess' house that night. Far prettier."

"Have you never seen her since?"

This was a pounce again and he was quite aware of it.

"Yes."

Feather gurgled.

"That was really worthy of Lord Coombe," she said. "I wasn't being pushing, really, Mr. Muir. If any one asks you your intentions it will be the Dowager—not little Miss Gareth-Lawless' mother. I never pretended to chaperon Robin. She might run about all over London without my asking any questions. I am afraid I am not much of a mother. I am not in the least like yours."

"Like mine?" He wondered why his mother should be so suddenly dragged in.

She laughed with a bright air of being much entertained.

"Do you remember how Mrs. Muir whisked you away from London the day after she found out that you were playing with my vagabond of a Robin—unknowing of your danger? There was a mother for you! It nearly killed my little pariah."

She rose and held out her hand.

"I have not really had my three minutes, but 'I must not detain you any longer,' as Royal Highnesses say. I must go."

"Why?" he ejaculated with involuntary impatience.

"Because Eileen Erwyn is standing with her back markedly turned towards us, pretending to talk. I know the expression of her little ears and she has just laid them back close to her head, which means business. Why do you all at once look *quite* like Lord Coombe?"

Perhaps he did look a trifle like his relative. He had risen to his feet.

"I was not aware that I was whisked away from London," he said.

"I was," with pretty impudence. "You were bundled back to Scotland almost before daylight. Lord Coombe knew about it. We laughed immensely together. It was a great joke because Robin fainted and fell into the mud, or something of the sort, when you didn't turn up the next morning. She almost pined away and died of grief, tiresome little thing! I told you Eileen was preparing to assault. Here she is! Hordes of girls will now advance upon you. So glad to have had you even for a few treasured seconds. *Good* afternoon."

Chapter 9

It was not a long time before he had left the house, but it seemed long and as if he had thought a great many rather incoherent things before he had reached the street and presently parted from his gay acquaintance and was on his way to his mother's house where she was spending a week, having come down from Scotland as she did often.

He walked all the way home because he wanted movement. He also wanted time to think things over because the intensity of his own mood troubled him. It was new for him to think much about himself, but lately he had found himself sometimes wondering at, as well as shaken by, emotional mental phases through which he passed. A certain moving fancy always held its own in his thoughts—as a sort of background to them. It was in his feeling that he was in those weeks a Donal Muir who was unknown and unseen by the passing world. No one but himself—and Robin—could know the meaning, the feeling, the nature of this Donal. It was as if he lived in a new Dimension of whose existence other people did not know. He could not have explained because it would not have been understood. He could vaguely imagine that effort at explanation would end—even begin—by being so clumsy that it would be met by puzzled or unbelieving smiles.

To walk about—to sleep—to awaken surrounded by rarefied light and air in which no object or act or even word or thought wore its past familiar meaning, or to go about the common streets, feeling as though somehow one were apart and unseen, was a singular thing. Having had a youth filled with quite virile pleasures and delightful emotions—and to be lifted above them into other air and among other visions—was, he told himself, like walking in a dream. To be filled continually with one thought, to rebel against any obstacle in the path to one desire, and from morning until night to be impelled by one eagerness for some moment or hour for which there was reason enough for its having place in the movings of the universe, if it brought him face to face with what he must stand near to—see—hear—perhaps touch.

It was because of the world's madness, because of the human fear and weeping everywhere, because of the new abysses which seemed to yawn every day on every side, that both soul and senses were so abnormally overstrung. He was overwhelmed by exquisite compassions in his thoughts of Robin, he was afraid for her youngness, her sweetness, the innocent defencelessness which was like a child's. He was afraid of his own young rashness and the entrancement of the dream. The great lunging chariot of War might plunge over them both.

But never for one moment could he force himself to regret or repent. Boys in their twenties already lay in their thousands on the fields over there. And she would far, far rather remember the kind hours and know that they were hidden in his heart for him to remember as he died—if he died! She had lain upon his breast holding him close and fast and she had sobbed hard—hard—but she had said it again and again and over and over when he had asked her.

It was this aspect of her and things akin to it which had risen in his incoherent thoughts when he was manoeuvering to get away from the drawing-room full of chattering people. He knew himself overwhelmed again by the exquisite compassion because the thing Mrs. Gareth-Lawless had told him had brought back all the silent anguish of impotent childish rebellion the morning when he had been awakened before the day, and during the day when he had thought his small breast would burst as the train rushed on with him—away—away!

And Robin had told him the rest—sitting one afternoon in the same chair with him—a roomy, dingy red arm-chair in an old riverside inn where they had managed to meet and had spent a long rainy day together. She had told him—in a queer little strained voice—about the waiting—and waiting—and waiting. And about the certainty of her belief in his coming. And the tiny foot which grew numb. And the slow lump climbing in her throat. And the rush under the shrubs—and the beating hands—and cries—and of the rose dress and socks and crushed hat covered with mud. She had not been piteous or dramatic. She had been so simple that she had broken his heart in two and he had actually hidden his face in her hair.

"Oh! Donal, dear. You're crying!" she had said and she had broken down too and for a few seconds they had cried together rocking in each other's arms, while the rain streamed down the window panes and beautifully shut them in, since there are few places more enclosing than the little, dingy private parlour of a remote English inn on a ceaselessly rainy day.

It had all come back before he reached the house in Kensington whose windows looked into the thick leaves of the plane trees. And at the same time he knew that the burning anger which kept rising in him was perhaps undue and not quite fair. But he was thinking it had *not* been mere cruel chance—it could have been helped—it need never have been! It had been the narrow cold hard planning of grown-up people who knew that they were powerful enough to enforce any hideous cruelty on creatures who had no defence. He actually found his heated mind making a statement of the case as wild as this and its very mercilessness of phrase checked him. The grown-up person had been his mother—his long-beloved—and he was absolutely calling her names. He pulled himself up vigorously and walked very fast. But the heat did not quite die down and other thoughts surged up in spite of his desire to keep his head and be reasonably calm. There *had* been a certain narrowness in the tragic separation of two happy children if the only reason for it had been that the mother of one was a pretty, frivolous, much gossiped about woman belonging to a rather too rapid set. And if it had been a reason then, how would it present itself now? What would happen to an untouched dream if argument and disapproval crashed into it? If his first intensely passionate impulse had been his desire to save it even from the mere touch of ordinary talk and smiling glances because he had felt that they would spoil the perfect joy of it, what would not open displeasure and opposition make of the down on the butterfly's wing—the bloom on the peach? It was not so he phrased in his thoughts the things which tormented him, but the figures would have expressed his feeling. What if his mother were angry—though he had never seen her angry in his life and could only approach the idea because he had just found out that she had once been cruel—yes, it had been cruel! What if Coombe actually chose to interfere. Coombe with his unmoving face, his perfection of exact phrase and his cold almost inhuman eye! After all the matter concerned him closely.

"While Houses threaten to crumble and Heads may fall into the basket there are things we must remember until we disappear," he had said not long ago with this same grey eye fixed on him. "I have no son. If Marquisates continue to exist you will be the Head of the House of Coombe."

What would *he* make of a dream if he handled it? What would there be left? Donal's heart burned in his side when he recalled Feather's impudent little laugh as she had talked of her "vagabond Robin," her "small pariah." He was a boy entranced and exalted by his first passion and because he was a sort of young superman it was not a common one, though it shared all the unreason and impetuous simplicities of the most rudimentary of its kind. He could not think very calmly or logically; both the heaven and the earth in him swept him along as with the rush of the spheres. It was Robin who was foremost in all his thoughts. It was because she was so apart from all the world that it had seemed beautiful to keep her so in his heart. She had always been so aloof a little creature—so unclaimed and naturally left alone. Perhaps that was why she had retained through the years the untouched look which he had recognised even at the dance, in the eyes which only waited exquisitely for kindness and asked for love. No one had ever owned her, no one really knew her—people only saw her loveliness—no one knew her but himself—the little beautiful thing—his own—his *own* little thing! Nothing on earth should touch her!

Because his thinking ended—as it naturally always did—in such thoughts as these last, he was obliged to turn back when he saw the plane trees and walk a few hundred feet in the opposite direction to give himself time. He even turned a corner and walked down another street. It was just as he turned that poignant chance brought him face to face with a girl in deep new mourning with the border of white crêpe in the brim of her close hat. Her eyes were red and half-closed with recent crying and she had a piteous face. He knew what it all meant and involuntarily raised his hand in salute. He scarcely knew he did it and for a second she seemed not to understand. But the next second she burst out crying and hurriedly took out her handkerchief and hid her face as she passed. One of the boys lying on the blood-wet mire in Flanders, was Donal's bitter thought, but he had had his kind hours to recall at the last moment—and even now she had them too.

Helen Muir from her seat at the window looking into the thick leafage of the trees saw him turn at the entrance and heard him mount the steps. The days between them and approaching separation were growing shorter and shorter. She thought this every morning when she awakened and realised anew that the worst of it all was that neither knew how short they were and that the thing which was to happen would be sudden—as death is always sudden however long one waits. He had never reached even that *beginning* of the telling—whatsoever he had to tell. Perhaps it was coming now. She had tried to prepare herself by endeavouring to imagine how he would look when he began—a little shy—even a little lovably awkward? But his engaging smile—his quite darling smile—would show itself in spite of him as it always did.

But when he came into the room his look was a new one to her. It was not happy—it was not a free look. There was something like troubled mental reservation in it—and when had there ever been mental reservation between them? Oh, no—that must not—must not be *now*! Not now!

He sat down with his cap in his hand as if he had forgotten to lay it aside or as if he were making a brief call.

"What has happened, Donal?" she said. "Have you come to tell me that—?"

"No, not that—though that may come any moment now. It is something else."

"What else?"

"I don't know how to begin," he said. "There has never been anything like this before. But I must know from you that a—silly

74

woman—has not been telling me spiteful lies. She is the kind of woman who would say anything it amused her to say."

"What was it she said?"

"I was dragged into a house by Clonmel. He said he had promised to drop in to tea. There were a lot of people. Mrs. Gareth-Lawless was there and began to talk to me."

"Why did you think she might be telling you spiteful lies?"

"That is it," he broke out miserably impetuous. "Perhaps it may all seem childish and unimportant to you. But you have always been perfect. You were the one perfect being. I have never doubted you—"

"Do you doubt me now?"

"Perhaps no one but myself could realise that a sort of sore spot—yes, a sore spot—was left in my mind for years because of a wretched thing which happened when I was a child. *Did* you deliberately take me back to Scotland so suddenly that early morning? Was it a thing which could have been helped?"

"I thought not, Donal. Perhaps I was wrong, perhaps I was right."

"Was it because you wanted to separate me from a child I was fond of?"

"Yes."

"And your idea was that because her mother was a flighty woman with bad taste and the wrong surrounding her poor little girl would contaminate me?"

"It was because her mother was a light woman and all her friends were like her. And your affection for the child was not like a child's affection."

"No, it wasn't," he said and he leaned forward with his forehead in his hands.

"I wanted to put an end to it before it was too late. I saw nothing but pain in it for you. It filled me with heart-broken fear to think of the girl such a mother and such a life would make."

"She was such a little thing—" said Donal, "—such a tender mite of a thing! She's such a little thing even now."

"Is she?" said Helen.

Now she knew he would not tell her. And she was right. Up to that afternoon there had always been the chance that he would. Night

75

after night he had been on the brink of telling her of the dream. Only as the beauty and wonder of it grew he had each day given himself another day, and yet another and another. But he had always thought the hour would come and he had been sure she would not grudge him a moment he had held from her. Now he shut everything within himself.

"I wish you had not done it. It was a mistake," was all he said. Suddenly he felt thrown back upon himself, heartsick and cold. For the first time in his life he could not see her side of the question. The impassioned egotism of first love overwhelmed him.

"You met her on the night of the old Duchess' dance," Helen said.

"Yes."

"You have met her since?"

"Yes."

"It is useless for older people to interfere," she said. "We have loved each other very much. We have been happy together. But I can do nothing to help you. Oh! Donal, my own dear!"

Her involuntary movement of putting her hand to her throat was a piteous gesture.

"You are going away," she pleaded. "Don't let anything come between us—not *now*! It is not as if you were going to stay. When you come back perhaps—"

"I may never come back," he answered and as he said it he saw again the widowed girl who had hurried past him crying because he had saluted her. And he saw Robin as he had seen her the night before—Robin who belonged to no one—whom no one missed at any time when she went in or out—who could come and go and meet a man anywhere as if she were the only little soul in London. And yet who had always that pretty, untouched air.

"I only wanted to be sure. It was a mistake. We will never speak of it again," he added.

"If it was a mistake, forgive it. It was only because I could not hear that your life should not be beautiful. These are not like other days. Oh! Donal my dear, my dear!" And she broke into weeping and took him in her arms and he held her and kissed her tenderly. But whatsoever happened—whatsoever he did he knew that if he was to save and hold his bliss to the end he could not tell her now.

Chapter 10

Mrs. Bennett's cottage on the edge of Mersham Wood seemed to Robin when she first saw it to be only a part of a fairy tale. It is true that only in certain bits of England and in pictures in books of fairy tales did one see cottages of its kind, and in them always lived with their grandmothers—in the fairy stories as Robin remembered—girls who would in good time be discovered by wandering youngest sons of fairy story kings. The wood of great oaks and beeches spread behind and at each side of it and seemed to have no end in any land on earth. It nestled against its primæval looking background in a nook of its own. Under the broad branches of the oaks and beeches tall ferns grew so thick that they formed a forest of their own—a lower, lighter, lacy forest where foxglove spires pierced here and there, and rabbits burrowed and sniffed and nibbled, and pheasants hid nests and sometimes sprang up rocketing startlingly. Birds were thick in the wood and trilled love songs, or twittered and sang low in the hour before their bedtime, filling the twilight with clear adorable sounds. The fairy-tale cottage was whitewashed and its broad eaved roof was thatched. Hollyhocks stood in haughty splendour against its walls and on either side its path. The latticed windows were diamond-paned and their inside ledges filled with flourishing fuchsias and trailing white campanula, and mignonette. The same flowers grew thick in the crowded blooming garden. And there were nests in the hawthorn hedge. And there was a small wicket gate.

When Robin caught sight of it she wondered—for a moment—if she were going to cry. Only because it was part of the dream and could be nothing else—unless one wakened.

On the tiny porch covered with honeysuckle in bloom, a little, old fairy woman was sitting knitting a khaki sock very fast. She wore a clean print gown and a white apron and a white cap with a frilled border. She had a stick and a nutcracker face and a pair of large iron bowed spectacles. She was so busy that she did not seem to hear Robin as she walked up the path between the borders of pinks and snapdragons, but when she was quite close to her she glanced up.

Robin thought she looked almost frightened when she saw her. She got up and made an apologetic curtsey.

"Eh!" she ejaculated, "to think of me not hearing you. I do beg your pardon, Miss, I do that. I was really waiting here to be ready for you."

"Thank you. Thank you, Mrs. Bennett," Robin answered in a sweet hurry to reassure her. "I hope you are very well." And she held out her hand.

Mrs. Bennett had only been shocked at her own apparent inattention to duty. She was not really frightened and her nutcracker face illuminated itself with delighted smiles.

"I don't hear very well at the best of times," she said. "And I've got a bit of a cold. Just worry, Miss, just worry it is—along of this 'ere war and my grandsons going marching off every few days seems like. Dick, that's the youngest as was always my pet, he's the last and he'll be off any minute—and these is his socks."

Robin actually picked up a sock and patted it softly—with a childish quiver of her chin. It seemed alive.

"Yes, yes!" she said. "Oh! dear! Oh! dear!"

Mrs. Bennett winked tears out of her eyes hastily.

"Me being hard of hearing is no excuse for me talking about myself first thing. Dick, he's an Englishman—and they're all Englishmen—and it's Englishmen that's got to stand up and do their duty—same as they did at Waterloo." She swallowed valiantly the lump in her throat. "Her grace wrote to me about you, Miss, with her own kind hand. She said the cottage was so quiet and pretty you wouldn't mind it being little—and me being a bit deaf."

"I shall mind nothing," said Robin. She raised her voice and tried to speak very distinctly so as to make sure that the old fairy woman would hear her. "It is the most beautiful cottage I ever saw in my life. It is like a cottage in a fairy story."

"That's what the vicar says, Miss, my dear," was Mrs. Bennett's cheerful reply. "He says it ought to be hid some way because if the cheap trippers found it out they'd wear the life out of me with pestering me to give 'em six-penny teas. They'd get none from me!" quite fiercely. "Her grace give it to me her own self and it's on Mersham land and not a lawyer on earth could put me out."

She became quite active and bustling—picking a spray of honeysuckle and a few sprigs of mignonette from near the doorway and handing them to Robin.

"Your room's full of 'em," she said, "them and musk and roses. You'll sleep and wake in the midst of flowers and birds singing and bees humming. And I can give you rich milk and home-baked bread, God bless you! You *are* welcome. Come in, my pretty dear—Miss."

The girl came down from London to the cottage on the wood's edge several times during the weeks that followed. It was easy to reach and too beautiful and lone and strange to stay away from. The War ceased where the wood began. Mrs. Bennett delighted in her and, regarding the Duchess as a sort of adored deity, would have served her lodger on bended knee if custom had permitted. Robin could always make her hear, and she sat and listened so tenderly to her stories of her grandsons that there grew up between them an absolute affection.

"And yet we don't see each other often," the old fairy woman had said. "You flit in like, and flit away again as if you was a butterfly, I think sometimes when I'm sitting here alone. When you come to stay you're mostly flitting about the wood and I only see you bit by bit. But I couldn't tell you, Miss, my dear, what it's like to me. You do love the wood, don't you? It's a fairy place too—same as this is."

"It's all fairy, Mrs. Bennett," Robin said. "Perhaps I am a fairy too when I am here. Nothing seems quite earthly."

She bent forward suddenly and took the old face in her hands and kissed it.

"Eh! I shouldn't wonder," the old fairy woman chuckled sweetly. "I used to hear tales of fairies in Devonshire in my young days. And you do look like something witched—but you've been witched for happiness. Babies look that way for a bit sometimes—as if they brought something with them when they come to earth."

"Yes," answered Robin. "Yes."

It was true that she only flitted in and out, and that she spent hours in the depths of the wood, and always came back as if from fairy land.

Once she had a holiday of nearly a week. She came down from town one afternoon in a pretty white frock and hat and white shoes and with an air of such delicate radiance about her that Mrs. Bennett would have clutched her to her breast, but for long-ago gained knowledge of the respect due to those connected with great duchesses.

"Like a new young bride you look, my pretty dear—Miss," she cried out when she first saw her as she came up the path between the hollyhocks in the garden. "God's surely been good to you this day. There's something like heaven in your face." Robin stood still a moment looking like the light at dawn and breathing with soft quickness as if she had come in haste.

"God has been good to me for a long time," she said.

In the deep wood she walked with Donal night after night when the stillness was like heaven itself. Now and then a faint rustle among the ferns or the half awakened movement and sleepy note of a bird in the leaves slightly stirred the silence, but that was all. Lances of moonlight pierced through the branches and their slow feet made no sound upon the thick moss. Here and there pale foxglove spires held up their late blossoms like flower spirits in the dim light.

Donal thought—the first night she came to him softly through the ferns—that her coming was like that of some fair thing not of earth—a vision out of some old legend or ancient poem of faëry. But he marched towards her, soldierly—like a young Lohengrin whose silver mail had changed to khaki. There was no longer war in the world—there never had been.

"I brought it with me," he said and took her close in his arms. For a few minutes the wood seemed more still than before.

"Do you hear my heart beat?" he said at last.

"I feel it. Do you hear mine?" she whispered.

"We love each other so!" he breathed. "We love each other so!"

"Yes," she answered. "Yes."

Did every one who saw him know how beautiful he was? Oh his smile that loved her so and made her feel there was no fear or loneliness left on earth! He was so tall and straight and strong—a young soldier statue! When he laughed her heart always gave a strange little leap. It was such a lovely sound. His very hands were beautiful—with long, strong smooth fingers and smooth firm palms. Oh! Donal! Donal! And while she smiled as a little angel might smile, small sobs of joy filled her throat.

They sat together among the ferns, close side by side. He showed her the thing he had brought with him. It was a very slender chain of gold with a plain gold ring hung on it. He put the chain around her neck but slipped the ring on her finger and kissed it again and again.

"Wear it when we are together," he whispered. "I want to see it. It makes you mine as much as if I had put it on in a church with a huge organ playing."

"I should be yours without it," answered Robin. "I *am* yours."

"Yes," he whispered again. "You are mine. And I am yours. It always was so—since the morning stars sang together."

Chapter 11

"There are more women than those in Belgium who are being swept over by the chariots of war and trampled on by marching feet," the Duchess of Darte said to a group of her women friends on a certain afternoon.

The group had met to work and some one had touched on a woeful little servant-maid drama which had painfully disclosed itself in her household. A small, plain kitchen maid had "walked out" in triumphant ecstasy with a soldier who, a few weeks after bidding her good-bye, had been killed in Belgium. She had been brought home to her employer's house by a policeman who had dragged her out of the Serpentine. An old story had become a modern one. In her childish ignorance and terror of her plight she had seen no other way, but she had not had courage to face more than very shallow water, with the result of finding herself merely sticking in the mud and wailing aloud.

"The policeman was a kind-hearted, sensible fellow," said the relator of the incident. "He had a family of his own and what he said was 'She looked such a poor little drowned rat of a thing I couldn't make up my mind to run her in, ma'am. This 'ere war's responsible for a lot more than what the newspapers tell about. Young chaps in uniform having to brace up and perhaps lying awake in the night thinking over what the evening papers said—and young women they've been sweet-heartin' with—they get wild, in a way, and cling to each other and feel desperate—and he talks and she cries—and he may have his head blown off in a week's time. And who wonders that there's trouble.' Do you know he actually told me that there were a number of girls he was keeping a watch on. He said he'd begun to recognise a certain look in their eyes when they walked alone in the park. He said it was a 'stark, frightened look.' I didn't know what he meant, but it gave me a shudder."

"I think I know," said the Duchess. "Poor, wretched children! There ought to be a sort of moratorium in the matter of social laws. The old rules don't hold. We are facing new conditions. This is a thing for women to take in hand, practically, as they are taking in hand other work. It must be done absolutely without prejudice. There is no time to lecture or condemn or even deplore. There is only time to try to heal wounds and quiet maddening pain and save life."

Lady Lothwell took the subject up.

"In the country places and villages, where the new army is swarming to be billeted, the clergymen and their wives are greatly agitated. Even in times of peace one's vicar's wife tells one stories in shocked whispers of 'immorality'—though the rustic mind does not seem to regard it as particularly immoral. An illegal baby is generally accepted with simple resignation or merely a little fretful complaint even in quite decent cottages. It is called—rather prettily, I think—'a love child' and the nicer the grandparents are, the better they treat it. Mrs. Gracey, the wife of our rector at Mowbray Wells told me a few days ago that she and her husband were quite in despair over the excited, almost lawless, holiday air of the village girls. There are so many young men about and uniforms have what she calls 'such a dreadful effect.' Giddy and unreliable young women are wandering about the lanes and fields with stranger sweethearts at all hours. Even girls who have been good Sunday-school scholars are becoming insubordinate. She did not in the least mean to be improperly humorous—in fact she was quite tragic when she said that the rector felt that he ought to marry, on the spot, every rambling couple he met. He had already performed the ceremony in a number of cases when he felt it was almost criminally rash and idiotic, or would have been in time of peace."

"That was what I meant by speaking of the women who were being swept over by the chariot of war," said the Duchess. "It involves issues the women who can think must hold in their minds and treat judicially. One cannot moralise and be shocked before an advancing tidal wave. It has always been part of the unreason and frenzy of times of war.

When Death is near, Life fights hard for itself. It does not care who or what it strikes."

The tidal wave swept on and the uninitiated who formed the mass of humanity in every country in the world, reading with feverish anxiety almost hourly newspaper extras every day, tried to hide a secret fear that no one knew what was really happening or could trust to the absolute truth of any spoken or published statement. The exultant hope of to-day was dashed to-morrow. The despair of the morning was lightened by gleams of hope before night closed, and was darkened and lightened again and again. Great cities and towns aroused themselves from a half-somnolent belief in security. Village by village England awakened to what she faced in common with an amazed and half incredulous world. The amazement and incredulity were founded upon a certain mistaken belief in a world predominance of the laws of decency and civilisation. The statement of piety and morality that the world in question was a bad one, filled with crime, had somehow so far been accepted with a guileless reservation in the matter of a ruling majority whose lapses from virtue were at least not openly vaunted treachery, blows struck at any unprepared back presenting itself, merciless attacks on innocence and weakness, and savage gluttings of lust, of fury, with exultant pæans of self-glorification and praise of a justly applauding God. Before such novelty of onslaught the British mind had breathless moments of feeling itself stupid and incapably aghast. But after its first deep draughts of the cup of staggering the nation braced up a really muscular back and stood upon hard, stout legs and firm feet, immovable and fixed on solid British earth.

Incompetent raw troops gathered from fields, shops and desks, half trained, half clad, half armed, according to pessimistic report, fared forth across the narrow Channel and did strangely competent things—this being man's way when in dire moments needs must be. Riff-raff exalted itself and also died competently enough. The apparently aimless male offspring of the so-called useless rich and great died competently enough with the rest. The Roll of Honour raked fore and aft. The youngsters who had tangoed best and had shone in *cabarets* were swept away as grass by scythes.

"Will any one be left?" white Robin shuddered, clinging to Donal in the wood at night. "Every day there are new ones. Almost every one who has gone! Kathryn says that no one—*no one* will ever come back!"

"Hush—sh! Hush—sh!" whispered Donal. "Hush—sh! little lovely love!" And his arms closed so tightly around her that she could for a few moments scarcely breathe.

The Duchess had much work for her to do and was glad to see that the girl looked well and untired. When she was at home in Eaton Square her grace was even more strict about the walks and country holidays than she had been when she was away.

"Health and strength were never so much needed," she said. "We must keep our bodies in readiness for any test or strain."

This notwithstanding, there was at last a morning when Robin looked as though she had not slept well. It was so unusual a thing that the Duchess spoke of it.

"I hope you have not been sitting up late at your work?" she said.

"No. Thank you," Robin answered. "I went to bed last night at ten o'clock."

The Duchess looked at her seriously. Never before had she seen her with eyes whose misted heaviness suggested tears. Was it possible that there seemed something at once strained and quivering about her mouth—as if she were making an effort to force the muscles to hold it still.

"I hope you would tell me if you had a headache. You must, you know, my dear."

Robin's slight movement nearer to her had the air of being almost involuntary—as if it were impelled by an uncontrollable yearning to be a little near *something*—some one. The strained and quivering look was even more noticeable and her lifted eyes singularly expressed something she was trying to hold back.

"Thank you—indeed!" she said. "But it isn't headache. It is—things I could not help thinking about in the night."

The Duchess took her hand and patted it with firm gentleness.

"You mustn't, my dear. You must try hard *not* to do it. We shall be of no use if we let our minds go. We must try to force ourselves into a sort of deafness and blindness in certain directions. I am trying—with all my might."

"I know I must," Robin answered not too steadily. "I must—more than most people. I'm not brave and strong. I'm weak and cowardly—cowardly." Her breath caught itself and she went on quickly, "Work helps more than anything else. I want to *work* all the time. Please may I begin the letters now?"

She was bending over her desk when Lord Coombe came in earlier than was his custom. The perfection of his dress, his smooth creaselessness and quiet harmony of color and line seemed actually to add to the aged look of his face. His fine rigidity was worn and sallowed. After his greeting phrases he stood for a space quite silent while the Duchess watched him as if waiting.

"He has gone?" she said presently. She spoke in quite a low voice, but it reached Robin's desk.

"Yes. At dawn. The suddenness and secrecy of these goings add to the poignancy of them. I saw him but he did not see me. I found out the hour and made an effort. He is not my boy, but I wanted to *look* at him. It was perhaps for the last time. Good God! What a crime!"

He spoke low himself and rather quickly and with a new tone in his voice—as if he had been wrenched and was in pain.

"I am not in a heroic mood. I was only sick and furious when I watched them go by. They were a handsome, clean-built lot. But he stood out—the finest among them. His mere beauty and strength brought hideous thoughts into one's mind—thoughts of German deviltries born of hell."

Robin was looking at her hand which had stopped writing. She could not keep it still. She must get up and go to her own rooms. Would her knees shake under her like that when she tried to stand on her feet? The low talking went on and she scarcely heard what was said. She and Donal had always known this was coming; they had known it even the first day they had talked together in the Garden. The knowledge had been the spectre always waiting hidden at some turn in the path ahead. That was why they had been so frightened and desperate and hurried. They had clung together and shut their eyes and caught at the few hours—the few heavenly hours. He had said it would come suddenly. But she had not thought it would be as sudden as this. Last night a soldier had brought a few wild, passionate blotted lines to her. Yes, they had been blotted and blistered. She pushed her chair back and began to rise from it.

There had been a few seconds of dead silence. Lord Coombe had been standing thinking and biting his lip. "He is gone!" he said. "*Gone!*"

They did not notice Robin as she left the room. Outside the door she stood in the hall and looked up the staircase piteously. It looked so long and steep that she felt it was like a path up a mountain. But she moved towards the bottom step and began to climb stair by stair—stair by stair—dragging at the rail of the balustrade.

When she reached her room she went in and shut the door. She fell down upon the floor and sat there. Long ago his mother had taken him away from her. Now the War had taken him. The spectre stood straight in the path before her.

"It was such a short time," she said, shaking. "And he is gone. And the fairy wood is there still—and the ferns!—All the nights—always!"

And what happened next was not a thing to be written about—though at the time the same thing was perhaps at that very hour happening in houses all over England.

Chapter 12

The effect of something like unreality produced in the mind of the mature and experienced by a girl creature, can only be equaled by the intensity of the sense of realness in the girl herself. That centre of the world in which each human being exists is in her case more poignantly a centre than any other. She passes smiling or serious, a thing of untried eyes and fair unmarked smoothness of texture, and onlookers who have lived longer than she know that the unmarked untriedness is a sign that so far "nothing" has happened in her life and in most cases believe that "nothing" is happening. They are quite sure they know—long after the thing has ceased to be true. The surface of her is so soft and fair, and its lack of any suggestion of abysses or chasms seems to make them incredible things. But the centre of the world contains all things and when one is at the beginning of life and sees them for the first time they assume strange proportions. It enters a room, it talks lightly or sweetly, it whirls about in an airy dance, this pretty untested thing; and, among those for whom the belief in the reality of strange proportions has modified itself through long experience, only those of the thinking habit realise that at any moment the testing—the marking with deep scores may begin or has perhaps begun already. At eighteen or twenty a fluctuation of flower-petal tint which may mean an imperfect night can signify no really important cause. What could eighteen or twenty have found to think about in night watches? But in its centre of the world as it stands on the stage with the curtain rolling up, those who have lived longer—so very long—are only the dim audience sitting in the shadowy auditorium looking on at passionately real life with which they have really nothing whatever to do, because what they have seen is past and what they have learned has lost its importance and meaning with the changing of the years. The lying awake and tossing on pillows—if lying awake there is—has its cause in *real* joys—or griefs—not in things atrophied by time. So it seems on the stage, in the first act. If the curtain goes down on anguish and despair it seems equally the pitiless truth that it can never rise again; the play is ended; the lights go out forever; the theatre crumbles to dust; the world comes to an end. But the dim audience sitting in the shadow do not generally know this.

To those who came in and out of the house in Eaton Square the figure sitting at the desk writing letters or taking orders from the Duchess was that of the unconsidered and unreal girl. Among the changing groups of women with intensely absorbed and often strained faces the kind-hearted observing ones were given to noticing Robin and speaking to her almost affectionately because she was so attractive an object as well as so industriously faithful to her work. Girls who were Jacqueminot-rose flushed and who looked up to answer people with eyes like an antelope's were not customarily capable of concentrating their attention entirely upon brief letters of request and lists of necessaries for hospitals and comfort kits. This type was admitted to be frequently found readier for service in the preparation of entertainments "for the benefit of"—more especially when such benefits took the form of dancing. But the Duchess' little Miss Lawless came and went on errands, wasting no time. She never forgot things or was slack in any way. Her antelope eyes expressed a kind of yearning eagerness to do all she could without a moment's delay.

"She works as if it were a personal thing with her," Lady Lothwell once said thoughtfully. "I have seen girls wear that look when they are war brides or have lovers or brothers at the front."

But she remained to the world generally only a rather specially lovely specimen of the somewhat unreal young being with whom great agonies and terrors had but little to do.

On a day when the Duchess had a cold and was obliged to remain in her room Robin was with her, writing and making notes of instruction at her bedside. In the afternoon a cold and watery sun making its way through the window threw a chill light on her as she drew near with some papers in her hand. It was the revealing of this light which made the Duchess look at her curiously.

"You are not quite as blooming as you were, my child," she said. "About two months ago you were particularly blooming. Lady Lothwell and Lord Coombe and several other people noticed it. You have not been taking your walks as regularly as you did. Let me look at you." She took her hand and drew her nearer. "No. This will not do."

Robin stood very still.

"How could *any* one be blooming!" broke from her.

"You are thinking about things in the night again," said the Duchess.

"Yes," said Robin. "Every night. Sometimes all night."

The Duchess watched her anxiously.

"It's so—lonely!" There was a hint of hysteric breakdown in the exclamation. "How can I—*bear* it!" She turned and went back to her writing table and there she sat down and hid her face, trembling in an extraordinary way.

"You are as unhappy as that?" said the Duchess. "And you are *lonely?*"

"All the world is lonely," Robin cried—not weeping, only shaking. "Everything is left to itself to suffer. God has gone away."

The Duchess trembled a little herself. She too had hideously felt something like the same thing at times of late. But this soft shaking thing—! There shot into her mind like a bolt a sudden thought. Was this something less inevitable—something more personal? She wondered what would be best to say.

"Even older people lose their nerve sometimes," she decided on at last. "When you said that work was the greatest help you were right. Work—and as much sleep as one can get, and walking and fresh air. And we must help each other—old and young. I want you to help *me*, child. I need you."

Robin stood up and steadied herself somehow. She took up a letter in a hand not yet quite still.

"Please need me," she said. "Please let me do everything—anything—and never stop. If I never stop in the day time perhaps I shall sleep better at night."

As there came surging in day by day bitter and cruel waves of war news—stories of slaughter by land and sea, of massacre in simple places, of savagery wrought on wounded men and prisoners in a hydrophobia of hate let loose, it was ill lying awake in the dark remembering loved beings surrounded by the worst of all the world has ever known. Robin was afraid to look at the newspapers which her very duties themselves obliged her to familiarise herself with, and she could not close her ears. With battleship raids on harmless coast towns, planned merely to the end of the wanton killing of such unconsidered trifles of humanity as little children and women and men at their every-day work, the circle of horror seemed to draw itself in closely.

Zeppelin raids leaving fragments of bodies on pavements and broken things under fallen walls, were not so near as the women who dragged themselves back to their work with death in their faces written large—the death of husband or son or lover. These brought realities close indeed.

"I don't know how he died," one of them said to the Duchess. "I don't know how long it took him to die. I don't want to be told. I am glad he is dead. Yes, I am glad. I wish the other two were dead too. I'm not splendid and heroic. I thought I was at first, but I couldn't keep it up—after I heard about Mrs. Foster's boy. If I believed there was anything to thank, I should say 'Thank God I have no more sons.'"

That night Robin lay in the dark thinking of the dream. Had there been a dream—or had it only been like the other things one dreamed about? Sometimes an eerie fearfulness beset her vaguely. If there were letters each day! But letters belonged to a time when rivers of blood did not run through the world. She sat up in bed and clasped her hands round her knees gazing into the blackness which seemed to enclose and shut her in. It *had* been true! She could see the wood and the foxglove spires piercing the ferns. She could hear the ferns rustle and the little bird sounds and stirrings. And oh! she could hear Donal whispering. "Can you hear my heart beat?"

He had said it over and over again. His heart seemed to be so big and to beat so strongly. She had thought it was because he was so big and marvellous himself. It had been rapture to lay her cheek and ear against his breast and listen. Everything had been so still. They had been so still—so still themselves for pure joy in their close, close nearness. Yes, the dream had been true. But here she sat in the dark and Donal—where was Donal? Where millions of men were marching, marching—only to kill each other—thinking of nothing but killing. Donal too. He must kill. If he were a brave soldier he must only think of killing and not be afraid because at any moment he might be killed too. She clutched her knees and shuddered, feeling her forehead grow damp. Donal killing a man—perhaps a boy like himself—a boy who might have a dream of his own! How would his blue eyes look while he was killing a man? Oh! No! No! No! Not Donal!

With her forehead still damp and her hands damp also she found herself getting out of bed and walking up and down in the dark. She was wringing her hands and sobbing. She must not think of things like these. She must shut them out of her mind and think only of the dream. It had been true—it had! And then the strange thought came to her that out of all the world only he and she had known of their dreaming. And if he never came back—! (Oh! please, God, let him come back!) no one need ever know. It was their own, own dream and how could she bear to speak of it to any one and why should she? He had said he wanted to have this one thing of his very own before his life ended—if it was going to end. If it ended it would be his sacred secret and hers forever. She might live to be an old woman with white hair and no one would ever guess that since the morning stars sang together they two had belonged to each other.

Night after night she lay awake with thoughts like these. Through the waiting days she began to find an anguished comfort in the feeling that she was keeping their secret for him and that no one need ever know. More than once she went on quietly with her writing when people stood near her and spoke of him and his regiment, which every one was interested in because he was so handsome and so young and new to the leading of men. There were rumours that he must have been plunged into fierce fighting though definite news did not come through without delay.

"Boys like that," she heard. "They ought to be kept at home. All the greatest names will be extinct. And they are the splendid, silly ones who expose themselves most. Young Lord Elphinstowe a week ago—the last of his line! Scarcely a fragment of him to put together." There were women who had a hysterical desire to talk about such things and make gruesome pictures even of slightly founded stories. But when she heard them she did not even lift her eyes from her work.

One marked feature of their meetings—though they themselves had not marked it—had been that they had never talked of the future. It had been as though there were no future. To live perfectly through the few hours—even for the one hour or half hour they could snatch—was all that they could plan and hope for. Could they meet to-morrow in this place or that? When they met were they quite safe and blissfully alone? The spectre had always been waiting and they had always been trying to forget it. Each meeting had seemed so brief and crowded and breathlessly sweet.

Only a boy and a girl could have so lost sight of all but their hour and perhaps also only this boy and girl, because their hour had struck at a time when all futures seemed to hold only chances that at any moment might come to an end.

"Do you hear my heart beat? There is no time—no time!" these two things had been the beginning, the middle and the end.

Sometimes Robin went and sat in the Gardens and one day in coming out she met her mother whom she had not seen for months. Feather had been exultingly gay and fashionably patriotic and she was walking round the corner to a meeting to be held at her club. The khaki colouring of her coat and brief skirt and cap added to their military air with pipings and cords and a small upright feather of scarlet. She wore a badge and a jewelled pin or so. She was about to pass Robin unrecognised but took a second glance at her and stopped.

"I didn't know you," she exclaimed. "What is the matter?"

"Nothing—thank you," Robin answered pausing.

"Something *is*! You are losing your looks. Is your mistress working you to death?"

"The Duchess is very kind indeed. She is most careful that I don't do too much. I like my work more every day."

Feather took her in with a sharp scrutinising. She seemed to look her over from her hat to her shoes before she broke into her queer little critical laugh.

"Well, I can't congratulate her on the result. You are thin. You've lost your colour and your mouth is beginning to drag at the corners." And she nodded and marched away, the high heels of her beautiful small brown boots striking the pavement with a military click.

As she had dressed in the morning Robin had wondered if she was mistaken in thinking that the awful nights had made her look different.

If there had been letters to read—even a few lines such as are all a soldier may write—to read over and over again, to hide in her breast all day, to kiss and cry over and lay her cheek upon at night. Such a small letter would have been such a huge comfort and would have made the dream seem less far away. But everybody waited for letters—and waited and waited. And sometimes they went astray or were lost forever and people were left waiting.

Chapter 13

But there were no letters. And she was obliged to sit at her desk in the corner and listen to what people said about what was happening, and now and then to Lord Coombe speaking in low tones to the Duchess of his anxiety and uncertainty about Donal. Anxiety was increasing on every side and such of the unthinking multitude as had at last ceased to believe that one magnificent English blow would rid the earth of Germany, had begun to lean towards belief in a vision of German millions adding themselves each day to other millions advancing upon France, Belgium, England itself, a grey encroaching mass rolling forward and ever forward, overwhelming even neutral countries until not only Europe but the whole world was covered, and the mailed fist beat its fragments into such dust as it chose. Even those who had not lost their heads and who knew more than the general public, wore grave faces because they felt they knew too little and could not know more. Coombe's face was hard and grey many days.

"It seems as if one lost them in the flood sometimes," Robin heard him say to the Duchess. "I saw his mother yesterday and could give her no definite news. She believes that he is where the worst fighting is going on. I could not tell her he was not."

As, when they had been together, the two had not thought of any future, so, now Robin was alone, she could not think of any to-morrow—perhaps she would not. She lived only in the day which was passing. She rose, dressed and presented herself to the Duchess for orders; she did the work given her to do, she saw the day gradually die and the lights lighted; she worked as long as she was allowed to do so—and then the day was over and she climbed the staircase to her room.

Sometimes she sat and wrote letters to Donal—long yearning letters, but when they were written she tore them into pieces or burned them. If they were to keep their secret she could not send such letters because there were so many chances that they would be lost. Still there was a hopeless comfort in writing them, in pouring out what she would not have written even if she had been sure that it would reach him safely. No girl who loved a man who was at the Front would let him know that it seemed as if her heart were slowly breaking. She must be brave—brave! But she was not brave, that she knew. The news from the Front was worse every day; there were more women with awful faces; some workers had dropped out and came no more. One of them who had lost three sons in one battle had died a few days after the news arrived because the shock had been too great for her strength to endure. There were new phases of anguish on all sides. She did all she was called on to do with a secret passion of eagerness; each smallest detail was the sacred thing. She begged the Duchess to allow her to visit and help the mothers of sons who were fighting—or wounded or missing. That made her feel nearer to things she wanted to feel near to. When they cried or told her stories, she could understand. When she worked she might be doing things which might somehow reach Donal or boys like Donal.

Howsoever long her life was she knew one thing would never be blotted out by time—the day she went down to Mersham Wood to see Mrs. Bennett, whose three grandsons had been killed within a few days of each other. She had received the news in one telegram. There was no fairy wood any longer, there were only bare branched trees standing holding out naked arms to the greyness of the world. They looked as if they were protesting against something. The grass and ferns were brown and sodden with late rains and there were no hollyhocks and snapdragons in the cottage garden—only on either side of the brick path dead brown stalks, some of them broken by the wind. Things had not been neatly cut down and burned and swept away. The grandsons had made the garden autumn-tidy every year before this one.

The old fairy woman sat on a clean print-covered arm chair by a very small fire. She had a black print dress on and a black shawl and a black ribbon round her cap. Her Bible lay on a little table near her but it was closed.

"Don't get up, please, Mrs. Bennett," Robin said when she lifted the latch and entered.

The old fairy woman looked at her in a dazed way.

"I'm so eye-dimmed with crying that I can scarcely see," she said.

Robin came to her and knelt down on the hearth.

"I'm your lodger," she faltered, "who—who used to love the fairy wood so."

She had not known what she would say when she spoke first but she had certainly not thought of saying anything like this. And she certainly had not known that she would suddenly find herself overwhelmed by a rising tidal wave of unbearable woe and drop her face on to the old woman's lap with wild sobbing. She had not come down from London to do this—but away from the world—in the clean, still little cottage room which seemed to hold only grief and silence and death the wave rose and broke and swept her with it.

Mrs. Bennett only gave herself up to the small clutching hands and sat and shivered.

"No one—will come in—will they?" Robin was gasping. "There is no one to hear, is there?"

"No one on earth," said the old fairy woman. "Quiet and loneliness are left if there's naught else."

What she thought it would be hard to say. The blow which had come to her at the end of a long life had, as it were, felled her as a tree might have been felled in Mersham Wood. As the tree might have lain for a short time with its leaves still seeming alive on its branches so she seemed living. But she had been severed from her root. She listened to the girl's sobbing and stroked her hair.

"Don't be afraid. There's no one left to hear but the walls and the bare trees in the wood," she said.

Robin sobbed on.

"You've a kind heart, but you're not crying for me," she said next. "You've a black trouble of your own. There's few that hasn't these days. And it's worse for the young that's got to live through it and after it. When Mary Ann comes to see after me to-morrow morning I may be lying dead, thank God. But you're a child." The small clutching hands clutched more piteously because it was so true—so true. Whatsoever befell there were all the long, long years to come—with only the secret left and the awful fear that sometime she might begin to be afraid that it was not a real thing—since no one had ever known or ever would know and since she could never speak of it or hear it spoken of.

"I'm so afraid," she shuddered at last in a small low voice. "I'm so *lonely*!" The old fairy woman's stroking hand stopped short.

"Is there—anything—you'd like to tell me—anything in the world?" she asked tremulously. "There's nothing I'd mind."

The pretty head on her lap shook itself to and fro.

"No! No! No! No!" the small choked voice gave out. "Nothing—nothing! Nothing. That's why it's so lonely."

As she had waited alone through the night in her cradle, as she had watched the sparrows on the roofs above her in the nursery, as she had played alone until Donal came, so it was her fate to be alone now.

"But you came away from London because there were too many people there and you wanted to be in a place where there was nothing but an empty cottage and an old woman. Some would call it lonelier here."

"The wood is here—the fairy wood!" she cried and her sobbing broke forth tenfold more bitterly.

Mrs. Bennett had seen in her day much of the troubles of others and many of the things she had seen had been the troubles of women who were young. Sometimes it had been possible to help them, sometimes it had not, but in any case she had always known that help could be given only if one asked careful questions. The old established rules with regard to one's behaviour in connection with duchesses and their belongings had strangely faded away since the severing of her root as all things on earth had faded and lost consequence. She remembered no rules as she bent her head over the girl and almost whispered to her.

"I won't ask no questions after this one, Miss dear," she said quaking. "But was there ever—a young gentleman—in the wood?"

"No! No! No! No!" four times again Robin cried it. "Never! Never!" And she lifted her face and let her see it white and streaming and with eyes which desperately defied and as they defied implored for love and aid and mercy.

The old fairy woman's nutcracker mouth trembled. It mumbled pathetically before she was able to control it. She knew she had heard this kind of thing before though in cases with which great ladies had nothing whatever to do. And at the same time there was something in this case that was somehow different.

"I don't know what to say or do," she faltered helplessly. "With the world like this—we've got to try to comfort each other—and we don't know how."

"Let me come into your arms," said Robin like a child. "Hold me and let me hold you." She crept near and folding soft arms about the old figure laid her cheek against the black shawl. "Let us cry. There's nothing for either of us to do but cry until our hearts break in two. We are all alone and no one can hear us."

"There's naught but the wood outside," moaned the old fairy woman.

The voice against the shawl was a moan also.

"Perhaps the wood hears us—perhaps it hears. Oh! me! Oh! me!"

When she reached London she saw that there were excited groups of people talking together in the streets. Among them were women who were crying, or protesting angrily or comforting others. But she had seen the same thing before and would not let herself look at people or hear anything she could shut her ears against. Some new thing had happened, perhaps the Germans had taken some important town and wreaked their vengeance on the inhabitants, perhaps some new alarming move had been made and disaster stared the Allies in the face. She staggered through the crowds in the station and did not really know how she reached Eaton Square.

Half an hour later she was sitting at her desk quiet and neat in her house dress. She had told the Duchess all she could tell her of her visit to old Mrs. Bennett.

"We both cried a good deal," she explained when she saw her employer look at her stained eyes. "She keeps remembering what they were like when they were babies—how rosy and fat they were and how they learned to walk and tumbled about on her little kitchen floor. And then how big they grew and how fine they looked in their khaki. She says the worst thing is wondering how they look now. I told her she mustn't wonder. She mustn't think at all. She is quite well taken care of. A girl called Mary Ann comes in three times a day to wait on her—and her daughter comes when she can but her trouble has made her almost wander in her mind. It's because they are *all* gone. When she comes in she forgets everything and sits and says over and over again, 'If it had only been Tom—or only Tom and Will—or if it had been Jem—or only Jem and Tom—but it's Will—and Jem—and Tom,'—over and over again. I am not at all sure I know how to comfort people. But she was glad I came."

When Lord Coombe came in to make his daily visit he looked rigid indeed—as if he were stiff and cold though it was not a cold night.

He sat down by the Duchess and took a telegram from his pocket. Glancing up at him, Robin was struck by a whiteness about his mouth. He did not speak at once. It was as though even his lips were stiff.

"It has come," he said at last. "Killed. A shell." The Duchess repeated his words after him. Her lips seemed stiff also.

"Killed. A shell."

He handed the telegram to her. It was the customary officially sympathetic announcement. She read it more than once. Her hands began to tremble. But Coombe sat with face hidden. He was bowed like an old man.

"A shell," he said slowly as if thinking the awful thing out. "That I heard unofficially." Then he added a strange thing, dragging the words out. "How could that—be blown to atoms?"

The Duchess scarcely breathed her answer which was as strange as his questioning.

"Oh! How *could* it!"

She put out her shaking hand and touched his sleeve, watching his face as if something in it awed her.

"You *loved* him?" She whispered it. But Robin heard.

"I did not know I had loved anything—but I suppose that has been it. His physical perfection attracted me at first—his extraordinary contrast to Henry. It was mere pride in him as an heir and successor. Afterwards it was a *beautiful* look his young blue eyes had. Beautiful seems an unmasculine word for such a masculine lad, but no other word expresses it. It was a sort of valiant brightness and joy in living and being friends with the world. I saw it every time he came to talk to me. I wished he were my son. I even tried to think of him as my son." He uttered a curious low sound like a sudden groan, "My son has been killed."

When he was about to leave the house and stood in the candle-lighted hall he was thinking of many dark things which passed unformedly through his mind and made him move slowly. He was slow in his movements as the elderly maid servant assisted him to put on his overcoat, and he was as slowly drawing on his gloves when his eyes—slow also—travelled up the staircase and stopped at the first landing, where he seemed to see an indefinite heap of something lying.

"Am I mistaken or is—something—lying on the landing?" he said to the woman.

The fact that he was impelled to make the inquiry seemed to him part of his abnormal state of mind. What affair of his after all were curiously dropped bundles upon his hostess' staircase? But—

"Please go and look at it," he added, and the woman gave him a troubled look and went up the stairs.

He himself was only a moment behind her. He actually found himself following her as if he were guessing something. When the maid cried out, he vaguely knew what he had been guessing.

"Oh!" the woman gasped, bending down. "It's poor little Miss Lawless! Oh, my lord," wildly after a nearer glance, "She looks as if she was dead!"

Chapter 14

"Now no one will ever know."

Robin waking from long unconsciousness found her mind saying this before consciousness which was clear had actually brought her back to the world.

"Now no one will ever know—ever."

She seemed to have been away somewhere in the dark for a very long time. She was too tired to try to remember what had happened before she began to climb the staircase, which grew steeper and longer as she dragged herself from step to step. But in the back of her mind there was one particular fact she knew without trying to remember how she learned it. A shell had fallen somewhere and when it had burst Donal was "blown to atoms." How big were atoms—how small were they? Several times when she reached this point she descended into the abyss of blackness and fainted again, though people were doing things to her and trying to keep her awake in ways which troubled her greatly. Why should they disturb her so when sinking into blackness was better?

"Now no one will ever know."

She was lying in her bed in her own room. Some one had undressed her. It was a nice room and very quiet and there was only a dim light burning. It was a long time before she came back, after one of the descents into the black abyss, and became slowly aware that Something was near her bed. She did not actually see it because at first she could not have lifted or turned her eyes. She could only lie still. But she knew that it was near her and she wished it were not. At last—by degrees it ceased to be a mere *thing* and evolved into a person. It was a man who was holding her wrist and watching her quietly and steadily—as if he had been doing it for some time. No one else was in the room. The people who had been disturbing her by doing things had gone away.

"Now," she whispered dragging out word after word, "no one will—ever—ever know." But she was not conscious she had said it even in a whisper which could be heard. She thought the thing had only passed again through her mind.

"Donal! Blown—to—atoms," she said in the same way. "How small is—an atom?" She was sinking into the blackness again when the man dropped her wrist quickly and did something to her which brought her back.

"Don't!" she moaned. "Please—don't."

But he would not let her go.

Perhaps days and nights passed—or perhaps only one day and night before she found herself still lying in her bed but feeling somehow more awake when she opened her eyes and found the same man sitting close to her holding her wrist again.

"I am Dr. Redcliff," he said in a quiet voice. "You are much better. I want to ask you some questions. I will not tire you."

He began to ask her questions very gently as if he did not wish to alarm or disturb her. She had been found in a dead faint lying on the landing. She had remained unconscious for an abnormally long time. When she had been brought out of one faint she had fallen into another and this had happened again and again. The indication was that she had been struck down by some shock. In examining her he had found that she was underweight. He wished to discover if she had been secretly working too late at night in her deep interest in what she was doing. What exactly had her diet been? Had she taken enough exercise in the open air? How had she slept? The Duchess was seriously anxious.

They were the questions doctors always asked people except that he seemed more desirous of being sure of the amount of exercise she had taken than about anything else. He was specially interested in the times when she had been in the country. She was obliged to tell him she had always been alone. He thought it would have been better

104

if she had had some companion. Once when he was asking her about her visits to Mrs. Bennett's cottage the blackness almost engulfed her again. But he was watching her very closely and perhaps seeing her turn white—gave her some stimulant in time. He had a clever face which was not unkind, but she wished that it had not had such a keenly watchful look. More than once the watchfulness tired her and she closed her eyes because she did not want him to look into them—as if he were asking questions which were not altogether doctors' questions.

When he left her and went downstairs to talk to the Duchess he asked a good many quiet questions again. He was a man whose intense interest in his profession did not confine itself wholly to its scientific aspect. An extraordinarily beautiful child swooning into death was not a mere pathological incident to him. And he knew many strange things brought about by the abnormal conditions of war. He himself was conscious of being overstrung with the rest of a tormented world.

He knew of Mrs. Gareth-Lawless and he had heard more stories of her household, her loveliness and Lord Coombe than he had time to remember. He had, of course, heard the unsavoury rumours of the child who was being brought up for some nefarious object. As he knew Lord Coombe rather well he did not believe stories about him which went beyond a certain limit. Not until he had talked to the Duchess for some time did he discover that the hard-smitten child lying half-lifeless in her bed was the very young heroine of the quite favourite scandal. The knowledge gave him furiously to think. It was Coombe who had interested the Duchess in her. The Duchess had no doubt taken her under her protection for generously benign reasons. He pursued his questioning delicately.

"Has she had any young friends? She seems to have taken her walks alone and even to have gone into the country by herself."

"The life of the young people in its ordinary sense of companionship and amusement has been stopped by the War. There may be some who go on in the old way but she has not been one of them," the Duchess said.

"Visits to old women in remote country places are not stimulating enough. Has she had *no* companions?"

"I tried—" said the Duchess wearily. She was rather pale herself. "The news of the Sarajevo tragedy arrived on the day I gave a small dance for her—to bring some young people together." Her waxen pallor became even more manifest. "How they danced!" she said woefully. "What living things they were! Oh!" the exclamation broke forth at a suddenly overwhelming memory. "The beautiful boy—the splendid lad who was blown to atoms—the news came only yesterday—was there dancing with the rest!"

Dr. Redcliff leaned forward slightly.

"To hear that *any* boy has been blown to atoms is a hideous thing," he said. "Who brought the news? Was Miss Lawless in the room when it was brought?"

"I think so though I am not sure. She comes in and goes out very quietly. I am afraid I forgot everything else. The shock was a great one. My old friend Lord Coombe brought the news. The boy would have succeeded him. We hear again and again of great families becoming extinct. The house of Coombe has not been prolific. The War has taken its toll. Donal Muir was the last of them. One has felt as though it was of great importance that—that a thing like that should be carried on." She began to speak in a half-numbed introspective way. "What does it matter really? Only one boy of thousands—perhaps hundreds of thousands before it is over? But—but it's the youngness—the power—the potential meaning—wasted—torn— scattered in fragments." She stopped and sat quite still, gazing before her as though into space.

"She is very young. She has been absorbed in war work and living in a highly charged atmosphere for some time." Dr. Redcliff said presently, "If she knew the poor lad—"

"She did not really know him well, though they had met as children. They danced together that night and sat and talked in the conservatory. But she never saw him again," the Duchess explained.

"It might have been too much, even if she did not know him well. We must keep her quiet," said Dr. Redcliff.

Very shortly afterwards he rose and went away.

An hour later he was sitting in a room at Coombe House alone with Lord Coombe. It was the room in which Mademoiselle Vallé had found his lordship on the night of Robin's disappearance. No one knew now where Mademoiselle was or if she were still alive. She had been living with her old parents in a serene Belgian village which had been destroyed by the Germans. Black tales had been told of which Robin had been allowed to hear nothing. She had been protected in many ways.

Though they had not been intimates the two men knew each other well. To each individually the type of the other was one he could understand. It was plain to Lord Coombe that Redcliff found his case of rather special interest, which he felt was scarcely to be wondered at. As he himself had seen the too slender prostrate figure and the bloodless small face with its curtain of lashes lying too heavily close to the cold cheek, he had realised that their helpless beauty alone was enough to arrest more than ordinary attention. She had, as the woman had cried out, looked as if she were dead, and dead loveliness is a reaching power.

Dr. Redcliff spoke of her thoughtfully and with a certain gentleness. He at first included her with many other girls, the changes in whose methods of life he had been observing.

"The closed gates in their paths are suddenly thrown open for them because no one has to lock and unlock them," he said. "It produces curious effects. The light-minded ones take advantage of the fact and find dangerous amusement in it sometimes. The serious ones go about the work they have taken in hand. Miss Lawless is, I gather, one of the thinking and feeling ones and has gone about a great deal."

"Yes. The Duchess has tried to save her from her own ardour, but perhaps she has worked too steadily."

"Has the Duchess always known where she has gone and what people she has seen?"

"That would have been impossible. She wished her to feel free and if we had not wished it, one can see that it would not have been possible to stand guard over her. Neither was it necessary."

But he began to listen with special attention. There awakened in his mind the consciousness that he was being asked questions which suggested an object. The next one added to his awakening sense of the thing.

"Her exercise and holidays were always taken alone?" Redcliff said.

"The Duchess believed so."

"She has evidently been living under a poignant strain and some ghastly shock has struck her down. I think she must have been in the room when you brought the news of young Muir's terrible death."

"She was," said Coombe. "I saw her and then forgot."

"I thought so," Redcliff went on. "She cried out several times, 'Blown to atoms—atoms! Donal!' She was not conscious of the cries."

"Are you sure she said 'Donal'?" Coombe asked.

"Quite sure. It was that which set me thinking. I have thought a great deal. She has touched me horribly. The mere sight of her was enough. There is desolation in her childlikeness."

Lord Coombe sat extremely still. The room was very silent till Redcliff went on in dropped voice.

"There was another thing she said. She whispered it brokenly word by word. She did not know that, either. She whispered, 'Now—no one—will ever—know—ever.'"

Lord Coombe still sat silent. What he was thinking could not be read in his face but being a man of astute perception and used to the study of faces Dr. Redcliff knew that suddenly some startling thought had leaped within him.

"You were right to come to me," he said. "What is it you—suspect?"

That Dr. Redcliff was almost unbearably moved was manifest. He was not a man of surface emotions but his face actually twitched and he hastily gulped something down.

"She is a heartbreakingly beautiful thing," he said. "She has been left—through sheer kindness—in her own young hands. They were too young—and these are hours of cataclysm. She knows nothing. She does not know that—she will probably have a child."

Chapter 15

The swiftness of the process by which the glowing little Miss Lawless, at whom people had found themselves involuntarily looking so often, changed from a rose of a girl into something strangely like a small waxen image which walked, called forth frequent startled comment. She was glanced at even oftener than ever.

"Is she going into galloping consumption? Her little chin has grown quite pointed and her eyes are actually frightening," was an early observation. But girls who are going into galloping consumption cough and look hectic and are weaker day by day and she had no cough, nor was she hectic and, though it was known that Dr. Redcliff saw her frequently, she insisted that she was not ill and begged the Duchess to let her go on with her work.

"But the *done for* woe in her face is inexplicable—in a girl who has had no love affairs and has not even known any one who could have flirted with her and ridden away. The little thing's *done for*. It cries out aloud. I can't bear to look at her," one woman protested.

"I shall send her away if she does not improve," the Duchess said. "She shall go to some remote place in the Highlands and she shall not be allowed to remember that there is a war in the world. If I can manage to send her old nurse Dowie with her she will stand guard over her like an old shepherd."

She also had been struck by the look which had been spoken of as "done for." Girls did not look like that for any common reason. She asked herself questions and with great care sat on foot a gradual and delicate cross-examination of Robin herself. But she discovered no reason common or uncommon for the thing she recognised each time she looked at her. It was inevitable that she should talk to Lord

Coombe but she met in him a sort of barrier. She could not avoid seeing that he was preoccupied. She remotely felt that he was turning over in his mind something which precluded the possibility of his giving attention to other questions.

"I almost feel as if your interest in her had lapsed," she said at last.

"No. It has taken a—an entirely new form," was his answer.

It was when his glance encountered hers after he said this that each regarded the other with a slow growing anxiousness. Something came to life in each pair of eyes and it was something disturbed and reluctant. The Duchess spoke first.

"She has had no companions," she said painfully. "The War put an end to what I thought I might do for her. There has been *nobody*."

"At present it is a curious fact that in one sense we know very little of each other's lives," he answered. "The old leisurely habit of observing details no longer exists. As Redcliff said in speaking of her—and girls generally—all the gates are thrown wide open."

The Duchess was very silent for a space before she made her reply. "Yes."

"You do not know her mother?"

"No."

"Two weeks ago she gave me something to reflect on. Her feeling for her daughter is that of a pretty cat-like woman for something enragingly younger than herself. She always resented her. She was infuriated by your interest in her. She said to me one afternoon, 'I hope the Duchess is still pleased with her companion. I saw her to-day in Bond Street and she looked like a housemaid I once had to dismiss rather suddenly. I am glad she is in her grace's house and not in mine.'"

After a few seconds—

"*I* am glad she is in my house and not in hers," the Duchess said.

"After I had spoken to her at some length and she had quite lost her temper, she added 'You evidently don't know that she has been meeting Donal Muir. He told me so himself at the Erwyn's. I asked him if he had seen her since the dance and he owned that he had—and then was cross at himself for making the slip. I did not ask him how *often* he had met her. He would not have told me. But if he met her once he met her as often as he chose.' She was not lying when she said it. I know her. I have been thinking constantly ever since." There was a brief silence between them; then he proceeded. "Robin worshipped him when she was a mere baby. They were very beautiful together on the night of the dance. She fainted on the stairway after hearing of his death. She had been crawling up to hide herself in her room, poor child! It is one of the tragedies. Perhaps you and I together—"

The Duchess was seeing again the two who had come forth shining from the conservatory. She continued to see them as Lord Coombe went on speaking, telling her what Dr. Redcliff had told him.

On her part Robin scarcely understood anything which was happening because nothing seemed to matter. On the morning when the Duchess told her that Dr. Redcliff wished to see her alone that fact mattered as little as the rest. She was indifferently conscious that the Duchess regarded her in an anxious kind way, but if she had been unkind instead of kind that would have meant nothing. There was only room for one thing in the world. She wondered sometimes if she were really dead—as Donal was—and did not know she was so. Perhaps after people died they walked about as she did and did not understand that others could not see them and they were not alive. But if she were dead she would surely see Donal.

Before she went to Dr. Redcliff the Duchess took her hand and held it closely in both her own. She looked at her with a curious sort of pitifulness—as if she were sorry.

"My poor child," she said. "Whatsoever he tells you don't be frightened. Don't think you are without friends. I will take care of you."

"Thank you," she said. "I don't think anything would frighten me. Nothing seems frightening—now." After which she went into the room where Dr. Redcliff was waiting for her.

The Duchess sat alone and thought deeply. What she thought of chiefly was the Head of the House of Coombe. She had always known that more than probably his attitude towards a circumstance of this sort would not even remotely approach in likeness that of other people. His point of view would detach itself from ordinary theories of moralities and immoralities. He would see with singular clearness all sides of the incident. He would not be indignant, or annoyed or embarrassed. He had had an interest in Robin as a creature representing peculiar loveliness and undefended potentialities. Sometimes she had felt that this had even verged on a tenderness of which he was himself remotely, if at all, conscious. Concerning the boy Donal she had realised that he felt something stronger and deeper than any words of his own had at any time expressed. He had believed fine things of him and had watched him silently. He had wished he had been his own flesh and blood. Perhaps he had always felt a longing for a son who might have been his companion as well as his successor. Who knew whether a thwarted paternal instinct might not now be giving him such thinking to do as he might have done if Donal Muir had been the son of his body—dead on the battlefield but leaving behind him something to be gravely considered? What would a man think—what would a man *do* under such circumstances?

"One might imagine what some men would do—but it would depend entirely upon the type," she thought. "What he will do will be different. It might seem cold; it might be merely judicial—but it might be surprising."

She was quite haunted by the haggard look of his face as he had exclaimed:

"I wish to God I had known him better! I wish to God I had talked to him more!"

What he had done this morning was to go to Mersham Wood to see Mrs. Bennett. There were things it might be possible to learn by amiable and carefully considered expression of interest in her loss and loneliness. Concerning such things as she did not already know she would learn nothing from his conversation, but concerning such things as she had become aware of he would learn everything without alarming her.

"If those unhappy children met at her cottage and wandered about in Mersham Wood together the tragedy is understandable."

The Duchess' thinking ended pityingly because just at this time it was that Robin opened the door and stood looking at her.

It seemed as though Dr. Redcliff must have talked to her for a long time. But she had on her small hat and coat and what the Duchess seemed chiefly to see was the wide darkness of her eyes set in a face suddenly pinched, small and snow white. She looked like a starved baby.

"Please," she said with her hands clasped against her chest, "please—may I go to Mersham Wood?"

"To—Mersham Wood," the Duchess felt aghast—and then suddenly a flood of thought rushed upon her.

"It is not very far," the little gasping voice uttered. "I must go, please! Oh! I must! Just—to Mersham Wood!"

Something almost uncontrollable rose in the Duchess' throat.

"Child," she said. "Come here!"

Robin went to her—oh, poor little soul!—in utter obedience. As she drew close to her she went down upon her knees holding up her hands like a little nun at prayer.

"*Please* let me go," she said again. "Only to Mersham Wood."

"Stay here, my poor child and talk to me," the Duchess said. "The time has come when you must talk to some one."

"When I come back—I will try. I—I want to ask—the Wood," said Robin. She caught at a fold of the Duchess' dress and went on rapidly.

"It is not far. Dr. Redcliff said I might go. Mrs. Bennett is there. She loves me."

"Are you going to talk to Mrs. Bennett?"

"No! No! No! No! Not to any one in the world."

Hapless young creatures in her plight must always be touching, but her touchingness was indescribable—almost unendurable to the ripe aged woman of the world who watched and heard her. It was as if she knew nothing of the meaning of things—as if some little spirit had been torn from heaven and flung down upon the dark earth. One felt that one must weep aloud over the exquisite incomprehensible remoteness of her. And it was so awfully plain that there was some tragic connection with the Wood and that her whole soul cried out to it. And she would not speak to any one in the world. Such things had been known. Was the child's brain wavering? Why not? All the world was mad was the older woman's thought, and she herself after all the years, had for this moment no sense of balance and felt as if all old reasons for things had been swept away.

"If you will come back," she said. "I will let you go."

After the poor child had gone there formulated itself in her mind the thought that if Lord Coombe and Mrs. Bennett met her together some clarity might be reached. But then again she said to herself, "Oh why, after all, should she be asked questions? What can it matter to the rest of the woeful world if she hides it forever in her heart?"

And she sat with drooped head knowing that she was tired of living because some things were so helpless.

Chapter 16

The Wood was gradually growing darker. It had been almost brilliant during a part of the afternoon because the bareness of the branches let in the wintry sun. There were no leaves to keep it out and there had been a rare, chill blue sky. All seemed cold blue sky where it was not brown or sodden yellow fern and moss. The trunks of the trees looked stark and the tall, slender white stems of the birches stood out here and there among the darker growth like ghosts who were sentinels. It was always a silent place and now its stillness seemed even added to by the one sound which broke it—the sound of sobbing—sobbing—sobbing.

It had been going on for some time. There had stolen through the narrow trodden pathway a dark slight figure and this had dropped upon the ground under a large tree which was one of a group whose branches had made a few months ago a canopy of green where birds had built nests and where one nightingale had sung night after night to the moon.

Later—Robin had said to herself—she would go to the cottage, and she would sit upon the hearth and lay her head on Mrs. Bennett's knee and they would cling together and sob and talk of the battlefields and the boys lying dead there. But she had no thought of saying any other thing to her, because there was nothing left to say. She had said nothing to Dr. Redcliff; she had only sat listening to him and feeling her eyes widening as she tried to follow and understand what he was saying in such a grave, low-toned cautious way—as if he himself were almost afraid as he went on. What he said would once have been strange and wonderful, but now it was not, because wonder had gone out of the world. She only seemed to sit stunned before the feeling that now the dream was not a sacred secret any longer and there grew within her, as she heard, a wild longing to fly to the Wood as if it were a living human thing who would hear her and understand—as if it would be like arms enclosing her. Something would be there listening and she could talk to it and ask it what to do.

She had spoken to it as she staggered down the path—she had cried out to it with wild broken words, and then when she heard nothing she had fallen down upon the earth and the sobbing—sobbing—had begun.

"Donal!" she said. "Donal!" And again, "Donal!" over and over. But nothing answered, for even that which had been Donal—with the heavenly laugh and the blue in his gay eyes and the fine, long smooth hands—had been blown to fragments in a field somewhere—and there was nothing anywhere.

She had heard no footsteps and she was sobbing still when a voice spoke at her side—the voice of some one standing near.

"It is Donal you want, poor child—no one else," it said.

That it should be this voice—Lord Coombe's! And that amazing as it was to hear it, she was not amazed and did not care! Her sobbing ceased so far as sobbing can cease on full flow. She lay still but for low shuddering breaths.

"I have come because it is Donal," he said. "You told me once that you had always hated me. Hatred is useless now. Don't feel it."

But she did not answer.

"You probably will not believe anything I say. Well I must speak to you whether you believe me or not."

She lay still and he himself was silent. His voice seemed to be a sudden thing when he spoke.

"I loved him too. I found it out the morning I saw him march away."

He had seen him! Since she had looked at his beautiful face this man had looked at it!

"You!" She sat up on the earth and gazed, swaying. So he knew he could go on.

"I wanted a son. I once lay on the moss in a wood and sobbed as you have sobbed. *She* was killed too."

But Robin was thinking only of Donal.

"What—was his face like? Did you—see him near?"

"Quite near. I stood on the street. I followed. He did not see me. He saw nothing."

The sobbing broke forth again.

"Did—did his eyes look as if he had been crying? He did cry—he did!"

The Head of the House of Coombe showed no muscular facial sign of emotion and stood stiffly still. But what was this which leaped scalding to his glazed eyes and felt hot?

"Yes," he answered huskily. "I saw—even as he marched past—that his eyes were heavy and had circles round them. There were other eyes like his—some were boys' eyes and some were the eyes of men. They held their heads up—but they had all said 'Good-bye'—as he had."

The Wood echoed to a sound which was a heart-wrung wail and she dropped forward on the moss again and lay there.

"He said, 'Oh, let us cry—together—together! Oh little—lovely love'!"

She who would have borne torment rather than betray the secret of the dream, now that it could no longer be a secret lay reft of all but memories and the wild longing to hold to her breast some shred which was her own. He let her wail, but when her wailing ceased helplessly he bent over her.

"Listen to me," he said. "If Donal were here he would tell you to listen. You are a child. You are too young to know what has come upon you—both."

She did not speak.

"You were both too young—and you were driven by fate. If he had been more than a boy—and if he had not been in a frenzy—he would have remembered. He would have thought—"

Yes—yes! She knew how young! But oh, what mattered youth—or thought—or remembering! Her small hand beat in soft impatience on the ground.

He was—strangely—on one knee beside her, his head bent close, and in his voice there was a new strong insistence—as if he would not let her alone— Oh! Donal! Donal!

"He would have remembered—that he might leave a child!"

His voice was almost hard. She did not know that in his mind was a memory which now in secret broke him—a memory of a belief which was a thing he had held as a gift—a certain faith in a clear young highness and strength of body and soul in this one scion of his house, which even in youth's madness would have *remembered*. If the lad had been his own son he might have felt something of the same pang.

His words brought back what she had heard Redcliff say to her earlier in the day—the thing which had only struck her again to the earth.

"It—will have—no father," she shuddered. "There is not even a grave."

He put his hand on her shoulder—he even tried to force her to lift her head.

"It *must* have a father," he said, harshly. "Look at me. It *must*."

Stupefied and lost to all things as she was, she heard something in his harshness she could not understand and was startled by. Her small starved face stared at him piteously. There was no one but herself left in the world.

"There is no time—" he broke forth.

"He said so too," she cried out. "There was no time!"

"But he should have remembered," the harsh voice revealed more than he knew. "He could have given his child all that life holds that men call happiness. How could even a lad forget! He loved you—you loved him. If he had married you—"

He stopped in the midst of the words. The little starved face stared at him with a kind of awfulness of woe. She spoke as if she scarcely knew the words she uttered, and not, he saw, in the least as if she were defending herself—or as if she cared whether he believed her or not—or as if it mattered.

"Did you—think we were—not married?" the words dragged out.

Something turned over in his side. He had heard it said that hearts did such things. It turned—because she did not care. She knew what love and death were—what they *were*—not merely what they were called—and life and shame and loss meant nothing.

"Do you know what you are saying?" he heard the harshness of his voice break. "For God's sake, child, let me hear the truth."

She did not even care then and only put her childish elbows on her knees and her face in her hands and wept and wept.

"There was—no time," she said. "Every day he said it. He knew—he *knew*. Before he was killed he wanted *something* that was his own. It was our secret. I wanted to keep it his secret till I died."

"Where," he spoke low and tensely, "were you married?"

"I do not know. It was a little house in a poor crowded street. Donal took me. Suddenly we were frightened because we thought he was to go away in three days. A young chaplain who was going away too was his friend. He had just been married himself. He did it because he was sorry for us. There was no time. His wife lent me a ring. They were young too and they were sorry."

"What was the man's name?"

"I can't remember. I was trembling all the time. I knew nothing. That was like a dream too. It was all a dream."

"You do not remember?" he persisted. "You were married—and have no proof."

"We came away so quickly. Donal held me in his arm in the cab because I trembled. Donal knew. Donal knew everything."

He was a man who had lived through tragedy but that had been long ago. Since then he had only known the things of the world. He had seen struggles and tricks and paltry craftiness. He had known of women caught in traps of folly and passion and weakness and had learned how terror taught them to lie and shift and even show abnormal cleverness. Above all he knew exactly what the world would say if a poor wretch of a girl told a story like this of a youngster like Donal—when he was no longer on earth to refute it.

And yet if these wild things were true, here in a wintry wood she sat a desolate and undefended thing—with but one thought. And in that which was most remote in his being he was conscious that he was for the moment relieved because even worldly wisdom was not strong enough to overcome his desire to believe in a certain thing which was—that the boy would have played fair even when his brain whirled and all his fierce youth beset him.

As he regarded her he saw that it would be difficult to reach her mind which was so torn and stunned. But by some method he must reach it.

"You must answer all the questions I ask," he said. "It is for Donal's sake."

She did not lift her face and made no protest.

He began to ask such questions as a sane man would know must be answered clearly and as he heard her reply to each he gradually reached the realisation of what her empty-handed, naked helplessness confronted. That he himself comprehended what no outsider would, was due to his memories of heart-wrung hours, of days and nights when he too had been unable to think quite sanely or to reason with a normal brain. Youth is a remorseless master. He could see the tempest of it all—the hours of heaven—and the glimpses of hell's self—on whose brink the two had stood clinging breast to breast. With subtle carefulness he slowly gleaned it all. He followed the rising of the tide which at first had borne them along unquestioning. They had not even asked where they were going because the way led through young paradise. Then terror had awakened them. There had come to them the news of death day after day—lads they knew and had seen laughing a few weeks before—Halwyn, Meredith, Jack or Harry or Phil. A false rumour of a sudden order to the Front and they had stood and gazed into each other's eyes in a fateful hour. Robin did not know of the picture her disjointed, sobbed-forth sentences and words made clear. Coombe could see the lad as he stood before her in this very Wood and then went slowly down upon his knees and kissed her small feet in the moss as he made his prayer. There had been something rarely beautiful in the ecstasy of his tenderness—and she had given herself as a flower gives itself to be gathered. She seemed to have seen nothing, noted nothing, on the morning of the mad marriage, but Donal, who held her trembling in his arms as they drove through the crowded streets in the shabby neighbourhood she had never seen before, to the house crowded between others all like itself. She had actually not heard the young chaplain's name in her shyness and tremor. He would scarcely have been an entity but for the one moving fact that he himself had just hastily married a girl he adored and must leave, and so sympathised and understood the stress of their hour. On their way home they had been afraid of chance recognition and had tried to shield themselves by sitting as far back as possible in the cab.

"I could not think. I could not see. It was all frightening—and unreal."

She had not dreamed of asking questions. Donal had taken care of her and tried to help her to be less afraid of seeing people who might recognise her. She had tilted her hat over her face and worn a veil. She had gone home to Eaton Square—and then in the afternoon to the cottage at Mersham Wood.

They had not written letters to each other. Robin had been afraid and they had met almost every day. Once Lord Coombe thought himself on the track of some clue when she touched vaguely on some paper Donal had meant to send her and had perhaps forgotten in the haste and pressure of the last few hours because his orders had been so sudden. But there was no trace. There had been something he wished her to have. But if this had meant that his brain had by chance cleared to sane reasoning and he had, for a few moments touched earth and intended to send her some proof which would be protection if she needed it—the moment had been too late and, at the last, action had proved impossible. And Death had come so soon. It was as though a tornado had swept him out of her arms and dashed him broken to earth. And she was left with nothing because she asked nothing—wanted nothing.

The obviousness of this, when he had ended his questioning and exhausted his resources, was a staggering thing.

"Do you know," he said grimly, after it was all over, "—that no one will believe you?"

"Donal knew," she said. "There is no one—no one else."

"You mean that there is no one whose belief or disbelief would affect you?"

The Wood was growing darker still and she had ceased crying and sat still like a small ghost in the dim light.

"There never *was* any one but Donal, you know," she said. To all the rest of the world she was as a creature utterly unawake and to a man who was of the world and who had lived a long life in it the contemplation of her was a strange and baffling thing.

"You do not ask whether *I* believe you?" he spoke quite low.

The silence of the darkening wood was unearthly and her dropped word scarcely stirred it.

"No." She had never even thought of it.

He himself was inwardly shaken by his own feeling.

"I will believe you if—you will believe me," was what he said, a singular sharp new desire impelling him.

She merely lifted her face a little so that her eyes rested upon him.

"Because of this tragic thing you must believe me. It will be necessary that you should. What you have thought of me with regard to your mother is not true. You believed it because the world did. Denial on my part would merely have called forth laughter. Why not? When a man who has money and power takes charge of a pretty, penniless woman and pays her bills, the pose of Joseph or Galahad is not a good one for him. My statement would no more have been believed than yours will be believed if you can produce no proof. What you say is what any girl might say in your dilemma, what I should have said would have been what any man might have said. But—I believe you. Do you believe *me*?"

She did not understand why suddenly—though languidly—she knew that he was telling her a thing which was true. It was no longer of consequence but she knew it. And if it was true all she had hated him for so long had been founded on nothing. He had not been bad—he had only *looked* bad and that he could not help. But what did that matter, either? She could not feel even sorry.

"I will—try," she answered.

It was no use as yet, he saw. What he was trying to deal with was in a new Dimension.

He held out his hands and helped her to her feet.

"The Wood is growing very dark," he said. "We must go. I will take you to Mrs. Bennett's and you can spend the night with her."

The Wood was growing dark indeed. He was obliged to guide her through the closeness of the undergrowth. They threaded their way along the narrow path and the shadows seemed to close in behind them. Before they reached the end which would have led them out into the open he put his hand on her shoulder and held her back.

"In this Wood—even now—there is Something which must be saved from suffering. It is helpless—it is blameless. It is not you—it is not Donal. God help it."

He spoke steadily but strangely and his voice was so low that it was almost a whisper—though it was not one. For the first time she felt something stir in her stunned mind—as if thought were wakening—fear—a vague quaking. Her wan small face began to wonder and in the dark roundness of her eyes a question was to be seen like a drowned thing slowly rising from the deeps of a pool. But she asked no question. She only waited a few moments and let him look at her until she said at last in a voice as near a whisper as his own.

"I—will believe you."

Chapter 17

He was alone with the Duchess. The doors were closed, and the world shut out by her own order. She leaned against the high back of her chair, watching him intently as she listened. He walked slowly up and down the room with long paces. He had been doing it for some time and he had told her from beginning to end the singular story of what had happened when he found Robin lying face downward on the moss in Mersham Wood.

This is what he was saying in a low, steady voice.

"She had not once thought of what most women would have thought of before anything else. If I were speaking to another person than yourself I should say that she was too ignorant of the world. To you I will say that she is not merely a girl—she is the unearthly luckless embodiment of the pure spirit of Love. She knew only worship and the rapt giving of gifts. Her unearthliness made him forget earth himself. Folly and madness of course! Incredible madness—it would seem to most people—a decently intelligent lad losing his head wholly and not regaining his senses until it was too late to act sanely. But perhaps not quite incredible to you and me. There must have been days which seemed to him—and lads like him—like the last hours of a condemned man. In the midst of love and terror and the agony of farewells—what time was there for sanity?"

"You *believe* her?" the Duchess said.

"Yes," impersonally. "In spite of the world, the flesh and the devil. I also know that no one else will. To most people her story will seem a thing trumped up out of a fourth rate novel. The law will not listen to it. You will—when you see her unawakened face."

"I have seen it," was the Duchess' interpolation. "I saw it when she went upon her knees and prayed that I would let her go to Mersham Wood. There was something inexplicable in her remoteness from fear and shame. She was only woe's self. I did not comprehend. I was merely a baffled old woman of the world. Now I begin to see. I believe her as you do. The world and the law will laugh at us because we have none of the accepted reasons for our belief. But I believe her as you do—absurd as it will seem to others."

"Yes, it will seem absurd," Coombe said slowly pacing. "But here she is—and here *we* are!"

"What do you see before us?" she asked of his deep thought.

"I see a helpless girl in a dark plight. As far as knowledge of how to defend herself goes, she is as powerless as a child fresh from a nursery. She lives among people with observing eyes already noting the change in her piteous face. Her place in your house makes her a centre of attention. The observation of her beauty and happiness has been good-natured so far. The observation will continue, but in time its character will change. I see that before anything else."

"It is the first thing to be considered," she answered.

"The next—" she paused and thought seriously, "is her mother. Perhaps Mrs. Gareth-Lawless has sharp eyes. She said to you something rather vulgarly hideous about being glad her daughter was in my house and not in hers."

"Her last words to Robin were to warn her not to come to her for refuge 'if she got herself into a mess.' She is in what Mrs. Gareth-Lawless would call 'a mess.'"

"It is what a good many people would call it," the Duchess said. "And she does not even know that her tragedy would express itself in a mere vulgar colloquialism with a modern snigger in it. Presently, poor child, when she awakens a little more she will begin to go about looking like a little saint. Do you see that—as I do?"

She thought he did and that he was moved by it though he did not say so.

"I am thinking first of her mother. Mrs. Gareth-Lawless must see and hear nothing. She is not a criminal or malignant creature, but her light malice is capable of playing flimsily with any atrocity. She has not brain enough to know that she can be atrocious. Robin can be protected only if she is shut out of the whole affair. She was simply speaking the truth when she warned the girl not to come to her in case of need."

"For a little longer I can keep her here," the Duchess said. "As she looks ill it will not be unnatural that the doctor should advise me to send her away from London. It is not possible to remember anything long in the life we live now. She will be forgotten in a week. That part of it will be simple."

"Yes," he answered. "Yes."

He paced the length of the room twice—three times and said nothing. She watched him as he walked and she knew he was going to say more. She also wondered what curious thing it might be. She had said to herself that what he said and did would be entirely detached from ordinary or archaic views. Also she had guessed that it might be extraordinary—perhaps as extraordinary as his long intimacy with Mrs. Gareth-Lawless. Was there a possibility that he was going to express himself now?

"But that is not all," he said at last and he ended his pondering walk by coming nearer to her. He sat down and touched the newspapers lying on the table.

"You have been poring over these," he said, "and I have been doing the same thing. I have also been talking to the people who know things and to those who ought to know them but don't. Just now the news is worse each day. In the midst of the roar and thunder of cataclysms to talk about a mere girl 'in trouble' appears disproportionate. But because our world seems crumbling to pieces about us she assumes proportions of her own. I was born of the old obstinate passions of belief in certain established things and in their way they have had their will of me. Lately it has forced itself upon me that I am not as modern as I have professed to be. The new life has gripped me, but the old has not let me go. There are things I cannot bear to see lost forever without a struggle."

"Such as—" she said it very low.

"I conceal things from myself," he answered, "but they rise and confront me. There were days when we at least believed—quite obstinately—in a number of things."

"Sometimes quite heroically," she admitted. "'God Save the Queen' in its long day had actual glow and passion. I have thrilled and glowed myself at the shouting song of it."

"Yes," he drew a little nearer to her and his cold face gained a slight colour. "In those days when a son—or a grandson—was born to the head of a house it was a serious and impressive affair."

"Yes." And he knew she at once recalled her own son—and George in Flanders.

"It meant new generations, and generations counted for decent dignity as well as power. A farmer would say with huge pride, 'Me and mine have worked the place for four generations,' as he would say of the owner of the land, 'Him and his have held it for six centuries.' Centuries and generations are in danger of no longer inspiring special reverence. It is the future and the things to be which count."

"The things to be—yes," the Duchess said and knew that he was drawing near the thing he had to say.

"I suppose I was born a dogged sort of devil," he went on almost in a monotone. "The fact did not manifest itself to me until I came to the time when—all the rest of me dropped into a bottomless gulf. That perhaps describes it. I found myself suddenly standing on the edge of it. And youth, and future, and belief in the use of hoping and real enjoyment of things dropped into the blackness and were gone while I looked on. If I had not been born a dogged devil I should have blown my brains out. If I had been born gentler or kinder or more patient I should perhaps have lived it down and found there was something left. A man's way of facing things depends upon the kind of thing he was born. I went on living *without*—the rest of myself. I closed my mouth and not only my mouth but my life—as far as other men and women were concerned. When I found an interest stirring in me I shut another door—that was all. Whatsoever went on did it behind a shut door."

"But there were things which went on?" the Duchess gently suggested.

"In a hidden way—yes. That is what I am coming to. When I first saw Mrs. Gareth-Lawless sitting under her tree—" He suddenly stopped. "No," harshly, "I need not put it into words to *you*." Then a pause as if for breath. "She had a way of lifting her eyes as a very young angel might—she had a quivering spirit of a smile—and soft, deep curled corners to her mouth. You saw the same things in the old photograph you bought. The likeness was—Oh! it was hellish that such a resemblance could be! In less than half an hour after she spoke to me I had shut another door. But I was obliged to go and *look* at her again and again. The resemblance drew me. By the time her husband died I knew her well enough to be sure what would happen. Some man would pick her up and throw her aside—and then some one else. She could have held nothing long. She would have passed from one hand to another until she was tossed into the gutter and swept away—quivering spirit of a smile and all of it. I could not have shut any door on that. I prevented it—and kept her clean—by shutting doors right and left. I have watched over her. At times it has bored me frightfully. But after a year or so—behind another door I had shut the child."

"Robin? I had sometimes thought so," said the Duchess.

"I did not know why exactly. It was not affection or attraction. It was a sort of resentment of the beastly unfairness of things. The bottomless gulf seemed to yawn in her path when she was nothing but a baby. Everything was being tossed into it before she had taken a step. I began to keep an eye on her and prevent things—or assist them. It was more fury than benevolence, but it has gone on for years—behind the shut door."

"Are you quite sure you have been entirely free from all affection for her?" The Duchess asked the question impersonally though with a degree of interest.

"I think so. I am less sure that I have the power to feel what is called 'affection' for any one. I think that I have felt something nearer it for Donal—and for you—than for any one else. But when the child talked to me in the wood I felt for the first time that I wished her to know that my relation to her mother was not the reason for her hating me which she had believed."

"She shall be made to understand," said the Duchess.

"She must," he said, "*because of the rest.*"

The last four words were, as it were, italicised. Now, she felt, she was probably about to hear the chief thing he had been approaching. So she waited attentively.

"Behind a door has been shut another thing," he said and he endeavoured to say it with his usual detached rigidity of calm, but did not wholly succeed. "It is the outcome of the generations and the centuries at present diminishing in value and dignity. The past having had its will of me and the present and future having gripped me—if I had had a son—"

As if in a flash she saw as he lingered on the words that he was speaking of a thing of which he had secretly thought often and much, though he had allowed no human being to suspect it. She had not suspected it herself. In a secretive, intense way he had passionately desired a son.

"If you had had a son—" she repeated.

"He would have stood for both—the past and the future—at the beginning of a New World," he ended.

He said it with such deliberate meaning that the magnitude of his possible significance caused her to draw a sudden breath.

"Is it going to be a New World?" she said.

"It cannot be the old one. I don't take it upon myself to describe the kind of world it will be. That will depend upon the men and women who build it. Those who were born during the last few years—those who are about to be born now."

Then she knew what he was thinking of.

"Donal's child will be one of them," she said.

"The Head of the House of Coombe—if there is a Head who starts fair—ought to have quite a lot to say—and do. Howsoever black things look," obstinately fierce, "England is not done for. At the worst no real Englishman believes she can be. She *can't*! You know the old saying, 'In all wars England loses battles, but she always wins one—the last one.' She always will. Afterwards she must do her bit for the New World."

Chapter 18

This then was it—the New World and the human creatures who were to build it, the unborn as well as those now in their cradles or tottering in their first step on the pathway leading to the place of building. Yet he himself had no thought of there being any touch of heroic splendour in his way of looking at it. He was not capable of drama. Behind his shut doors of immovability and stiff coldness, behind his cynic habit of treating all things with detached lightness, the generations and the centuries had continued their work in spite of his modernity. His British obstinacy would not relinquish the long past he and his had seemed to *own* in representing it. He had loved one woman, and one only—with a love like a deep wound; he had longed for a son; he had stubbornly undertaken to protect a creature he felt life had treated unfairly. The shattering of the old world had stirred in him a powerful interest in the future of the new one whose foundations were yet to be laid. The combination of these things might lead to curious developments.

They sat and talked long and the developments were perhaps more unusual than she had imagined they might be.

"If I had been able to express the something which approached affection which I felt for Donal, he would have found out that my limitations were not deliberately evil proclivities," was one of the things he said. "One day he would have ended by making a clean breast of it. He was afraid of me. I suspect he was afraid of his mother—fond as they were of each other. I should have taken the matter in hand and married the pair of them at once—quietly if they preferred it, but safely and sanely. God knows I should have comprehended their wish to keep a roaring world out of their paradise. It *was* paradise!"

"How you believe her!" she exclaimed.

"She is not a trivial thing, neither was he. If I did *not* believe her I should know that he *meant* to marry her, even if fate played them some ghastly trick and there was not time. Another girl's consciousness of herself might have saved her, but she had no consciousness but his. If—if a son is born he should be what his father would have been after my death."

"The Head of the House," the Duchess said.

"It is a curious thing," he deliberated, "that now there remains no possible head but what is left of myself—it ceases to seem the mere pompous phrase one laughed at—the Head of the House of Coombe. Here I, of all men, sit before you glaring into the empty future and demanding one. There ought to have been more males in the family. Only four were killed—and we are done for."

"If you had seen them married before he went away—" she began.

He rose to his feet as if involuntarily. He looked as she had never seen him look before.

"Allow me to make a fantastic confession to you," he said. "It will open doors. If all were as the law foolishly demands it should be—if she were safe in the ordinary way—absurdly incredible or not as the statement may seem—I should now be at her feet."

"At her feet!" she said slowly, because she felt herself facing actual revelation.

"Her child would be to me the child of the son who ought to have been born to me a life time ago. God, how I have wanted him! Robin would seem to be what another Madonna-like young creature might have been if she had been my wife. She would not know that she was a little saint on an altar. She would be the shrine of the past and the future. In my inexpressive way I should be worshipping before her. That her possible son would rescue the House of Coombe from extinction would have meant much, but it would be a mere detail. Now you understand."

Yes. She understood. Things she had never comprehended and had not expected to comprehend explained themselves with comparative clearness. He proceeded with a certain hard distinctness.

"The thing which grips me most strongly is that this one—who is one of those who have work before them—shall not be handicapped. He shall not begin life manacled and shamed by illegitimacy. He shall begin it with the background of all his father meant to give him. The law of England will not believe in his claims unless they can be proven. She can prove nothing. I can prove nothing for her. If she had been a little female costermonger she would have demanded her 'marriage lines' and clung to them fiercely. She would have known that to be able to flaunt them in the face of argument was indispensable."

"She probably did not know that there existed such documents," the Duchess said. "Neither of the pair knew anything for the time but that they were wild with love and were to be torn apart."

"Therefore," he said with distinctness even clearer and harder, "she must possess indisputable documentary evidence of marriage before the child is born—as soon as possible."

"Marriage!" she hesitated aghast. "But *who* will—?"

"I," he answered with absolute rigidity. "It will be difficult. It must be secret. But if it can be done—when his time comes the child can look his new world in the face. He will be the Head of the House of Coombe when it most needs a strong fellow who has no cause to fear anything and who holds money and power in his hands."

"You propose to suggest that she shall marry *you?*" she put it to him.

"Yes. It will be the devil's own job," he answered. "She has not begun to think of the child yet—and she has abhorred me all her life. To her the world means nothing. She does not know what it can do to her and she would not care if she did. Donal was her world and he is gone. But you and I know what she does not."

"So this is what you have been thinking?" she said. It was indeed an unarchaic point of view. But even as she heard him she realised that it was the almost inevitable outcome—not only of what was at the moment happening to the threatened and threatening world, but of his singularly secretive past—of all the things he had hidden and also of all the things he had professed not to hide but had baffled people with.

"Since the morning Redcliff dropped his bomb I have not been able to think of much else," he said. "It was a bomb, I own. Neither you nor I had reason for a shadow of suspicion. My mind has a trick of dragging back to me a memory of a village girl who was left as—as she is. She said her lover had married her—but he went away and never came back. The village she lived in was a few miles from Coombe Keep and she gave birth to a boy. His childhood must have been a sort of hell. When other boys had rows with him they used to shout 'Bastard' after him in the street. He had a shifty, sickened look and when he died of measles at seven years old no doubt he was glad of it. He used to run crying to his wretched mother and hide his miserable head in her apron."

"It sounds unendurable," the Duchess said sharply.

"I can defy the world as she cannot," he said with dangerous calm. "I can provide money for her. She may be hidden away. But only one thing will save her child—Donal's child—from being a sort of outcast and losing all he should possess—a quick and quiet marriage which will put all doubt out of the question."

"And you know perfectly well what the general opinion will be with regard to yourself?"

"Damned well. A debauched old degenerate marrying the daughter of his mistress because her eighteen years attracts his vicious decrepitude. My absolute indifference to that, may I say, can not easily be formulated. *She* shall be spared as much as possible. The thing can be kept secret for years. She can live in entire seclusion. No one need be told until I am dead—or until it is necessary for the boy's sake. By that time perhaps changes in opinion will have taken place. But now—as is the cry of the hour—there is no time. She said that Donal said it too." He stood still for a few moments and looked at the floor. "But as I said," he terminated, "it will be the devil's own job. When I first speak to her about it—she will almost be driven mad."

Chapter 19

Robin had spent the night at the cottage and Mrs. Bennett had been very good to her. They had sat by the fire together for a long time and had talked of the dead boys on the battlefield, while Robin's head had rested against the old fairy woman's knee and the shrivelled hand had stroked and patted her tremulously. It had been nearing dawn when the girl went to bed and at the last Mrs. Bennett had held on to her dress and asked her a pleading question.

"Isn't there anything you'd like me to do for you—anything on earth, Miss, dear? Sometimes there's things an old woman can do that young ones can't. If there was anything you'd like to tell me about—that I could keep private—? It'd be as safe with me as if I was a dumb woman. And it might just happen that—me being so old—I might be a help some way." She was giving her her chance, as in the course of her long life she had given it to other poor girls she loved less. One had to make ways and open gates for them.

But Robin only kissed her as lovingly as a child.

"I don't know what is going to happen to me," she said. "I can't think yet. I may want to ask you to let me come here—if—if I am frightened and don't know what to do. I know you would let me come and—talk to you—?"

The old fairy woman almost clutched her in enfolding arms. Her answer was a hoarse and trembling whisper.

"You come to me, my poor pretty," she said. "You come to me day or night—*whatsoever*. I'm not so old but what I can do anything—you want done."

The railroad journey back to London seemed unnaturally long because her brain began to work when she found herself half blindly gazing at the country swiftly flying past the carriage window. Perhaps the anxiousness in Mrs. Bennett's face had wakened thought in connecting itself with Lord Coombe's words and looks in the wood.

When the door of the house in Eaton Square opened for her she was conscious of shrinking from the sympathetic eyes of the war-substituted woman-servant who was the one who had found her lying on the landing. She knew that her face was white and that her eyelids were stained and heavy and that the woman saw them and was sorry for her.

The mountain climb of the stairs seemed long and steep but she reached her room at last and took off her hat and coat and put on her house dress. She did it automatically as if she were going downstairs to her work, as though there had been no break in the order of her living.

But as she was fastening the little hooks and buttons her stunned brain went on with the thought to which it had begun to awaken in the train. Since the hour when she had fallen unconscious on the landing she had not seemed to think at all. She had only *felt* things which had nothing to do with the real world.

There was a fire in the grate and when the last button was fastened she sat down on a seat before it and looked into the redness of the coals, her hands loosely clasped on her knee. She sat there for several minutes and then she turned her head and looked slowly round the room. She did it because she was impelled by a sense of its emptiness—by the fact that she was quite alone in it. There was only herself—only Robin in it.

That was her first feeling—the aloneness—and then she thought of something else. She seemed to feel again the hand of Lord Coombe on her shoulder when he held her back in the darkened wood and she could hear his almost whispered words.

"In this Wood—even now—there is Something which must be saved from suffering. It is helpless—it is blameless. It is not you—it is not Donal—God help it."

Then she was not alone—even as she sat in the emptiness of the room. She put up her hands and covered her face with them.

"What—will happen?" she murmured. But she did not cry.

The deadliness of the blow which had stupefied her still left her barely conscious of earthly significances. But something of the dark mistiness was beginning to lift slowly and reveal to her vague shadows and shapes, as it were. If no one would believe that she was married to Donal, then people would think that she had been the kind of girl who is sent away from decent houses, if she is a servant, and cut off in awful disgrace from her family and never spoken to again, if she belongs to the upper classes. Books and Benevolent Societies speak of her as "fallen" and "lost." Her vision of such things was at once vague and primitive. It took the form of pathetic fictional figures or memories of some hushed rumour heard by mere chance, rather than of anything more realistic. She dropped her hands upon her lap and looked at the fire again.

"Now I shall be like that," she said listlessly. "And it does not matter. Donal knew. And I do not care—I do not care."

"The Duchess will send me away," she whispered next. "Perhaps she will send me away to-day. Where shall I go!" The hands on her lap began to tremble and she suddenly felt cold in spite of the fire. The sound of a knock on the door made her start to her feet. The woman who had looked sorry for her when she came in had brought a message.

"Her grace wishes to see you, Miss," she said.

"Thank you," Robin answered.

After the servant had gone away she stood still a moment or so.

"Perhaps she is going to tell me now," she said to the empty room.

Two aspects of her face rose before the Duchess as the girl entered the room where she waited for her with Lord Coombe. One was that which had met her glance when Mademoiselle Vallé had brought her charge on her first visit. She recalled her impression of the childlikeness which seemed all the dark dew of appealing eyes, which were like a young doe's or a bird's rather than a girl's. The other was the star-like radiance of joy which had swept down the ballroom in Donal's arms with dancing whirls and swayings and pretty swoops. About them had laughed and swirled the boys now lying dead under the heavy earth of Flemish fields. And Donal—!

This face looked small and almost thin and younger than ever. The eyes were like those of a doe who was lost and frightened—as if it heard quite near it the baying of hounds, but knew it could not get away.

She hesitated a moment at the door.

"Come here, my dear," the Duchess said.

Lord Coombe stood by a chair he had evidently placed for her, but she did not sit down when she reached it. She hesitated again and looked from one to the other.

"Did you send for me to tell me I must go away?" she said.

"What do you mean, child?" said the Duchess.

"Sit down," Lord Coombe said and spoke in an undertone rapidly. "She thinks you mean to turn her out of the house as if she were a kitchen-maid."

Robin sat down with her listless small hands clasped in her lap.

"Nothing matters at all," she said, "but I don't know what to do."

"There is a great deal to do," the Duchess said to her and she did not speak as if she were angry. Her expression was not an angry one. She looked as if she were wondering at something and the wondering was almost tender.

"We know what to do. But it must be done without delay," said Lord Coombe and his voice reminded her of Mersham Wood.

"Come nearer to me. Come quite close. I want—" the Duchess did not explain what she wanted but she pointed to a small square ottoman which would place Robin almost at her knee. Her own early training had been of the statelier Victorian type and it was not easy for her to deal freely with outward expression of emotion. And here emotion sprang at her throat, so to speak, as she watched this childish thing with the frightened doe's eyes. The girl had been an inmate of her house for months; she had been kind to her and had become fond of her, but they had never reached even the borders of intimacy.

And yet emotion had seized upon her and they were in the midst of strange and powerful drama.

Robin did as she was told. It struck the Duchess that she always did as she was told and she spoke to her hoping that her voice was not ungentle.

"Don't look at me as if you were afraid. We are going to take care of you," she said.

But the doe's eyes were still great with hopeless fearfulness.

"Lord Coombe said—that no one would believe me," Robin faltered. "He thought I was not married to Donal. But I was—I was. I *wanted* to be married to him. I wanted to do everything he wanted me to do. We loved each other so much. And we were afraid every one would be angry. And so many were killed every day—and before he was killed—Oh!" with a sharp little cry, "I am glad—I am glad! Whatever happens to me I am *glad* I was married to him before he was killed!"

"You poor children!" broke from the Duchess. "You poor—poor mad young things!" and she put an arm about Robin because the barrier built by lack of intimacy was wholly overthrown.

Robin trembled all over and looked up in her face.

"I may begin to cry," she quavered. "I do not want to trouble you by beginning to cry. I must not."

"Cry if you want to cry," the Duchess answered.

"It will be better," said Lord Coombe, "if you can keep calm. It is necessary that you should be calm enough to think—and understand. Will you try? It is for Donal's sake."

"I will try," she answered, but her amazed eyes still yearningly wondered at the Duchess. Her arm had felt almost like Dowie's.

"Which of us shall begin to explain to her?" the Duchess questioned.

"Will you? It may be better."

They were going to take care of her. She was not to be turned into the street—though perhaps if she were turned into the street without money she would die somewhere—and that would not matter because she would be thankful.

The Duchess took one of her hands and held it on her knee. She looked kind still but she was grave.

"Do not be frightened when I tell you that most people will *not* believe what you say about your marriage," she said. "That is because it is too much like the stories other girls have told when they were in trouble. It is an easy story to tell when a man is dead. And in Donal's case so much is involved that the law would demand proofs which could not be denied. Donal not only owned the estate of

Braemarnie, but he would have been the next Marquis of Coombe. You have not remembered this and—" more slowly and with a certain watchful care—"you have been too unhappy and ill—you have not had time to realise that if Donal has a son—"

She heard Robin's caught breath.

"What his father would have inherited he would inherit also. Braemarnie would be his and in his turn he would be the Marquis of Coombe. It is because of these important things that it would be said that it would be immensely to your interest to insist that you were married to Donal Muir and the law would not allow of any shade of doubt."

"People would think I wanted the money and the castles—for myself?" Robin said blankly.

"They would think that if you were a dishonest woman—you wanted all you could get. Even if you were not actually dishonest they would see you would want it for your son. You might think it ought to be his—whether his father had married you or not. Most women love their children."

Robin sat very still. The stunned brain was slowly working for itself.

"A child whose mother seems bad—is very lonely," she said.

"It is not likely to have many friends."

"It seems to belong to no one. It *must* be unhappy. If—Donal's mother had not been married—even he would have been unhappy."

No one made any reply.

"If he had been poor it would have made it even worse. If he had belonged to nobody and had been poor too—! How could he have borne it!"

Lord Coombe took the matter up gently, as it were removing it from the Duchess' hands.

"But he had everything he wished for from his birth," he said. "He was always happy. I like to remember the look in his eyes. Thank God for it!"

"That beautiful look!" she cried. "That beautiful laughing look—as if all the world were joyful!"

"Thank God for it," Coombe said again. "I once knew a wretched village boy who had no legal father though his mother swore she had been married. His eyes looked like a hunted ferret's. It was through being shamed and flouted and bullied. The village lads used to shout 'Bastard' after him."

It was then that the baying of the hounds suddenly seemed at hand. The large eyes quailed before the stark emptiness of the space they gazed into.

"What shall I do—what shall I do?" Robin said and having said it she did not know that she turned to Lord Coombe.

"You must try to do what we tell you to do—even if you do not wish to do it," he said. "It shall be made as little difficult for you as is possible."

The expression of the Duchess as she looked on and heard was a changing one because her mind included so many aspects of the singular situation. She had thought it not unlikely that he would do something unusual. Could anything much more unusual have been provided than that a man, who had absolute splendour of rank and wealth to offer, should for strange reasons of his own use the tact of courts and the fine astuteness of diplomatists in preparing the way to offer marriage to a penniless, friendless and disgraced young "companion" in what is known as "trouble"? It was because he was himself that he understood what he was dealing with—that splendour and safety would hold no lure, that protection from disgrace counted as nothing, that only one thing had existence and meaning for her. And even as this passed through her mind, Robin's answer repeated it.

"I will do it whether it is difficult or not," she said, "but—" she actually got up from her ottoman with a quiet soft movement and stood before them—not a defiant young figure, only simple and elementally sweet— "I am not ashamed," she said. "I am not ashamed and I do not matter at all."

There was that instant written upon Coombe's face—so far at least as his old friend was concerned—his response to the significance of this. It was the elemental thing which that which moved him required; it was what the generations and centuries of the house of Coombe required—a primitive creature unashamed and with no cowardice or weak vanity lurking in its being. The Duchess recognised it in the brief moment of almost breathless silence which followed.

"You are very splendid, child," he said after it, "though you are not at all conscious of it."

"Sit down again." The Duchess put out a hand which drew Robin still nearer to her. "Explain to her now," she said.

Robin's light soft body rested against her when it obeyed. It responded to more than the mere touch of her hand; its yielding was to something which promised kindness and even comfort—that something which Dowie and Mademoiselle had given in those days which now seemed to have belonged to another world. But though she leaned against the Duchess' knee she still lifted her eyes to Lord Coombe.

"This is what I must ask you to listen to," he said. "We believe what you have told us but we know that no one else will—without legal proof. We also know that some form may have been neglected because all was done in haste and ignorance of formalities. You can give no clue—the ordinary methods of investigation are in confusion as the whole country is. This is what remains for us to face. *You* are not ashamed, but if you cannot prove legal marriage Donal's son will know bitter humiliation; he will be robbed of all he should possess—his life will be ruined. Do you understand?"

"Yes," she answered without moving her eyes from his face. She seemed to him again as he stood before her in the upper room of Lady Etynge's house when, in his clear aloof voice, he had told her that he had come to save her. He had saved her then, but now it was not she who needed saving.

"There is only one man who can give Donal's child what his father would have given him," he went on.

"Who is he?" she asked.

"I am the man," he answered, and he stood quite still.

"How—can you do it?" she asked again.

"I can marry you," his clear, aloof voice replied.

"You!—You!—You!" she only breathed it out—but it was a cry. Then he held up his hand as if to calm her.

"I told you in the wood that hatred was useless now and that your reason for hating me had no foundation. I know how you will abhor what I suggest. But it will not be as bad as it seems. You need not even endure the ignominy of being known as the Marchioness of Coombe. But when I am dead Donal's son will be my successor. It will not be held against him that I married his beautiful young mother and chose to keep the matter a secret. I have long been known as a peculiar person given to arranging my affairs according to my own liking. The Head of the House of Coombe"—with an ironic twitch of the mouth—"will have the law on his side and will not be asked for explanations. A romantic story will add to public interest in him. If your child is a daughter she will be protected. She will not be lonely, she will have friends. She will have all the chances of happiness a girl naturally longs for—all of them. Because you are her mother."

Robin rose and stood before him as involuntarily as she had risen before, but now she looked different. Her hands were wrung together and she was the blanched embodiment of terror. She remembered things Fräulein Hirsh had said.

"I could not marry you—if I were to be killed because I didn't," was all she could say. Because marriage had meant only Donal and the dream, and being saved from the world this one man had represented to her girl mind.

"You say that because you have no doubt heard that it has been rumoured that I have a depraved old man's fancy for you and that I have always hoped to marry you. That is as false as the other story I denied. I am not in love with you even in an antediluvian way. You would not marry me for your own sake. That goes without saying. But I will repeat what I said in the Wood when you told me you would believe me. There is Something—not you—not Donal—to be saved from suffering."

"That is true," the Duchess said and put out her hand as before. "And there is something longer drawn out and more miserable than mere dying—a dreary outcast sort of life. We know more about such things than you do."

"You may better comprehend my action if I add a purely selfish reason for it," Coombe went on. "I will give you one. I do not wish to be the last Marquis of Coombe."

He took from the table a piece of paper. He had actually made notes upon it.

"Do not be alarmed by this formality," he said. "I wish to spare words. If you consent to the performance of a private ceremony you will not be required to see me again unless you yourself request it. I have a quiet place in a remote part of Scotland where you can live with Dowie to take care of you. Dowie can be trusted and will understand what I tell her. You will be safe. You will be left alone. You will be known as a young widow. There are young widows everywhere."

Her eyes had not for a moment left his. By the time he had ended they looked immense in her thin and white small face. Her old horror of him had been founded on a false belief in things which had not existed, but a feeling which has lasted almost a lifetime has formed for itself an atmosphere from whose influence it is not easy to escape. And he stood now before her looking as he had always looked when she had felt him to be the finely finished embodiment of evil. But—

"You are—doing it—for Donal," she faltered.

"You yourself would be doing it for Donal," he answered.

"Yes. And—I do not matter."

"Donal's wife and the mother of Donal's boy or girl matters very much," he gave back to her. He did not alter the impassive aloofness of his manner, knowing that it was better not to do so. An astute nerve specialist might have used the same method with a patient.

There was a moment or so of silence in which the immense eyes gazed before her almost *through* him—piteously.

"I will do anything I am told to do," she said at last. After she had said it she turned and looked at the Duchess.

The Duchess held out both her hands. They were held so far apart that it seemed almost as if they were her arms. Robin swept towards the broad footstool but reaching it she pushed it aside and knelt down laying her face upon the silken lap sobbing soft and low.

"All the world is covered with dead—beautiful boys!" her sobbing said. "All alone and dead—dead!"

Chapter 20

No immediate change was made in her life during the days that followed. She sat at her desk, writing letters, referring to notes and lists and answering questions as sweetly and faithfully as she had always done from the first. She tried to remember every detail and she also tried to keep before her mind that she must not let people guess that she was thinking of other things—or rather trying not to think of them. It was as though she stood guard over a dark background of thought, of which others must know nothing. It was a background which belonged to herself and which would always be there. Sometimes when she lifted her eyes she found the Duchess looking at her and then she realised that the Duchess knew it was there too.

She began to notice that almost everybody looked at her in a kindly slightly troubled way. Very important matrons and busy excited girls who ran in and out on errands had the same order of rather evasive glance.

"You have no cough, my dear, have you?" more than one amiable grand lady asked her.

"No, thank you—none at all," Robin answered and she was nearly always patted on the shoulder as her questioner left her.

Kathryn sitting by her desk one morning, watching her as she wrote a note, suddenly put her hand out and stopped her.

"Let me look at your wrist, Robin," she said and she took it between her fingers.

"Oh! What a little wrist!" she exclaimed. "I—I am sure Grandmamma has not seen it. Grandmamma—" aloud to the Duchess, "*Have* you seen Robin's wrist? It looks as if it would snap in two."

There were only three or four people in the room and they were all intimates and looked interested.

"It is only that I am a little thin," said Robin. "Everybody is thinner than usual. It is nothing."

The Duchess' kind look somehow took in those about her in her answer.

"You are too thin, my dear," she said. "I must tell you frankly, Kathryn, that you will be called upon to take her place. I am going to send her away into the wilds. The War only ceases for people who are sent into wild places. Dr. Redcliff is quite fixed in that opinion. People who need taking care of must be literally hidden away in corners where war vibrations cannot reach them. He has sent Emily Clare away and even her friends do not know where she is."

Later in the day Lady Lothwell came and in the course of a few minutes drew near to her mother and sat by her chair rather closely. She spoke in a lowered voice.

"I am so glad, mamma darling, that you are going to send poor little Miss Lawless into retreat for a rest cure," she began. "It's so tactless to continually chivy people about their health, but I own that I can scarcely resist saying to the child every time I see her, 'Are you any better today?' or, 'Have you any cough?' or, 'How is your appetite?' I have not wanted to trouble you about her but the truth is we all find ourselves talking her over. The point of her chin is growing actually sharp. What is Mrs. Gareth-Lawless doing?" curtly.

"Giving dinners and bridge parties to officers on leave. Robin never sees her."

"Of course the woman does not want her about. She is too lovely for officers' bridge parties," rather sharply again.

"Mrs. Gareth-Lawless is not the person one would naturally turn to for sympathy in trouble. Illness would present itself to her mind as a sort of outrage." The Duchess herself spoke in a low tone and her eyes wandered for a moment or so to the corner where Robin sat among her papers.

"She is a sensitive child," she said, "and I have not wanted to alarm her by telling her she must give up the work her heart is in. I have seen for some time that she must have an entire holiday and that she must leave London behind her utterly for a while. Dr. Redcliff knows of the right remote sort of place for her. It is really quite settled. She will do as I advise her. She is very obedient."

"Mamma," murmured Lady Lothwell who was furtively regarding Robin also—and it must be confessed with a dewy eye—"I suppose it is because I have Kathryn—but I feel a sort of pull at my heart when I remember how the little thing *bloomed* only a few months ago! She was radiant with life and joy and youngness. It's the contrast that almost frightens one. Something has actually gone. Does Doctor Redcliff think—*Could* she be going to die? Somehow," with a tremulous breath, "one always thinks of death now."

"No! No!" the Duchess answered. "Dr. Redcliff says she is not in real danger. Nourishment and relaxed strain and quiet will supply what she needs. But I will ask you, Millicent, to explain to people. I am too tired to answer questions. I realise that I have actually begun to love the child and I don't want to hear amiable people continuously suggesting the probability that she is in galloping consumption—and proposing remedies."

"Will she go soon?" Lady Lothwell asked.

"As soon as Dr. Redcliff has decided between two heavenly little places—one in Scotland and one in Wales. Perhaps next week or a week later. Things must be prepared for her comfort."

Lady Lothwell went home and talked a little to Kathryn who listened with sympathetic intelligence.

"It would have been better not to have noticed her poor little wrists," she said. "Years ago I believe that telling people that they looked ill and asking anxiously about their symptoms was regarded as a form of affection and politeness, but it isn't done at all now."

"I know, mamma!" Kathryn returned remorsefully. "But somehow there was something so pathetic in her little thin hand writing so fast—and the way her eyelashes lay on a sort of hollow of shadow instead of a soft cheek—I took it in suddenly all at once—And I almost burst out crying without intending to do it. Oh, mamma!" throwing out her hand to clutch her mother's, "Since—since George—! I seem to cry so suddenly! Don't—don't you?"

"Yes—yes!" as they slipped into each other's arms. "We all do—everybody—everybody!"

Their weeping was not loud but soft. Kathryn's girl voice had a low violin-string wail in it and was infinitely touching in its innocent love and pity.

"It's because one feels as if it *couldn't* be true—as if he *must* be somewhere! George—good nice George. So good looking and happy and silly and dear! And we played and fought together when we were children. Oh! To *kill* George—George!"

When they sat upright again with wet eyes and faces Kathryn added,

"And he was only *one*! And that beautiful Donal Muir who danced with Robin at Grandmamma's party! And people actually *stared* at them, they looked so happy and beautiful." She paused and thought a moment. "Do you know, mamma, I couldn't help believing he would fall in love with her if he saw her often—and I wondered what Lord Coombe would think. But he never did see her again. And now—! You know what they said about—not even *finding* him!"

"It is better that they did not meet again. If they had it would be easy to understand why the poor girl looks so ill."

"Yes, I'm glad for her that it isn't that. That would have been much worse. Being sent away to quiet places to rest might have been no good."

"But even as it is, mamma is more anxious I am sure than she likes to own to herself. You and I must manage to convey to people that it is better not even to verge on making fussy inquiries. Mamma has too many burdens on her mind to be as calm as she used to be."

It was an entirely uncomplicated situation. It became understood that the Duchess had become much attached to her companion as a result of her sweet faithfulness to her work. She and Dr. Redcliff had taken her in charge and prepared for her comfort and well-being in the most complete manner. A few months would probably end in a complete recovery. There were really no special questions even for the curious to ask and no one was curious. There was no time for curiosity. So Robin disappeared from her place at the small desk in the corner of the Duchess' sitting room and Kathryn took her place and used her pen.

Chapter 21

In the front window of one of the row of little flat-faced brick houses on a narrow street in Manchester, Dowie sat holding Henrietta's new baby upon her lap. They were what is known as "weekly" houses, their rent being paid by the week and they were very small. There was a parlour about the size of a compartment in a workbox, there was a still smaller room behind it which was called a dining room and there was a diminutive kitchen in which all the meals were eaten unless there was "company to tea" which in these days was almost unknown. Dowie had felt it very small when she first came to it from the fine spaces and heights of the house in Eaton Square and found it seemingly full of very small children and a hysterically weeping girl awaiting the impending arrival of one who would be smaller than the rest.

"You'll never stay here," said Henrietta, crying and clutching the untidy half-buttoned front of her blouse. "You come straight from duchesses and grandeur and you don't know how people like us live. How can you stand us and our dirt, Aunt Sarah Ann?"

"There needn't be dirt, Henrietta, my girl," said Dowie with quite uncritical courage. "There wouldn't be if you were yourself, poor lass. I'm not a duchess, you know. I've only been a respectable servant. And I'm going to see you through your trouble."

Her sober, kindly capableness evolved from the slovenly little house and the untended children, from the dusty rooms and neglected kitchen the kind of order and neatness which had been plain to see in Robin's more fortune-favoured apartment. The children became as fresh and neat as Robin's nursery self. They wore clean pinafores and began to behave tidily at table.

"I don't know how you do it, Aunt Sarah Ann," sighed Henrietta. But she washed her blouse and put buttons on it.

"It's just seeing things and picking up and giving a touch here and there," said Dowie. She bought little comforts almost every day and Henrietta was cheered by cups of hot tea in the afternoon and found herself helping to prepare decent meals and sitting down to them with appetite before a clean tablecloth. She began to look better and recovered her pleasure in sitting at the front window to watch the people passing by and notice how many new black dresses and bonnets went to church each Sunday.

When the new baby was born there was neither turmoil nor terror.

"Somehow it was different from the other times. It seemed sort of natural," Henrietta said. "And it's so quiet to lie like this in a comfortable clean bed, with everything in its place and nothing upset in the room. And a bright bit of fire in the grate—and a tidy, swept-up hearth—and the baby breathing so soft in his flannels."

She was a pretty thing and quite unfit to take care of herself even if she had had no children. Dowie knew that she was not beset by sentimental views of life and that all she wanted was a warm and comfortable corner to settle down into. Some masculine creature would be sure to begin to want her very soon. It was only to be hoped that youth and flightiness would not descend upon her—though three children might be supposed to form a barrier. But she had a girlish figure and her hair was reddish gold and curly and her full and not too small mouth was red and curly also. The first time she went to church in her little widow's bonnet with the reddish gold showing itself under the pathetic little white crêpe border, she was looked at a good deal. Especially was she looked at by an extremely respectable middle-aged widower who had been a friend of her dead husband's. His wife had been dead six years, he had a comfortable house and a comfortable shop which had thriven greatly through a connection with army supplies.

He came to see Henrietta and he had the good sense to treat Dowie as if she were her mother. He explained himself and his circumstances to her and his previous friendship for her nephew. He asked Dowie if she objected to his coming to see her niece and bringing toys to the children.

"I'm fond of young ones. I wanted 'em myself. I never had any," he said bluntly. "There's plenty of room in my house. It's a cheerful place with good solid furniture in it from top to bottom. There's one room we used to call 'the Nursery' sometimes just for a joke—not often. I choked up one day when I said it and Mary Jane burst out crying. I could do with six."

He was stout about the waist but his small blue eyes sparkled in his red face and Henrietta's slimness unromantically but practically approved of him.

One evening Dowie came into the little parlour to find her sitting upon his knee and he restrained her when she tried to rise hastily.

"Don't get up, Hetty," he said. "Your Aunt Sarah Ann'll understand. We've had a talk and she's a sensible woman. She says she'll marry me, Mrs. Dowson—as soon as it's right and proper."

"Yes, we've had a talk," Dowie replied in her nice steady voice. "He'll be a good husband to you, Henrietta—kind to the children."

"I'd be kind to them even if she wouldn't marry me," the stout lover answered. "I want 'em. I've told myself sometimes that I ought to have been the mother of six—not the father but the mother. And I'm not joking."

"I don't believe you are, Mr. Jenkinson," said Dowie.

As she sat before the window in the scrap of a parlour and held the sleeping new baby on her comfortable lap, she was thinking of this and feeling glad that poor Jem's widow and children were so well provided for. It would be highly respectable and proper. The ardour of Mr. Jenkinson would not interfere with his waiting until Henrietta's weeds could be decorously laid aside and then the family would be joyfully established in his well-furnished and decent house. During his probation he would visit Henrietta and bring presents to the children and unostentatiously protect them all and "do" for them.

"They won't really need me now that Henrietta's well and cheerful and has got some one to make much of her and look after her," Dowie reflected, trotting the baby gently. "I can't help believing her grace would take me on again if I wrote and asked her. And I should be near Miss Robin, thank God. It seems a long time since—"

She suddenly leaned forward and looked up the narrow street where the wind was blowing the dust about and whirling some scraps of paper. She watched a moment and then lifted the baby and stood up so that she might make more sure of the identity of a tall gentleman she saw approaching. She only looked at him for a few seconds and then she left the parlour quickly and went to the back room where she had been aware of Mr. Jenkinson's voice rumbling amiably along as a background to her thoughts.

"Henrietta," she said, "his lordship's coming down the street and he's coming here. I'm afraid something's happened to Miss Robin or her grace. Perhaps I'm needed at Eaton Square. Please take the baby."

"Give him to me," said Jenkinson and it was he who took him with quite an experienced air.

Henrietta was agitated.

"Oh, my goodness! Aunt Sarah Ann! I feel all shaky. I never saw a lord—and he's a marquis, isn't it? I shan't know what to do."

"You won't have to do anything," answered Dowie. "He'll only say what he's come to say and go away."

She went out of the room as quickly as she had come into it because she heard the sound of the cheap little door knocker. She was pale with anxiety when she opened the door and Lord Coombe saw her troubled look and understood its reason.

"I am afraid I have rather alarmed you, Dowie," he said as he stepped into the narrow lobby and shook hands with her.

"It's not bad news of her grace or Miss Robin?" she faltered.

"I have come to ask you to come back to London. Her grace is well but Miss Robin needs you," was what he said.

But Dowie knew the words did not tell her everything she was to hear. She took him into the parlour for which she realised he was much too tall. When she discreetly closed the door after he had entered, he said seriously, "Thank you," before he seated himself. And she knew that this meant that they must be undisturbed.

"Will you sit down too," he said as she stood a moment waiting respectfully. "We must talk together."

She took a chair opposite to him and waited respectfully again. Yes, he had something grave on his mind. He had come to tell her something—to ask her questions perhaps—to require something of her. Her superiors had often required things of her in the course of her experience—such things as they would not have asked of a less sensible and reliable woman. And she had always been ready.

When he began to talk to her he spoke as he always did, in a tone which sounded unemotional but held one's attention. But his face had changed since she had last seen it. It had aged and there was something different in the eyes. That was the War. Since the War began so many faces had altered.

During the years in the slice of a house he had never talked to her very much. It was with Mademoiselle he had talked and his interviews with her had not taken place in the nursery. How was it then that he seemed to know her so well. Had Mademoiselle told him that she was a woman to be trusted safely with any serious and intimate confidence—that being given any grave secret to shield, she would guard it as silently and discreetly as a great lady might guard such a thing if it were personal to her own family—as her grace herself might guard it. That he knew this fact without a shadow of doubt was subtly manifest in every word he spoke, in each tone of his voice. There was strange dark trouble to face—and keep secret—and he had come straight to her—Sarah Ann Dowson—because he was sure of her and knew her ways. It was her *ways* he knew and understood—her steadiness and that she had the kind of manners that keep a woman from talking about things and teach her how to keep other people from being too familiar and asking questions. And he knew what that kind of manners was built on—just decent faithfulness and honest feeling. He didn't say it in so many words, of course, but as Dowie listened it was exactly as if he said it in gentleman's language.

England was full of strange and cruel tragedies. And they were not all tragedies of battle and sudden death. Many of them were near enough to seem even worse—if worse could be. Dowie had heard some hints of them and had wondered what the world was coming to. As her visitor talked her heart began to thump in her side. Whatsoever had happened was no secret from her grace. And together she and his lordship were going to keep it a secret from the world. Dowie could scarcely have told what phrase or word at last suddenly brought up before her a picture of the nursery in the house in Mayfair—the feeling of a warm soft childish body pressed close to her knee, the look of a tender, dewy-eyed small face and the sound of a small yearning voice saying:

"I want to *kiss* you, Dowie." And so hearing it, Dowie's heart cried out to itself, "Oh! Dear Lord!"

"It's Miss Robin that trouble's come to," involuntarily broke from her.

"A trouble she must be protected in. She cannot protect herself." For a few seconds he sat and looked at her very steadily. It was as though he were asking a question. Dowie did not know she was going to rise from her chair. But for some reason she got up and stood quite firmly before him. And her good heart went thump-thump-thump.

"Your lordship," she said and in spite of the thumping her voice actually did not shake. "It was one of those War weddings. And perhaps he's dead."

Then it was Lord Coombe who left his chair.

"Thank you, Dowie," he said and before he began to walk up and down the tiny room she felt as if he made a slight bow to her.

She had said something that he had wished her to say. She had removed some trying barrier for him instead of obliging him to help her to cross it and perhaps stumbling on her way. She had neither stumbled nor clambered, she had swept it away out of his path and hers. That was because she knew Miss Robin and had known her from her babyhood.

Though for some time he walked to and fro slowly as he talked she saw that it was easier for him to complete the relation of his story. But as it proceeded it was necessary for her to make an effort to recall herself to a realisation of the atmosphere of the parlour and the narrow street outside the window—and she was glad to be assisted by the amiable rumble of Mr. Jenkinson's voice as heard from the back room when she found herself involuntarily leaning forward in her chair, vaguely conscious that she was drawing short breaths, as she listened to what he was telling her. The things she was listening to stood out from a background of unreality so startling. She was even faintly tormented by shadowy memories of a play she had seen years ago at Drury Lane. And Drury Lane incidents were of a world so incongruously remote from the house in Eaton Square and her grace's clever aquiline ivory face—and his lordship with his quiet bearing and his unromantic and elderly, tired fineness. And yet he was going to undertake to do a thing which was of the order of deed the sober everyday mind could only expect from the race of persons known as "heroes" in theatres and in books. And he was noticeably and wholly untheatrical about it. His plans were those of a farseeing and practical man in every detail. To Dowie the working perfection of his preparations was amazing. They included every contingency and seemed to forget nothing and ignore no possibility. He had thought of things the cleverest woman might have thought of, he had achieved effects as only a sensible man accustomed to power and obedience could have achieved them. And from first to last he kept before Dowie the one thing which held the strongest appeal. In her helpless heartbreak and tragedy Robin needed her as she needed no one else in the world.

"She is so broken and weakened that she may not live," he said in the end. "No one can care for her as you can."

"I can care for her, poor lamb. I'll come when your lordship's ready for me, be it soon or late."

"Thank you, Dowie," he said again. "It will be soon."

And when he shook hands with her and she opened the front door for him, she stood and watched him, thinking very deeply as he walked down the street with the wind-blown dust and scraps of paper whirling about him.

Chapter 22

In little more than two weeks Dowie descended from her train in the London station and took a hansom cab which carried her through the familiar streets to Eaton Square. She was comforted somewhat by the mere familiarity of things—even by the grade of smoke which seemed in some way to be different from the smoke of Manchester's cotton factory chimneys—by the order of rattle and roar and rumble, which had a homelike sound. She had not felt at home in Manchester and she had not felt quite at home with Henrietta though she had done her duty by her. Their worlds had been far apart and daily adjustment to circumstances is not easy though it may be accomplished without the betrayal of any outward sign. His lordship's summons had come soon, as he had said it would, but he had made it possible for her to leave in the little house a steady and decent woman to take her place when she gave it up.

She had made her journey from the North with an anxiously heavy heart in her breast. She was going to "take on" a responsibility which included elements previously quite unknown to her. She was going to help to hide something, to live with a strange secret trouble and while she did so must wear her accustomed, respectable and decorous manner and aspect. Whatsoever alarmed or startled her, she must not seem to be startled or alarmed. As his lordship had carried himself with his usual bearing, spoken in his high-bred calm voice and not once failed in the naturalness of his expression—even when he had told her the whole strange plan—so she must in any circumstances which arose and in any difficult situation wear always the aspect of a well-bred and trained servant who knew nothing which did not concern her and did nothing which ordinary domestic service did not require that she should do. She must always seem to be only Sarah Ann Dowson and never forget. But delicate and unusual as this problem was, it was not the thing which made her heart heavy. Several times during her journey she had been obliged to turn her face towards the window of the railway carriage and away from her fellow passengers so that she might very quickly and furtively touch her eyes with her handkerchief because she did not want any one to see the tear which obstinately welled up in spite of her efforts to keep it back.

She had heard of "trouble" in good families, had even been related to it. She knew how awful it was and what desperate efforts were made, what desperate means resorted to, in the concealment of it. And how difficult and almost impossible it was to cope with it and how it seemed sometimes as if the whole fabric of society and custom combined to draw attention to mere trifles which in the end proved damning evidence.

And it was Miss Robin she was going to—her own Miss Robin who had never known a child of her own age or had a girl friend—who had been cut off from innocent youth and youth's happiness and intimacies.

"It's been one of those poor mad young war weddings," she kept saying to herself, "though no one will believe her. If she hadn't been so ignorant of life and so lonely! But just as she fell down worshipping that dear little chap in the Gardens because he was the first she'd ever seen—it's only nature that the first beautiful young thing her own age that looked at her with love rising up in him should set it rising in her—where God had surely put it if ever He put love as part of life in any girl creature His hand made. But Oh! I can *see* no one will believe her! The world's heart's so wicked. I know, poor lamb. Her Dowie knows. And her left like this!"

It was when her thoughts reached this point that the tear would gather in the corner of her eye and would have trickled down her cheek if she had not turned away towards the window.

But above all things she told herself she must present only Dowie's face when she reached Eaton Square. There were the servants who knew nothing and must know nothing but that Mrs. Dowson had come to take care of poor Miss Lawless who had worked too hard and was looking ill and was to be sent into the country to some retreat her grace had chosen because it was far enough away to allow of her being cut off from war news and work, if her attendants were faithful and firm. Every one knew Mrs. Dowson would be firm and faithful. Then there were the ladies who went in and out of the house in these days. If they saw her by any chance they might ask kind interested questions about the pretty creature they had liked. They might inquire as to symptoms, they might ask where she was to be taken to be nursed. Dowie knew that after she had seen Robin herself she could provide suitable symptoms and she knew, as she knew how to breathe and walk, exactly the respectful voice and manner in which she could make her replies and how natural she could cause it to appear that she had not yet been told their destination—her grace being still undecided. Dowie's decent intelligence knew the methods of her class and their value when perfectly applied. A nurse or a young lady's maid knew only what she was told and did not ask questions.

But what she thought of most anxiously was Robin herself. His lordship had given her no instructions. Part of his seeming to understand her was that he had seemed to be sure that she would know what to say and what to leave unsaid. She was glad of that because it left her free to think the thing over and make her own quiet plans. She drew more than one tremulous sigh as she thought it out. In the first place—little Miss Robin seemed like a baby to her yet! Oh, she *was* a baby! Little Miss Robin just in her teens and with her childish asking eyes and her soft childish mouth! Her a young married lady and needing to be taken care of! She was too young to be married—if it was ever so! And if everything had been done all right and proper with wedding cake and veil, orange blossoms and St. George's, Hanover Square, she still would have been too young and would have looked almost cruelly like a child. And at a time such as this Dowie would have known she was one to be treated with great delicacy and tender reserve. But as it was—a little shamed thing to be hidden away—to be saved from the worst of fates for any girl—with nothing in her hand to help her—how would it be wisest to face her, how could one best be a comfort and a help?

How the sensible and tender creature gave her heart and brain to her reflections! How she balanced one chance and one emotion against another! Her conclusion was, as Coombe had known it would be, drawn from the experience of practical wisdom and an affection as deep as the experience was broad.

"She won't be afraid of Dowie," she thought, "if it's just Dowie that looks at her exactly as she always did. In her little soul she may be frightened to death but if it's only Dowie she sees—not asking questions or looking curious and unnatural, she'll get over it and know she's got something to hold on to. What she needs is something she can hold on to—something that won't tremble when she does—and that looks at her in the way she was used to when she was happy and safe. What I must do with her is what I must do with the others—just look and talk and act as Dowie always did, however hard it is. Perhaps when we get away to the quiet place we're going to hide in, she may begin to want to talk to me. But not a question do I ask or look until she's ready to open her poor heart to me."

She had herself well under control when she reached her destination. She had bathed her face and freshened herself with a cup of hot tea at the station. She entered the house quite with her usual manner and was greeted with obvious welcome by her fellow servants. They had missed her and were glad to see her again. She reported herself respectfully to Mrs. James in the housekeeper's sitting room and they had tea again and a confidential talk.

"I'm glad you could leave your niece, Mrs. Dowson," the housekeeper said. "It's high time poor little Miss Lawless was sent away from London. She's not fit for war work now or for anything but lying in bed in a quiet place where she can get fresh country air and plenty of fresh eggs, and good milk and chicken broth. And she needs a motherly woman like you to watch her carefully."

"Does she look as delicate as all that?" said Dowie concernedly.

"She'll lie in the graveyard in a few months if something's not done. I've seen girls look like her before this." And Mrs. James said it almost sharply.

But even with this preparation and though Lord Coombe had spoken seriously of the state of the girl's health, Dowie was not ready to encounter without a fearful sense of shock what she confronted a little later when she went to Robin's sitting room as she was asked to.

When she tapped upon the door and in response to a faint sounding "Come in" entered the pretty place, Robin rose from her seat by the fire and came towards her holding out her arms.

"I'm so glad you came, Dowie dear," she said, "I'm *so* glad." She put the arms close round Dowie's neck and kissed her and held her cheek against the comfortable warm one a moment before she let go. "I'm so *glad*, dear," she murmured and it was even as she felt the arms close about her neck and the cheek press hers that Dowie caught her breath and held it so that she might not seem to gasp. They were such thin frail arms, the young body on which the dress hung loose was only a shadow of the round slimness which had been so sweet.

But it was when the arm released her and they stood apart and looked at each other that she felt the shock in full force while Robin continued her greetings.

"Did you leave Henrietta and the children quite well?" she was saying. "Is the new baby a pretty one?"

Dowie had not been one of those who had seen the gradual development of the physical change in her. It came upon her suddenly. She had left a young creature all softly rounded girlhood, sweet curves and life glow and bloom. She found herself holding a thin hand and looking into a transparent, sharpened small face whose eyes were hollowed. The silk of the curls on the forehead had a dankness and lifelessness which almost made her catch her breath again. Like Mrs. James she herself had more than once had the experience of watching young creatures slip into what the nurses of her day called "rapid decline" and she knew all the piteous portents of the early stages—the waxen transparency of sharpened features and the damp clinging hair. These two last were to her mind the most significant of the early terrors.

And in less than five minutes she knew that the child was not going to talk about herself and that she had been right in making up her own mind to wait. Whatsoever the strain of silence, there would be no speech now. The piteous darkness of her eye held a stillness that

159

was heart-breaking. It was a stillness of such touching endurance of something inevitable. Whatsoever had happened to her, whatsoever was going to happen to her, she would make no sound. She would outwardly be affectionate, pretty-mannered Miss Robin just as Dowie herself would give all her strength to trying to seem to be nothing and nobody but Dowie. And what it would cost of effort to do it well!

When they sat down together it was because she drew Robin by the thin little hand to an easy chair and she still held the thin hand when she sat near her.

"Henrietta's quite well, I'm glad to say," she answered. "And the baby's a nice plump little fellow. I left them very comfortable—and I think in time Henrietta will be married again."

"Married again!" said Robin. "Again!"

"He's a nice well-to-do man and he's fond of her and he's fond of children. He's never had any and he's always wanted them."

"Has he?" Robin murmured. "That's very nice for Henrietta." But there was a shadow in her eyes which was rather like frightened bewilderment.

Dowie still holding the mere nothing of a hand, stroked and patted it now and then as she described Mr. Jenkinson and the children and the life in the house in Manchester. She wanted to gain time and commonplace talk helped her.

"She won't be married again until her year's up," she explained. "And it's the best thing she could do—being left a young widow with children and nothing to live on. Mr. Jenkinson can give her more than she's ever had in the way of comforts."

"Did she love poor Jem very much?" Robin asked.

"She was very much taken with him in her way when she married him," Dowie said. "He was a cheerful, joking sort of young man and girls like Henrietta like jokes and fun. But they were neither of them romantic and it had begun to be a bit hard when the children came. She'll be very comfortable with Mr. Jenkinson and being comfortable means being happy—to Henrietta."

Then Robin smiled a strange little ghost of a smile—but there were no dimples near it.

"You haven't told me that I am thin, Dowie," she said. "I know I am thin, but it doesn't matter. And I am glad you kissed me first. That made me sure that you were Dowie and not only a dream. Everything has been seeming as if it were a dream—everything—myself—everybody—even you—*you*!" And the small hand clutched her hard.

A large lump climbed into Dowie's throat but she managed it bravely.

"It's no use telling people they're thin," she answered with stout good cheer. "It doesn't help to put flesh on them. And there are a good many young ladies working themselves thin in these days. You're just one of them that's going to be taken care of. I'm not a dream, Miss Robin, my dear. I'm just your own Dowie and I'm going to take care of you as I did when you were six."

She actually felt the bones of the small hand as it held her own still closer. It began to tremble because Robin had begun to tremble. But though she was trembling and her eyes looked very large and frightened, the silence was still deep within them.

"Yes," the low voice faltered, "you will take care of me. Thank you, Dowie dear. I—must let people take care of me. I know that. I am like Henrietta."

And that was all.

"She's very much changed, your grace," Dowie said breathlessly when she went to the Duchess afterwards. There had been no explanation or going into detail but she knew that she might allow herself to be breathless when she stood face to face with her grace. "Does she cough? Has she night sweats? Has she any appetite?"

"She does not cough yet," the Duchess answered, but her grave eyes were as troubled as Dowie's own. "Doctor Redcliff will tell you everything. He will see you alone. We are sending her away with you because you love her and will know how to take care of her. We are very anxious."

"Your grace," Dowie faltered and one of the tears she had forced back when she was in the railway carriage rose insubordinately and rolled down her cheek, "just once I nursed a young lady who—looked as she does now. I did my best with all my heart, the doctors did their best, everybody that loved her did their best—and there were a good many. We watched over her for six months."

"Six months?" the Duchess' voice was an unsteady thing.

"At the end of six months we laid her away in a pretty country churchyard, with flowers heaped all over her—and her white little hands full of them. And she hadn't—as much to contend with—as Miss Robin has."

And in the minute of dead silence which followed more tears fell. No one tried to hold them back and some of them were the tears of the old Duchess.

Chapter 23

There are old and forgotten churches in overgrown corners of London whose neglected remoteness suggests the possibility of any ecclesiastical ceremony being performed quite unobserved except by the parties concerned in it. If entries and departures were discreetly arranged, a baptismal or a marriage ceremony might take place almost as in a tomb. A dark wet day in which few pass by and such as pass are absorbed in their own discomforts beneath their umbrellas, offers a curiously entire aloofness of seclusion. In the neglected graveyards about them there is no longer any room to bury any one in the damp black earth where the ancient tombs are dark with mossy growth and mould, heavy broken slabs slant sidewise perilously, sad and thin cats prowl, and from a soot-blackened tree or so the rain drops with hollow, plashing sounds.

The rain was so plashing and streaming in rivulets among the mounds and stones of the burial ground of one of the most ancient and forgotten looking of such churches, when on a certain afternoon there came to the narrow soot-darkened Vicarage attached to it a tall, elderly man who wished to see and talk to the Vicar.

The Vicar in question was an old clergyman who had spent nearly fifty years in the silent, ecclesiastical-atmosphered small house. He was an unmarried man whose few relatives living in the far North of England were too poor and unenterprising to travel to London. His days were spent in unsatisfactory work among crowded and poverty-stricken human creatures before whom he felt helpless because he was an unpractical old Oxford bookworm. He read such services as he held in his dim church, to empty pews and echoing hollowness. He was nevertheless a deeply thinking man who was a gentleman of a scarcely remembered school; he was a peculiarly silent man and of dignified understanding. Through the long years he had existed in detached seclusion in his corner of his world around which great London roared and swept almost unheard by him in his remoteness.

When the visitor's card was brought to him where he sat in his dingy, book-packed study, he stood—after he had told his servant to announce the caller—gazing dreamily at the name upon the white surface. It was a stately name and brought back vague memories. Long ago—very long ago, he seemed to recall that he had slightly known the then bearer of it. He himself had been young then—quite young. The man he had known was dead and this one, his successor, must by this time have left youth behind him. What had led him to come?

Then the visitor was shown into the study. The Vicar felt that he was a man of singular suggestions. His straight build, his height, his carriage arrested the attention and the clear cut of his cold face held it. One of his marked suggestions was that there was unusual lack of revelation in his rather fine almond eye. It might have revealed much but its intention was to reveal nothing but courteous detachment from all but well-bred approach to the demand of the present moment.

"I think I remember seeing you when you were a boy, Lord Coombe," the Vicar said. "My father was rector of St. Andrews." St. Andrews was the Norman-towered church on the edge of the park enclosing Coombe Keep.

"I came to you because I also remembered that," was Coombe's reply.

Their meeting was a very quiet one. But every incident of life was quiet in the Vicarage. Only low sounds were ever heard, only almost soundless movements made. The two men seated themselves and talked calmly while the rain pattered on the window panes and streaming down them seemed to shut out the world.

What the Vicar realised was that, since his visitor had announced that he had come because he remembered their old though slight acquaintance, he had obviously come for some purpose to which the connection formed a sort of support or background. This man, whose modernity of bearing and externals seemed to separate them by a lifetime of experience, clearly belonged to the London which surrounded and enclosed his own silences with civilised roar and the tumult of swift passings. On the surface the small, dingy book-crammed study obviously held nothing this outer world could require. The Vicar said as much courteously and he glanced round the room as he spoke, gently smiling.

"But it is exactly this which brings me," Lord Coombe answered.

With great clearness and never raising the note of quiet to which the walls were accustomed, he made his explanation. He related no incidents and entered into no detail. When he had at length concluded the presentation of his desires, his hearer knew nothing whatever, save what was absolutely necessary, of those concerned in the matter. Utterly detached from all curiosities as he was, this crossed the Vicar's mind. There was a marriage ceremony to be performed. That only the contracting parties should be aware of its performance was absolutely necessary. That there should be no chance of opportunity given for question or comment was imperative. Apart from this the legality of the contract was all that concerned those entering into it; and that must be assured beyond shadow of possible doubt.

In the half-hidden and forgotten old church to which the Vicarage was attached such a ceremony could obviously be performed, and to an incumbent detached from the outer world, as it were, and one who was capable of comprehending the occasional gravity of reasons for silence, it could remain so long as was necessary a confidence securely guarded.

"It is possible," the Vicar said at the end of the explanation. "I have performed the ceremony before under somewhat similar circumstances."

A man of less breeding and with even normal curiosities might have made the mistake of asking innocent questions. He asked none except such as related to the customary form of procedure in such matters. He did not, in fact, ask questions of himself. He was also fully aware that Lord Coombe would have given no answer to any form of inquiry. The marriage was purely his own singular affair. It was he himself who chose in this way to be married—in a forgotten church in whose shadowy emptiness the event would be as a thing brought to be buried unseen and unmarked by any stone, but would yet be a contract binding in the face and courts of the world if it should for any reason be exhumed.

When he rose to go and the Vicar rose with him, there was a moment of pause which was rather curious. The men's eyes met and for a few moments rested upon each other. The Vicar's were still and grave, but there was a growth of deep feeling in them. This suggested a sort of profound human reflection.

Lord Coombe's expression itself changed a shade. It might perhaps be said that his eyes had before this moment scarcely seemed to hold expression.

"She is very young," he said in an unusual voice. "In this—holocaust—she needs protection. I can protect her."

"It is a holocaust," the Vicar said, "—a holocaust." And singularly the words seemed an answer.

On a morning of one of London's dark days when the rain was again splashing and streaming in rivulets among the mounds and leaning and tumbling stones of the forgotten churchyard, there came to the church three persons who if they had appeared in more frequented edifices would have attracted some attention without doubt, unnoticeably as they were dressed and inconspicuous as was their manner and bearing.

They did not all three present themselves at the same time. First there appeared the tall elderly man who had visited and conferred with the Vicar. He went at once to the vestry where he spent some time with the incumbent who awaited him.

Somewhat later there stepped through the little arched doorway a respectable looking elderly woman and a childlike white-faced girl in a close black frock. That the church looked to them so dark as to be almost black with shadows was manifest when they found themselves inside peering into the dimness. The outer darkness seemed to have crowded itself through the low doorway to fill the groined arches with gloom.

"Where must we go to, Dowie?" Robin whispered holding to the warm, stout arm.

"Don't be timid, my dearie," Dowie whispered back. "His lordship will be ready for us now we've come."

His lordship was ready. He came forward to meet them and when he did so, Robin knew—though he seemed to be part of the dimness and to come out of a dream—that she need feel no further uncertainties or fears. That which was to take place would move forward without let or hindrance to its end. That was what one always felt in his presence.

In a few minutes they were standing in a part of the church which would have seemed darker than any other shadow-filled corner but that a dim light burned on a small altar and a clergyman whose white vestments made him look wraithlike and very tall waited before it and after a few moments of solemn silence began to read from the prayer book he held in his hand.

There were strange passings and repassings through Robin's mind as she made her low responses—memories of the hours when she had asked herself if she were still alive—if she were not dead as Donal was, but walking about without having found it out. It was as though this must be true now and her own voice and Lord Coombe's and the clergyman's only ghosts' voices. They were so low and unlike real voices and when they floated away among the shadows, low ghastly echoes seemed to float with them.

"I will," she heard herself say, and also other things the clergyman told her to repeat after him and when Lord Coombe spoke she could scarcely understand because it was all like a dream and did not matter.

Once she turned so cold and white and trembled so that Dowie made an involuntary movement towards her, but Lord Coombe's quiet firmness held her swaying body and though the clergyman paused a moment the trembling passed away and the ceremony went on. She had begun to tremble because she remembered that the other marriage had seemed like a dream in another world than this—a world which was so alive that she had trembled and thrilled with exquisite living. And because Donal knew how frightened she was he had stood so close to her that she had felt the dear warmness of his body. And he had held her hand quite tight when he took it and his "I will" had been beautiful and clear. And when he had put on the borrowed ring he had drawn her eyes up to the blue tarn of his own. Donal was killed! Perhaps the young chaplain had been killed too. And she was being married to Lord Coombe who was an old man and did not stand close to her, whose hand scarcely held hers at all—but who was putting on a ring.

Her eyes—her hunted young doe's eyes—lifted themselves. Lord Coombe met them and understood. Strangely she knew he understood—that he knew what she was thinking about. For that one moment there came into his eyes a look which might not have been his own, and vaguely she knew that it held strange understanding and he was sorry for her—and for Donal and for everything in the world.

Chapter 24

The little feudal fastness in the Highlands which was called Darreuch
Castle—when it was mentioned by any one, which was rarely—had
been little more than a small ruin when Lord Coombe inherited it as
an unconsidered trifle among more imposing and available property.
It had indeed presented the aspect not so much of an asset as of an
entirely useless relic. The remote and—as far as record dwelt on
him—obviously unnotable ancestor who had built it as a stronghold
in an almost unreachable spot upon the highest moors had doubtlessly
had picturesque reasons for the structure, but these were lost in the
dim past and appeared on the surface, unexplainable to a modern
mind. Lord Coombe himself had not explained an interest he chose
to feel in it, or his own reasons for repairing it a few years after it
came into his possession. He rebuilt certain breaches in the walls and
made certain rooms sufficiently comfortable to allow of his spending
a few nights or weeks in it at rare intervals. He always went alone,
taking no servant with him, and made his retreat after his own mood,
served only by the farmer and his wife who lived in charge from year's
end to year's end, herding a few sheep and cultivating a few acres for
their own needs.

They were a silent pair without children and plainly not feeling the
lack of them. They had lived in remote moorland places since their
birth. They had so little to say to each other that Lord Coombe
sometimes felt a slight curiosity as to why they had married instead
of remaining silent singly. There was however neither sullenness nor
resentment in their lack of expression. Coombe thought they liked
each other but found words unnecessary. Jock Macaur driving his
sheep to fold in the westering sun wore the look of a man not unpleased

with life and at least undisturbed by it. Maggy Macaur doing her housework, churning or clucking to her hens, was peacefully cheerful and seemed to ask no more of life than food and sleep and comfortable work which could be done without haste. There were no signs of knowledge on her part or Jock's of the fact that they were surrounded by wonders of moorland and hillside colour and beauty. Sunrise which leaped in delicate flames of dawn meant only that they must leave their bed; sunset which lighted the moorland world with splendour meant that a good night's sleep was coming.

Jock had heard from a roaming shepherd or so that the world was at war and that lads were being killed in their thousands. One good man had said that the sons of the great gentry were being killed with the rest. Jock did not say that he did not believe it and in fact expressed no opinion at all. If he and Maggy gave credit to the story, they were little disturbed by any sense of its reality. They had no neighbours and their few stray kinfolk lived at remote distances and were not given to visits or communications. There had been vague rumours of far away wars in the years past, but they had assumed no more reality than legends. This war was a shadow too and after Jock came home one night and mentioned it as he might have mentioned the death of a cow or the buying of a moor pony the subject was forgotten by both.

"His lordship" it was who reminded them of it. He even bestowed upon the rumour a certain reality. He appeared at the stout little old castle one day without having sent them warning, which was unusual. He came to give some detailed orders and to instruct them in the matter of changes. He had shown forethought in bringing with him a selection of illustrated newspapers. This saved time and trouble in the matter of making the situation clear. The knowledge which conveyed itself to Maggy and Jock produced the effect of making them even more silent than usual if such a condition were possible. They stared fixedly and listened with respect but beyond a rare "Hech!" they had no opinion to express. It became plain that the war was more than a mere rumour— The lads who had been blown to bits or bayoneted! The widows and orphans that were left! Some of the youngest of the lads had lost their senses and married young things only to go off to the ill place folk called "The Front" and leave them widows in a few days' or weeks' time. There were hundreds of bits of girls left lonely waiting for their bairns to come into the world—Some with scarce a penny unless friends took care of them. There was a bit widow in her teens who was a distant kinswoman of his lordship's, and her poor lad was among those who were killed. He had been a fine lad and he would never see his bairn. The poor young widow had been ill with grief and the doctors said she must be hidden away in some quiet place where she would never hear of battles or see a newspaper. She must be kept in peace and taken great care of if she was to gain strength to live through her time. She had no family to watch over her and his lordship and an old lady who was fond of her had taken her trouble in hand. The well-trained woman who had nursed her as a child would bring her to Darreuch Castle and there would stay.

His lordship had been plainly much interested in the long time past when he had put the place in order for his own convenience. Now he seemed even more interested and more serious. He went from room to room with a grave face and looked things over carefully. He had provided himself with comforts and even luxuries before his first coming and they had been of the solid baronial kind which does not deteriorate. It was a little castle and a forgotten one, but his rooms had beauty and had not been allowed to be as gloomy as they might have been if stone walls and black oak had not been warmed by the rich colours of tapestry and pictures which held light and glow. But other things were coming from London. He himself would wait to see them arrive and installed. The Macaurs wondered what more the "young leddy" and her woman could want but took their orders obediently. Her woman's name was Mrs. Dowson and she was a quiet decent body who would manage the household. That the young widow was to be well taken care of was evident. A doctor was to ride up the moorland road each day to see her, which seemed a great precaution even though the Macaurs did not know that he had consented to live temporarily in the locality because he had been well paid to do so. Lord Coombe had chosen him with as discreet selection as he had used in his choice of the vicar of the ancient and forsaken church. A rather young specialist who was an enthusiast in his work and as ambitious as he was poor, could contemplate selling some months of his time for value received if the terms offered were high enough. That silence and discretion were required formed no objections.

The rain poured down on the steep moorland road when the carriage slowly climbed it to the castle. Robin, seeming to gaze out at the sodden heath, did not really see it because she was thinking of Dowie who sat silently by her side. Dowie had taken her from the church to the station and they had made the long journey together. They had talked very little in the train though Dowie had been tenderly careful and kind. Robin knew she would ask no questions and she dully felt that the blows which were falling on everybody every day must have stunned her also. What she herself was thinking as she seemed to gaze at the sodden heather was a thing of piteous and helpless pain. She was achingly wondering what Dowie was thinking—what she knew and what she thought of the girl she had taken such care of and who was being sent away to be hidden in a ruined castle whose existence was a forgotten thing. The good respectable face told nothing but it seemed to be trying to keep itself from looking too serious; and once Robin had thought that it looked as if Dowie might suddenly have broken down if she would have allowed herself but she would not allow herself.

The truth was that the two or three days at Eaton Square had been very hard for Dowie to manage perfectly. To play her accepted part before her fellow servants required much steady strength. They were all fond of "poor little Miss Lawless" and had the tendency of their class to discuss and dwell upon symptoms with sympathetic harrowingness of detail. It seemed that all of them had had some friend or relative who had "gone off in a quick decline. It's strange how many young people do!" A head housemaid actually brought her heart into her throat one afternoon by saying at the servants' hall tea:

"If she was one of the war brides, I should say she was just like my cousin Lucy—poor girl. She and her husband were that fond of each other that it was a pleasure to see them. He was killed in an accident. She was expecting. And they'd been that happy. She went off in three months. She couldn't live without him. She wasn't as pretty as Miss Lawless, of course, but she had big brown eyes and it was the way they looked that reminded me. Quick decline always makes people's eyes look big and—just as poor little Miss Lawless does."

To sit and eat buttered toast quietly and only look normally sad and slowly shake one's head and say, "Yes indeed. I know what you mean, Miss Tompkins," was an achievement entitled to much respect.

The first night Dowie had put her charge to bed and had seen the faint outline under the bedclothes and the sunken eyes under the pale closed lids whose heaviness was so plain because it was a heaviness which had no will to lift itself again and look at the morning, she could scarcely bear her woe. As she dressed the child when morning came and saw the delicate bones sharply denoting themselves, and the hollows in neck and throat where smooth fairness had been, her hands almost shook as she touched. And hardest of all to bear was the still, patient look in the enduring eyes. She was being patient—*patient*, poor lamb, and only God himself knew how she cried when she was left alone in her white bed, the door closed between her and all the house.

"Does she think I am wicked?" was what was passing through Robin's mind as the carriage climbed the moor through the rain. "It would break my heart if Dowie thought I was wicked. But even that does not matter. It is only *my* heart."

In memory she was looking again into Donal's eyes as he had looked into hers when he knelt before her in the wood. Afterwards he had kissed her dress and her feet when she said she would go with him to be married so that he could have her for his own before he went away to be killed.

It would have been *his* heart that would have been broken if she had said "No" instead of whispering the soft "Yes" of a little mating bird, which had always been her answer when he had asked anything of her.

When the carriage drew up at last before the entrance to the castle, the Macaurs awaited them with patient respectful faces. They saw the "decent body" assist with care the descent of a young thing the mere lift of whose eyes almost caused both of them to move a trifle backward.

"You and Dowie are going to take care of me," she said quiet and low and with a childish kindness. "Thank you."

She was taken to a room in whose thick wall Lord Coombe had opened a window for sunlight and the sight of hill and heather. It was a room warm and full of comfort—a strange room to find in a little feudal stronghold hidden from the world. Other rooms were near it, as comfortable and well prepared. One in a tower adjoining was hung with tapestry and filled with wonderful old things, uncrowded and harmonious and so arranged as to produce the effect of a small retreat for rest, the reading of books or refuge in stillness.

When Robin went into it she stood for a few moments looking about her—looking and wondering.

"Lord Coombe remembers everything," she said very slowly at last, "—everything. He remembers."

"He always did remember," said Dowie watching her. "That's it."

"I did not know—at first," Robin said as slowly as before. "I do—now."

In the evening she sat long before the fire and Dowie, sewing near her, looked askance now and then at her white face with the lost eyes. It was Dowie's own thought that they were "lost." She had never before seen anything like them. She could not help glancing sideways at them as they gazed into the red glow of the coal. What was her mind dwelling on? Was she thinking of words to say? Would she begin to feel that they were far enough from all the world—remote and all alone enough for words not to be sounds too terrible to hear even as they were spoken?

"Oh! dear Lord," Dowie prayed, "help her to ease her poor, timid young heart that's so crushed with cruel weight."

"You must go to bed early, my dear," she said at length. "But why don't you get a book and read?"

The lost eyes left the fire and met hers.

"I want to talk," Robin said. "I want to ask you things."

"I'll tell you anything you want to know," answered Dowie. "You're only a child and you need an older woman to talk to."

"I want to talk to you about—*me*," said Robin. She sat straight in her chair, her hands clasped on her knee. "Do you know about—me, Dowie?" she asked.

"Yes, my dear," Dowie answered.

"Tell me what Lord Coombe told you."

Dowie put down her sewing because she was afraid her hands would tremble when she tried to find the proper phrase in which to tell as briefly as she could the extraordinary story.

"He said that you were married to a young gentleman who was killed at the Front—and that because you were both so young and hurried and upset you perhaps hadn't done things as regular as you thought. And that you hadn't the papers you ought to have for proof. And it might take too much time to search for them now. And—and—Oh, my love, he's a good man, for all you've hated him so! He won't let a child be born with shame to blight it. And he's given you and it—poor helpless innocent—his own name, God bless him!"

Robin sat still and straight, with clasped hands on her knee, and her eyes more lost than before, as she questioned Dowie remorselessly. There was something she must know.

"He said—and the Duchess said—that no one would believe me if I told them I was married. Do *you* believe me, Dowie? Would Mademoiselle believe me—if she is alive—for Oh! I believe she is dead! Would you *both* believe me?"

Dowie's work fell upon the rug and she held out both her comfortable nursing arms, choking:

"Come here, my lamb," she cried out, with suddenly streaming eyes. "Come and sit on your old Dowie's knee like you used to do in the nursery."

"You *do* believe me—you *do*!" As she had looked in the nursery days—the Robin who left her chair and was swept into the well known embrace—looked now. She hid her face on Dowie's shoulder and clung to her with shaking hands.

"I prayed to Jesus Christ that you would believe me, Dowie!" she cried. "And that Mademoiselle would come if she is not killed. I wanted you to *know* that it was true—I wanted you to *know*!"

"That was it, my pet lamb!" Dowie kept hugging her to her breast "We'd both of us know! We know *you*—we do! No one need prove things to us. We *know*!"

"It frightened me so to think of asking you," shivered Robin. "When you came to Eaton Square I could not bear it. If your dear face had looked different I should have died. But I couldn't go to bed to-night without finding out. The Duchess and Lord Coombe are very kind and sorry for me and they say they believe me—but I can't feel sure they really do. And nobody else would. But you and Mademoiselle. You loved me always and I loved you. And I prayed you would."

Dowie knew how Mademoiselle had died—of the heap of innocent village people on which she had fallen bullet-riddled. But she said nothing of her knowledge.

"Mademoiselle would say what I do and she would stay and take care of you as I'm going to do," she faltered. "God bless you for asking me straight out, my dear! I was waiting for you to speak and praying you'd do it before I went to bed myself. I couldn't have slept a wink if you hadn't."

For a space they sat silent—Robin on her knee like a child drooping against her warm breast. Outside was the night stillness of the moor, inside the night stillness held within the thick walls of stone rooms and passages, in their hearts the stillness of something which yet waited—unsaid.

At last—

"Did Lord Coombe tell you who—he was, Dowie?"

"He said perhaps you would tell me yourself—if you felt you'd like me to know. He said it was to be as you chose."

Robin fumbled with a thin hand at the neck of her dress. She drew from it a chain with a silk bag attached. Out of the bag she took first a small folded package.

"Do you remember the dry leaves I wanted to keep when I was so little?" she whispered woefully. "I was too little to know how to save them. And you made me this tiny silk bag."

Dowie's face was almost frightened as she drew back to look. There was in her motherly soul the sudden sense of panic she had felt in the nursery so long ago.

"My blessed child!" she breathed. "Not that one—after all that time!"

"Yes," said Robin. "Look, Dowie—look."

She had taken a locket out of the silk bag and she opened it and Dowie looked.

Perhaps any woman would have felt what she felt when she saw the face which seemed to laugh rejoicing into hers, as if Life were such a supernal thing—as if it were literally the blessed gift of God as all the ages have preached to us even while they have railed at the burden of living and called it cruel nothingness. The radiance in the eyes' clearness, the splendid strength and joy in being, could have built themselves into nothing less than such beauty as this.

Dowie looked at it in dead silence, her breast heaving fast.

"Oh! blessed God!" she broke out with a gasp. "Did they kill—that!"

"Yes," said Robin, her voice scarcely more than a breath, "Donal."

Chapter 25

Dowie put her to bed as she had done when she was a child, feeling as if the days in the nursery had come back again. She saw gradually die out of the white face the unnatural restraint which she had grieved over. It had suggested the look of a girl who was not only desolate but afraid and she wondered how long she had worn it and what she had been most afraid of.

In the depths of her comfortable being there lay hidden a maternal pleasure in the nature of her responsibility. She had cared for young mothers before, and that she should be called to watch over Robin, whose child forlornness she had rescued, filled her heart with a glowing. As she moved about the room quietly preparing for the comfort of the night she knew that the soft dark of the lost eyes followed her and that it was not quite so lost as it had looked in the church and on their singularly silent journey.

When her work was done and she turned to the bed again Robin's arms were held out to her.

"I want to kiss you, Dowie—I want to kiss you," she said with just the yearning dwelling on the one word, which had so moved the good soul long ago with its innocent suggestion of tender reverence for some sacred rite.

Dowie hurriedly knelt by the bedside.

"Never you be frightened, my lamb—because you're so young and don't know things," she whispered, holding her as if she were a baby. "Never you let yourself be frightened for a moment. Your own Dowie's here and always will be—and Dowie knows all about it."

"Until you took me on your knee to-night," very low and in broken phrases, "I was so lonely. I was as lonely as I used to be in the old nursery before you and Mademoiselle came. Afterwards—" with a shudder, "there were so many long, long nights. There—always—will be so many. One after every day. I lie in my bed in the dark. And there is *Nothing*! Oh! Dowie, *let* me tell you!" her voice was a sweet longing wail. "When Donal came back all the world was full and shining and warm! It was full. There was no loneliness anywhere. We wanted nothing but each other. And when he was gone there was only emptiness! And I was not alive and I could not think. I can scarcely think now."

"You'll begin to think soon, my lamb," Dowie whispered. "You've got something to think of. After a while the emptiness won't be so big and black."

She ventured it very carefully. Her wise soul knew that the Emptiness must come first—the awful world-old Emptiness which for an endless-seeming time nothing can fill— And all smug preachers of the claims of life and duty must be chary of approaching those who stand desolate gazing into it.

"I could only *remember*," the broken heart-wringing voice went on. "And it seemed as if the remembering was killing me over and over again—It is like that now. But in the Wood Lord Coombe said something strange—which seemed to make me begin to think a little. Only it was like beginning to try to write with a broken arm. I can't go on—I can only think of Donal— And be lonely—lonely—lonely."

The very words—the mere sound of them in her own ears made her voice trail away into bitter helpless crying—which would not stop. It was the awful weeping of utter woe and weakness whose convulsive sobs go on and on until they almost cease to seem human sounds. Dowie's practical knowledge told her what she had to face. This was what she had guessed at when she had known that there had been crying in the night. Mere soothing of the tenderest would not check it.

"I had been lonely—always—And then the loneliness was gone. And then—! If it had never gone—!"

"I know, my dear, I know," said Dowie watching her with practised, anxious eye. And she went away for a few moments and came back with an unobtrusive calming draught and coaxed her into taking it and sat down and prayed as she held the little hands which unknowingly beat upon the pillow. Something of her steadiness and love flowed from her through her own warm restraining palms and something in her tender steady voice spoke for and helped her—though it seemed long and long before the cruelty of the storm had lessened and the shadow of a body under the bed-clothes lay deadly still and the heavy eyelids closed as if they would never lift again.

Dowie did not leave her for an hour or more but sat by her bedside and watched. Like this had been the crying in the night. And she had been alone.

As she sat and watched she thought deeply after her lights. She did not think only of the sweet shattered thing she so well loved. She thought much of Lord Coombe. Being a relic of a class which may be regarded as forever extinct, her views on the subject of the rights and responsibilities of rank were of an unswerving reverence verging on the feudal. Even in early days her perfection of type was rare. To her unwavering mind the remarkable story she had become a part of was almost august in its subjection of ordinary views to the future of a great house and its noble name. With the world falling to pieces and great houses crumbling into nothingness, that this one should be rescued from the general holocaust was a deed worthy of its head. But where was there another man who would have done this thing as he had done it—remaining totally indifferent to the ignomity which would fall upon his memory in the years to come when the marriage was revealed. That the explanation of his action would always be believed to be an unseemly and shameful one was to her respectable serving-class mind a bitter thing. That it would always be contemptuously said that a vicious elderly man had educated the daughter of his mistress, that he might marry her and leave an heir of her blooming youth, was almost worse than if he had been known to have committed some decent crime like honest murder. Even the servants' hall in the slice of a house, discussing the ugly whisper had somewhat revolted at it and thought it "a bit too steep even for these times." But he had plainly looked the whole situation in the face and had made up his mind to do what he had done. He hadn't cared for himself; he had only cared that the child who was to be born should be his legitimatised successor and that there should remain after him a Head of the House of Coombe. That such houses should have heads to succeed to their dignities was a simple reverential belief of Dowie's and—apart from all other feeling—the charge she had undertaken wore to her somewhat the aspect of a religious duty. His lordship was as one who had a place on a sort of altar.

"It's because he's so high in his way that he can bear it," was her thought. "He's so high that nothing upsets him. He's above things—that's what he is." And there was something else too—something she did not quite follow but felt vaguely moved by. What was happening to England came into it—and something else that was connected with himself in some way that was his own affair. In his long talk with her he had said some strange things—though all in his own way.

"Howsoever the tide of war turns, men and women will be needed as the world never needed them before," was one of them. "This one small unknown thing I want. It will be the child of my old age. I *want* it. Her whole being has been torn to pieces. Dr. Redcliff says that she might have died before this if her delicate body had not been stronger than it looks."

"She has never been ill, my lord," Dowie had answered, "—but she is ill now."

"Save her—save *it* for me," he broke out in a voice she had never heard and with a face she had never seen.

That in this plainly overwrought hour he should allow himself a moment of forgetfulness drew him touchingly near to her.

"My lord," she said, "I've watched over her since she was five. I know the ways young things in her state need to have about them to give them strength and help. Thank the Lord she's one of the loving ones and if we can hold her until she—wakes up to natural feelings she'll begin to try to live for the sake of what'll need her—and what's his as well as hers."

Of this she thought almost religiously as she sat by the bedside and watched.

Chapter 26

The doctor rode up the climbing moorland road the next morning and paid a long visit to his patient. He was not portentous in manner and he did not confine his conversation to the subject of symptoms. He however included something of subtle cross examination in his friendly talk. The girl's thinness, her sometimes panting breath and the hollow eyes made larger by the black ring of her lashes startled him on first sight of her. He found that the smallness of her appetite presented to Dowie a grave problem.

"I'm trying to coax good milk into her by degrees. She does her best. But she can't eat." When they were alone she said, "I shall keep her windows open and make her rest on her sofa near them. I shall try to get her to walk out with me if her strength will let her. We can go slowly and she'll like the moor. If we could stop the awful crying in the night— It's been shaking her to pieces for weeks and weeks— It's the kind that there's no checking when it once begins. It's beyond her poor bit of strength to hold it back. I saw how hard she tried—for my sake. It's the crying that's most dangerous of all."

"Nothing could be worse," the doctor said and he went away with a grave face, a deeply troubled man.

When Dowie went back to the Tower room she found Robin standing at a window looking out on the moorside. She turned and spoke and Dowie saw that intuition had told her what had been talked about.

"I will try to be good, Dowie," she said. "But it comes—it comes because—suddenly I know all over again that I can never *see* him any more. If I could only *see* him—even a long way off! But suddenly it all comes back that I can never *see* him again—Never!"

Later she begged Dowie not to come to her in the night if she heard sounds in her room.

"It will not hurt you so much if you don't see me," she said. "I'm used to being by myself. When I was at Eaton Square I used to hide my face deep in the pillow and press it against my mouth. No one heard. But no one was listening as you will be. Don't come in, Dowie darling. Please don't!"

All she wanted, Dowie found out as the days went by, was to be quiet and to give no trouble. No other desires on earth had been left to her. Her life had not taught her to want many things. And now—:

"Oh! please don't be unhappy! If I could only keep you from being unhappy—until it is over!" she broke out all unconsciously one day. And then was smitten to the heart by the grief in Dowie's face.

That was the worst of it all and sometimes caused Dowie's desperate hope and courage to tremble on the brink of collapse. The child was thinking that before her lay the time when it would be "all over."

A patient who held to such thoughts as her hidden comfort did not give herself much chance.

Sometimes she lay for long hours on the sofa by the open window but sometimes a restlessness came upon her and she wandered about the empty rooms of the little castle as though she were vaguely searching for something which was not there. Dowie furtively followed her at a distance knowing that she wanted to be alone. The wide stretches of the moor seemed to draw her. At times she stood gazing at them out of a window, sometimes she sat in a deep window seat with her hands lying listlessly upon her lap but with her eyes always resting on the farthest line of the heather. Once she sat thus so long that Dowie crept out of the empty stone chamber where she had been waiting and went and stood behind her. At first Robin did not seem conscious of her presence but presently she turned her head. There was a faintly bewildered look in her eyes.

"I don't know why—when I look at the edge where the hill seems to end—it always seems as if there might be something coming from the place we can't see—" she said in a helpless-sounding voice. "We can only see the sky behind as if the world ended there. But I feel as if something might be coming from the other side. The horizon always looks like that—now. There must be so much—where there seems to be nothing more. I want to go."

She tried to smile a little as though at her own childish fancifulness but suddenly a heavy shining tear fell on her hand. And her head dropped and she murmured, "I'm sorry, Dowie," as if it were a fault.

The Macaurs watched her from afar with their own special order of silent interest. But the sight of the slowly flitting and each day frailer young body began to move them even to the length of low-uttered expression of fear and pity.

"Some days she fair frights me passing by so slow and thin in her bit black dress," Maggy said. "She minds me o' a lost birdie fluttering about wi' a broken wing. She's gey young she is, to be a widow woman—left like that."

The doctor came up the moor road every day and talked more to Dowie than to his patient. As the weeks went by he could not sanely be hopeful. Dowie's brave face seemed to have lost some of its colour at times. She asked eager questions but his answers did not teach her any new thing. Yet he was of a modern school.

"There was a time, Mrs. Dowson," he said, "when a doctor believed—or thought he believed—that healing was carried in bottles. For thinking men that time has passed. I know very little more of such a case as this than you know yourself. You are practical and kind and watchful. You are doing all that can be done. So am I. But I am sorry to say that it seems as if only a sort of miracle—! If—as you said once—she would 'wake up'—there would be an added chance."

"Yes, sir," Dowie answered. "If she would. But it seems as if her mind has stopped thinking about things that are to come. You see it in her face. She can only remember. The days are nothing but dreams to her."

Dowie had written weekly letters to Lord Coombe in accordance with his request. She wrote a good clear hand and her method was as clear as her calligraphy. He invariably gathered from her what he most desired to know and learned that her courageous good sense was plainly to be counted upon. From the first her respectful phrases had not attempted to conceal from him the anxiety she had felt.

"It was the way she looked and that I hadn't expected to see such a change, that took the strength out of me the first time I saw her. And what your lordship had told me. It seemed as if the two things together were too much for her to face. I watch over her day and night though I try to hide from her that I watch so close. If she could be made to eat something, and to sleep, and not to break her little body to pieces with those dreadful fits of crying, there would be something to hold on to. But I shall hold on to her, my lord, whether there is anything to hold on to or not."

He knew she would hold on but as the weeks passed and she faithfully told him what record the days held he saw that in each she felt that she had less and less to grasp. And then came a letter which plainly could not conceal ominous discouragement in the face of symptoms not to be denied—increasing weakness, even more rapid loss of weight, and less sleep and great exhaustion after the convulsions of grief.

"It couldn't go on and not bring on the worst. It is my duty to warn your lordship," the letter ended.

For she had not "wakened up" though somehow Dowie had gone on from day to day wistfully believing that it would be only "Nature" that she should. Dowie had always believed strongly in "Nature." But at last there grew within her mind the fearsome thought that somehow the very look of her charge was the look of a young thing who had done with Nature—and between whom and Nature the link had been broken.

There were beginning to be young lambs on the hillside and Jock Macaur was tending them and their mothers with careful shepherding. Once or twice he brought a newborn and orphaned one home wrapped in his plaid and it was kept warm by the kitchen fire and fed with milk by Maggy to whom motherless lambs were an accustomed care.

There was no lamb in his plaid on the afternoon when he startled Dowie by suddenly appearing at the door of the room where she sat sewing—It was a thing which had never happened before. He had kept as closely to his own part of the place as if there had been no means of egress from the rooms he and Maggy lived in. His face sometimes wore an anxious look when he brought back a half-dead lamb, and now though his plaid was empty his weather-beaten countenance had trouble in it—so much trouble that Dowie left her work quickly.

"I was oot o' the moor and I heard a lamb cryin'," he said uncertainly. "I thought it had lost its mither. It was cryin' pitifu'. I searched an' couldna find it. But the cryin' went on. It was waur than a lamb's cry—It was waur—" he spoke in reluctant jerks. "I followed until I cam' to it. There was a cluster o' young rowans with broom and gorse thick under them. The cryin' was there. It was na a lamb cryin'. It was the young leddy—lyin' twisted on the heather. I daurna speak to her. It was no place for a man body. I cam' awa' to ye, Mistress Dowson. You an' Maggy maun go to her. I'll follow an' help to carry her back, if ye need me."

Dowie's colour left her.

"I thought she was asleep on her bed," she said. "Sometimes she slips away alone and wanders about a bit. But not far and I always follow her. To-day I didn't know."

The sound like a lost lamb's crying had ceased when they reached her. The worst was over but she lay on the heather shut in by the little thicket of gorse and broom—white and with heavily closed lids. She had not wandered far and had plainly crept into the enclosing growth for utter seclusion. Finding it she had lost hold and been overwhelmed. That was all. But as Jock Macaur carried her back to Darreuch, Dowie followed with slow heavy feet and heart. They took her to the Tower room and laid her on her sofa because she had faintly whispered.

"Please let me lie by the window," as they mounted the stone stairs.

"Open it wide," she whispered again when Macaur had left them alone.

"Are you—are you short of breath, my dear?" Dowie asked opening the window very wide indeed.

"No," still in a whisper and with closed eyes. "But—when I am not so tired—I want to—look—"

She was silent for a few moments and Dowie stood by her side and watched her.

"—At the end of the heather," the faint voice ended its sentence after a pause. "I feel as if—something is there." She opened her eyes, "Something—I don't know what. 'Something.' Dowie!" frightened, "Are you—crying?"

Dowie frankly and helplessly took out a handkerchief and sat down beside her. She had never done such a thing before.

"You cry yourself, my lamb," she said. "Let Dowie cry a bit."

Chapter 27

And the next morning came the "waking up" for which Dowie had so long waited and prayed. But not as Dowie had expected it or in the way she hard thought "Nature."

She had scarcely left her charge during the night though she had pretended that she had slept as usual in an adjoining room. She stole in and out, she sat by the bed and watched the face on the pillow and thanked God that—strangely enough—the child slept. She had not dared to hope that she would sleep, but before midnight she became still and fell into a deep quiet slumber. It seemed deep, for she ceased to stir and it was so quiet that once or twice Dowie became a little anxious and bent over her to look at her closely and listen to her breathing. But, though the small white face was always a touching sight, it was no whiter than usual and her breathing though low and very soft was regular.

"But where the strength's to come from the good God alone knows!" was Dowie's inward sigh.

The clock had just struck one when she leaned forward again. What she saw would not have disturbed her if she had not been overstrung by long anxiety. But now—after the woeful day—in the middle of the night with the echo of the clock's solitary sound still in the solitary room—in the utter stillness of moor and castle emptiness she was startled almost to fright. Something had happened to the pitiful face. A change had come over it—not a change which had stolen gradually but a change which was actually sudden. It was smiling—it had begun to smile that pretty smile which was a very gift of God in itself.

Dowie drew back and put her hand over her mouth. "Oh!" she said "Can she be—going—in her sleep?"

But she was not going. Even Dowie's fright saw that in a few moments more. Was it possible that a mist of colour was stealing over the whiteness—or something near colour? Was the smile deepening and growing brighter? Was that caught breath something almost like a little sob of a laugh—a tiny ghost of a sound more like a laugh than any other sound on earth?

Dowie slid down upon her knees and prayed devoutly—clutching at the robe of pity and holding hard—as women did in crowds nearly two thousand years ago.

"Oh, Lord Jesus," she was breathing behind the hands which hid her face—"if she can dream what makes her smile like that, let her go on, Lord Jesus—let her go on."

When she rose to her chair again and seated herself to watch it almost awed, it did not fade—the smile. It settled into a still radiance and stayed. And, fearful of the self-deception of longing as she was, Dowie could have sworn as the minutes passed that the mist of colour had been real and remained also and even made the whiteness a less deathly thing. And there was such a naturalness in the strange smiling that it radiated actual peace and rest and safety. When the clock struck three and there was no change and still the small face lay happy upon the pillow Dowie at last even felt that she dare steal into her own room and lie down for a short rest. She went very shortly thinking she would return in half an hour at most, but the moment she lay down, her tired eyelids dropped and she slept as she had not slept since her first night at Darreuch Castle.

When she wakened it was not with a start or sense of anxiety even though she found herself sitting up in the broad morning light. She wondered at her own sense of being rested and really not afraid. She told herself that it was all because of the smile she had left on Robin's face and remembered as her own eyes closed.

She got up and stole to the partly opened door of the next room and looked in. All was quite still. Robin herself seemed very still but she was awake. She lay upon her pillow with a long curly plait trailing over one shoulder—and she was smiling as she had smiled in her sleep—softly—wonderfully. "I thank God for that," Dowie thought as she went in.

The next moment her heart was in her throat.

"Dowie," Robin said and she spoke as quietly as Dowie had ever heard her speak in all their life together, "Donal came."

"Did he, my lamb?" said Dowie going to her quickly but trying to speak as naturally herself. "In a dream?"

Robin slowly shook her head.

"I don't think it was a dream. It wasn't like one. I think he was here. God sometimes lets them come—just sometimes—doesn't he? Since the War there have been so many stories about things like that. People used to come to see the Duchess and sit and whisper about them. Lady Maureen Darcy used to go to a place where there was a woman—quite a poor woman—who went into a kind of sleep and gave her messages from her husband who was killed at Liège only a few weeks after they were married. The woman said he was in the room and Lady Maureen was quite sure it was true because he told her true things no one knew but themselves. She said it kept her from going crazy. It made her quite happy."

"I've heard of such things," said Dowie, valiantly determined to keep her voice steady and her expression unalarmed. "Perhaps they are true. Now that the other world is so crowded with those that found themselves there sudden—perhaps they are crowded so close to earth that they try to speak across to the ones that are longing to hear them. It might be. Lie still, my dear, and I'll bring you a cup of good hot milk to drink. Do you think you could eat a new-laid egg and a shred of toast?"

"I will," answered Robin. "I *will*."

She sat up in bed and the faint colour on her cheeks deepened and spread like a rosy dawn. Dowie saw it and tried not to stare. She must not seem to watch her too fixedly—whatsoever alarming thing was happening.

"I can't tell you all he said to me," she went on softly. "There was too much that only belonged to us. He stayed a long time. I felt his arms holding me. I looked into the blue of his eyes—just as I always did. He was not dead. He was not an angel. He was Donal. He laughed and made me laugh too. He could not tell me now where he was. There was a reason. But he said he could come because we belonged to each other—because we loved each other so. He said beautiful things to me—" She began to speak very slowly as if in careful retrospection. "Some of them were like the things Lord Coombe said. But when Donal said them they seemed to go into my heart and I understood them. He told me things about England—needing new souls and new strong bodies—he loved England. He said beautiful—beautiful things."

Dowie made a magnificent effort to keep her eyes clear and her look straight. It was a soldierly thing to do, for there had leaped into her mind memories of the fears of the great physician who had taken charge of poor young Lady Maureen.

"I am sure he would do that—sure of it," she said without a tremor in her voice. "It's only things like that he's thought of his whole life through. And surely it was love that brought him back to you—both."

She wondered if she was not cautious enough in saying the last word. But her fear was a mistake.

"Yes—*both*," Robin gave back with a new high bravery. "Both," she repeated. "He will never be dead again. And I shall never be dead. When I could not think, it used to seem as if I must be—perhaps I was beginning to go crazy like poor Lady Maureen. I have come alive."

"Yes, my lamb," answered Dowie with fine courage. "You look it. We'll get you ready for your breakfast now. I will bring you the egg and toast—a nice crisp bit of hot buttered toast."

"Yes," said Robin. "He said he would come again and I know he will."

Dowie bustled about with inward trembling. Whatsoever strange thing had happened perhaps it had awakened the stunned instinct in the girl—perhaps some change had begun to take place and she *would* eat the bit of food. That would be sane and healthy enough in any case. The test would be the egg and the crisp toast—the real test. Sometimes a patient had a moment of uplift and then it died out too quickly to do good.

But when she had been made ready and the tray was brought Robin ate the small breakfast without shrinking from it, and the slight colour did not die away from her cheek. The lost look was in her eyes no more, her voice had a new tone. The exhaustion of the night before seemed mysteriously to have disappeared. Her voice was not tired and she herself was curiously less languid. Dowie could scarcely believe the evidence of her ears when, in the course of the morning, she suggested that they should go out together.

"The moor is beautiful to-day," she said. "I want to know it better. It seems as if I had never really looked at anything."

One of the chief difficulties Dowie often found she was called upon to brace herself to bear was that in these days she looked so pathetically like a child. Her small heart-shaped face had always been rather like a baby's, but in these months of her tragedy, her youngness at times seemed almost cruel. If she had been ten years old she could scarcely have presented herself to the mature vision as a more touching thing. It seemed incredible to Dowie that she should have so much of life and suffering behind and before her and yet look like that. It was not only the soft curve and droop of her mouth and the lift of her eyes—there was added to these something as indescribable as it was heart-moving. It was the thing before which Donal—boy as he was—had trembled with love and joy. He had felt its tenderest sacredness when he had knelt before her in the Wood and kissed her feet, almost afraid of his own voice when he poured forth his pleading. There were times when Dowie was obliged to hold herself still for a moment or so lest it should break down her determined calm.

It was to be faced this morning when Robin came down in her soft felt hat and short tweed skirt and coat for walking. Dowie saw Mrs. Macaur staring through a window at her, with slightly open mouth, as if suddenly struck with amazement which held in it a touch of shock. Dowie herself was obliged to make an affectionate joke.

"Your short skirts make such a child of you that I feel as if I was taking you out to walk in the park, and I must hold your hand," she said.

Robin glanced down at herself.

"They do make people look young," she agreed. "The Lady

Downstairs looked quite like a little girl when she went out in them. But it seems so long since I was little."

She walked with Dowie bravely though they did not go far from the Castle. It happened that they met the doctor driving up the road which twisted in and out among the heath and gorse. For a moment he looked startled but he managed to control himself quickly and left his dogcart to his groom so that he might walk with them. His eyes—at once grave and keen—scarcely left her as he strolled by her side.

When they reached the Castle he took Dowie aside and talked anxiously with her.

"There is a change," he said. "Has anything happened which might have raised her spirits? It looks like that kind of thing. She mustn't do too much. There is always that danger to guard against in a case of sudden mental stimulation."

"She had a dream last night," Dowie began.

"A dream!" he exclaimed disturbedly. "What kind of dream?"

"The dream did it. I saw the change the minute I went to her this morning," Dowie answered. "Last night she looked like a dying thing—after one of her worst breakdowns. This morning she lay there peaceful and smiling and almost rosy. She had dreamed that she saw her husband and talked to him. She believed it wasn't a common dream—that it wasn't a dream at all. She believes he really came to her."

Doctor Benton rubbed his chin and there was serious anxiety in the movement. Lines marked themselves on his forehead.

"I am not sure I like that—not at all sure. In fact I'm sure I don't like it. One can't say what it may lead to. It would be better not to encourage her to dwell on it, Mrs. Dowson."

"The one thing that's in my mind, sir," Dowie's respectfulness actually went to the length of hinting at firmness—"is that it's best not to *dis*courage her about anything just now. It brought a bit of natural colour to her cheeks and it made her eat her breakfast—which she hasn't been able to do before. They *must* be fed, sir," with the seriousness of experience. "You know that better than I do."

"Yes—yes. They must have food."

"She suggested the going out herself," said Dowie. "I'd thought she'd be too weak and listless to move. And they *ought* to have exercise."

"They *must* have exercise," agreed Doctor Benton, but he still rubbed his chin. "Did she seem excited or feverish?"

"No, sir, she didn't. That was the strange thing. It was me that was excited though I kept quiet on the outside. At first it frightened me. I was afraid of—what you're afraid of, sir. It was only her *not* being excited—and speaking in her own natural voice that helped me to behave as sense told me I ought to. She was *happy*—that's what she looked and what she was."

She stopped a moment here and looked at the man. Then she decided to go on because she saw chances that he might, to a certain degree, understand.

"When she told me that he was not dead when she saw him, she said that she was not dead any more herself—that she had come alive. If believing it will keep her feeling alive, sir, wouldn't you say it would be a help?"

The Doctor had ceased rubbing his chin but he looked deeply thoughtful. He had several reasons for thoughtfulness in connection with the matter. In the present whirl of strange happenings in a mad war-torn world, circumstances which would once have seemed singular seemed so no longer because nothing was any longer normal. He realised that he had been by no means told all the details surrounding this special case, but he had understood clearly that it was of serious importance that this girlish creature's child should be preserved. He wondered how much more the finely mannered old family nurse knew than he did.

"Her vitality must be kept up—Nothing could be worse than inordinate grief," he said. "We must not lose any advantage. But she must be closely watched."

"I'll watch her, sir," answered Dowie. "And every order you give I'll obey like clockwork. Might I take the liberty of saying that I believe it'll be best if you don't mention the dream to her!"

"Perhaps you are right. On the whole I think you are. It's not wise to pay attention to hallucinations."

He did not mention the dream to Robin, but his visit was longer than usual. After it he drove down the moor thinking of curious things. The agonised tension of the war, he told himself, seemed to be developing new phases—mental, nervous, psychic, as well as physiological. What unreality—or previously unknown reality—were they founded upon? It was curious how much one had begun to hear of telepathy and visions. He himself had been among the many who had discussed the psychopathic condition of Lady Maureen Darcy, whose black melancholia had been dispersed like a cloud after her visits to a little sewing woman who lived over an oil dealer's shop in the Seven Sisters Road. He also was a war tortured man mentally and the torments he must conceal beneath a steady professional calm had loosened old shackles.

"Good God! If there is help of any sort for such horrors of despair let them take it where they find it," he found himself saying aloud to the emptiness of the stretches of heath and bracken. "The old nurse will watch."

Dowie watched faithfully. She did not speak of the dream, but as she went about doing kindly and curiously wise things she never lost sight of any mood or expression of Robin's and they were all changed ones. On the night after she had "come alive" they talked together in the Tower room somewhat as they had talked on the night of their arrival.

A wind was blowing on the moor and making strange sounds as it whirled round the towers and seemed to cry at the narrow windows. By the fire there was drawn a broad low couch heaped with large cushions, and Robin lay upon them looking into the red hollow of coal.

"You told me I had something to think of," she said. "I am thinking now. I shall always be thinking."

"That's right, my dear," Dowie answered her with sane kindliness.

"I will do everything you tell me, Dowie. I will not cry any more and I will eat what you ask me to eat. I will sleep as much as I can and I will walk every day. Then I shall get strong."

"That's the way to look at things. It's a brave way," Dowie answered. "What we want most is strength and good spirits, my dear."

"That was one of the things Donal said," Robin went on quite naturally and simply. "He told me I need not be ill. He said a rose was not ill when a new bud was blooming on it. That was one of the lovely things he told me. There were so many."

"It was a beautiful thing, to be sure," said Dowie.

To her wholly untranscendental mind, long trained by patent facts and duties, any suggestion of the occult was vaguely ominous. She had spent her early years among people who regarded such things with terror. In the stories of her youth those who saw visions usually died or met with calamity. That their visions were, as a rule, gruesome and included pale and ghastly faces and voices hollow with portent was now a supporting recollection. "He was not dead. He was not an angel. He was Donal," Robin had said in her undoubting voice. And she had stood the test—that real test of earthly egg and buttered toast. Dowie was a sensible and experienced creature and had been prepared before the doctor's suggestion to lose no advantage. If the child began to sleep and eat her food, and the fits of crying could be controlled, why should she not be allowed to believe what supported her? When her baby came she'd forget less natural things. Dowie knew how her eyes would look as she bent over it—how they would melt and glow and brood and how her childish mouth would quiver with wonder and love. Who knew but that the Lord himself had sent her that dream to comfort her because she had always been such a loving, lonely little thing with nothing but tender goodness in her whole body and soul? She had never had an untender thought of anybody but for that queer dislike to his lordship—And when you came to think of what had been forced into her innocent mind about him, who wondered?—And she was beginning to see that differently too, in these strange days. She was nothing now but softness and sorrow. It seemed only right that some pity should be shown to her.

Dowie noticed that she did not stay up late that night and that when she went to bed she knelt a long time by her bedside saying her prayers. Oh! What a little girl she looked, Dowie thought,—in her white night gown with her long curly plait hanging down her back tied with a blue ribbon! And she to be the mother of a child—that was no more than one herself!

When all the prayers were ended and Dowie came back to the room to tuck her in, her face was marvellously still-looking and somehow remotely sweet as if she had not quite returned from some place of wonderful calm.

She nestled into the softness of the pillow with her hand under her cheek and her lids dropped quietly at once.

"Good night, Dowie dear," she murmured. "I am going to sleep."

To sleep in a moment or so Dowie saw she went—with the soft suddenness of a baby in its cradle.

But it could not be said that Dowie slept soon. She found herself lying awake listening to the wind whirling and crying round the tower. The sound had something painfully human in it which made her conscious of a shivering inward tremor.

"It sounds as if something—that has been hurt and is cold and lonely wants to get in where things are human and warm," was her troubled thought.

It was a thought so troubled that she could not rest and in spite of her efforts to lie still she turned from side to side listening in an abnormal mood.

"I'm foolish," she whispered. "If I don't get hold of myself I shall lose my senses. I don't feel like myself. Would it be too silly if I got up and opened a tower window?"

She actually got out of her bed quietly and crept to the tower room and opened one. The crying wind rushed in and past her with a soft cold sweep. It was not a bitter wind, only a piteous one.

"It's—it's come in," she said, quaking a little, and went back to her bed.

When she awakened in the morning she realised that she must have fallen asleep as quickly as Robin had, for she remembered nothing after her head had touched the pillow. The wind had ceased and the daylight found her herself again.

"It was silly," she said, "but it did something for me as silliness will sometimes. Walls and shut windows are nothing to them. If he came, he came without my help. But it pacified the foolish part of me."

She went into Robin's room with a sense of holding her breath, but firm in her determination to breathe and speak as a matter of fact woman should.

Robin was standing at her window already dressed in the short skirt and soft hat. She turned and showed that her thin small face was radiant.

"I have been out on the moor. I wakened just after sunrise, and I heard a skylark singing high up in the sky. I went out to listen and say my prayers," she said. "You don't know what the moor is like, Dowie, until you stand out on it at sunrise."

She met Dowie's approach half way and slipped her arms round her neck and kissed her several times. Dowie had for a moment quailed before a thought that she looked too much like a young angel, but her arms held close and her kisses were warm and human.

"Well, well!" Dowie's pats on her shoulder took courage. "That's a good sign—to get up and dress yourself and go into the open air. It would give you an appetite if anything would."

"Perhaps I can eat two eggs this morning," with a pretty laugh. "Wouldn't that be wonderful?" and she took off her hat and laid it aside on the lounge as if she meant to go out again soon.

Dowie tried not to watch her too obviously, but she could scarcely keep her eyes from her. She knew that she must not ask her questions at the risk of "losing an advantage." She had, in fact, never been one of the women who must ask questions. There was however something eerie in remembering her queer feeling about the crying of the wind, silly though she had decided it to be, and something which made it difficult to go about all day knowing nothing but seeing strange signs. She had been more afraid for Robin than she would have admitted even to herself. And when the girl sat down at the table by the window overlooking the moor and ate her breakfast without effort or distaste, it was far from easy to look quite as if she had been doing it every morning.

Then there was the look in her eyes, as if she was either listening to something or remembering it. She went out twice during the day and she carried it with her even when she talked of other things. Dowie saw it specially when she lay down on the big lounge to rest. But she did not lie down often or long at a time. It was as though she was no longer unnaturally tired and languid. She did little things for herself, moving about naturally, and she was pleased when a messenger brought flowers, explaining that his lordship had ordered that they should be sent every other day from the nearest town. She spent an hour filling crystal bowls and clear slim vases with them and the look never left her.

But she said nothing until she went out with Dowie at sunset. They only walked for a short time and they did not keep to the road but went on to the moor itself and walked among the heath and bracken. After a little while they sat down and gave themselves up to the vast silence with here and there the last evening twitter of a bird in it. The note made the stillness greater. The flame of the sky was beyond compare and, after gazing at it for a while, Dowie turned a slow furtive look on Robin.

But Robin was looking at her with clear soft naturalness—loving and untroubled and kindly sweet.

"He came back, Dowie. He came again," she said. And her voice was still as natural as the good woman had ever known it.

Chapter 28

But even after this Dowie did not ask questions. She only watched more carefully and waited to be told what the depths of her being most yearned to hear. The gradually founded belief of her careful prosaic life prevented ease of mind or a sense of security. She could not be certain that it would be the part of wisdom to allow herself to feel secure. She did not wish to arouse Doctor Benton's professional anxiety by asking questions about Lady Maureen Darcy, but, by a clever and adroitly gradual system of what was really cross examination which did not involve actual questions, she drew from him the name of the woman who had been Lady Maureen's chief nurse when the worst seemed impending. It was by fortunate chance the name of a woman she had once known well during a case of dangerous illness in an important household. She herself had had charge of the nursery and Nurse Darian had liked her because she had proved prompt and intelligent in an alarming crisis. They had become friends and Dowie knew she might write to her and ask for information and advice. She wrote a careful respectful letter which revealed nothing but that she was anxious about a case she had temporary charge of. She managed to have the letter posted in London and the answer forwarded to her from there. Nurse Darian's reply was generously full for a hard-working woman. It answered questions and was friendly. But the woman's war work had plainly led her to see and reflect upon the opening up of new and singular vistas.

"What we hear oftenest is that the whole world is somehow changing," she ended by saying. "You hear it so often that you get tired. But something *is* happening—something strange—Even the doctors find themselves facing things medical science does not explain.

They don't like it. I sometimes think doctors hate change more than anybody. But the cleverest and biggest ones talk together. It's this looking at a thing lying on a bed alive and talking perhaps, one minute—and *gone out* the next, that sets you asking yourself questions. In these days a nurse seems to see nothing else day and night. You can't make yourself believe they have gone far—And when you keep hearing stories about them coming back—knocking on tables, writing on queer boards—just any way so that they can get at those they belong to—! Well, I shouldn't be sure myself that a comforting dream means that a girl's mind's giving away. Of course a nurse is obliged to watch—But Lady Maureen found *something*—And she *was* going mad and now she is as sane as I am."

Dowie was vaguely supported because the woman was an intelligent person and knew her business thoroughly. Nevertheless one must train one's eyes to observe everything without seeming to do so at all.

Every morning when the weather was fine Robin got up early and went out on the moor to say her prayers and listen to the skylarks singing.

"When I stand and turn my face up to the sky—and watch one going higher into heaven—and singing all the time without stopping," she said, "I feel as if the singing were carrying what I want to say with it. Sometimes he goes so high that you can't see him any more—He's not even a little speck in the highest sky—Then I think perhaps he has gone in and taken my prayer with him. But he always comes back. And perhaps if I could understand he could tell me what the answer is."

She ate her breakfast each day and was sweetly faithful to her promise to Dowie in every detail. Dowie used to think that she was like a child who wanted very much to learn her lesson well and follow every rule.

"I want to be good, Dowie," she said once. "I should like to be very good. I am so *grateful*."

Doctor Benton driving up the moor road for his daily visits made careful observation of every detail of her case and pondered in secret. The alarming thinness and sharpening of the delicate features was he saw, actually becoming less marked day by day; the transparent hands were less transparent; the movements were no longer languid.

"She spends most of the day out of doors when the weather's decent," Dowie said. "She eats what I give her. And she sleeps."

Doctor Benton asked many questions and the answers given seemed to provide him with food for reflection.

"Has she spoken of having had the dream again?" he inquired at last.

"Yes, sir," was Dowie's brief reply.

"Did she say it was the same dream?"

"She told me her husband had come back. She said nothing more."

"Has she told you that more than once?"

"No, sir. Only once so far."

Doctor Benton looked at the sensible face very hard. He hesitated before he put his next question.

"But you think she has seen him since she spoke to you? You feel that she might speak of it again—at almost any time?"

"She might, sir, and she might not. It may seem like a sacred thing to her. And it's no business of mine to ask her about things she'd perhaps rather not talk about."

"Do you think that she believes that she sees her husband every night?"

"I don't know *what* I think, sir," said Dowie in honourable distress.

"Well neither do I for that matter," Benton answered brusquely. "Neither do thousands of other people who want to be honest with themselves. Physically the effect of this abnormal fancy is excellent. If this goes on she will end by being in a perfectly normal condition."

"That's what I'm working for, sir," said Dowie.

Whereupon Dr. Benton went away and thought still stranger and deeper things as he drove home over the moor road which twisted through the heather.

The next day's post delivered by Macaur himself brought as it did weekly a package of books and carefully chosen periodicals. Robin had, before this, not been equal even to looking them over and Dowie had arranged them neatly on shelves in the Tower room.

To-day when the package was opened Robin sat down near the table on which they were placed and began to look at them.

Out of the corner of her eye as she arranged books decorously on a shelf Dowie saw the still transparent hand open first one book and then another. At last it paused at a delicately coloured pamphlet. It was the last alluring note of modern advertisement, sent out by a firm which made a specialty of children's outfits and belongings. It came from an elect and expensive shop which prided itself on its dainty presentation of small beings attired in entrancing garments such as might have been designed for fairies and elves.

"If she begins to turn over the pages she'll go on. It'll be just Nature," Dowie yearned.

The awakening she had thought Nature would bring about was not like the perilous miracle she had seen take place and had watched tremulously from hour to hour. Dreams, however much one had to thank God for them, were not exactly "Nature." They were not the blessed healing and strengthening she felt familiar with. You were never sure when they might melt away into space and leave only emptiness behind them.

"But if she would wake up the other way it would be healthy—just healthy and to be depended upon," was her thought. Robin turned over the leaves in no hurried way. She had never carelessly turned over the leaves of her picture books in her nursery. As she had looked at her picture books she looked at this one. There were pages given to the tiniest and most exquisite things of all, and it was the illustrations of these, Dowie's careful sidelong eye saw she had first been attracted by.

"These are for very little—ones?" she said presently.

"Yes. For the new ones," answered Dowie.

There was moment or so of silence.

"How little—how little!" Robin said softly. She rose softly and went to her couch and lay down on it. She was very quiet and Dowie wondered if she were thinking or if she were falling into a doze. She wished she had looked at the pamphlet longer. As the weeks had gone by Dowie had even secretly grieved a little at her seeming unconsciousness of certain tender things. If she had only looked at it a little longer.

"Was there a sound of movement in the next room?"

The thought awakened Dowie in the night. She did not know what the hour was, but she was sure of the sound as soon as she was fully awake. Robin had got up and was crossing the corridor to the Tower room.

"Does she want something? What could she want? I must go to her."

She must never quite lose sight of her or let her be entirely out of hearing. Perhaps she was walking in her sleep. Perhaps the dream—Dowie was a little awed. Was he with her? In obedience to a weird impulse she always opened a window in the Tower room every night before going to bed. She had left it open to-night.

It was still open when she entered the room herself.

There was nothing unusual in the aspect of the place but that Robin was there and it was just midnight. She was not walking in her sleep. She was awake and standing by the table with the pamphlet in her hand.

"I couldn't go to sleep," she said. "I kept thinking of the little things in this book. I kept seeing them."

"That's quite natural," Dowie answered. "Sit down and look at them a bit. That'll satisfy you and you'll sleep easy enough. I must shut the window for you."

She shut the window and moved a book or so as if such things were usually done at midnight. She went about in a quiet matter-of-fact way which was even gentler than her customary gentleness because in these days, while trying to preserve a quite ordinary demeanour, she felt as though she must move as one would move in making sure that one would not startle a bird one loved.

Robin sat and looked at the pictures. When she turned a page and looked at it she turned it again and looked at it with dwelling eyes. Presently she ceased turning pages and sat still with the book open on her lap as if she were thinking not only of what she held but of something else.

When her eyes lifted to meet Dowie's there was a troubled wondering look in them.

"It's so strange—I never seemed to think of it before," the words came slowly. "I forgot because I was always—remembering."

"You'll think now," Dowie answered. "It's only Nature."

"Yes—it's only Nature."

The touch of her hand on the pamphlet was a sort of caress—it was a touch which clung.

"Dowie," timidly. "I want to begin to make some little clothes like these. Do you think I can?"

"Well, my dear," answered Dowie composedly—no less so because it was past midnight and the stillness of moor and deserted castle rooms was like a presence in itself. "I taught you to sew very neatly before you were twelve. You liked to do it and you learned to make beautiful small stitches. And Mademoiselle taught you to do fine embroidery. She'd learned it in a convent herself and I never saw finer work anywhere."

"I did like to do it," said Robin. "I never seemed to get tired of sitting in my little chair in the bay window where the flowers grew, and making tiny stitches."

"You had a gift for it. Not all girls have," said Dowie. "Sometimes when you were embroidering a flower you didn't want to leave it to take your walk."

"I am glad I had a gift," Robin took her up. "You see I want to make these little things with my own hands. I don't want them sent up from London. I don't want them bought. Look at this, Dowie."

Dowie went to her side. Her heart was quickening happily as it beat.

Robin touched a design with her finger.

"I should like to begin by making that," she suggested. "Do you think that if I bought one for a pattern I could copy it?"

Dowie studied it with care.

"Yes," she said. "You could copy it and make as many more as you liked. They need a good many."

"I am glad of that," said Robin. "I should like to make a great many." The slim fingers slid over the page. "I should like to make that one—and that—and that." Her face, bent over the picture, wore its touching *young* look thrilled with something new. "They are so *pretty*—they are so pretty," she murmured like a dove.

"They're the prettiest things in the world," Dowie said. "There never was anything prettier."

"It must be wonderful to make them and to know all the time you are putting in the tiny stitches, that they are for something little—and warm—and alive!"

"Those that have done it never forget it," said Dowie. Robin lifted her face, but her hands still held the book with the touch which clung.

"I am beginning to realise what a strange life mine has been," she said. "Don't you think it has, Dowie? I haven't known things. I didn't know what mothers were. I never knew another child until I met Donal in the Gardens. No one had ever kissed me until he did. When I was older I didn't know anything about love and marrying—really. It seemed only something one read about in books until Donal came. You and Mademoiselle made me happy, but I was like a little nun." She paused a moment and then said thoughtfully, "Do you know, Dowie, I have never touched a baby?"

"I never thought of it before," Dowie answered with a slightly caught breath, "but I believe you never have."

The girl leaned forward and her own light breath came a shade more quickly, and the faint colour on her cheek flickered into a sweeter warm tone.

"Are they very soft, Dowie?" she asked—and the asking was actually a wistful thing. "When you hold them do they feel very light—and soft—and warm? When you kiss them isn't it something like kissing a little flower?"

"That's what it is," said Dowie firmly as one who knows. "A baby that's loved and taken care of is just nothing but fine soft lawns and white downiness with the scent of fresh violets under leaves in the rain."

A vaguely dreamy smile touched Robin's face and she bent over the pictures again.

"I felt as if they must be like that though I had never held one," she murmured. "And Donal—told me." She did not say when he had told her but Dowie knew. And unearthly as the thing was, regarded from her standpoint, she was not frightened, because she said mentally to herself, what was happening was downright healthy and no harm could come of it. She felt safe and her mind was at ease even when Robin shut the little book and placed it on the table again.

"I'll go to bed again," she said. "I shall sleep now."

"To be sure you will," Dowie said.

And they went out of the Tower room together, but before she followed her Dowie slipped aside and quietly opened the window.

Chapter 29

Coombe House had been transformed into one of the most practical nursing homes in London. The celebrated ballroom and picture gallery were filled with cots; a spacious bedroom had become a perfectly equipped operating room; nurses and doctors moved everywhere with quiet swiftness. Things were said to be marvellously well done because Lord Coombe himself held reins which diplomatically guided and restrained amateurishness and emotional infelicities.

He spent most of his time, when he was in the house, in the room on the entrance floor where Mademoiselle had found him when she had come to him in her search for Robin.

He had faced ghastly hours there as the war news struck its hideous variant note from day to day. Every sound which rolled through the street had its meaning for him, and there were few which were not terrible. They all meant inhuman struggle, inhuman suffering, inhuman passions, and wounds or death. He carried an unmoved face and a well-held head through the crowded thoroughfares. The men in the cots in his picture gallery and his ballroom were the better for the outward calm he brought when he sat and talked to them, but he often hid a mad fury in his breast or a heavy and sick fatigue.

Even in London a man saw and heard and was able, if he had an imagination, to visualise too much to remain quite normal. He had seen what was left of strong men brought back from the Front, men who could scarcely longer be counted as really living human beings; he had talked to men on leave who had a hideous hardness in their haggard eyes and who did not know that they gnawed at their lips sometimes as they told the things they had seen. He saw the people going into the churches and chapels. He sometimes went into such places himself and he always found there huddled forms kneeling in the pews, even when no service was being held. Sometimes they were men, sometimes women, and often they writhed and sobbed horribly. He did not know why he went in; his going seemed only part of some surging misery.

He heard weird stories again and again of occult happenings. He had been told all the details of Lady Maureen's case and of a number of other cases somewhat resembling it. He was of those who have advanced through experience to the point where entire disbelief in anything is not easy. This was the more so because almost all previously accepted laws had been shaken as by an earthquake. He had fallen upon a new sort of book drifting about. He had had such books put into his hands by acquaintances, some of whom were of the impressionable hysteric order, but many of whom were as analytically minded as himself. He found much of such literature in the book shops. He began to look over the best written and ended by reading them with deep attention. He was amazed to discover that for many years profoundly scientific men had been seriously investigating and experimenting with mysteries unexplainable by the accepted laws of material science. They had discussed, argued and written grave books upon them. They had been doing all this before any society for psychical research had founded itself and the intention of new logic was to be scientific rather than psychological. They had written books, scattered through the years, on mesmerism, hypnosis, abnormal mental conditions, the powers of suggestion, even unexplored dimensions and in modern days psychotherapeutics.

"What has amazed me is my own ignorance of the prolonged and serious nature of the investigation of an astonishing subject," he said in talking with the Duchess. "To realise that analytical minds have been doing grave work of which one has known nothing is an actual shock to one's pride. I suppose the tendency would have been to pooh-pooh it. The cheap, modern popular form is often fantastic and crude, but there remains the fact that it all contains truths not to be explained by the rules we have always been familiar with."

The Duchess had read the book he had brought her and held it in her hands.

"Perhaps the time has come, in which we are to learn the new ones," she said.

"Perhaps we are being forced to learn them—as a result of our pooh-poohing," was his answer. "Some of us may learn that clear-cut disbelief is at least indiscreet."

Therefore upon a certain morning he sat long in reflection over a letter which had arrived from Dowie. He read it a number of times.

"I don't know what your lordship may think," Dowie said and he felt she held herself with a tight rein. "If I may say so, it's what's going to come out of it that matters and not what any of us think of it. So far it seems as if a miracle had happened. About a week ago she wakened in the morning looking as I'd been afraid she'd never look again. There was actually colour in her thin little face that almost made it look not so thin. There was a light in her eyes that quite startled me. She lay on her bed and smiled like a child that's suddenly put out of pain. She said—quite quiet and natural—that she'd seen her husband. She said he had *come* and talked to her a long time and that it was not a dream, and he was not an angel—he was himself. At first I was terrified by a dreadful thought that her poor young mind had given way. But she had no fever and she was as sweet and sensible as if she was talking to her Dowie in her own nursery. And, my lord, this is what does matter. She sat up and *ate her breakfast* and said she would take a walk with me. And walk she did—stronger and better than I'd have believed. She had a cup of tea and a glass of milk and a fresh egg and a slice of hot buttered toast. That's what I hold on to, my lord—without any thinking. I daren't write about it at first because I didn't trust it to last. But she has wakened in the same way every morning since. And she's eaten the bits of nice meals I've put before her. I've been careful not to put her appetite off by giving her more than a little at a time. And she's slept like a baby and walked every day. I believe she thinks she sees Captain Muir every night. I wouldn't ask questions, but she spoke of it once again to me.

"Your obedient servant, SARAH ANN DOWSON."

Lord Coombe sat in interested reflection. He felt curiously uplifted above the rolling sounds in the street and the headlines of the pile of newspapers on the table.

"If it had not been for the tea and egg and buttered toast she would have been sure the poor child was mad." He thought it out. "An egg and a slice of buttered toast guarantee even spiritual things. Why not? We are material creatures who have only material sight and touch and taste to employ as arguments. I suppose that is why tables are tipped, and banjos fly about for beginners. It's because we cannot see other things, and what we cannot see—Oh! fools that we are! The child said he was not an angel—he was himself. Why not? Where did he come from? Personally I believe that he *came*."

Chapter 30

"It was Lord Coombe who sent the book," said Robin.

She was sitting in the Tower room, watching Dowie open the packages which had come from London. She herself had opened the one which held the models and she was holding a tiny film of lawn and fine embroidery in her hands. Dowie could see that she was quite unconscious that she loosely held it against her breast as if she were nursing it.

"It's his lordship's way to think of things," the discreet answer came impersonally.

Robin looked slowly round the small and really quite wonderful room.

"You know I said that, the first night we came here."

"Yes?" Dowie answered.

Robin turned her eyes upon her. They were no longer hollowed, but they still looked much too large.

"Dowie," she said. "He *knows* things."

"He always did," said Dowie. "Some do and some don't."

"He *knows* things—as Donal does. The secret things you can't talk about—the meaning of things."

She went on as if she were remembering bit by bit. "When we were in the Wood in the dark, he said the first thing that made my mind begin to move—almost to think. That was because he *knew*. Knowing things made him send the book."

The fact was that he knew much of which it was not possible for him to speak, and in passing a shop window he had been fantastically arrested by a mere pair of small sleeves—the garment to which they belonged having by chance so fallen that they seemed to be tiny arms holding themselves out in surrendering appeal. They had held him a moment or so staring and then he had gone into the shop and asked for their catalogue.

"Yes, he knew," Dowie replied.

A letter had been written to London signed by Dowie and the models and patterns had been sent to the village and brought to the castle by Jock Macaur. Later there had come rolls of fine flannel and lawn, with gossamer thread and fairy needles and embroidery floss. Then the sewing began.

Doctor Benton had gradually begun to look forward to his daily visits with an interest stimulated by a curiosity become eager. The most casual looker-on might have seen the change taking place in his patient day by day and he was not a casual looker-on. Was the improvement to be relied upon? Would the mysterious support suddenly fail them?

"What in God's name should we do if it did?" he broke out unconsciously aloud one day when Dowie and he were alone together.

"If it did what, sir?" she asked.

"If it stopped—the dream?"

Dowie understood. By this time she knew that, when he asked questions, took notes and was professionally exact, he had ceased to think of Robin merely as a patient. She had touched him in some unusual way which had drawn him within the circle of her innocent woe. He was under the spell of her pathetic youngness which made Dowie herself feel as if they were watching over a child called upon to bear something it was unnatural for a child to endure.

"It won't stop," she said obstinately, but she lost her ruddy colour because she was not sure.

But after the sewing began there grew up within her a sort of courage. A girl whose material embodiment has melted away until she has worn the aspect of a wraith is not restored to normal bloom in a week. But what Dowie seemed to see was the lamp of life relighted and the first flickering flame strengthening to a glow. The hands which fitted together on the table in the Tower room delicate puzzles in bits of lawn and paper, did not in these days tremble with weakness. Instead of the lost look there had returned to the young doe's eyes the pretty trusting smile. The girl seemed to smile as if to herself nearly all the time, Dowie thought, and often she broke into a happy laugh at her own small blunders—and sometimes only at the sweet littleness of the things she was making.

One fact revealed itself clearly to Dowie, which was that she had lost all sense of the aspect which the dream must wear to others than herself. This was because there had been no others than Dowie who had uttered no suggestion of doubt and had never touched upon the subject unless it had been first broached by Robin herself. She had hidden her bewilderment and anxieties and had outwardly accepted the girl's own acceptance of the situation.

Of the incident of the sewing Lord Coombe had been informed later with other details.

"She sits and sews and sews," wrote Dowie. "She sewed beautifully even before she was out of the nursery. I have never seen a picture of a little saint sewing. If I had, perhaps I should say she looked like it."

Coombe read the letter to his old friend at Eaton Square.

There was a pause as he refolded it. After the silence he added as out of deep thinking, "I wish that I could see her."

"So do I," the Duchess said. "So do I. But if I were to go to her, questioning would begin at once."

"My going to Darreuch would attract no attention. It never did after the first year. But she has not said she wished to see me. I gave my word. I shall never see her again unless she asks me to come. She does not need me. She has Donal."

"What do you believe?" she asked.

"What do *you* believe?" he replied.

After a moment of speculative gravity came her reply.

"As without proof I believed in the marriage, so without proof I believe that in some mysterious way he comes to her—God be thanked!"

"So do I," said Coombe. "We are living in a changing world and new things are happening. I do not know what they are, but they shake me inwardly."

"You want to see her because—?" the Duchess put it to him.

"Perhaps I am changing with the rest of the world, or it may be that instincts which have always been part of me have been shaken to the surface of my being. Perhaps I was by nature an effusively affectionate and domestic creature. I cannot say that I have ever observed any signs of the tendency, but it may have lurked secretly within me."

"It caused you to rescue a child from torment and watch over its helplessness as if it had been your own flesh and blood," interposed the Duchess.

"It may have been. Who knows? And now the unnatural emotional upheaval of the times has broken down all my artificialities. I feel old and tired—perhaps childish. Shrines are being torn down and blown to pieces all over the world. And I long for a quite simple shrine to cleanse my soul before. A white little soul hidden away in peace, and sitting smiling over her sewing of small garments is worth making a pilgrimage to. Do you remember the childish purity of her eyelids? I want to see them dropped down as she sews. I want to *see* her."

"Alixe—and her children—would have been your shrine." The Duchess thought it out slowly.

"Yes."

He was the last of men to fall into an unconventional posture, but he dropped forward in his seat, his elbows on his knees, his forehead in his hands.

"If she lives and the child lives I shall long intolerably to see them. As her mother seemed to live in Alixe's exquisite body without its soul, so Alixe's soul seems to possess this child's body. Do I appear to be talking nonsense? Things without precedent have always been supposed to be nonsense."

"We are not so sure of that as we used to be," commented the Duchess.

"I shall long to be allowed to be near them," he added. "But I may go out of existence without seeing them at all. I gave my word."

Chapter 31

After the first day of cutting out patterns from the models and finely sewing tiny pieces of lawn together, Dowie saw that, before going to her bedroom for the night, Robin began to gather together all she had done and used in doing her work. She had ordered from London one of the pretty silk-lined lace-frilled baskets women are familiar with, and she neatly folded and laid her sewing in it. She touched each thing with fingers that lingered; she smoothed and once or twice patted something. She made exquisitely orderly little piles. Her down-dropped white lids quivered with joy as she did it. When she lifted them to look at Dowie her eyes were like those of a stray young spirit.

"I am going to take them into my room," she said. "I shall take them every night. I want to keep them on a chair quite near me so that I can put out my hand and touch them."

"Yes, my lamb," Dowie agreed cheerfully. But she knew she was going to hear something else. And this would be the third time.

"I want to show them to Donal." The very perfection of her naturalness gave Dowie a cold chill, even while she thanked God. She had shivered inwardly when she had opened the Tower room window, and so she shivered now despite her serene exterior. A simple unexalted body could not but think of those fragments which were never even found. And she, standing there with her lips and eyes smiling, just like any other radiant girl mother whose young husband is her lover, enraptured and amazed by this new miracle of hers!

Robin touched her with the tip of her finger.

"It can't be only a dream, Dowie," she said. "He's too real. I am too real. We are too happy." She hesitated a second. "If he were here at Darreuch in the daytime—I should not always know where he had been when he was away. Only his coming back would matter. He can't tell me now just where he comes from. He says 'Not yet.' But he comes. Every night, Dowie."

Every day she sewed in the Tower room, her white eyelids drooping over her work. Each night the basket was carried to her room. And each day Dowie watched with amazement the hollows in her temples and cheeks and under her eyes fill out, the small bones cover themselves, the thinned throat grow round with young tissue and smooth with satin skin. Her hair became light curled silk again; the faint colour deepened into the Jacqueminot glow at which passers by had turned to look in the street when she was little more than a baby. But she never talked of the dream. The third time was the last for many weeks.

Between Doctor Benton and Dowie there grew up an increased reserve concerning the dream. Never before had the man encountered an experience which so absorbed him. He was a student of the advanced order. He also had seen the books which had fallen into the hands of Coombe—some the work of scientific men—some the purely commercial outcome of the need of the hour written by the jackals of the literary profession. He would have been ready to sit by the bedside of his patient through the night watching over her sleep, holding her wrist with fingers on her pulse. Even his most advanced thinking involuntarily harked back to pulse and temperature and blood pressure. The rapidity of the change taking place in the girl was abnormal, but it expressed itself physically as well as mentally. How closely involved physiology and psychology were after all! Which was which? Where did one end and the other begin? Where was the line drawn? Was there a line at all? He had seen no chances for the apparently almost dying young thing when he first met her. She could not have lived through what lay before her. She had had a dream which she believed was real, and, through the pure joy and comfort of it, the life forces had begun to flow through her being and combine to build actual firm tissue and supply blood cells. The results were physical enough. The inexplicable in this case was that the curative agency was that she believed that her husband, who had been blown to atoms on the battle field, came to her alive each night—talked with her—held her in warm arms. Nothing else had aided her. And there you were—thrown upon occultism and what not!

He became conscious that, though he would have been glad to question Dowie daily and closely, a certain reluctance of mind held him back. Also he realised that, being a primitive though excellent woman, Dowie herself was secretly awed into avoidance of the subject. He believed that she knelt by her bedside each night in actual fear, but faithfully praying that for some months at least the dream might be allowed to go on. Had not he himself involuntarily said,

"She is marvellously well. We have nothing to fear if this continues."

It did continue and her bloom became a thing to marvel at. And not her bloom alone. Her strength increased with her blooming until no one could have felt fear for or doubt of her. She walked upon the moor without fatigue, she even worked in a garden Jock Macaur had laid out for her inside the ruined walls of what had once been the castle's banquet hall. So much of her life had been spent in London that wild moor and sky and the growing of things thrilled her. She ran in and out and to and fro like a little girl. There seemed no limit to the young vigour that appeared day by day to increase rather than diminish.

"It's a wonderful thing and God be thankit," said Mrs. Macaur.

Only Dowie in secret trembled sometimes before the marvel of her. As Doctor Benton had imagined, she prayed forcefully.

"Lord, forgive me if I am a sinner—but for Christ's sake don't take the strange thing away from her until she's got something to hold on to. What would she do—What could she!"

Robin came into the Tower room on a fair morning carrying her pretty basket as she always did. She put it down on its table and went and stood a few minutes at a window looking out. The back of her neck, Dowie realised, was now as slenderly round and velvet white as it had been when she had dressed her hair on the night of the Duchess' dance. Dowie did not know that its loveliness had been poor George's temporary undoing; she only thought of it as a sign of the wonderful change. It had been waxen pallid and had shown piteous hollows.

She turned about and spoke.

"Dowie, dear, I am going to write to Lord Coombe."

Dowie's heart hastened its beat and she herself being conscious of the fact, hastened to answer in an unexcited manner.

"That'll be nice, my dear. His lordship'll be glad to get the good news you can give him."

She asked herself if she would not perhaps tell her something—something which would make the fourth time.

"Perhaps he's asked her to do it," she thought.

But Robin said nothing which could make a fourth time. After she had eaten her breakfast she sat down and wrote a letter. It did not seem a long one and when she had finished it she sent it to the post by Jock Macaur.

There had been dark news both by land and sea that day, and Coombe had been out for many hours. He did not return to Coombe House until late in the evening. He was tired almost beyond endurance, and his fatigue was not merely a thing of muscle and nerve. After he sat down it was some time before he even glanced at the letters upon his writing table.

There were always a great many and usually a number of them were addressed in feminine handwriting. His hospital and other war work brought him numerous letters from women. Even their most impatient masculine opponents found themselves admitting that the women were being amazing.

Coombe was so accustomed to opening such letters that he felt no surprise when he took up an envelope without official lettering upon it, and addressed in a girlish hand. Girls were being as amazing as older women.

But this was not a letter about war work or Red Cross efforts. It was Robin's letter. It was not long and was as simple as a school girl's. She had never been clever—only exquisite and adorable, and never dull or stupid.

"Dear Lord Coombe,

"You were kind enough to say that you would come to see me when I asked you. Please will you come now? I hope I am not asking you to take a long journey when you are engaged in work too important to leave. If I am please pardon me, and I will wait until you are less occupied.

"Robin."

That was all. Coombe sat and gazed at it and read it several times. The thing which had always touched him most in her was her simple obedience to the laws about her. Curiously it had never seemed insipid—only a sort of lovely desire to be in harmony with all near her—things and people alike. It had been an innocent modesty which could not express rebellion. Her lifelong repelling of himself had been her one variation from type. Even that had been quiet except in one demonstration of her babyhood when she had obstinately refused to give him her hand. When Fate's self had sprung upon her with a wild-beast leap she had only lain still and panted like a young fawn in the clutch of a lion. She had only thought of Donal and his child. He remembered the eyes she had lifted to his own when he had put the ring on her finger in the shadow-filled old church—and he had understood that she was thinking of the warm young hand clasp and the glow of eyes she had looked up into when love and youth had stood in his place.

The phrasing of the letter brought it all back. His precision of mind and resolve would have enabled him to go to his grave without having looked on her face again—but he was conscious that she was an integral part of his daily thought and planning and that he longed inexpressibly to see her. He sometimes told himself that she and the child had become a sort of obsession with him. He believed that this was because Alixe had shown the same soft obedience to fate, and the same look in her sorrowful young eyes. Alixe had been then as she was now—but he had not been able to save her. She had died and he was one of the few abnormal male creatures who know utter loneliness to the end of life because of utter loss. He knew such things were not normal. It had seemed that Robin would die, though not as Alixe did. If she lived and he might watch over her, there lay hidden in the back of his mind a vague feeling that it would be rather as though his care of all detail—his power to palliate—to guard—would be near the semblance of the tenderness he would have shown to

Alixe. His old habit of mind caused him to call it an obsession, but he admitted he was obsessed.

"I want to *see* her!" he thought.

Chapter 32

Many other thoughts filled his mind on his railroad journey to Scotland. He questioned himself as to how deeply he still felt the importance of there coming into the racked world a Head of the House of Coombe, how strongly he was still inspired by the centuries old instinct that a House of Coombe must continue to exist as part of the bulwarks of England. The ancient instinct still had its power, but he was curiously awakening to a slackening of the bonds which caused a man to specialise. It was a reluctant awakening—he himself had no part in the slackening. The upheaval of the whole world had done it and of the world England herself was a huge part—small, huge, obstinate, fighting England. Bereft of her old stately beauties, her picturesque splendours of habit and custom, he could not see a vision of her, and owned himself desolate and homesick. He was tired. So many men and women were tired—worn out with thinking, fearing, holding their heads up while their hearts were lead. When all was said and done, when all was over, what would the new England want—what would she need? And England was only a part. What would the ravaged world need as it lay—quiet at last—in ruins physical, moral and mental? He had no answer. Wiser men than he had no answer. Only time would tell. But the commonest brain cells in the thickest skull could argue to the end which proved that only men and women could do the work to be done. The task would be one for gods, or demigods, or supermen—but there remained so far only men and women to face it—to rebuild, to reinspire with life, to heal unearthly gaping wounds of mind and soul. Each man or woman born strong and given the chance to increase in vigour which would build belief in life and living, in a future, was needed as breath and air are needed—even such an one as in the past would have wielded a sort of unearned sceptre as a Head of the House of Coombe. A man born a blacksmith, if he were of like quality, would meet equally the world's needs, but each would be doing in his way his part of that work which it seemed to-day only demigod and superman could fairly confront.

There was time for much thinking in long hours spent shut in a railroad carriage and his mind was, in these days, not given to letting him rest.

He had talked with many men back from the Front on leave and he had always noted the marvel of both minds and bodies at the relief from strain—from maddening noise, from sights of death and horror, from the needs of decency and common comfort and cleanliness which had become unheard of luxury. London, which to the Londoner seemed caught in the tumult and turmoil of war, was to these men rest and peace.

Coombe felt, when he descended at the small isolated station and stood looking at the climbing moor, that he was like one of those who had left the roar of battle behind and reached utter quiet. London was a world's width away and here the War did not exist. In Flanders and in France it filled the skies with thunders and drenched the soil with blood. But here it was not.

The partly rebuilt ruin of Darreuch rose at last before his view high on the moor as he drove up the winding road. The space and the blue sky above and behind it made it seem the embodiment of remote stillness. Nothing had reached nor could touch it. It did not know that green fields and deep woods were strewn with dead and mangled youth and all it had meant of the world's future. Its crumbled walls and remaining grey towers stood calm in the clear air and birds' nests were hidden safely in their thick ivy.

Robin was there and each night she believed that a dead man came to her a seeming living being. He was not like Dowie, but his realisation of the mystery of this thing touched his nerves as a wild unexplainable sound heard in the darkness at midnight might have done. He wondered if he should see some look which was not quite normal in her eyes and hear some unearthly note in her voice. Physically the effect upon her had been good, but might he not be aware of the presence of some mental sign?

"I think you'll be amazed when you see her, my lord," said Dowie, who met him. "I am myself, every day."

She led him up to the Tower room and when he entered it Robin was sitting by a window sewing with her eyelids dropped as he had pictured them. The truth was that Dowie had not previously announced him because she had wanted him to come upon just this.

Robin rose from her chair and laid her bit of sewing aside. For a moment he almost expected her to make the little curtsey Mademoiselle had taught her to make when older people came into the schoolroom. She looked so exactly as she had looked before life had touched her. There was very little change in her girlish figure; the child curve of her cheek had returned; the Jacqueminot rose glowed on it and her eyes were liquid wonders of trust. She came to him holding out both hands.

"Thank you for coming," she said in her pretty way. "Thank you, Lord Coombe, for coming."

"Thank you, my child, for asking me to come," he answered and he feared that his voice was not wholly steady.

There was no mystic sign to be seen about her. The only mystery was in her absolutely blooming health and naturalness and in the gentle and clear happiness of her voice and eyes. She was not tired; she was not dragged or anxious looking as he had seen even fortunate young wives and mothers at times. There actually flashed back upon him the morning, months ago, when he had met her in the street and said to himself that she was like a lovely child on her birthday with all her gifts about her. Her radiance had been quiet even then because she was always quiet.

She led him to a seat near her window and she sat by him.

"I put this chair here for you because it is so lovely to look out at the moor," she said.

That moved him to begin with. She had been thinking simply and kindly of him even before he came. He had always been prepared for, waited upon either with flattering attentions or ceremonial service, but the quiet pretty things mothers and sisters and wives did had not been part of his life and he had always noticed and liked them and sometimes wondered that most men received them with a casual air. This small thing alone caused the roar he had left behind to recede still farther.

"I was afraid that you might be too busy to come," she went on. "You see, I remembered how important the work was and that there are things which cannot wait for an hour. I could have waited as long as you told me to wait. But I am so *glad* you could come!"

"I will always come," was his answer. "I have helpers who could be wholly trusted if I died to-night. I have thought of that. One must."

She hesitated a moment and then said, "I am quite away here as you wanted me to be. I see it was the only thing. I read nothing, hear nothing. London—the War—" her voice fell a little.

"They go on. Will you be kind to me and help me to forget them for a while?" He looked through the window at the sky and the moor. "They are not here—they never have been. The men who come back will do anything to make themselves forget for a little while. This place makes me feel that I am a man who has come back."

"I will do anything—everything—you wish me to do," she said eagerly. "Dowie wondered if you would not want to be very quiet and not be reminded. I—wondered too."

"You were both right. I want to feel that I am in another world. This seems like a new planet."

"Would you—" she spoke rather shyly, "would you be able to stay a few days?"

"I can stay a week," he answered. "Thank you, Robin."

"I am so glad," she said. "I am so glad."

So they did not talk about the War or about London, though she inquired about the Duchess and Lady Lothwell and Kathryn.

"Would you like to go out and walk over the moor?" she asked after a short time. "It's so scented and sweet, and darling things scurry about. I don't think they are really frightened, because I try to walk softly. Sometimes there are nests with eggs or soft little things in them."

They went out together and walked side by side, sometimes on the winding road and sometimes through the heather. He found himself watching every step she made and keeping his eye on the path ahead of them to make sure she would avoid roughness or irregularities. In some inner part of his being there remotely worked the thought that this was the way in which he might have walked side by side with Alixe, watching over each step taken by her sacred little feet.

The day was a wonder of peace and relaxation to him. Farther and farther, until lost in nothingness, receded the roar and the tensely strung sense of waiting for news of unbearable things. As they went on he realised that he need not even watch the path before her because she knew it so well and her step was as light and firm as a young roe's. Her very movements seemed to express the natural physical enjoyment of exercise.

He knew nothing of her mind but that Mademoiselle had told him that she was intelligent. They had never talked together and so her mentality was an unexplored field to him. She did not chatter. She said fresh picturesque things about life on the moor, about the faithful silent Macaurs, about Dowie, and now and then about something she had read. She showed him beauties and small curious things she plainly loved. It struck him that the whole trend of her being lay in the direction of being fond of people and things—of loving and being happy,—and even merry if life had been kind to her. Her soft laugh had a naturally merry note. He heard it first when she held him quite still at her side as they watched the frisking of some baby rabbits.

There was a curious relief in realising, as the hours passed, that her old dislike and dread of him had melted into nothingness like a mist blown away in the night. She was thinking of him as if he were some mature and wise friend who had always been kind to her. He need not rigidly watch his words and hers. She was not afraid of him at all; there was no shrinking in her eyes when they met his. If Alixe had had a daughter who was his own, she might have lifted such lovely eyes to him.

They lunched together and Dowie served them with deft ability and an expression which Coombe was able to comprehend the at once watchful and directing meaning of. It directed him to observation of Robin's appetite and watched for his encouraged realisation of it as a supporting fact.

He went to his own rooms in the afternoon that she might be alone and rest. He read an old book for an hour and then talked with the Macaurs about the place and their work and their new charge. He wanted to hear what they were thinking of her.

"It's wonderful, my lord!" was Mrs. Macaur's repeated contribution. "She came here a wee ghost. She frighted me. I couldna see how she could go through what's before her. I lay awake in my bed expectin' Mrs. Dowie to ca' me any hour. An' betwixt one night and anither the change cam. She's a well bairn—for woman she isna, puir wee thing! It's a wonder—a wonder—a wonder, my lord!"

When he saw Dowie alone he asked her a question.

"Does she know that you have told me of the dream?"

"No, my lord. The dream's a thing we don't talk about. She's only mentioned it three times. It's in my mind that she feels it's too sacred to be made common by words."

He had wondered if Robin had been aware of his knowledge. After Dowie's answer he wondered if she would speak to him about the dream herself. Perhaps she would not. It might be that she had asked him to come to Darreuch because her thought of him had so changed that she had realised something of his grave anxiety for her health and a gentle consideration had made her wish to give him the opportunity to see her face to face. Perhaps she had intended only this.

"I want to see her," he had said to himself. The relief of the mere seeing had been curiously great. He had the relief of sinking, as it were, into the deep waters of pure peace on this new planet. In this realisation every look at the child's face, every movement she made, every tone of her voice, aided. Did she know that she soothed him? Did she intend to try to soothe? When they were together she gave him a feeling that she was strangely near and soft and warm. He had felt it on the moor. It was actually as if she wanted to be quieting to him—almost as if she had realised that he had been stretched upon a mental rack with maddening tumult all around him. It was part of her pretty thought of him in the matter of the waiting chair and he felt it very sweet.

But she had had other things in her mind when she had asked him
to come. This he knew later.

Chapter 33

After they had dined they sat together in the long Highland twilight before her window in the Tower room where he had found her sitting when he arrived. Her work basket was near her and she took a piece of sheer lawn from it and began to embroider. And he sat and watched her draw delicate threads through the tiny leaves and flowers she was making. So he might have watched Alixe if she had been some unroyal girl given to him in one of life's kinder hours. She seemed to draw near out of the land of lost shadows as he sat in the clear twilight stillness and looked on. As he might have watched Alixe.

The silence, the paling daffodil tints of the sky, the non-existence of any other things than calm and stillness seemed to fill his whole being as a cup might be filled by pure water falling slowly. She said nothing and did not even seem to be waiting for anything. It was he who first broke the rather long silence and his voice was quite low.

"Do you know you are very good to me?" he said. "How did you learn to be so kind to a man—with your quietness?"

He saw the hand holding her work tremble a very little. She let it fall upon her knee, still holding the embroidery. She leaned forward slightly and in her look there was actually something rather like a sort of timid prayer.

"Please let me," she said. "Please let me—if you can!"

"Let you!" was all that he could say.

"Let me try to help you to rest—to feel quiet and forget for just a little while. It's such a small thing. And it's all I can ever *try* to do."

"You do it very perfectly," he answered, touched and wondering.

"You have been kind to me ever since I was a child—and I did not know," she said. "Now I know, because I understand. Oh! *will* you forgive me? *Please*—will you?"

"Don't, my dear," he said. "You were a baby. *I* understood. That prevented there being anything to forgive—anything."

"I ought to have loved you as I loved Mademoiselle and Dowie." Her eyes filled with tears. "And I think I hated you. It began with Donal," in a soft wail. "I heard Andrews say that his mother wouldn't let him know me because you were my mother's friend. And then as I grew older—"

"Even if I had known what you thought I could not have defended myself," he answered, faintly smiling. "You must not let yourself think of it. It is nothing now."

The hand holding the embroidery lifted itself to touch her breast. There was even a shade of awe of him in her eyes.

"It is something to me—and to Donal. You have never defended yourself. You endure things and endure them. You watched for years over an ignorant child who loathed you. It was not that a child's hatred is of importance—but if I had died and never asked you to forgive me, how could I have looked into Donal's eyes? I want to go down on my knees to you!"

He rose from his chair, and took in his own the unsteady hand holding the embroidery. He even bent and lightly touched it with his lips, with his finished air.

"You will not die," he said. "And you will not go upon your knees. Thank you for being a warm hearted child, Robin."

But still her eyes held the touch of awe of him.

"But what I have spoken of is the least." Her voice almost broke. "In the Wood—in the dark you said there was something that must be saved from suffering. I could not think then—I could scarcely care. But you cared, and you made me come awake. To save a poor little child who was not born, you have done something which will make people believe you were vicious and hideous—even when all this is over forever and ever. And there will be no one to defend you. Oh! What shall I do!"

"There are myriads of worlds," was his answer. "And this is only one of them. And I am only one man among the myriads on it. Let us be very quiet again and watch the coming out of the stars."

In the pale saffron of the sky which was mysteriously darkening, sparks like deep-set brilliants were lighting themselves here and there. They sat and watched them together for long. But first Robin murmured something barely above her lowest breath. Coombe was not sure that she expected him to hear it.

"I want to be your little slave. Oh! Let me!"

Chapter 34

This was what she had been thinking of. This had been the meaning of the tender thought for him he had recognised uncomprehendingly in her look: it had been the cause of her desire to enfold him in healing and restful peace. When he had felt that she drew so close to him that they were scarcely separated by physical being, it was because she had suddenly awakened to a new comprehension. The awakening must have been a sudden one. He had known at the church that it had taken all her last remnant of strength to aid her to lay her cold hand in his and he had seen shrinking terror in her eyes when she lifted them to his as he put on her wedding ring. He had also known perfectly what memory had beset her at the moment and he had thrown all the force of his will into the look which had answered her—the look which had told her that he understood. Yes, the awakening must have been sudden and he asked himself how it had come about—what had made all clear?

He had never been a mystic, but during the cataclysmic hours through which men were living, many of them stunned into half blindness and then shocked into an unearthly clarity of thought and sight, he had come upon previously unheard of signs of mysticism on all sides. People talked—most of them blunderingly—of things they would not have mentioned without derision in pre-war days. Premonitions, dreams, visions, telepathy were not by any means always flouted with raucous laughter and crude witticisms. Even unorthodox people had begun to hold tentatively religious views.

Was he becoming a mystic at last? As he walked by Robin's side on the moor, as he dined with her, talked with her, sat and watched her at her sewing, more than ever each hour he believed that her dream was no ordinary fantasy of the unguided brain. She had in some strange way seen Donal. Where—how—where he had come from—where he returned after their meeting—he ceased to ask himself. What did it matter after all if souls could so comfort and sustain each other? The blessedness of it was enough.

He wondered as Dowie had done whether she would reveal anything to him or remain silent. There was no actual reason why she should speak. No remotest reference to the subject would come from himself.

It was in truth a new planet he lived on during this marvel of a week. The child was wonderful, he told himself. He had not realised that a feminine creature could be so exquisitely enfolding and yet leave a man so wholly free. She was not always with him, but her spirit was so near that he began to feel that no faintest wish could form itself within his mind without her mysteriously knowing of its existence and realising it while she seemed to make no effort. She did pretty things for him and her gladness in his pleasure in them touched him to the core. He also knew that she wished him to see that she was well and strong and never tired or languid. There was, perhaps, one thing she could do for him and she wanted to prove to him that he might be sure she would not fail him. He allowed her to perform small services for him because of the dearness of the smile it brought to her lips—almost a sort of mothering smile. It was really true that she wanted to be his little slave and he had imagination enough to guess that she comforted herself by saying the thing to herself again and again; childlike and fantastic as it was.

She taught him to sleep as he had not slept for a year; she gave him back the power to look at his food without a sense of being repelled; she restored to him the ability to sit still in a chair as though it were meant to rest in. His nerves relaxed; his deadly fatigue left him; and it was the quiet nearness of Robin that had done it. He felt younger and knew that on his return to London he should be more inclined to disbelieve exaggerated rumours than to believe them.

On the evening before he left Darreuch they sat at the Tower window again. She did not take her sewing from its basket, but sat very quietly for a while looking at the purple folds of moor.

"You will go away very early in the morning," she began at last.

"Yes. You must promise me that you will not awaken."

"I do not waken early. If I do I shall come to you, but I think I shall be asleep."

"Try to be asleep."

He saw that she was going to say something else—something not connected with his departure. It was growing in her eyes and after a silent moment or so she began.

"There is something I want to tell you," she said.

"Yes?"

"I have waited because I wanted to make sure that you could believe it. I did not think you would not wish to believe it, but sometimes there are people who *cannot* believe even when they try. Perhaps once I should not have been able to believe myself. But now—I *know*. And to-night I feel that you are one of those who *can* believe."

She was going to speak of it.

"In these days when all the forces of the world are in upheaval people are learning that there are many new things to be believed," was his answer.

She turned towards him, extending her arms that he might see her well.

"See!" she said, "I am alive again. I am alive because Donal came back to me. He comes every night and when he comes he is not dead. Can you believe it?"

"When I look at you and remember, I can believe anything. I do not understand. I do not know where he comes from—or how, but I believe that in some way you see him."

She had always been a natural and simple girl and it struck him that her manner had never been a more natural one.

"*I* do not know where he comes from," the clearness of a bell in her voice. "He does not want me to ask him. He did not say so but I know. When he is with me we know things without speaking words. We only talk of happy things. I have not told him that—that I have been unhappy and that I thought that perhaps I was really dead. He made me understand about you—but he does not know anything—else. Yes—" eagerly, eagerly, "you are believing—you are!"

"Yes—I am believing."

234

"If everything were as it used to be—I should see him and talk to him in the day time. Now I see him and talk to him at night instead. You see, it is almost the same thing. But we are really happier. We are afraid of nothing and we only tell each other of happy things. We know how wonderful everything is and that it was *meant* to be like that. You don't know how beautiful it is when you only think and talk about joyful things! The other things fly away. Sometimes we go out onto the moor together and the darkness is not darkness—it is a soft lovely thing as beautiful as the light. We love it—and we can go as far as we like because we are never tired. Being tired is one of the things that has flown away and left us quite light. That is why I feel light in the day and I am never tired or afraid. I *remember* all the day."

As he listened, keeping his eyes on her serenely radiant face, he asked himself what he should have been thinking if he had been a psychopathic specialist studying her case. He at the same time realised that a psychopathic specialist's opinion of what he himself—Lord Coombe—thought would doubtless have been scientifically disconcerting. For what he found that he thought was that, through some mysteriously beneficent opening of portals kept closed through all the eons of time, she who was purest love's self had strangely passed to places where vision revealed things as they were created by that First Intention—of which people sometimes glibly talked in London drawing-rooms. He had not seen life so. He was not on her plane, but, as he heard her, he for the time believed in its existence and felt a remote nostalgia.

"Dowie is very brave and tries not to be frightened," she went on; "but she is really afraid that something may happen to my mind. She thinks it is only a queer dream which may turn out unhealthy. But it is not. It is Donal."

"Yes, it is Donal," he answered gravely. And he believed he was speaking a truth, though he was aware of no material process of reasoning by which such a conclusion could be reached. One had to overleap gaps—even abysses—where material reasoning came to a full stop. One could only argue that there might be yet unknown processes to be revealed. Mere earthly invention was revealing on this plane unknown processes year by year—why not on other planes?

"I wanted to tell you because I want you to know everything about me. It seems as if I belong to you, Lord Coombe," there was actual sweet pleading in her voice. "You watched and made my life for me. I should not have been this Robin if you had not watched. When Donal came back he found me in the house you had taken me to because I could be safe in it. Everything has come from you ... I am yours as well as Donal's."

"You give me extraordinary comfort, dear child," he said. "I did not know that I needed it, but I see that I did. Perhaps I have longed for it without knowing it. You have opened closed doors."

"I will do anything—everything—you wish me to do. I will *obey* you always," she said.

"You are doing everything I most desire," he answered.

"Then I will try more every day."

She meant it as she had always meant everything she said. It was her innocent pledge of faithful service, because, understanding at last, she had laid her white young heart in gratitude at his feet. No living man could have read her more clearly than this one whom half Europe had secretly smiled at as its most finished debauchée. When she took her pretty basket upon her knee and began to fold its bits of lawn delicately for the night, he felt as if he were watching some stainless acolyte laying away the fine cloths of an altar.

Though no one would have accused him of being a sentimentalist or an emotional man, his emotions overpowered him for once and swept doubt of emotion and truth into some outer world.

The morning rose fair and the soft wind blowing across the gorse and heather brought scents with it. Dowie waited upon him at his early breakfast and took the liberty of indulging in open speech.

"You go away looking rested, my lord," she respectfully ventured. "And you leave us feeling safe."

"Quite safe," he answered; "she is beautifully well."

"That's it, my lord—beautifully—thank God. I've never seen a young thing bloom as she does and I've seen many."

The cart was at the door and he stood in the shadows of the hall when a slight sound made him look up at the staircase. It was an ancient winding stone descent with its feudal hand rope for balustrade. Robin was coming down it in a loose white dress. Her morning face was wonderful. It was inevitable that he should ask himself where she had come from—what she had brought with her unknowing. She looked like a white blossom drifting from the bough—like a feather from a dove's wing floating downward to earth. But she was only Robin.

"You awakened," he reproached her.

She came quite near him.

"I wanted to awake. Donal wanted me to."

She had never been quite so near him before. She put out a hand and laid it on the rough tweed covering his breast.

"I wanted to see you. Will you come again—when you are tired? I shall always be here waiting."

"Thank you, dear child," he answered. "I will come as often as I can leave London. This is a new planet."

He was almost as afraid to move as if a bird had alighted near him.

But she was not afraid. Her eyes were clear pools of pure light.

"Before you go away—" she said as simply as she had said it to Dowie years before, "—may I kiss you, Lord Coombe? I want to kiss you."

His old friend had told him the story of Dowie and it had extraordinarily touched him though he had said but little. And now it repeated itself. He had never seen anything so movingly lovely in his life as her sweet gravity.

She lifted her slight arms and laid them around his neck as she kissed him gently, as if she had been his daughter—his own daughter and delight—whose mother might have been Alixe.

Chapter 35

"It was the strangest experience of my existence. It seemed suddenly to change me to another type of man."

He said it to the Duchess as he sat with her in her private room at Eaton Square. He had told her the whole story of his week at Darreuch and she had listened with an interest at moments almost breathless.

"Do you feel that you shall remain the new type of man, or was it only a temporary phase?" she inquired.

"I told her that I felt I was living on a new planet. London is the old planet and I have returned to it. But not as I left it. Something has come back with me."

"It must have seemed another planet," the Duchess pondered. "The stillness of huge unbroken moors—no war—no khaki in sight—utter peace and remoteness. A girl brought back to life by pure love, drawing a spirit out of the unknown to her side on earth."

"She is like a spirit herself—but that she remains Robin—in an extraordinary new blooming."

"Yes, she remains Robin." The Duchess thought it out slowly. "Not once did she disturb you or herself by remembering that you were her husband."

"A girl who existed on the old planet would have remembered, and I should have detested her. To her, marriage means only Donal. The form we went through she sees only as a supreme sacrifice I made for the sake of Donal's child. If you could have heard her heart-wrung cry, 'There will be no one to defend you! Oh! What shall I do!'"

"The stainless little soul of her!" the Duchess exclaimed. "Her world holds only love and tenderness. Her goodbye to you meant that in her penitence she wanted to take you into it in the one way she feels most sacred. She will not die. She will live to give you the child. If it is a son there will be a Head of the House of Coombe."

"On the new planet one ceases to feel the vital importance of 'houses,'" Coombe half reflected aloud.

"Even on the old planet," the Duchess spoke as a woman very tired, "one is beginning to contemplate changes in values."

The slice of a house in Mayfair had never within the memory of man been so brilliant. The things done in it were called War Work and necessitated much active gaiety. Persons of both sexes, the majority of them in becoming uniform, flashed in and out in high spirits. If you were a personable and feminine creature, it was necessary to look as much like an attractive boy as possible when you were doing War Work. If one could achieve something like leggings in addition to a masculine cut of coat, one could swagger about most alluringly. There were numbers of things to be done which did not involve frumpish utilitarian costumes, all caps and aprons. Very short skirts were the most utilitarian of garments because they were easy to get about in. Smart military little hats were utilitarian also—and could be worn at any inspiring angle which would most attract the passing eye. Even before the War, shapely legs, feet and ankles had begun to play an increasingly interesting part in the scheme of the Universe—as a result of the brevity of skirts and the prevalence of cabaret dancing. During the War, as a consequence of the War Work done in such centres of activity as the slice of a house in Mayfair, these attractive members were allowed opportunities such as the world had not before contemplated.

"Skirts must be short when people are doing real work," Feather said. "And then of course one's shoes and stockings require attention. I'm not always sure I like leggings however smart they are. Still I often wear them—as a sort of example."

"Of what?" inquired Coombe who was present

"Oh, well—of what women are willing to do for their country—in time of war. Wearing unbecoming things—and doing without proper food. These food restrictions are enough to cause a revolution."

She was specially bitter against the food restrictions. If there was one thing men back from the Front—particularly officers—were entitled to, it was unlimited food. The Government ought to attend to it. When a man came back and you invited him to dinner, a nice patriotic thing it was to restrict the number of courses and actually deny him savouries and entrées because they are called luxuries. Who should have luxuries if not the men who were defending England?

"Of course the Tommies don't need them," she leniently added. "They never had them and never will. But men who are officers in smart regiments are starving for them. I consider that my best War Work is giving as many dinner parties as possible, and paying as little attention to food restrictions as I can manage by using my wits."

For some time—in certain quarters even from early days—there had been flowing through many places a current of talk about America. What was she going to do? Was she going to do anything at all? Would it be possible for her hugeness, her power, her wealth to remain inert in a world crisis? Would she be content tacitly to admit the truth of old accusations of commerciality by securing as her part in the superhuman conflict the simple and unadorned making of money through the dire necessities of the world? There was bitterness, there were sneers, there were vague hopes and scathing injustices born of torment and racking dread. Some few were patiently just, because they knew something of the country and its political and social workings and were by chance of those whose points of view included the powers and significances of things not readily to be seen upon the surface of events.

"If there were dollars to be made out of it, of course America would rush in," was Feather's decision. "Americans never do anything unless they can make dollars. I never saw a dollar myself, but I believe they are made of green paper. It would be very exciting if they did rush in. They would bring so much money and they spend it as if it were water. Of course they haven't any proper army, so they'd have to build one up out of all sorts of people."

"Which was what we were obliged to do ourselves, by the way," Coombe threw in as a contribution.

"But they will probably have stockbrokers and Wall Street men for officers. Then some of them might give one 'tips' about how to make millions in 'corners.' I don't know what corners are but they make enormities out of them. Starling!" with a hilarious tinkle of a laugh, "you know that appallingly gorgeous house of Cherry Cheston's in Palace Garden—did she ever tell you that it was the result of a 'tip' a queer Chicago man managed for her? He liked her. He used to call her 'Cherry Ripe' when they were alone. He was big and red and half boyish—sentimental and half blustering. Cherry *was* ripe, you know, and he liked the ripe style. I should like to have a Chicago stockbroker of my own. I wish the Americans *would* come in!"

The Dowager Duchess of Darte and Lord Coombe had been of those who had begun their talk of this in the early days.

"Personally I believe they will come in," Coombe had always said. And on different occasions he had added reasons which, combined, formulated themselves into the following arguments. "We don't really know much of the Americans though they have been buying and selling and marrying us for some time. Our insular trick of feeling superior has held us mentally aloof from half the globe. But presumably the United States was from the first, in itself, an ideal, pure and simple. It was. It is asinine to pooh-pooh it. A good deal is said about that sort of thing in their histories and speeches. They keep it before each other and it has had the effect of suggesting ideals on all sides. Which has resulted in laying a sort of foundation of men who believe in the ideals and would fight for them. They are good fighters and, when the sincere ones begin, they will plant their flag where the insincere and mere politicians will be forced to stand by it to save their faces. A few louder brays from Berlin, a few more threats of hoofs trampling on the Star Spangled Banner and the fuse will be fired. An American fuse might turn out an amazing thing—because the ideals do exist and ideals are inflammable."

This had been in the early days spoken of.

Chapter 36

Harrowby and the rest did not carry on their War Work in the slice of a house. It was of an order requiring a more serious atmosphere. Feather saw even the Starling less and less.

"Since the Dowager took her up she's far too grand for the likes of us," she said.

So to speak, Feather blew about from one place to another. She had never found life so exciting and excitement had become more vitally necessary to her existence as the years had passed. She still looked extraordinarily youthful and if her face was at times rather marvellous in its white and red, and her lips daring in their pomegranate scarlet, the fine grain of her skin aided her effects and she was dazzlingly in the fashion. She had never worn such enchanting clothes and never had seemed to possess so many.

"I twist my rags together myself," she used to laugh. "That's my gift. Hélène says I have genius. I don't mean that I sit and sew. I have a little slave woman who does that by the day. She admires me and will do anything that I tell her. Things are so delightfully scant and short now that you can cut two or three frocks out of one of your old petticoats—and mine were never very old."

There was probably a modicum of truth in this—the fact remained that the garments which were more scant and shorter than those of any other feathery person were also more numerous and exquisite. Her patriotic entertainment of soldiers who required her special order of support and recreation was fast and furious. She danced with them at cabarets; she danced as a nymph for patriotic entertainments, with snow-white bare feet and legs and a swathing of Spring woodland green tulle and leaves and primroses. She was such a success that important personages smiled on her and asked her to appear under undreamed of auspices. Secretly triumphant though she was, she never so far lost her head as to do anything which would bore her or cause her to appear at less than an alluring advantage. When she could invent a particularly unique and inspiring shred of a garment to startle the public with, she danced for some noble object and intoxicated herself with the dazzle of light and applause. She found herself strung to her highest pitch of excitement by the air raids, which in the midst of their terrors had the singular effect of exciting many people and filling them with an insane recklessness. Those so excited somehow seemed to feel themselves immune. Feather chattered about "Zepps" as if bombs could only wreak their vengeance upon coast towns and the lower orders.

When Lord Coombe definitely refused to allow her to fit up the roof of the slice of a house as a sort of luxurious Royal Box from which she and her friends might watch the spectacle, she found among her circle acquaintances who shared her thrills and had prepared places for themselves. Sometimes she was even rather indecently exhilarated by her sense of high adventure. The fact was that the excitement of the seething world about her had overstrung her trivial being and turned her light head until it whirled too fast.

"It may seem horrid to say so and I'm not horrid—but I *like* the war. You know what I mean. London never was so thrilling—with things happening every minute—and all sorts of silly solemn fads swept away so that one can do as one likes. And interesting heroic men coming and going in swarms and being so grateful for kindness and entertainment. One is really doing good all the time—and being adored for it. I own I like being adored myself—and of course one likes doing good. I never was so happy in my life."

"I used to be rather a coward, I suppose," she chattered gaily on another occasion. "I was horribly afraid of things. I believe the War and living among soldiers has had an effect on me and made me braver. The Zepps don't frighten me at all—at least they excite me so that they make me forget to be frightened. I don't know what they do to me exactly. The whole thing gets into my head and makes me want to rush about and *see* everything. I wouldn't go into a cellar for worlds. I want to *see*!"

She saw Lord Coombe but infrequently at this time, the truth being that her exhilaration and her War Work fatigued him, apart from which his hours were filled. He also objected to a certain raffishness which in an extremely mixed crowd of patriots rather too obviously "swept away silly old fads" and left the truly advanced to do as they liked. What they liked he did not and was wholly undisturbed by the circumstances of being considered a rigid old fossil. Feather herself had no need of him. An athletic and particularly well favoured young actor who shared her thrills of elation seemed to permeate the atmosphere about her. He and Feather together at times achieved the effect, between raids, of waiting impatiently for a performance and feeling themselves ill treated by the long delays between the acts.

"Are we growing callous, or are we losing our wits through living at such high temperature?" the Duchess asked. "There's a delirium in the air. Among those who are not shuddering in cellars there are some who seem possessed by a sort of light insanity, half defiance, half excited curiosity. People say exultantly, 'I had a perfectly splendid view of the last Zepp!' A mother whose daughter was paying her a visit said to her, 'I wish you could have seen the Zepps while you were here. It is such an experience.'"

"They have not been able to bring about the wholesale disaster Germany hoped for and when nothing serious happens there is a relieved feeling that the things are futile after all," said Coombe. "When the results are tragic they must be hushed up as far as is possible to prevent panic."

Dowie faithfully sent him her private bulletin. Her first fears of peril had died away, but her sense of mystification had increased and was more deeply touched with awe. She opened certain windows every night and felt that she was living in the world of supernatural things. Robin's eyes sometimes gave her a ghost of a shock when she came upon her sitting alone with her work in her idle hands. But supported by the testimony of such realities as breakfasts, long untiring walks and unvarying blooming healthfulness, she thanked God hourly.

"Doctor Benton says plain that he has never had such a beautiful case and one that promised so well," she wrote. "He says she's as strong as a young doe bounding about on the heather. What he holds is that it's natural she should be. He is a clever gentleman with some wonderful comforting new ideas about things, my lord. And he tells me I need not look forward with dread as perhaps I had been doing."

Robin herself wrote to Coombe—letters whose tender-hearted comprehension of what he was doing always held the desire to surround him with the soothing quiet he had so felt when he was with her. What he discovered was that she had been born of the elect,—the women who know what to say, what to let others say and what to beautifully leave unsaid. Her unconscious genius was quite exquisite.

Now and then he made the night journey to Darreuch Castle and each time she met him with her frank childlike kiss he was more amazed and uplifted by her aspect. Their quiet talks together were wonderful things to remember. She had done much fine and dainty work which she showed him with unaffected sweetness. She told him stories of Dowie and Mademoiselle and how they had taught her to sew and embroider. Once she told him the story of her first meeting with Donal—but she passed over the tragedy of their first parting.

"It was too sad," she said.

He noticed that she never spoke of sad and dark hours. He was convinced that she purposely avoided them and he was profoundly glad.

"I know," she said once, "that you do not want me to talk to you about the War."

"Thank you for knowing it," he answered. "I come here on a pilgrimage to a shrine where peace is. Darreuch is my shrine."

"It is mine, too," was her low response.

"Yes, I think it is," his look at her was deep. Suddenly but gently he laid his hand on her shoulder.

"I beg you," he said fervently, "I *beg* you never to allow yourself to think of it. Blot the accursed thing out of the Universe while—you are here. For you there must be no war."

"How kind his face looked," was Robin's thought as he hesitated a second and then went on:

"I know very little of such—sacrosanct things as mothers and children, but lately I have had fancies of a place for them where there are only smiles and happiness and beauty—as a beginning."

It was she who now put her hand on his arm. "Little Darreuch is like that—and you gave it to me," she said.

Chapter 37

Lord Coombe was ushered into the little drawing-room by an extremely immature young footman who—doubtless as a consequence of his immaturity—appeared upon the scene too suddenly. The War left one only servants who were idiots or barely out of Board Schools, Feather said. And in fact it was something suggesting "a scene" upon which Coombe was announced. The athletic and personable young actor—entitled upon programmes Owen Delamore—was striding to and fro talking excitedly. There was theatrical emotion in the air and Feather, delicately flushed and elate, was listening with an air half frightened, half pleased. The immaturity of the footman immediately took fright and the youth turning at once produced the fatal effect of fleeing precipitately.

Mr. Owen Delamore suddenly ceased speaking and would doubtless have flushed vividly if he had not already been so high of colour as to preclude the possibility of his flushing at all. The scene, which was plainly one of emotion, being intruded upon in its midst left him transfixed on his expression of anguish, pleading and reproachful protest—all thrilling and confusing things.

The very serenity of Lord Coombe's apparently unobserving entrance was perhaps a shock as well as a relief. It took even Feather two or three seconds to break into her bell of a laugh as she shook hands with her visitor.

"Mr. Delamore is going over his big scene in the new play," she explained with apt swiftness of resource. "It's very good, but it excites him dreadfully. I've been told that great actors don't let themselves get excited at all, so he ought not to do it, ought he, Lord Coombe?"

Coombe was transcendently well behaved.

"I am a yawning abyss of ignorance in such matters, but I cannot agree with the people who say that emotion can be expressed without feeling." He himself expressed exteriorly merely intelligent consideration of the idea. "That however may be solely the opinion of one benighted."

It was so well done that the young athlete, in the relief of relaxed nerves, was almost hysterically inclined to believe in Feather's adroit statement and to feel that he really had been acting. He was at least able to pull himself together, to become less flushed and to sit down with some approach to an air of being lightly amused at himself.

"Well it is proved that I am not a great actor," he achieved. "I can't come anywhere near doing it. I don't believe Irving ever did—or Coquelin. But perhaps it is one of my recommendations that I don't aspire to be great. At any rate people only ask to be amused and helped out just now. It will be a long time before they want anything else, it's my opinion."

They conversed amiably together for nearly a quarter of an hour before Mr. Owen Delamore went on his way murmuring polite regrets concerning impending rehearsals, his secret gratitude expressing itself in special courtesy to Lord Coombe.

As he was leaving the room, Feather called to him airily:

"If you hear any more of the Zepps—just dash in and tell me!—Don't lose a minute! Just dash!"

When the front door was heard to close upon him, Coombe remarked casually:

"I will ask you to put an immediate stop to that sort of thing."

He observed that Feather fluttered—though she had lightly moved to a table as if to rearrange a flower in a group.

"Put a stop to letting Mr. Delamore go over his scene here?"

"Put a stop to Mr. Delamore, if you please."

It was at this moment more than ever true that her light being was overstrung and that her light head whirled too fast. This one particular also overstrung young man had shared all her amusements with her and had ended by pleasing her immensely—perhaps to the verge of inspiring a touch of fevered sentiment she had previously never known. She told herself that it was the War when she thought of it. She had however not been clever enough to realise that she was a little losing her head in a way which might not be to her advantage. For the moment she lost it completely. She almost whirled around as she came to Coombe.

"I won't," she exclaimed. "I won't!"

It was a sort of shock to him. She had never done anything like it before. It struck him that he had never before seen her look as she looked at the moment. She was a shade too dazzlingly made up—she had crossed the line on one side of which lies the art which is perfect. Even her dress had a suggestion of wartime lack of restraint in its style and colours.

It was of a strange green and a very long scarf of an intensely vivid violet spangled with silver paillettes was swathed around her bare shoulders and floated from her arms. One of the signs of her excitement was that she kept twisting its ends without knowing that she was touching it. He noted that she wore a big purple amethyst ring—the amethyst too big. Her very voice was less fine in its inflections and as he swiftly took in these points Coombe recognised that they were the actual result of the slight tone of raffishness he had observed as denoting the character of her increasingly mixed circle.

She threw herself into a chair palpitating in one of her rages of a little cat—wreathing her scarf round and round her wrist and singularly striking him with the effect of almost spitting and hissing out her words.

"I won't give up everything I like and that likes me," she flung out. "The War has done something to us all. It's made us let ourselves go. It's done something to me too. It's made me less frightened. I won't be bullied into—into things."

"Do I seem to bully you? I am sorry."

The fact that she had let herself go with the rest of the world got the better of her.

"You have not been near me for weeks and now you turn up with your air of a grand Bashawe and order people out of my house. You have not been near me."

The next instant it was as though she tore off some last shred of mental veiling and threw it aside in her reckless mounting heat of temper.

"Near me!" she laughed scathingly, "For the matter of that when have you ever been *near* me? It's always been the same. I've known it for years. As the Yankees say, you 'wouldn't touch me with a ten-foot pole.' I'm sick of it. What did you *do* it for?"

"Do what?"

"Take possession of me as if I were your property. You never were in love with me—never for a second. If you had been you'd have married me."

"Yes. I should have married you."

"There was no reason why you should not. I was pretty. I was young. I'd been decently brought up—and it would have settled everything. Why *didn't* you instead of letting people think I was your mistress when I didn't count for as much as a straw in your life?"

"You represented more than that," he answered. "Kindly listen to me."

That she had lost her head completely was sufficiently manifested by the fact that she had begun to cry—which made it necessary for her to use her handkerchief with inimitable skill to prevent the tears from encroaching on her brilliant white and rose.

"If you had been in love with me—" she chafed bitterly.

"On the morning some years ago when I came to you I made myself clear to the best of my ability," he said. "I did not mention love. I told you that I had no intention of marrying you. I called your attention to what the world would assume. I left the decision to you."

"What could I do—without a penny? Some other man would have had to do it if you had not," the letting go rushed her into saying.

"Or you would have been obliged to return to your parents in Jersey—which you refused to contemplate."

"Of course I refused. It would have been mad to do it. And there were other people who would have paid my bills."

"Solely because I knew that, I made my proposition. Being much older than you I realised that other people might not feel the responsibility binding—and permanent."

She sat up and stared at him. There was no touch of the rancour of recrimination in his presentation of detached facts. He *was* different from the rest. He was always better dressed and the perfection of his impersonal manner belonged to a world being swept away. He made Mr. Owen Delamore seem by contrast a bounder and an outsider. But the fact which had in the secret places of her small mind been the fly in her ointment—the one fact that he had never for a moment cared a straw for her—caused her actually to hate him as he again made it, quite without prejudice, crystal clear. It was true that he had more than kept his word—that he had never broken a convention in his bearing towards her—that in his rigid way he had behaved like a prince—but she had been dirt under his feet—she had been dirt under his feet! She wanted to rave like a fishwife—though there were no fishwives in Mayfair.

It was at this very moment of climax that a sudden memory beset her.

"Rob always said that if a woman who was pretty could see a man often enough—again and again—he couldn't *help* himself—unless there *was* some one else!"

Her last words were fiercely accusing. She quite glared at him a few seconds, her chest heaving pantingly.

She suddenly sprang from her sofa and dashed towards a table where a pile of photographs lay in an untidy little heap. She threw them about with angrily shaking hands until at last she caught at one and brought it back to him.

"There *was* some one else," she laughed shrilly. "You were in love with that creature."

It was one of the photographs of Alixe such as the Bond Street shop had shown in its windows.

She made a movement as if to throw it into the grate and he took it from her hand, saying nothing whatever.

"I'd forgotten about it until Owen Delamore reminded me only yesterday," she said. "He's a romantic thing and he heard that you had been in attendance and had been sent to their castle in Germany. He worked the thing out in his own way. He said you had chosen me because I was like her. I can see now! I *was* like her!"

"If you had been like her," his voice was intensely bitter, "I should have asked you to be my wife. You are as unlike her as one human being can be to another."

"But I was enough like her to make you take me up!" she cried furiously.

"I have neither taken you up nor put you down," he answered. "Be good enough never to refer to the subject again."

"I'll refer to any subject I like. If you think I shall not you are mistaken. It will be worth talking about. An Early Victorian romance is worth something in these days."

The trend of her new circle had indeed carried her far. He was privately appalled by her. She was hysterically, passionately spiteful—almost to the point of malignance.

"Do you realise that this is a scene? It has not been our habit to indulge in scenes," he said.

"I shall speak about it as freely as I shall speak about Robin," she flaunted at him, wholly unrestrained. "Do you think I know nothing about Robin? I'm an affectionate mother and I've been making inquiries. She's not with the Dowager at Eaton Square. She got ill and was sent away to be hidden in the country. Girls are, sometimes. I thought she would be sent away somewhere, the day I met her in the street. She looked exactly like that sort of thing. Where is she? I demand to know."

There is nothing so dangerous to others as the mere spitefully malignant temper of an empty headed creature giving itself up to its own weak fury. It knows no restraint, no limit in its folly. In her fantastic broodings over her daughter's undue exaltation of position Feather had many times invented for her own entertainment little scenes in which she could score satisfactorily. Such scenes had always included Coombe, the Dowager, Robin and Mrs. Muir.

"I am her mother. She is not of age. I *can* demand to see her. I can make her come home and stay with me while I see her through her 'trouble,' as pious people call it. She's got herself into trouble—just like a housemaid. I knew she would—I warned her," and her laugh was actually shrill.

It was inevitable—and ghastly—that he should suddenly see Robin with her white eyelids dropped over her basket of sewing by the window in the Tower room at Darreuch. It rose as clear as a picture on a screen and he felt sick with actual terror.

"I'll go to the Duchess and ask her questions until she can't face me without telling the truth. If she's nasty I'll talk to the War Work people who crowd her house. They all saw Robin and the wide-awake ones will understand when I'm maternal and tragic and insist on knowing. I'll go to Mrs. Muir and talk to her. It will be fun to see her face and the Duchess'."

He had never suspected her of malice such as this. And even in the midst of his ghastly dismay he saw that it was merely the malice of an angrily spiteful selfish child of bad training and with no heart. There was nothing to appeal to—nothing to arrest and control. She might repent her insanity in a few days but for the period of her mood she would do her senseless worst.

"Your daughter has not done what you profess to believe," he said. "You do not believe it. Will you tell me why you propose to do these things?"

She had worked herself up to utter recklessness.

"Because of *everything*," she spat forth. "Because I'm in a rage—because I'm sick of her and her duchesses. And I'm most sick of you hovering about her as if she were a princess of the blood and you were her Grand Chamberlain. Why don't you marry her yourself—baby and all! Then you'll be sure there'll be another Head of the House of Coombe!"

She knew then that she had raved like a fishwife—that, even though there had before been no fishwives in Mayfair, he saw one standing shrilling before him. It was in his eyes and she knew it before she had finished speaking, for his look was maddening. It enraged her even further and she shook in the air the hand with the big purple amethyst ring, still clutching the end of the bedizened purple scarf. She was intoxicated with triumph—for she had reached him.

"I will! I will!" she cried. "I will—to-morrow!"

"You will not!" his voice rang out as she had never heard it before. He even took a step forward. Then came the hurried leap of feet up the narrow staircase and Owen Delamore flung the door wide, panting:

"You told me to dash in," he almost shouted. "They're coming! We can rush round to the Sinclairs'. They're on the roof already!"

She caught the purple scarf around her and ran towards him, for at this new excitement her frenzy reached its highest note.

"I will! I will!" she called back to Coombe as she fled out of the room and she held up and waved at him again the hand with the big amethyst. "I will, to-morrow!"

Lord Coombe was left standing in the garish, crowded little drawing-room listening to ominous sounds in the street—to cries, running feet and men on fleeing bicycles shouting warnings as they sped at top speed and strove to clear the way.

Chapter 38

It was one of the raids which left hellish things behind it—things hushed with desperate combined effort to restrain panic, but which blighted the air people strove to breathe and kept men and women shuddering for long after and made people waken with sharp cries from nightmares of horror. Certain paled faces belonged to those who had seen things and would never forget them. Others strove to look defiant and cheerful and did not find it easy. Some tried to get past policemen to certain parts of the city and some, getting past, returned livid and less adventurous in spirit because they had heard things it was gruesome to hear. Lord Coombe went the next morning to the slice of a house and found the servants rather hysterical. Feather had not returned, but they were not hysterical for that reason. She had probably remained at the house to which she had gone to see the Zepps. After the excitement was over, people like the Sinclairs were rather inclined to restore themselves by making a night of it, so to speak.

As "to-morrow" had now arrived, Lord Coombe wished to see her on her return. He had in fact lain awake thinking of plans of defence but had so far been able to decide on none. If there had been anything to touch, to appeal to, there might have been some hope, but she had left taste and fastidiousness scattered in shreds behind her. The War, as she put it, had made her less afraid of life. She had in fact joined the army of women who could always live so long as their beauty lasted. At the beginning of her relations with Lord Coombe she had belonged in a sense to a world which now no longer existed in its old form. Possibly there would soon be neither courts nor duchesses and so why should anything particularly matter? There were those who were taking cataclysms lightly and she was among them. If her airy mind chanced to have veered and her temper died down, money or jewels might induce her to keep quiet if one could endure the unspeakable indignity of forcing oneself to offer them. She would feel such an offer no indignity and would probably regard it as a tremendous joke. But she could no more be trusted than a female monkey or jackdaw.

Lord Coombe sat among the gewgaws in the drawing room and waited because he must see her when she came in and at least discover if the weather cock had veered.

After waiting an hour or more he heard a taxi arrive at the front door and stop there. He went to the window to see who got out of the vehicle. It gave him a slight shock to recognise a man he knew well. He wore plain clothes, but he was a member of the police force.

He evidently came into the house and stopped in the hall to talk to the immature footman who presently appeared at the drawing-room door, looking shaken because he had been questioned and did not know what it portended.

"What is the matter?" Lord Coombe assisted him with.

"Some one who is asking about Mrs. Gareth-Lawless. He doesn't seem satisfied with what I tell him. I took the liberty of saying your lordship was here and perhaps you'd see him."

"Bring him upstairs."

It was in fact a man who knew Lord Coombe well enough to be aware that he need make no delay.

"It was one of the worst, my lord," he said in answer to Coombe's first question. "We've had hard work—and the hardest of it was to hold things—people—back." He looked hag-ridden as he went on without any preparation. He was too tired for prefaces.

"There was a lady who went out of here last night. She was with a gentleman. They were running to a friend's house to see things from the roof. They didn't get there. The gentleman is in the hospital delirious to-day. He doesn't know what happened. It's supposed something frightened her and she lost her wits and ran away. The gentleman tried to follow her but the lights were out and he couldn't find her in the dark streets. The running about and all the noises and crashes sent him rather wild perhaps. Trying to find a frightened woman in the midst of all that—and not finding her—"

"What ghastly—damnable thing has happened?" Coombe asked with stiff lips.

"It's both," the man said, "—it's both."

He produced a package and opened it. There was a torn and stained piece of spangled violet gauze folded in it and on top was a little cardboard box which he opened also to show a ring with a big amethyst in it set with pearls.

"Good God!" Coombe ejaculated, getting up from his chair hastily, "Oh! Good God!"

"You know them?" the man asked.

"Yes. I saw them last night—before she went out."

"She ran the wrong way—she must have been crazy with fright. This—" the man hesitated a second here and pulled himself together, "—this is all that was found except—"

"Good God!" said Lord Coombe again and he walked to and fro rapidly, trying to hold his body rigid.

"The gentleman—his name is Delamore—went on looking—after the raid was over. Some one saw him running here and there as if he had gone crazy. He was found afterwards where he'd fainted—near a woman's hand with this ring on and the piece of scarf in it. He's a strong young chap but he'd fainted dead. He was carried to the hospital and to-day he's delirious."

"There—was nothing more?" shuddered Coombe.

"Nothing, my lord."

Out of unbounded space embodied nothingness had seemed to float across the world of living things, and into space the nothingness had disappeared—leaving behind a trinket and a rent scrap of purple gauze.

Chapter 39

Six weeks later Coombe was driven again up the climbing road to Darreuch. There was something less of colour than usual in his face, but the slightly vivid look of shock observing persons had been commenting upon had died out. As he had travelled, leaning back upon the cushions of the railway carriage, he had kept his eyes closed for the greater part of the journey. When at last he began to open them and look out at the increasingly beautiful country he also began to look rested and calm. He already felt the nearing peace of the shrine and added to it was an immense relaxing and uplift. A girl of a type entirely different from Robin's might, he knew, have made him feel during the past months as if he were taking part in a melodrama. This she had wholly saved him from by the clear simplicity of her natural acceptance of all things as they were. She had taken and given without a word. He was, as it were, going home to her now, as deeply thrilled and moved as a totally different type of man might have gone—a man who was simpler.

The things he might once have been and felt were at work within him. Again he longed to see the girl—he *wanted* to see her. He was going to the castle in response to a telegram from Dowie. All was well over. She was safe. For the rest, all calamity had been kept from her knowledge and, as he had arranged it, the worst would never reach her. In course of time she would learn all it was necessary that she should know of her mother's death.

When Mrs. Macaur led him to one of his own rooms she glowed red and expectantly triumphant.

"The young lady, your lordship—it was wonderful!"

But before she had time to say more Dowie had appeared and her face was smooth and serene to marvellousness.

"The Almighty himself has been in this place, my lord," she said devoutly. "I didn't send more than a word, because she's like a schoolroom child about it. She wants to tell you herself." The woman was quivering with pure joy.

"May I see her?"

"She's waiting, my lord."

Honey scents of gorse and heather blew softly through the open windows of the room he was taken to. He did not know enough of such things to be at all sure what he had expected to see—but what he moved quickly towards, the moment after his entrance, was Robin lying fair as a wild rose on her pillows—not pale, not tragic, but with her eyes wide and radiant as a shining child's.

Her smiling made his heart stand still. He really could not speak. But she could and turned back the covering to show him what lay in her soft curved arm.

"He is not like me at all," was her joyous exulting. "He is exactly like Donal."

The warm, tender breathing, semi-dormant, scarcely sentient-seeming thing might indeed have been the reincarnation of what had in the past so peculiarly reached bodily perfection. Robin, who mysteriously knew every line and curve of the new-born body, could point out how each limb and feature was an embryonic replica.

"Though he looks so tiny, he is not really little," was her lovely yearning boast. "He is really very big. Dowie has known hundreds of babies and they were none of them as big as he is. He is a giant—an angel giant," burying her face in the soft red neck.

"It seemed to change me into another type of man," Coombe once said to the Duchess.

The man into whom he had been transformed was he who lived through the next few days at Darreuch even as though life were a kindly faithful thing. Many other men, he told himself, must have lived as he did and he wondered if any of them ever forgot it. It was a thing set apart.

He sat by Robin's side; they talked together; he retired to his own rooms or went out for a long walk, coming back to her to talk again, or read aloud, or to consider with her the marvel of the small thing by her side, examining curled hands and feet with curious interest.

"But though they look so little, they are not really," she always said. "See how long his fingers are and how they taper. And his foot is long, too, and narrow and arched. Donal's was like it."

"Was," she said, and he wondered if she might not feel a pang as he himself did.

He wondered often and sometimes, when he sat alone in his room at night, found something more than wonder in his mind—something that, if she had not forbidden it, would have been fear because of strange things he saw in her.

He could not question her. He dared not even remotely touch on the dream. She was so well, her child was so well. She was as any young mother might have been who could be serene in her husband's absence because she knew he was safe and would soon return.

"Is she always as calm?" he once asked Dowie. "Does she never seem to be reminded of what would have been if he were alive?"

Dowie shook her head and he saw that the old anxiousness came back upon her.

"My lord, she believes he *is* alive when she sees him. That's what troubles me even in my thankfulness. I don't understand, God help me! I was afraid when she saw the child that it might all come over her again in a way that would do her awful harm. But when I laid the little thing down by her she just lay there herself and looked at it as if something was uplifting her. And in a few seconds she whispered, 'He is like Donal.' And then she said to herself, soft but quite clear, 'Donal, Donal!' And never a tear rose. Perhaps," hesitating over it, "it's the blessedness of *time*. A child's a wonderful thing—and so is time. Sometimes," a queer sigh broke from her, "when I've been hard put to it by trouble, I've said to myself, 'Well the Almighty did give us *time*—whatever else he takes away.'"

But Coombe mysteriously felt that it was not merely time which had calmed her, though any explanation founded on material reasoning became more remote each day. The thought which came to him at times had no connection with temporal things. He found he was gravely asking himself what aspect mere life would have worn if Alixe had come to him every night in such form as had given him belief in the absolute reality of her being. If he had been convinced that he heard the voice of Alixe—if she had smiled and touched him with her white hands as she had never touched him in life—if her eyes had been unafraid and they had spoken together "only of happy things"—and had understood as one soul—what could the mere days have held of hurt? There was only one possible reply and it seemed to explain his feeling that she was sustained by something which was not alone the mere blessedness of time.

He became conscious one morning of the presence of a new expression in her eyes. There was a brave radiance in them and, before, he had known that in their radiance there had been no necessity for bravery. He felt a subtle but curious difference.

Her child had been long asleep and she lay like a white dove on her pillows when he came to make his brief good-night visit. She was very still and seemed to be thinking. Her touch on his arm was as the touch of a butterfly when she at last put out her hand to him.

"He may not come to-night," she said.

He put his own hand over hers and hoped it was done quietly.

"But to-morrow night?" trusting that his tone was quiet also. It must be quiet.

"Perhaps not for a good many nights. He does not know. I must not ask things. I never do."

"But it has been so wonderful that you know—"

On what plane was he—on what plane was she? What plane were they talking about with such undoubtingness? Heaven be praised his voice actually sounded natural.

"I do not know much—except that he is Donal. And I can never feel as if I were dead again—never."

"No," he answered. "Never!"

She lay so still for a few minutes that if her eyes had not been open he would have thought she was falling asleep. They were so dreamy that perhaps she was falling asleep and he softly rose to leave her.

"I think—he is trying to come nearer," she murmured. "Good-night, dear."

Chapter 40

Ominous hours had come and gone; waves of gloom had surged in and receded, but never receded far enough. It was as though the rising and falling of some primæval storm was the background of all thought and life and its pandemonium of sound foretold the far-off heaving of some vast tidal wave, gathering its unearthly power as it swelled.

Coombe talking to his close friend in her few quiet hours at Eaton Square, found a support in the very atmosphere surrounding her.

"The world at war creates a prehistoric uproar," he said. "The earth called out of chaos to take form may have produced some such tempestuous crash. But there is a far-off glow—"

"You believe—something—I believe too. But the prehistoric darkness and uproar are so appalling. One loses hold." The Duchess leaned forward her voice dropping. "What do you know that I do not?"

"The light usually breaks in the East," Coombe answered.

"It is breaking in the West to-day. It has always been there and it has been spreading from the first. At any moment it may set the sky aflame."

For as time had gone on the world had beheld the colossal spectacle of a huge nation in the melting pot. And, as it was as a nation the composite result of the fusion of all the countries of the earth, the breath-suspended lookers-on beheld it in effect, passionately commercial, passionately generous, passionately sordid, passionately romantic, chivalrous, cautious, limited, bounded. As American wealth and sympathy poured in where need was most dire, bitterness became silent through sheer discretion's sake, when for no more honest reason.

As the commercial tendency expressed itself in readiness and efficiency, sneering condemnation had become less loud.

"It will happen. It is the result of the ideals really," Coombe said further. "And it will come to pass at the exact psychological moment. If they had come in at the beginning they would have faced the first full force of the monstrous tidal wave of the colossal German belief in its own omnipotence—and they would have faced it unawakened, unenraged by monstrosities and half incredulous of the truth. It was not even their fight then—and raw fighters need a flaming cause. But the tower of agonies has built itself to its tottering height before their blazing eyes. Now it is their fight because it is the fight of the whole world. Others have borne the first fierce heat and burden of the day, but they will rush in young and untouched by calamity—bounding, shouting and singing. They will come armed with all that long-borne horrors and maddening human fatigue most need. I repeat—it will occur at the exact psychological moment. They will bring red-hot blood and furious unbounded courage—And it will be the end."

In fact Coombe waited with a tense sensation of being too tightly strung. He had hours when he felt that something might snap. But nothing must snap yet. He was too inextricably entangled in the arduous work even to go to Darreuch for rest. He did not go for weeks. All was well there however—marvellously well it seemed, even when he held in mind a letter from Robin which had ended:—

"He has not come back. But I am not afraid. I promised him I would never be afraid again."

In dark and tired hours he steadied himself with a singular half-realised belief that she would not—that somehow some strange thing would be left to her, whatsoever was taken away. It was because he felt as if he were nearing the end of his tether. He had become hypersensitive to noises, to the sounds in the streets, to the strain and grief in faces he saw as he walked or drove.

After lying awake all one night without a moment of blank peace he came down pale and saw that his hand shook as he held his coffee cup. It was a livid sort of morning and when he went out for the sake of exercise he found he was looking at each of the strained faces as if it held some answer to an unformed question. He realised that the tenseness of both mind and body had increased. For no reason whatever he was restrung by a sense of waiting for something—as if something were going to happen.

He went back to Coombe House and when he crossed the threshold he confronted the elderly unliveried man who had stood at his place for years—and the usually unperturbed face was agitated so nearly to panic that he stopped and addressed him.

"Has anything happened?"

"My lord—a Red Cross nurse—has brought"—he was actually quite unsteady—too unsteady to finish, for the next moment the Red Cross nurse was at his side—looking very whitely fresh and clean and with a nice, serious youngish face.

"I need not prepare you for good news—even if it is a sort of shock," she said, watching him closely. "I have brought Captain Muir back to you."

"You have brought—?" he exclaimed.

"He has been in one of the worst German prisons. He was left for dead on the field and taken prisoner. We must not ask him questions. I don't know why he is alive. He escaped, God knows how. At this time he does not know himself. I saw him on the boat. He asked me to take charge of him," she spoke very quickly. "He is a skeleton, poor boy. Come."

She led the way to his own private room. She went on talking short hurried sentences, but he scarcely heard her. This, then, was what he had been waiting for. Why had he not known? This tremendous thing was really not so tremendous after all because it had happened in other cases before—Yet he had never once thought of it.

"He would not let his wife or his mother see him until he looked more like himself," he heard the Red Cross nurse say as he entered the room.

Donal was lying stretched at full length on a sofa. He looked abnormally long, because he was so thin that he was, as the nurse had said, a skeleton. His face was almost a death's head, but his blue eyes looked out of their great hollow sockets clear as tarn water, and with the smile which Coombe would not have forgotten howsoever long life had dragged out.

"Be very careful!" whispered the nurse.

He knew he must be careful. Only the eyes were alive. The body was a collapsed thing. He seemed scarcely breathing, his voice was a thread.

"Robin!" Coombe caught as he bent close to him. "Robin!"

"She is well, dear boy!" How his voice shook! "I have taken care of her."

The light leaped up into the blue for a second. The next the lids dropped and the nurse sprang forward because he had slipped into a faint so much like death that it might well have rent hope from a looker-on.

For the next hour, and indeed for many following, there was unflagging work to be done. The Red Cross Nurse was a capable, swiftly moving woman, with her resources at her finger's ends, and her quick wits about her. Almost immediately two doctors from the staff, in charge of the rooms upstairs were on the spot and at work with her. By what lightning-flashed sentences she conveyed to them, without pausing for a second, the facts it was necessary for them to know, was incomprehensible to Coombe, who could only stand afar off and wait, watching the dead face. Its sunken temples, cheeks and eyes, and the sharply carven bone outline were heart gripping.

It seemed hours before one of the doctors as he bent over the couch whispered,

"The breathing is a little better—"

It was not possible that he should be moved, but the couch was broad and deeply upholstered and could be used temporarily as a bed. Every resource of medical science was within reach. Nurse Jones, who had been on her way home to take a rest, was so far ensnared by unusual interest that she wished to be allowed to remain on duty. There were other nurses who could be called on at any moment of either night or day. There were doctors of indisputable skill who were also fired by the mere histrionic features of the case. The handsome, fortunate young fellow who had been supposed torn to fragments had by some incomprehensible luck been aided to drag himself home—perhaps to die of pure exhaustion.

Was it really hours before Coombe saw the closed eyes weakly open? But the smile was gone and they seemed to be looking at something not in the room.

"They will come—in," the words dragged out scarcely to be heard. "Jackson—said—said—they—would." The eyes dropped again and the breathing was a mere flutter.

Nurse Jones was in fact filled with much curiosity concerning and interest in the Marquis of Coombe. She was a clever and well trained person, but socially a simple creature, who in an inoffensive way "loved a lord." If her work had not absorbed her she could not have kept her eyes from this finely conventional and rather unbending-looking man who—keeping himself out of the way of all who were in charge of the seemingly almost dead boy—still would not leave the room, and watched him with a restrained passion of such feeling as it was not natural to see in the eyes of men. Marquis or not he had gone through frightful things in his life and this boy meant something tremendous to him. If he couldn't be brought back—! Despite the work her swift eye darted sideways at the Marquis.

When at length another nurse took her place and she was going out of the room, he moved quickly towards her and spoke.

"May I ask if I may speak to you alone for a few minutes? I have no right to keep you from your rest. I assure you I won't."

"I'll come," she answered. What she saw in the man's face was that, because she had brought the boy, he actually clung to her. She had been clung to many times before, but never by a man who looked quite like this. There was *more* than you could see.

He led her to a smaller room near by. He made her sit down, but he did not sit himself. It was plain that he did not mean to keep her from her bed—though he was in hard case if ever man was. His very determination not to impose on her caused her to make up her mind to tell him all she could, though it wasn't much.

"Captain Muir's mother believes that he is dead," he said. "It is plain that no excitement must approach him—even another person's emotion. He was her idol. She is in London. *Must* I send for her—or would it be safe to wait?"

"There have been minutes to-day when if I'd known he had a mother I should have said she must be sent for," was her answer. "To-night I believe—yes, I *do*—that it would be better to wait and watch. Of course the doctors must really decide."

"Thank you. I will speak to them. But I confess I wanted to ask *you*." How he did cling to her!

"Thank you," he said again. "I will not keep you."

He opened the door and waited for her to pass—as if she had been a marchioness herself, she thought. In spite of his desperate eyes he didn't forget a single thing. He so moved her that she actually turned back.

"You don't know anything yet— Some one you're fond of coming back from the grave must make you half mad to know how it happened," she said. "I don't know much myself, but I'll tell you all I was able to find out. He was light headed when I found him trying to get on the boat. When I spoke to him he just caught my hand and begged me to stay with him. He wanted to get to you. He'd been wandering about, starved and hiding. If he'd been himself he could have got help earlier. But he'd been ill treated and had seen things that made him lose his balance. He couldn't tell a clear story. He was too weak to talk clearly. But I asked questions now and then and listened to every word he said when he rambled because of his fever. Jackson was a fellow prisoner who died of hemorrhage brought on by brutality. Often I couldn't understand him, but he kept bringing in the name of Jackson. One thing puzzled me very much. He said several times 'Jackson taught me to dream of Robin. I should never have seen Robin if I hadn't known Jackson.' Now 'Robin' is a boy's name—but he said 'her' and 'she' two or three times as if it were a girl's."

"Robin is his wife," said Coombe. He really found the support of the door he still held open, useful for the moment.

An odd new interest sharpened in her eyes.

"Then he's been dreaming of her." She almost jerked it out—as if in sudden illumination almost relief. "He's been dreaming of her—!

And it may have kept him alive." She paused as if she were asking questions of her own mind. "I wonder," dropped from her in slow speculation, "if she has been dreaming of *him*?"

"He was not dead—he was not an angel—he was Donal!" Robin had persisted from the first. He had not been dead. In some incredibly hideous German prison—in the midst of inhuman horrors and the blackness of what must have been despair—he had been alive, and had dreamed as she had.

Nurse Jones looked at him, waiting. Even if nurses had not been, presumably, under some such bond of honourable secrecy as constrained the medical profession, he knew she was to be trusted. Her very look told him.

"She did dream of him," he said. "She was slipping fast down the slope to death and he caught her back. He saved her life and her child's. She was going to have a child."

They were both quite silent for a few moments. The room was still. Then the woman drew her hand with a quick odd gesture across her forehead.

"Queer things happened in the last century, but queerer ones are going to happen in this—if people will let them. Doctors and nurses see and think a lot they can't talk about. They're always on the spot at what seems to be the beginning and the ending. These black times have opened up the ways. 'Queer things,' I said," with sudden forcefulness. "They're not queer. It's only laws we haven't known about. It's the writing on the scroll that we couldn't read. We're just learning the alphabet." Then after a minute more of thought, "Those two—were they particularly fond of each other—more to each other than most young couples?"

"They loved each other the hour they first met—when they were little children. It was an unnatural shock to them both when they were parted. They seemed to be born mated for life."

"That was the reason," she said quite relievedly. "I can understand that. It's as orderly as the stars." Then she added with a sudden, strong, quite normal conviction, and her tiredness seemed to drop from her, "He won't die—that beautiful boy," she said. "He can't. It's not meant. They're going on, those three. He's the most splendid human thing I ever handled—skeleton as he is. His very bones are magnificent as he lies there. And that smile of his that's deep in the blue his eyes are made of—it can only flicker up for a second now—but it can't go out. He's safe, even this minute, though you mayn't believe it."

"I do believe it," Coombe said.

And he stood there believing it, when she went through the open door and left him.

Chapter 41

It was long before the dropped eyelids could lift and hold themselves open for more than a few seconds and long before the eyes wore their old clear look. The depths of the collapse after prolonged tortures of strain and fear was such as demanded a fierce and unceasing fight of skill and unswerving determination on the part of both doctors and nurses. There were hours when what seemed to be strange, deathly drops into abysses of space struck terror into most of those who stood by looking on. But Nurse Jones always believed and so did Coombe.

"You needn't send for his mother yet," she said without flinching. "You and I know something the others don't know, Lord Coombe. That child and her baby are holding him back though they don't know anything about it."

It revealed itself to him that her interest in things occult and apparently unexplained by material processes had during the last few years intensely absorbed her in private. Her feeling, though intense, was intelligent and her processes of argument were often convincing. He became willing to answer her questions because he felt sure of her. He lent her the books he had been reading and in her hard-earned hours of leisure she plunged deep into them.

"Perhaps I read sometimes when I ought to be sleeping, but it rests me—I tell you it *rests* me. I'm finding out that there's strength outside of all this and you can draw on it. It's there waiting," she said. "Everybody will know about its being there—in course of time."

"But the time seems long," said Coombe.

Concerning the dream she had many interesting theories. She was at first disturbed and puzzled because it had stopped. She was anxious to find out whether it had come back again, but, like Lord Coombe, she realised that Robin's apparent calm must on no account be disturbed. If her health-giving serenity could be sustained for a certain length of time, the gates of Heaven would open to her. But at first Nurse Jones asked herself and Lord Coombe some troubled questions.

It came about at length that she appeared one night, in the room where their first private talk had taken place and she had presented herself on her way to bed, because she had something special to say.

"It came to me when I awakened this morning as if it had been told to me in the night. Things often seem to come that way. Do you remember, Lord Coombe, that she said they only talked about happy things?"

"Yes. She said it several times," Coombe answered.

"Do you remember that he never told her where he came from? And she knew that she must not ask questions? How *could* he have told her of that hell—how could he?"

"You are right—quite!"

"I feel sure I am. When he can talk he will tell you—if he remembers. I wonder how much they remember—except the relief and the blessed happiness of it? Lord Coombe, I believe as I believe I'm in this room, that when he knew he was going to face the awful risk of trying to escape, he knew he mustn't tell her. And he knew that in crawling through dangers and hiding in ditches he could never be sure of being able to lie down to sleep and concentrate on sending his soul to her. So he told her that he might not come for some time. Oh, lord! If he'd been caught and killed he could never—No! No!" obstinately, "even then he would have got back in some form—in some way. I've got to the point of believing as much as that. He was hers!"

"Yes. Yes. Yes," was all his slow answer. But there was deep thought in each detached word and when she went away he walked up and down the room with leisurely steps, looking down at the carpet.

As many hours of the day and night as those in authority would allow him Lord Coombe sat and watched by Donal's bed. He watched from well hidden anxiousness to see every subtle change recording itself on his being; he watched from throbbing affection and longing to see at once any tinge of growing natural colour, any unconscious movement perhaps a shade stronger than the last. It was his son who lay there, he told himself, it was the son he had remotely yearned for in his loneliness; if he had been his father watching his sunk lids with bated breath, he would have felt just these unmerciful pangs.

He also watched because in the boy's hours of fevered unconsciousness he could at times catch words—sometimes broken sentences, which threw ghastly light upon things past. Sometimes their significance was such as made him shudder. A condition the doctors most dreaded was one in which monstrous scenes seem lived again—scenes in which cruelties and maddening suffering and despairing death itself rose vividly from the depth of subconsciousness and cried aloud for vengeance. Sometimes Donal shuddered, tearing at his chest with both hands, more than once he lay sobbing until only skilled effort prevented his sobs from becoming choking danger.

"It may be years after he regains his strength," the chief physician said, "years before it will be safe to ask him for detail. On my own part I would *never* bring such horrors back to a man. You may have noticed how the men who have borne most, absolutely refuse to talk."

"It's an accursed fool who tries to make them," broke in one of the younger men. "There was a fellow who had been pinned up against a barn door and left to hang there—and a coarse, loud-mouthed lunatic asked him to describe how it felt. The chap couldn't stand it. Do you know what he did? He sprang at him and knocked him down. He apologized afterwards and said it was his nerves. But there's not a man who was there who will ever speak to that other brute again."

The man whose name was Jackson seemed to be a clinging memory to the skeleton when its mind wandered in the past Hades. He had been in some way very close to the boy. He had died somehow—cruelly. There had been blood—blood—and no one would help. Some devil had even laughed. When that scene came back the doctors and nurses held their breath and silently worked hard. Nothing seemed quite as heart-rending as what had happened to Jackson. But there were endless other things to shudder at.

So the time passed and Nurse Jones found many times that she must stop at his door on her way to her rest to say, "Don't look like that, Lord Coombe. You need not send for his mother yet."

Then at last—and it had been like travelling for months waterless in a desert—she came in one day with a new and elate countenance. "Mrs. Muir is a quiet, self-controlled woman, isn't she?" she asked.

"Entirely self-controlled and very quiet," he answered.

"Then if you will speak to Dr. Beresford about it I know he will allow her to see Captain Muir for a few minutes. And, thank God, it's not because if she doesn't see him now she'll never see him alive again. He has all his life before him."

"Please sit down, Nurse," Coombe spoke hastily and placed a chair as he spoke. He did so because he had perceiving eyes.

She sat down and covered her face with her apron for a moment. She made no sound or movement, but caught a deep quick breath two or three times. The relaxed strain had temporarily overpowered her. She uncovered her face and got up almost immediately. She was not likely to give way openly to her emotions.

"Thank you, Lord Coombe," she said. "I've never had a case that gripped hold of me as this has. I've often felt as though that poor half-killed boy was more to me than he is. You might speak to Dr. Beresford now. He's just gone in."

Therefore Lord Coombe went that afternoon to the house before which grew the plane trees whose leaves had rustled in the dawn's first wind on the morning Donal had sat and talked with his mother after the night of the Dowager Duchess of Darte's dance.

On his way his thoughts were almost uncontrollable things and he knew the first demand of good sense was that he should control them. But he was like an unbelievable messenger from another world—a dark world unknown, because shadows hid it, and would not let themselves be pierced by streaming human eyes. Donal was dead. This was what would fill this woman's mind when he entered her house. Donal was dead. It was the thought that had excluded all else from life for her, though he knew she had gone on working as other broken women had done. What did people say to women whose sons had been dead and had come back to life? It had happened before. What

274

could one say to prepare them for the transcendent shock of joy? What preparation could there be?

"God help me!" he said to himself with actual devoutness as he stood at the door.

He had seen Helen Muir once or twice since the news of her loss had reached her and she had looked like a most beautiful ghost and shadow of herself. When she came into her drawing-room to meet him she was more of a ghost and shadow than when they had last met and he saw her lips quiver at the mere sight of him, though she came forward very quietly.

Whatsoever helped him in response to his unconscious appeal brought to him suddenly a wave of comprehension of her and of himself as creatures unexpectedly near each other as they had never been before. The feeling was remotely akin to what had been awakened in him by the pure gravity and tenderness of Robin's baptismal good-bye kiss. He was human, she was human, they had both been forced to bear suffering. He was bringing joy to her.

He met her almost as she entered the door. He made several quick steps and he took both her hands in his and held them. It was a thing so unheard of that she stopped and stood quite still, looking up at him.

"Come and sit down here," he said, drawing her towards a sofa and he did not let her hands go, and sat down at her side while she stared at him and her breath began to come and go quickly.

"What—?" she began, "You are changed—quite different—"

"Yes, I am changed. Everything is changed—for us both!"

"For us—" She touched her breast weakly. "For me—as well as you?"

"Yes," he answered, and he still held her hands protectingly and kept his altered eyes—the eyes of a strangely new man—upon her. They were living, human, longing to help her—who had so long condemned him. His hands were even warm and held hers as if to give her support.

"You are a calm, well-balanced woman," he said. "And joy does not kill people—even hurt them."

There could be only one joy—only one! And she knew he knew there could be no other. She sprang from her seat.

"Donal!" she cried out so loud that the room rang. "Donal! Donal!"

He was on his feet also because he still wonderfully did not let her go.

"He is at my house. He has been there for weeks because we have had to fight for his life. We should have called you if he had been dying. Only an hour ago the doctor in charge gave me permission to come to you. You may see him—for a few minutes."

She began to tremble and sat down.

"I shall be quiet soon," she said. "Oh, dear God! God! God! Donal!"

Tears swept down her cheeks but he saw her begin to control herself even the next moment.

"May I speak to him at all?" she asked.

"Kiss him and tell him you are waiting in the next room and can come back any moment. What the hospital leaves free of Coombe House is at your disposal."

"God bless you! Oh, *forgive* me!"

"He escaped from a German prison by some miracle. He must be made to forget. He must hear of nothing but happiness. There is happiness before him—enough to force him to forget. You will accept anything he tells you as if it were a natural thing?"

"Accept!" she cried. "What would I *not* accept, praising God! You are preparing me for something. Ah! don't, don't be afraid! But—is it maiming—darkness?"

"No! No! It is a perfect thing. You must know it before you see him—and be ready. Before he went to the Front he was married."

"Married!" in a mere breath.

Coombe went on in quick sentences. She must be prepared and she could bear anything in the rapture of her joy.

"He married in secret a lonely child whom the Dowager Duchess of Darte had taken into her household. We have both taken charge of her since we discovered she was his wife. We thought she was his widow. She has a son. Before her marriage she was Robin Gareth-Lawless."

"Ah!" she cried brokenly. "He would have told me—he wanted to tell me—but he could not—because I was so hard! Oh! poor motherless children!"

"You never were hard, I could swear," Coombe said. "But perhaps you have changed—as I have. If he had not thought I was hard he might have told me— Shall we go to him at once?"

Together they went without a moment's delay.

Chapter 42

The dream had come back and Robin walked about the moor carrying her baby in her arms, even though Dowie followed her. She laid him on the heather and let him listen to the skylarks and there was in her face such a look, that, in times past if she had seen it, Dowie would have believed that it could only mean translation from earth.

But when Lord Coombe came for a brief visit he took Dowie to walk alone with him upon the moor. When they set out together she found herself involuntarily stealing furtive sidelong glances at him. There was that in his face which drew her eyes in spite of her. It was a look so intense and new that once she caught her breath, trembling. It was then that he turned to look at her and began to talk. He began—and went on—and as she listened there came to her sudden flooding tears and more than once a loud startled sob of joy.

"But he begs that she shall not see him until he is less ghastly to behold. He says the memory of such a face would tell her things she must never know. His one thought is that she must not know. Things happen to a man's nerves when he has seen and borne the ultimate horrors. Men have gone mad under the prolonged torture. He sometimes has moments of hideous collapse when he cannot shut out certain memories. He is more afraid of such times than of anything else. He feels he must get hold of himself."

Dowie's step slackened until it stopped. Her almost awed countenance told him what she felt she must know or perish. He felt that she had her rights and one of them was the right to be told. She had been a strong tower of honest faith and love.

"My lord, might I ask if you have told him—all about it?"

"Yes, Dowie," he answered. "All is well and no one but ourselves will ever know. The marriage in the dark old church is no longer a marriage. Only the first one—which he can prove—stands."

The telling of his story to Donal had been a marvellous thing because he had so controlled its drama that it had even been curiously undramatic. He had made it a mere catalogued statement of facts. As Donal had lain listening his heart had seemed to turn over in his breast.

"If I had *known* you!" he panted low. "If we had known each other! We did not!"

Later, bit by bit, he told him of Jackson—only of Jackson. He never spoke of other things. When put together the "bit by bit" amounted to this:

"He was a queer, simple sort of American. He was full of ideals and a kind of unbounded belief in his country. He had enlisted in Canada at the beginning. He always believed America would come in. He was sure the Germans knew she would and that was why they hated Americans. The more they saw her stirred up, the more they hated the fellows they caught—and the worse they treated them. They were hellish to Jackson!"

He had stopped at this point and Coombe had noted a dreaded look dawning in his eyes.

"Don't go on, my boy. It's bad for you," he broke in.

Donal shook his head a little as if to shake something away.

"I won't go on with—that," he said. "But the dream—I must tell you about that. It saved me from going mad—and Jackson did. He believed in a lot of things I'd not heard of except as jokes. He called them New Thought and Theosophy and Christian Science. He wasn't clever, but he *believed*. And it helped him. When I'm stronger I'll try to tell you. Subconscious mind and astral body came into it. I had begun to see things—just through starvation and agony. I told him about Robin when I scarcely knew what I was saying. He tried to hold me quiet by saying her name to me over and over. He'd pull me up with it. He began to talk to me about dreaming. When your body's not fed—you begin to see clear—if your spirit is not held down."

He was getting tired and panting a little. Coombe bent nearer to him.

"I can guess the rest. I have been reading books on such subjects. He told you how to concentrate on dreaming and try to get near her. He helped you by suggestion himself—"

"He used to lie awake night after night and do it—and I began to dream—No, it was not a dream. I believe I got to her—He did it—and they killed him!"

"Hush! hush!" cried Coombe. "Of all men he would most ardently implore you to hold yourself still—"

Donal made some strange effort. He lay still.

"Yes, he would! Yes—of all the souls in the other world he'd be strongest. He saved me—he saved Robin—he saved the child—you—all of us! Perhaps he's here now! He said he'd come if he could. He believed he could."

He lay quiet for a few seconds and then the Donal smile they had all adored lighted up his face.

"Jackson, old chap!" he said. "I can't see you—but I'll do what you want me to do—I'll do it."

He fainted the next minute and the doctors came to him.

The facts which came later still were that Jackson had developed consumption, and exposure and brutality had done their worst. And Donal had seen his heart wringing end.

"But he knew America would come in. I believed it too, because he did. Just at the right time. 'All the rest have fought like mad till they're tired—though they'll die fighting,' he said. 'America's not tired. She's got everything and she sees red with frenzy at the bestiality. She'll *burst* in—just at the right time!' Jackson *knew*!"

"I must not go trembling to her," Donal said on the morning when at last—long last, it seemed—he drove with Coombe up the moor road to Darreuch. "But," bravely, "what does it matter? I'm trembling because I'm going to her!"

He had been talking about her for weeks—for days he had been able to talk of nothing else—Coombe had listened as if he heard echoes from a past when he would have so talked and dared not utter a word. He had talked as a boy lover talks—as a young bridegroom might let himself pour his joy forth to his most sacredly trusted friend.

Her loveliness, the velvet of her lifting eyes—the wonder of her trusting soul—the wonder of her unearthly selfless sweetness!

"It was always the same kind of marvel every time you saw her," he said boyishly. "You couldn't believe there could be such sweetness on earth—until you saw her again. Even her eyes and her little mouth and her softness were like that. You had to tell yourself about them over and over again to make them real when she wasn't there!"

He was still thin, but the ghastly hollows had filled and his smile scarcely left his face—and he had waited as long as he could.

"And to see her with a little child in her arms!" he had murmured. "Robin! Holding it—and being careful! And showing it to me!"

After he first caught sight of the small old towers of Darreuch he could not drag his eyes from them.

"She's there! She's there! They're both there together!" he said over and over. Just before they left the carriage he wakened as it were and spoke to Coombe.

"She won't be frightened," he said. "I told her—last night."

Coombe had asked himself if he must go to her. But, marvellously even to him, there was no need.

When they stood in the dark little hall—as she had come down the stone stairway on the morning when she bade him her sacred little good-bye, so she came down again—like a white blossom drifting down from its branch—like a white feather from a dove's wing—But she held her baby in her arms and to Donal her cheeks and lips and eyes were as he had first seen them in the Gardens.

He trembled as he watched her and even found himself spellbound—waiting.

"Donal! Donal!"

And they were in his arms—the soft warm things—and he sat down upon the lowest step and held them—rocking—and trembling still more—but with the gates of peace open and earth and war shut out.

www.ingramcontent.com/pod-product-compliance
Ingram Content Group UK Ltd.
Pitfield, Milton Keynes, MK11 3LW, UK
UKHW040642280225
455688UK00003B/83

9 781447 268413